# HAVING THE COWBOY'S BABY

BY
JUDY DUARTE

MILLS & BOON

First Published in Great Britain 2016
By Mills & Boon, an imprint of HarperCollins*Publishers*
1 London Bridge Street, London, SE1 9GF

© 2016 Judy Duarte

ISBN: 978-0-263-91953-0

23-0116

Our policy is to use papers that are natural, renewable and recyclable products and made from wood grown in sustainable forests.The logging and manufacturing processes conform to the legal environmental regulations of the country of origin.

Printed and bound in Spain
by CPI, Barcelona

Since 2002, *USA TODAY* bestselling author **Judy Duarte** has written over forty books for Mills & Boon Special Edition, earned two RITA® Award finals, won two Maggies and received a National Readers' Choice Award. When she's not cooped up in her writing cave, she enjoys traveling with her husband and spending quality time with her grandchildren. You can learn more about Judy and her books at her website, www.judyduarte.com, or at facebook.com/judyduartenovelist.

To my daughter, Christy Jeffries, who is everything I could ever wish for in a daughter and more.

Congratulations on your sales to Special Edition, the first of which—*A Marine for His Mom*—shares a January release date with my book! I'm looking forward to sharing more of the crazy and fabulous life of being a Mills & Boon author with you.

## Chapter One

Carly Rayburn was back in town. Not that there'd been any big announcements, but news traveled fast in Brighton Valley. And even if it didn't, not much got past Ian McAllister.

She'd had a singing gig in San Antonio, but apparently that hadn't panned out for her, which was too bad. She had a dream to make it big in country music someday, a dream Ian no longer had. But he couldn't fault her for that.

Jason, her oldest brother, said she'd be staying on the Leaning R for a while, which wasn't a surprise. It seemed to Ian that she came home to the ranch whenever her life hit a snag. So that's what she would do, right after attending Jason's wedding in town.

As the foreman of the Leaning R, Ian had been

invited to the ceremony and reception, but he'd graciously declined and sent a gift instead. The only people attending were family and a few close friends, so Ian would have felt out of place—for more reasons than one. So he'd remained on the ranch.

Now, as darkness settled over Brighton Valley, he did what he often did in the evenings after dinner. He sat on the front porch of his small cabin and enjoyed the peaceful evening sounds, the scent of night-blooming jasmine and the vast expanse of stars in the Texas sky.

The Leaning R had been in Carly's family for years. It was run-down now, but it had great potential. It was also the perfect place for Ian to hide out, where people only knew him as a quiet cowboy who felt more comfortable around livestock than the bright lights of the big cities. And thanks to his granddaddy, who'd once owned a respectable spread near Dallas, that was true.

He glanced at the Australian shepherd puppy nestled in his lap. The sleepy pooch yawned, then stretched and squirmed.

"What's the matter, Cheyenne?" He stroked her black-and-white furry head. "Is your snooze over?"

When the pup gave a little yip, Ian set her down and watched as she padded around the wooden flooring, taking time to sniff at the potted geranium on the porch, her stub of a tail wagging. Then she waddled down the steps.

"Don't wander off too far," he told her. "It's dark out there, and you're still getting the lay of the land."

The pup glanced at him, as if she understood what he was saying, then trotted off.

Ian loved dogs. He'd grown up with several of them on his granddad's ranch, but after he'd moved out on his own, he hadn't been able to have one until now. Fortunately, his life was finally lining up the way he'd always hoped it would. Once the Leaning R went on the market, as Carly's brother said it would, Ian was prepared to buy it. As the trustee and executor of the Rayburn family estate, Jason was in charge now. The only thing holding him back from listing the property was getting Carly and their brother Braden to agree to the sale.

But Braden had his own spread about ten miles down the road, and Carly had no intention of being a rancher. When she'd left Brighton Valley the last time, she'd been hell-bent on making a name for herself. With her talent, there was no reason she wouldn't. There was always a price for fame, though, and Ian just hoped she was willing to pay it.

He reached for his guitar, which rested beside him near the cabin window, and settled it into his lap. As he strummed the new song he'd written, the chords filled the peaceful night. He might love ranching, but that didn't mean he'd given up music altogether. He just played for pleasure these days, in the evenings after a long workday. He'd learned the hard way that it beat the hell out of opening a bottle of whiskey to relax.

Now, as he sat outside singing the words to the tune he'd written about love gone wrong, he waited for Carly to return from the wedding she'd come home to attend, waited to see if anything had changed. To see if, by some strange twist of fate, she'd decided that she wanted something different out of life.

He'd only played a few bars when his cell phone rang. He set the guitar aside and answered on the third ring.

"Hey, Mac," the graveled smoker's voice said. "How's it going?"

It was Uncle Roy, one of the few people who called him Mac and who knew how to contact him. "Not bad. How's everything in Sarasota? How are Grandma and Granddad?"

"They're doing just fine. Mama's cholesterol is a bit high, but the doctor put her on some medication to lower it. Other than that, they're settling into retired life out here in Florida and making friends."

Ian was glad to hear it, although he'd been sorry when his grandparents had sold the family ranch. But his granddad had put in a long, successful life, first as a rodeo cowboy, then as a rancher. And Grandma had always wanted to live near the water. So Ian couldn't blame him for selling the place and moving closer to his sole remaining son—even if Ian felt more like his uncle's sibling than a nephew.

"Say," Roy said, "I called to let you know that it'll be their fiftieth wedding anniversary next month—on the fifteenth. So me and your aunt Helen are planning a party for them. We're going to try to keep it a surprise, although I'm not sure if we can pull it off. But it'd be great if you could come."

"I'll be there." Ian wasn't sure what he'd do about finding someone to look after the Leaning R for him, but there was no way he'd miss celebrating with the couple who'd raised him.

"Dad said you're thinking about buying that place where you've been working," Roy added.

"That's my plan."

"You made an offer yet?"

"Not yet." But Ian was ready to jump the minute the place was officially on the market.

"What's the holdup?"

"The ranch is held by a trust, and the trustees are three half siblings. They're not quite in agreement about selling. At least, they didn't used to be. I think it's finally coming together now."

"What *was* the holdup?"

"A couple of them wanted it to stay in the family, but no one was willing to move in and take over."

Uncle Roy seemed to chew on that for a while, then asked, "You sure it's a good deal?"

"Damned straight. The widow of the man who originally owned it took good care of it, but her grandson, the previous trustee, was some sort of big-shot, corporate-exec type who let it go to the dogs. It's a shame, too. You should have seen what it once was—and what it could become again with a little love and cash. I'm looking forward to having the right to invest in it the way Mrs. Rayburn would have if she were still alive."

"Well, Helen and I'll be praying for you. I hope it all works out. I know having your own place and running a spread has been a dream of yours for a long time."

And that dream had grown stronger these past three years. "Thanks, Uncle Roy."

"Never did understand why you wanted to give up the good life, though. Dad says you were always a rancher at heart and not a performer. And he knows you best. But damn, boy. You sure could play and sing."

Ian still could. It was the fame he'd never liked. He'd always been an introvert, and even though he hadn't been the lead singer in the group, the gigs had gotten harder and harder to handle without a couple of shots of tequila to get him through the night.

So when the lights had grown too bright, the crowds too big and his fear of following in his alcoholic father's stumbling boot steps too real, he'd left the groupies and Nashville behind for the quiet life of a cowboy.

"Listen, I gotta go," Roy said.

"Give everyone my love. I know it's an hour later there and Granddad turns in early, so I'll call them in the morning."

"Don't forget—that party's a secret," Roy added.

"I won't."

When the line disconnected, Ian scanned the yard for Cheyenne, only to find her sniffing around near the faucet in the middle of the yard. Then he began strumming his guitar again.

Not everyone understood why he'd given up the life he'd once led, but Ian was happy here on the Leaning R. Only trouble was, Carly had swept into his life and turned it upside down for a while.

And now she was back.

Carly Rayburn gripped the wheel of her red Toyota Tacoma, the radio filling the cab with the latest country-western hit. She was still dressed in the pale green dress she'd worn as the maid of honor at her half brother's wedding, although she'd slipped on a denim jacket to ward off the evening chill and traded her high heels for her favorite pair of cowboy boots.

Under normal circumstances, she usually came up with an excuse for why she couldn't attend weddings. For one reason, she found it difficult to feign happiness for the bride and groom because she was skeptical of the whole "until death do us part" philosophy.

But then, why wouldn't she be? Her father had a daughter and two sons by three different women. Then, after her parents' divorce, her mom had gone on to date a series of men, all celebrities who'd moved in and out of Carly's life as if it were a revolving door. So was it any wonder she thought "true love" was a myth and only something to sing about?

Today, however, when she stood at the altar and watched her oldest brother, Jason, vow to love, honor and cherish Juliana Bailey for the rest of their lives, she had to admit to not only being surprised by the rush of sentiment, but also feeling hopeful for the newlyweds, too. And that was a first.

Now, as she steered her pickup toward the Leaning R Ranch, she found herself happy for Jason and Juliana yet pondering her own future, which was now up in the air. Five weeks ago, she'd thought she'd finally gotten her start with a singing gig at a nightclub in San Antonio, but a stomach bug had ended that, leaving her between jobs again.

For the most part, she felt a lot better now. But every

time she thought the virus was a thing of the past, it flared up again. Like today, at her brother's reception. She was going to have a glass of champagne, but before she could even take a sip, a whiff of the popping bubbles set off her nausea. Yet now she was fine again.

When she'd first caught the flu or whatever it was, she'd gotten sick right before showtime in San Antonio. Her friend, Heather, had suggested that it might be stage fright, but there was no way that was the case. Carly had been performing ever since she could stand in front of her bedroom mirror and grip the mic on her child's karaoke machine.

She figured she was just tired and run-down. So, with a little R & R on her family's ranch, she'd kick this thing in no time at all and line up another gig before you could sing "Back in the Saddle Again."

When she got within a few miles of the ranch, her thoughts drifted to Ian, the handsome cowboy who was content living on the Leaning R and who had no intention of picking up stakes. The two of them had become intimately involved the last time she came home, and as nice as it had been, as heated, as *magical*, Carly didn't dare let it start up again.

So for that reason, she'd dragged her feet at the wedding reception, which was held at Maestro's, the new Italian restaurant on Main Street. It was a nice venue for a small but elegant celebration—probably too nice and upscale for Brighton Valley, though. Still, while everyone had raved about the food, she thought the chef had been way too heavy-handed with the garlic and basil. Just one sniff had caused her to push her plate aside. But then, she'd had a late lunch and hadn't been all that hungry anyway.

Once the newlyweds had taken off in a limousine bound for Houston, Carly had climbed into her pickup and left town. According to her plan, she would arrive at the Leaning R after dark, when it would be less likely for anyone—namely Ian—to see her. She just hoped she could slip unnoticed into the house and remain there until she figured out a plan B.

Yet, as luck would have it, when she pulled into the graveled drive at the Leaning R, Ian's lights blazed bright. And to make matters worse, he was sitting on the front porch of his cabin.

That meant she would have to face the one man in Brighton Valley who unwittingly had the power to thwart most any plan she might come up with—if she let him. But there was no chance of that. Maybe if she'd been like the other girls who grew up around here, content to settle for the country life on a homestead with some cowboy and their two-point-four kids, she'd be champing at the bit to let the sexy foreman make an honest woman of her. But Carly had never been like the other girls—her family life had been too dysfunctional—and she was even less like them now. She had big dreams to go on world tours, while Ian was content to stay in Brighton Valley.

Well, there was no avoiding him now. She got out of the truck and made her way toward his small cabin.

"Hey," she said. "How's it going?"

"All right." He set his guitar aside. "How was the wedding?"

"Small, but nice. That is, if you're into that sort of thing."

"And you're not." It was a statement, not a question. Ian was well aware of how Carly felt about love and forever-after, so she let it go with a half shrug. His easygoing and nonjudgmental attitude was the main reason she'd even allowed herself to have a brief fling with him four or five months back. Well, that and the way he looked in those faded jeans.

He'd taken off his hat, revealing thick, brown hair in need of a comb. Or a woman's touch.

She'd always found his green eyes intriguing—the way they lit up in mirth, the intensity in them during the heat of lovemaking.

His gaze raked over her as if he was hoping to pick up where they'd left off, and her heart rate stumbled before catching on to the proper beat again. But then, the guitar wasn't the only thing Ian was skilled at strumming.

If truth be told, there'd been a fleeting moment at the wedding when her own resolve had waffled. She'd seen her stuffy brother's eyes light up when his pretty bride walked down the aisle, and it had had touched her heart. She truly hoped that Jason and Juliana defied the odds and lived happily ever after. But she just couldn't quite see herself dressed in white lace and making lifelong promises to someone. After all, she'd never known anyone who'd actually met "the one" and managed to make a commitment that had lasted longer than a year or two.

She glanced at Ian, saw his legs stretched out while

seated in that patio chair, all long and lean, muscle and sinew. She did love a handsome cowboy, though. And Ian certainly fit the image to a tee. He also knew how to treat a lady—in all the ways that mattered.

Again, she shook it off. They'd ended things on a good note, both of them agreeing that their sexual fling—no matter how good it had been—would only end awkwardly if they let it go on any further. It had been a mutual agreement that she had every intention of sticking to.

"That's an interesting bridesmaid getup," he said as his gaze swept down to her boots and back up again.

"A bridesmaid *getup*?" That was a cowboy for you. "The wedding was so sudden that I didn't have time to shop. So I wore a dress I've had for a while." She glanced at her skirt, then twirled slightly to the right. "What's wrong with it?"

"Not a thing." His lips quirked into a crooked grin. "I was talking about the denim jacket and the boots. Juliana and Jason seem to be more traditional."

She smiled. "Well, that's true. I kicked off my heels the first chance I got. And since it's a bit chilly out tonight and this dress is sleeveless, I grabbed the only jacket I had handy."

"Either way, you make a good-looking bridesmaid, Carly."

Before she could change the subject to one that was much safer than brides or commitments of any kind, she noticed a bush at the side of the cabin shake and tremble.

Had that pesky raccoon come back again? If so,

it was certainly getting brave. But instead of Rocky, the nickname she and Ian had for the little rascal that knocked over the trash cans, a darling little black-and-white puppy trotted out from the bush.

"Oh my gosh," Carly said. "How cute is he?"

"It's a she. And her name is Cheyenne."

As Carly bent to pick up the pup, she must have moved too quickly, because a wave of dizziness struck. For a moment, everything around her seemed to spin. She wasn't going to faint, was she?

She paused a moment and blinked. Her head cleared, thank goodness. Then she pulled the hem of her dress out of the way, slowly got on her knees and reached out her hands. The pup came right over to her, but she held still for a while longer, making sure the world wouldn't start spinning again.

"Aren't you a sweetheart?" she said to the puppy. Then she glanced at Ian, who had a boyish grin splashed across his face. "Where'd you get her?"

"Paco, the owner of the feed store, had a litter of Australian shepherds for sale, so I bought her. It's something I've been planning to do for a while. A spread like this needs a good cattle dog."

Carly pulled the pup into her arms and stood. "But what if the new owners don't want you to stay on?"

He shrugged. "I'm not worried."

Ian didn't get too concerned about much. In fact, he always seemed to go with the flow, which was a plus in the casual relationship department, but another reason they'd never make a good match in the long run. He didn't have the same ambition she did.

For as long as Carly could remember, all she'd wanted was to stand out on her own and be recognized as more than a pretty little girl whose divorced parents, a wealthy businessman and a glamorous country-western singer, were both too busy to spend quality time with her. And she'd found the best place to do that was on the stage.

"That puppy is going to get your pretty dress all dirty," Ian said.

"I don't mind." She tossed him a smile as Cheyenne licked her nose. "I've always wanted a dog, but I never stay in one place long enough to have one."

"I'll share Cheyenne with you when you come home."

As nice as the offer was, it wouldn't work. "Jason plans to sell the ranch, remember?"

"Yep. I sure do."

"So I won't have a place to run home to anymore. At least, it won't be here. And like I said, you don't know for sure that the new owner will want you to stay on. I mean, I hope they do."

"Like I said…" His eyes sparkled, and a grin tickled his lips. "I'm not worried."

"Yes, but you have to be responsible for a puppy now."

"Having something to look after will do me good."

She thought about some of the homeless people she'd seen on the city streets, pushing a grocery cart laden with their belongings, a tethered dog trotting along beside them. Not that she had any reason to think Ian would ever find himself homeless. He'd built a good reputation with the other ranchers in town. He was also a hard worker and would undoubtedly find a job somewhere. But he seemed to be as carefree as a tumble-weed, especially when it came to making plans, which was yet another reason they'd never make a go of it. Their basic personalities were just too different.

"You're going to find that the ranch house is nearly all packed," Ian said. "Juliana had most everything boxed up by the time she left. So it might not be too comfortable sleeping in there. But you're welcome to stay with me, if you want."

Memories of the nights she'd spent in his bed swept over her, warming her blood and setting a flutter in her tummy. But that wouldn't do either of them any good. Well, maybe it would for as long as it lasted, but she couldn't afford to get too invested in him—or anyone—at this stage in her career.

"As tempting as that might be," she said, "I'd better pass. Besides, Juliana told me the kitchen is still in order. And the guest bed has fresh sheets. So I'll be okay."

"Suit yourself."

Their gazes locked for a moment, as a lover's moon shone brightly overhead. And while Ian didn't say another word, she felt compelled to continue arguing her case.

"We already discussed this," she said.

His smile dimpled his cheeks in a way that could tempt a good girl to rebel. "I didn't say anything about sleeping with me, although I won't turn you down if you insist."

She clicked her tongue and returned his smile.

"You're incorrigible, Ian McAllister. You're going to be the death of me."

"No, I'm not. You said it yourself, a relationship between us would crash and burn. And I agreed."

He had, and it was true. But that didn't lessen her attraction to him, which seemed to be just as strong as it ever had been. She'd just have to ratchet up her willpower and avoid him whenever possible.

So she walked up to the porch and placed Cheyenne next to his chair. As she did so, she caught a whiff of soap and leather, musk and cowboy. Dang, downplaying their chemistry wasn't going to be easy.

He reached for her hand, and as he did, his thumb grazed her wrist. Her heart quickened.

"It's good to have you back, Carly. I missed your company."

She'd missed him, too. The horseback rides, the sing-alongs on his porch, the lovemaking in his cabin, the mornings waking up in his arms… But she tugged her hand from his grip. She didn't have to pull very hard. She was free from his touch before she knew it.

"Well, I'd better turn in," she said. "It's been a long day."

"Good night."

No argument? Not that she wanted one. But she was used to men coming on to her.

So why wasn't she relieved that he'd taken no for an answer so easily?

Because life got complicated when hormones got in the way of good judgment, that's why.

"Sleep tight," she said as she turned and started for the house.

The chords of his guitar rang out in the night as he played a lively melody with a two-step beat, a tune she didn't recognize, a song she'd never heard. She turned, crossed her arms and shifted her weight to one hip. When she did, he stopped playing.

"That's nice," she said. "Is it something you wrote?"

"Yep. You like it?"

"I really do. You have a lot of talent, Ian. You ought to do something with it."

"I just did. And you heard it."

"That's not what I meant. You should let me—or somebody—record this song. Maybe it could be a hit."

"You have a beautiful voice, Carly. But I'm not interested in recording this song. It's something I wrote for my grandparents. It's going to be my gift to them."

"That's great, and I'll bet they'll love it. But what if you could do even more with it? Wouldn't that be an awesome tribute to them?"

"I'd like them to be the first to hear it performed at their wedding anniversary."

"But maybe afterward—"

"Sorry. My mind's made up."

So it was. And that should serve as a good reminder that Ian wasn't a go-getter like she was. Sure, he could put in the effort when it came to working the ranch, but he had no other goals besides living as simply as possible. Plus, she'd learned that, as carefree as Ian McAllister could be, he was as stubborn as Granny Rayburn's old milk cow when he *did* make a decision.

She nodded, then turned to go. As she made her way to the house, the melody followed her, and so did Ian's soulful voice as it sang of two lonely hearts finding each other one moonlit night, of them falling crazy in love and of the lifetime vow they'd made, one that would last forever and a day.

She would have liked to have met the couple that had inspired him to write such a beautiful song. If she had known them, maybe she would look forward to settling down herself one day. But not for a long time—and certainly not with Ian.

## *Chapter Two*

When Carly entered the front door of the ranch house, unexpected grief struck her like a wallop to the chest.

The inside walls were lined with boxes stacked two and three high, each one carefully labeled with what was inside. Carly had known that her new sister-in-law had first inventoried and then packed up Granny's belongings, but that still hadn't prepared her for the heartbreaking sight.

Seeing a lifetime of memories all boxed up, especially the plaques, pictures and knickknacks that made the ranch a home, reminded her that Granny was gone and the Leaning R would soon belong to someone else. And for the first time in Carly's life, coming home wasn't the least bit comforting.

As she wandered through the empty house like a

lost child, the ache in her chest grew as hard and cold as dry ice.

Needing comfort—or a sense of place—she hurried to the kitchen, where she and Granny had spent a lot of time together. She nearly cried with joy at the familiar surroundings. It was the only room that still bore Granny's touch, the only place that still offered a safe haven from the disappointment of the outside world.

She studied the faded blue wallpaper, with its straw baskets holding wildflowers. The colors, now yellowed with age, had once brightened the kitchen where Carly had often joined Granny before mealtimes and begged to help her cook and bake.

The elderly woman had been more of a mother to Carly than the one who'd given birth to her and then left her in the care of nannies for most of her childhood. Of course, Raelynn Fallon would say that wasn't true. And no one argued with Raelynn, least of all her daughter, who'd been asked to refer to her by her first name because *Mama* made her sound so old and matronly.

Was it any wonder their mother-daughter relationship hadn't been all that warm and loving?

Thank God for Granny, who'd been the only parental role model Carly had ever had. For that reason, she'd grieved more for her great-grandma's passing last year than she had when word came of her father's fatal car accident in Mexico four months ago.

Carly glanced at the cat-shaped clock on wall, its drooping black tail swinging back and forth with each tick-tock.

Life went on, she supposed. But now she was at a loss. There'd been plenty to do on her last trip home, but that was no longer the case. Jason had hired Juliana to inventory and pack Granny's belongings before he'd fallen in love with the woman and married her. And while Carly was tempted to unpack the boxes and return everything to where it belonged, she couldn't very well do that.

So what was she going to do with her time, especially since she was trying to avoid Ian?

Her gaze landed on the countertop, where she spotted Granny's old recipe box. She reached for the familiar, white metal container, with the scene of a mountain meadow hand painted on the outside. She lifted the lid and studied the yellowed tabs, bent from use.

Appetizers, beverages, breads, cakes...

She thumbed through the cookie recipes, which had always been her favorites. Granny had made little handwritten notes on the back of most of them. What a treat to be able to read her great-grandmother's thoughts tonight, especially when she knew sleep wouldn't come easy.

After rummaging through the pantry for a box of herbal tea, Carly filled the teapot with water, then put it on the stove to heat. Next, she took a seat at the antique oak table to begin reading through Granny's recipes as well as the notes on the backs of them.

She'd no more than pulled out the stack of cards listed under cookies when her cell phone rang. She glanced at the display. It was Heather, who was still performing in the show in San Antonio, the one Carly had once starred in and then had to quit.

"Hey," Carly said. "What's up?"

"I called to check on you. How are you feeling?"

"A lot better, although I've been pretty tired lately. I think that's from burning the candle at both ends—and that bug I had really wore me down."

"You probably ought to talk to a doctor."

"I plan to get some sleep while I'm on the ranch. I never rest as well as I do out here. If that doesn't work, I'll make an appointment to see mine."

"But how are you feeling otherwise? I mean, starring in that show was really important to you. And the director wasn't happy when you had to quit. Wasn't he the one who told you he'd put in a good word for you with his buddy in Nashville?"

"Yes, he was. So I doubt that he'll do that now. But I've been disappointed before." By people, by life events. Fortunately, Carly had learned to shake it off and to pivot in a new direction, if she needed to. "Don't worry. I'll find another gig soon."

"Good. You really need to get your career jump-started before you get to feeling maternal and lay that dream aside for a husband who doesn't appreciate you and a slew of whining kids."

Heather, who'd grown up as the oldest in a family of seven, had spent more time babysitting her younger siblings than being a child herself. So it wasn't any wonder she felt that way.

If truth be told, Carly had once dreamed of having a family of her own someday, with two kids, a dog and a house in the suburbs. She'd also told her-self she'd find a husband who would be willing to co-parent and who'd promise not to work or be absent on holidays. But two years ago, her gynecologist had nipped that wishful thinking in the bud when she'd told Carly that due to a hormonal imbalance and a sketchy menstrual cycle she probably wouldn't ever be able to conceive.

But true to form, Carly had shaken off that girlish dream, instead focusing on her career. Besides, she'd told herself, with the lack of parenting she'd experi-enced, what kind of mother would she make anyway?

"Don't worry about me falling in love and giving up my singing career, Heather. I'll make it happen."

"I'm glad to hear it. And I love your can-do atti-tude." Her friend blew out a sigh. "But please give me a call after you talk to the doctor. I've been worried about you."

Now that Granny was gone, there weren't too many people who actually worried about Carly. She sus-pected Braden did, and Jason. The two of them had become a lot closer lately, especially since love and romance had softened her oldest brother.

"Thanks, Heather. If it turns out that I have to make an appointment, I'll let you know."

When she disconnected the call, Carly glanced down at the recipe cards in her hand. She flipped through them until she spotted one of her favorites.

Sugar cookies. What fun Carly used to have roll-ing out the dough and cutting them into shapes, espe-cially at Christmas. Then she and Granny would frost them. She turned over the card. In blue ink, Granny had written:

Carly's favorite. The holidays aren't the same without these cookies. That precious child's eyes light up in pure joy. Warms my heart so.

Then, in pencil, she'd added: "It was a sad day when she grew too old to bake with me anymore."

Carly remembered Granny's last Christmas. She'd called and invited her to come over and bake cookies. "Just for old times' sake," Granny had added.

But Carly had been too busy. It hadn't been the first time she'd declined to visit Granny or to spend time in this old kitchen, but it had certainly been the last.

Was that the day Granny had penciled the note?

Guilt welled up in Carly's chest until it clogged her throat and brought tears to her eyes.

"Granny," she said aloud, "I'm going to bake a batch of sugar cookies for old times' sake. And before your kitchen is packed away."

Carly set the card aside and pulled out another. Brownies. No one made them like Granny. And this particular recipe had a fudge frosting that was to die for. On the back, Granny had written, "Men and boys can't say no to these! They make good peace offerings. And good bribes, too!"

The teapot on the stove whistled. After setting aside a stack of recipes she intended to bake, including Granny's Texas chocolate cake, Carly poured a cup of hot water into a cup, then tore open a packet of chamomile tea and let it steep.

With nothing on her agenda for this trip home—and most of the packing already done—she reached into the kitchen desk drawer, pulled out a sheet of paper and a pen. Then she began a long grocery list.

She had no idea what she was going to do with everything she intended to bake, but it was going to do her heart good. And right now, her heart needed all the good it could get.


As the summer sun climbed high in the Texas sky, Ian came out of the barn with Cheyenne tagging behind him. Carly had taken off a couple of hours ago, but he'd been in the south pasture at the time and had only watched her pickup driving down the county road.

He had no right to know where she was going, he supposed, but that didn't make him any less curious.

Still, as he headed for the corral, where Jesse Ramirez, one of the teenage boys Jason had hired, was painting the rails, Carly drove up. At least she hadn't taken one look at the packed-up house last night and blasted out of town at first light. Apparently, she planned to stick around for a while.

When she waved at him, his pulse spiked. But then why wouldn't it? Carly Rayburn was every cowboy's dream—a five-foot-two-inch blonde, blue-eyed beauty with a soft Southern twang and a body built for snug denim and white lace.

She was dressed to kill today in boots, black jeans and a blue frilly blouse. With her blond curls tumbling down her shoulders, she looked as though she was ready for one of the rides they used to take together, and he was half tempted to call it a day and suggest they do just that. But Carly had hitched her wagon to a different star and sought the fame and glory Ian had been happy to leave behind.

Of course, she had no idea who Ian had once been or why he'd given it all up. It was a secret he meant to keep now that he was living in small-town obscurity and going by his given name.

As she climbed from the truck and closed the driver's door, she said, "I don't suppose you'd want to help me carry some of this stuff into the house."

"Sure. What have you got there?"

"Groceries."

He glanced at the bags and boxes that filled the entire bed of her truck, then blew out a whistle. "What is all this? Flour, sugar, cocoa…? You planning to open a bakery?"

She laughed with that soft lilt that stirred his blood and lent a unique sound to her singing voice. "Maybe I should. I found Granny's recipe box last night. She made notes on the back of the cards. And since I couldn't sleep, I spent a long time reading over them and reminiscing. So I started making a grocery list, and… Well, it looks like I'm going to do some baking. I'll just have to find someone to give it to, or I'll end up looking like a Butterball turkey."

"Hey, don't forget where I live. I haven't had homemade goodies in ages. I favor chocolate, but I'm not fussy. If it's sweet, I'll give it a try."

She blessed him with a pretty smile. "I'll keep that in mind."

As they carried the groceries into the kitchen, she said, "Guess who I ran into at the market? Earl Tellis, the owner of the Stagecoach Inn."

"He was shopping?" Ian laughed. "I didn't figure him for being all that domestic."

"Neither did I, especially during daylight hours. But his wife had her appendix removed a couple of days ago, so he's helping out around the house."

Ian didn't respond. He sometimes drove out to the honky-tonk on weekend evenings, but for the most part, he didn't like crowds, especially as the night wore on and some folks tended to drink to excess and get rowdy. He'd certainly seen his share of it in the past. And he'd done his share of whooping it up, too. But he was pretty much a teetotaler now. He wanted to prove that he could say no and knew when to quit—unlike his old man.

"Earl asked if I'd come out and perform on Saturday night," Carly added.

"Good for you."

"Yeah, well, it's not the big time by any means, but it's a place to perform while I'm here." She bit down on her bottom lip.

Uh-oh. Ian had an idea where her thoughts were going.

"Earl asked if I had a band," she added. "I told him no, but that I might be able to find a guitarist."

"Who'd you have in mind?" He knew the answer, though, and his gut clenched.

"You, of course."

Ian shook his head. "I told you I'm not a performer."

"You don't know that yet—not if you don't try it first. Come on. Help me out this once. Without you, Earl's not going to want me." She bit down on her lip again, then blinked at him with those little ol' cocker spaniel eyes.

"Don't look at me like that."

Her lips parted, and her eyes grew wide. "Like what?"

He folded his arms across his chest. "I'm not your daddy who used to give in to that little sad face."

She slapped her hands on her denim clad hips and went from cocker spaniel to junkyard dog in nothing flat. "I'm not doing any such thing! And I never tried to work my dad like that."

Ian arched a brow in objection. "Come on, Carly. I saw you do it."

"When?"

"That first day you met me. When your dad stopped by and found out that the old foreman had retired and Granny chose me to replace him."

"My dad hadn't been happy to learn that Reuben Montoya had gone back to Mexico. And I was afraid he would do something…stupid."

"Like what?"

"Chase after him, I guess. Or fire you before we had a chance to see if you could handle Reuben's job." She gave a little shrug. "I was only trying to change the subject and give him something else to think about. But I didn't 'work' him the way you're implying."

"That wasn't the only time. And you were good at it, too. But it won't work on me."

"That's not fair, Ian. You make it sound like I'm a big flirt or a spoiled brat. And I'm neither."

Not by nature, he supposed. But when you grew up with an ultrarich father who thought throwing money at his kids was the same as saying I love you, it was probably hard not to try to get your way on occasion.

"I'm not trying to offend you or stir you up. And I don't want to thwart your chance at performing locally, but I'm not interested in playing guitar down at the Stagecoach Inn."

"Do you get nervous playing for a crowd?"

"Nope." Stage fright had never been an issue. "I just don't want to." That was the same reason he'd given Felicia Jamison, of country music fame, when he'd told her he was quitting the band. And she hadn't taken it any easier then than Carly was now. But he didn't figure he owed either of them any further explanation, although he probably should have given Felicia an earful.

Ten years ago, Felicia had been an up-and-coming singer when she'd hired Ian to be her lead guitarist. And the fit had been magical. Felicia could really rock the house with her voice, but it was Ian's songwriting that had helped her soar in popularity.

Most of her fans might not have heard of Mac McAllister, but he'd still earned a name for himself within the country music industry.

So far, no one in Brighton Valley knew who he was. Felicia had the face people would recognize. Ian had only been a member of her band, but if he put himself out in the limelight again, the greater chance he had of someone recognizing him and word of where he was getting out. And he'd been dead serious when he'd told Felicia that he was retiring.

"Then I guess you can't blame me if I try to change your mind," Carly said.

Ian wasn't sure how she intended to go about that, but the truth of the matter was, he still found Carly as sexy as hell. And while she'd made it clear that she didn't want their fling to start up all over again, he wasn't so sure he felt the same way.

Carly had never been one to take no for an answer—especially since she hadn't been entirely honest with Ian. Not only had Earl Tellis asked her to perform on Saturday night, but she'd already made the commitment—for both her *and* a guitarist.

And since Ian could be rather stubborn, she had her work cut out for her. She also had a batch of chewy, chocolaty brownies with fudge frosting that were sure to impress the handsome cowboy. After all, hadn't Granny said they made good bribes?

And that was exactly what Carly hoped to use them for this evening—a bribe to soften up Ian. So after dinner she put on a pretty yellow dress and slipped on her denim jacket and a pair of boots. Then she spent a little extra time on her makeup and hair before carrying a platter of brownies to his cabin.

Just like the night before, when she returned from the wedding, she found him sitting on his front porch, strumming his guitar. Only this time, he was playing a different tune, one that had a haunting melody, and singing the heart-stirring lyrics.

Not surprising, she thought it was just as memorable, just as good, as the one he'd written for his grandparents.

He stopped playing when she approached and cast her a heart-strumming smile instead.

"Was that another new song?" she asked, assuming it was and adjusting the platter in her arms.

"Yep."

Ian didn't realize how talented he was. Not only could he play and sing, but he had a way with lyrics, too. Most musicians would give up their birthrights to be able to write songs the way he could.

He set his guitar aside, next to where Cheyenne lay snoozing. "What do you have there? Did you bring dessert?"

Whoever said that the way to a man's heart was through his stomach must have been spot-on. She just hoped Granny's brownies were as persuasive as the note on the recipe suggested they were.

Carly stepped up on the porch and lifted the foil covering from the platter. "This is my first attempt to make Granny's blue-ribbon brownies. Tell me what you think."

Ian reached for one of the frosted squares and took a bite. As he chewed, his eyes closed and his expression morphed into one of such pleasure that she didn't need a verbal response. But when she got one, it was just what she'd expected.

"These are awesome, Carly. I had no idea you could bake like this."

She hoped he didn't get any ideas about her changing careers, because there was no way that would ever happen. "Thanks, but it was just a matter of following the directions on the recipe card. Granny was the baker in the family."

"That's for sure. A couple of days after I started working here, your great-grandmother asked me to have dinner with her." He burst into a broad grin, his eyes glimmering. "Fried chicken, mashed potatoes and gravy, fresh green beans. I'll never forget that meal— or any of the others that followed. I would have done anything Granny asked me to do just to get another invitation to sit at her table."

That's the magic Carly hoped the brownies would work for her. She offered Ian a warm smile. "Granny loved cooking and baking for people."

"She sure did. I really lucked out when I landed a job on the Leaning R. And not because I needed the work. I'd been homesick, so we kind of filled a need for each other."

Guilt swirled up inside again, twisting Carly's tummy into a knot. "I guess she was lonely after my brothers and I grew up and didn't need her to look after us anymore."

"She understood that kids should have a life of their own. But it was your father who seemed to abandon her. He got so caught up in his life and his business that she often felt neglected and forgotten."

"I know. Granny said as much to me. His parents

died in a small plane crash when he was a kid, and Granny raised him until his maternal grandfather insisted he attend college in California. That side of the family was very rich, and he was smitten by the glitz and glamour."

"Granny didn't hold that against him," Ian said. "But she still thought he should have called to check on her or stopped in to visit more often than he did."

Carly knew how the older woman felt. Heck, they all did. Charles Rayburn had been very generous with his money, but not with his time. And both of her brothers would agree.

"I hope I didn't let Granny down," she said.

"She never mentioned anything to me about you kids disappointing her."

Carly studied the handsome cowboy who seemed to have become her great-grandma's confidant at the end. "The two of you must have become pretty tight."

He gave a shrug. "I grew up with my grandparents, too. When I got tired of roaming and doing my own thing, I wanted to move back home. But by that time, Granddad had already retired, sold the ranch and moved to Florida to live near my uncle and his family. So I had to find another place to fall back on. That's when I met Granny. Three years ago. I was passing through Brighton Valley and stopped to have breakfast at Caroline's Diner. Granny needed an extra hand, and I wanted a job. Things ended up working out well for both of us."

"I guess it did. But there's something I've always wondered and never asked. Why did you stay on, especially now that things are so up in the air? It would seem to me that you'd look for work on a ranch that's more stable—and more successful."

Ian studied the pretty blonde, her curls tumbling along her shoulders, her blue eyes bright, the lashes thick and lush without the need for mascara.

She brushed the strand of hair from her eyes. "Was the question so difficult that you have to think about your answer? Most foremen would have moved on, especially when no one seemed to care about the Leaning R like my great-grandma did."

There was a lot Carly didn't know about Ian, a lot he hadn't shared. And he wasn't sure how much he wanted her to know.

He hadn't just been looking for work when he'd landed the job on the Leaning R, he'd been looking for a place to call home. And the elderly widow hadn't just found a ranch hand and future foreman, she'd found the grandson she'd always hoped Charles would be.

The two had looked after each other until her death. And even when Rosabelle Rayburn was gone and the late Charles Rayburn had taken charge of her estate, Ian had continued to look after her best interests. It soon became clear that Charles hadn't given a rip about the ranch, and if Ian hadn't been there, who knew what would have happened to the Leaning R?

Like Granddad used to say, *You can't buy loyalty, son. But when it's earned and real, it lasts beyond death*. And those words had proven to be true when it came to Rosabelle and the ranch she'd loved.

Ian shrugged. "I don't have anywhere else to go. Besides, I like Brighton Valley. And I plan to settle here and buy a piece of land."

After Charles died and his oldest son, Jason, became the trustee, Jason had announced that he intended to sell the ranch. When Ian heard that, he decided to purchase it himself. He'd developed more than a fondness for the Leaning R, and not just because he'd worked the land. He'd enjoyed all the stories Granny used to tell him about the history of the place, about the rugged Rayburn men who'd once run cattle here.

"I take it you've been putting some money aside," Carly said.

"You could say that."

"If you need any help, let me know. I'd be happy to loan you some." Carly had a trust fund, so she didn't have any financial worries. Apparently, she assumed Ian was little more than a drifter and needed her charity.

"Thanks, but I'll be all right."

It might come as a big surprise to Carly and her brothers—because it certainly had to Ralph Nettles, the Realtor who would be listing the property—but Ian had money stashed away from his days on the road with Felicia. He also had plenty of royalties coming in from the songs he'd written for her.

So, since he could no longer inherit or purchase the Rocking M from his granddad, buying the Leaning R was the next best thing.

"You know that song you were just playing?" Carly asked.

"What about it?"

"Would you sing it for me? From the beginning?"

Ian had written it right after she'd left the ranch the last time, after they'd both come to the decision that it would be best to end things between them. And while Carly had seemed to think their breakup had been permanent, he hadn't been convinced. She usually came running back to the Leaning R whenever life dealt her a blow, so he'd known she'd return—eventually.

Not that he'd expected her to fail. Hell, she had more talent than her mother and—from what Ian had seen and heard—more heart than either of her parents. And he suspected that, deep down, what she really yearned for was someone to love and appreciate her for who she really was.

Ian wasn't sure that he was that man, though.

Then again, he wasn't convinced that he wasn't, either.

He reached for his guitar, then nodded toward the empty chair on the porch, the one she used to sit on during those romantic nights she'd spent with him in his cabin.

Once she was seated beside him, he sang the song he'd written about the two of them, wondering if she'd connect the dots, if she'd guess that she'd inspired the words and music.

When the last guitar chords disappeared into the night, she clapped softly. "That was beautiful, Ian. I love it. But I have to ask you something. Did you write that song about...us?"

"No, not really," he lied. "When you left, I got to thinking about lovers ending a good thing for all the right reasons. And the words and music just seemed to flow out of me. I guess you could say the song almost wrote itself."

He wasn't about to admit that the words had actually come from his heart. He'd become so adept at hiding his feelings, especially from a woman who'd become—or who was about to become—an ex-lover, that it was easier to let the emotion flow through his guitar.

"You really should do something with that song," Carly said. "In the right hands—or with the right voice—it could be a hit."

No one knew that better than Ian. With one phone call to Felicia, the song would strike platinum in no time. But then, before he knew it, every agent and musician in Nashville would be knocking on his door, insisting he come out of retirement and write for them. And there'd go his quiet life and his privacy.

"Would you please let me sing that with you as a duet at the Stagecoach Inn on Saturday night?" Carly lifted the platter of brownies in a tempting fashion. "If you do, I'll leave the rest of these with you."

A smile slid across his face. He'd always found Carly to be tempting, especially when she was determined to have her way. Sometimes he even gave in to her, but this time he couldn't be swayed. "I may have one heck of a sweet tooth, but you can't bribe me with goodies. It won't work."

She blew out a sigh and pulled the platter back. "Don't make me ask Don Calhoun to play for me."

That little weasel? Surely she wasn't serious. "The guy who hit on you that night we stopped at the Filling

Station to have a drink on our way home from the movies in Wexler?"

"Don went to school with me, and we sometimes performed together at the county fair."

Ian clucked his tongue. "Calhoun's a jerk. I saw him watching you from across the room. And as soon as I excused myself to go to the restroom, he took my seat and asked you out."

"Like I said, Don and I are old friends. But if it makes you feel better, I told him no and let him know that you and I were dating."

But they weren't dating anymore. And, old friends or not, the guy was still a tool.

"What's the deal at the Stagecoach Inn on Saturday night?" Ian asked.

"They're having a local talent night. Our gig would just be a few songs—thirty minutes at the most. Will you please sing with me?"

"Now it's playing *and* singing?"

She held out the brownies, offering him the entire plate, and smiled.

But it wasn't the brownies that caused his resolve to waver, it was the beautiful blonde whose bright blue eyes and dimples turned him every which way but loose. He'd had all kinds of women throw themselves at him, and he'd never lost his head, never forgotten that there were some who weren't interested in the real man inside. But there was something about Carly Rayburn that reached deep into the heart of him, something sweet, something vulnerable.

"Damn it, Carly. I'll do it. But just this once."

"Thanks, Ian. You won't regret this."

She was wrong. They were going to have to practice together every evening from now until Saturday. And he was already regretting it.

## Chapter Three

Carly couldn't believe how talented Ian was on a guitar—and how good they sounded together. Of course, that hadn't made practicing with him any easier. In fact, over the past few nights, each session seemed to have gotten progressively harder to endure than the last, with this being the most difficult yet.

The air almost crackled with the soaring phero-mones, the heady scent of Ian's woodsy cologne and the soft Southern twang of his voice as they performed on the front porch of his cabin. Still, she sang her heart out.

As the music flowed between them, the words of the love songs they'd chosen taunted the raw emotion she'd once felt whenever she'd been in his arms. And it seemed to be truer now than ever, since this was their last chance to practice before singing at the local honky-tonk.

"Let's try 'Breathe' one last time," Ian said. "Then we can call it a night."

"All right," she said, but she feared that if she sang the sexy lyrics of that particular song once more time, she'd refuse to call it a night until she'd kissed the breath right out of her old lover. And then look at the fix she'd be in.

She stole a glance at the handsome cowboy and caught a sparkle in his eyes. The crooked grin tugging at his lips suggested that he knew exactly what he'd done. And that he'd planned all along to suggest the Faith Hill hit as their wrap-up tonight.

Darn him. He probably thought that after singing about the heated desire they shared she'd be more likely to suggest one last night of lovemaking—for old times' sake. But she couldn't do that, even though the idea was sorely tempting.

She had half a notion to scratch that particular song from their list. And she would have done it, too, if they hadn't sounded so good together.

When the song ended, she reached for the glass of water she'd left on the porch railing and took a sip.

"We should be ready for tomorrow night," Ian said, as he placed his guitar back into its case.

Had she been wrong about his intentions?

It appeared so, and while she should be relieved, she tamped down the momentary disappointment.

"Thanks for agreeing to sing with me," she said again.

He didn't respond, which suggested that he still wasn't happy about being forced— No, not forced. She'd only encouraged him. But he'd given his word, which meant he'd follow through on the commitment.

Carly glanced near the front door, at the spot on the wooden flooring where Cheyenne lay curled up asleep. She would have stooped to give the puppy an affectionate pat before leaving, but she hated to wake her.

Instead, she tucked her fingers into the front pocket of her jeans. "I think we're going to knock 'em dead at the Stagecoach Inn."

"You might be right," Ian said, "but keep in mind that it's only a one-shot deal."

That's what they'd agreed to, but she hoped it was actually their first of many performances. She kept that to herself. At this point, there was no need to provoke him any more than she had.

Once he performed with her, she knew the audience would convince him that they were a perfect duo. And then maybe Ian would finally come to the same indisputable conclusion she had—that their amazing chemistry went beyond the bedroom and was destined to light up the stage.

Ian had been in more than his share of honky-tonks during the early days of his career, and the Stagecoach Inn was no different than the others.

Once he crossed the graveled parking lot, climbed the wooden steps and opened the door, the smell of booze and smoke, as well as the sounds of a blaring jukebox and hoots of laughter, slammed into him, taking him back in time to a place he no longer wanted to be.

He stood in the doorway for a moment, watching the people mill about and chatter among themselves.

When he'd been known as Mac McAllister, one of Felicia's Wiley Five, he'd worn his hair long. A bristled face had given him a rugged look he'd favored back then.

Hopefully, no one would recognize him now that he'd shaved and cut his hair in a shorter style. He was also dressed differently, opting for a white button-down shirt and faded jeans, rather than the mostly black attire he'd worn on stage before.

It wasn't until a couple came up behind him that he finally stepped inside the honky-tonk. With his guitar in hand, he made his way across the scarred wood floor to the bar, which stretched across the far wall. In the old days, when he'd played with the Wiley Five, he'd relied on a couple of shots of tequila to get him through the performance. But that wasn't his problem as he headed toward the bar tonight—his throat was just dry.

He was also annoyed at Carly for forcing his hand— or maybe he was just plain angry at himself for rolling over and agreeing to perform with her. He didn't normally do anything he didn't feel like doing.

So why had he agreed to do it for her?

Why here? Why now?

And why had she asked him to meet her here instead of riding over together? Something didn't quite seem right. She might say she hadn't played her daddy, but that wasn't true. And while she might think she could wrap Ian around her little pinky, too, that definitely wasn't the case. After tonight, it wouldn't happen again.

The thirtysomething bartender, a busty brunette in a low-cut tank top, leaned forward across the polished oak bar and offered him an eyeful. "Can I get you a drink, cowboy? It's happy hour. Draft beers are two for one."

"No, thanks. I'm not looking for a deal."

"Ooh. Big spender. I like that in my men."

Ian liked his bartenders to keep quiet and do their job. Instead of serving the patrons, this flirty brunette ought to be seated on the other side of the bar, tempting the male customers to buy her a drink.

"I'll have a root beer," he said.

Her eyes widened, and her lips parted. "Seriously?"

"You got a problem with my order?"

"Nope." She straightened and her smile faded. "Coming right up."

He glanced over his shoulder at the door, wondering where Carly was. He doubted she'd be late. The performance was too important to her.

The busty barkeep set a can and a frosted mug in front of him. "Do you want to run a tab?"

"Nope." He placed a ten dollar bill on the bar, then took a swig of his soda pop.

"That's a shame. I was looking forward to serving you all night."

As the brunette turned to get Ian's change, Carly, who'd apparently just arrived, eased in beside him. She was wearing a brand-new outfit—at least, as far as he could tell. And with her makeup done to a tee, she was just as beautiful as ever, although he preferred to see her without all the hairspray and glitz.

"I'm sorry I'm late," she said.

"I haven't been here long."

She laughed, her eyes sparkling. "I'm just glad you showed up."

Ian reached for her hand and held it tight, his thumb pressing against her wrist, where her pulse rate kicked up a notch. "I said I'd be here, Carly. And while I'll admit I'm not happy about doing it, when I give my word about something, I keep it. So if you had any real doubts, you don't know me as well as you think."

Her glimmering eyes widened, and her lips parted. He wasn't sure if it was his words or his touch setting her emotions reeling. Either way, he didn't mind. There were a few things she needed to get straight about him. He was loyal and honest to a fault. But he wasn't anyone's lapdog.

He released her hand, his own heart rate pulsing through his veins, his own emotions swirling around in a slurpy mess. What was it about Carly Rayburn that set him off like this?

"I'm sorry for pushing you," she said, "but this is going to be fun. You won't be sorry once you see how people react to the two of us singing. Besides, we practiced—and we sound good together."

They had practiced. And they did do well. Carly had a beautiful voice, maybe even better than Felicia's. It had a sultrier edge to it, a sexy, intoxicating sound that the fans were going to eat up. Hell, Ian could listen to her talk or laugh or sing all night long.

"What time are we supposed to go on?" he asked.

"Around nine o'clock—give or take a few minutes. Do you want to find a table? Or would you rather sit here at the bar?"

He glanced at the bartender, who was laying down his change, her eyes and her sullen expression focused on Carly.

"I'd be more comfortable at one of the booths in the corner," he said. "Come on, let's go."

This time, he didn't give her a chance to argue.

Carly followed Ian as he made his way through the crowd to an out-of-the-way spot in the back. She hadn't meant to push him or to anger him. No matter what he might think, she wasn't that type of woman. But in this case, she felt she was doing him a favor.

She supposed she was doing herself one, too.

The only way the two of them could strike up any kind of romantic relationship again, one that might even prove lasting, was if they could perform together. Once they did, he'd see that he was meant to pursue a career in music, same as she. But even then, a commitment might be questionable. Carly was used to strong men. And Ian seemed so…quiet and unassuming. Perhaps he just needed a little push now and then to help build his self-confidence.

She'd struggled with that herself until Braden's mom encouraged her to sing in the Sunday choir one summer. And it had done wonders for her.

Yes, all Ian needed was to see that there was a future for him as a singer and musician—one that was more exciting and profitable than working someone else's cattle for the rest of his life.

Of course, when Ian had grabbed her hand this evening, when he'd admonished her for not trusting him to be a man of his word, he'd certainly given her reason to doubt her initial assessment of him.

Sure, she knew he was a good man, an honest one. And there was no question he was an amazing and considerate lover. She wouldn't have gotten involved with him in the first place if that hadn't been the case. It's just that they'd hit this fork in their road, and he wanted to go a different direction than she did.

She wouldn't claim it hadn't hurt her to end things between them, but it had been for the best. Really.

Now, as they sat in silence in a darkened corner booth, Ian's expression somber, she knew she had to think of something to say, something to change his mood. But before she could give it any thought, a blonde cocktail waitress stopped at their table.

"Can I get y'all a drink?" she asked.

Carly would have ordered a glass of wine, but her tummy had been bothering her again. Not as badly as it had in San Antonio, but she didn't dare risk a bout of nausea before performing. "I'll have a lemon-lime soda."

"You got it." The cocktail waitress looked at Ian and smiled. "How about you?"

"I'll have a shot of tequila—Patrón or the best you have."

Now that was a surprise. Ian never drank—at least, Carly hadn't seen him drink. But apparently, she didn't know him as well as she'd thought.

"I didn't realize you liked tequila," she said.

He didn't respond.

Maybe he was just taking the edge off his nerves. She probably should have been a little more understanding, but there was only one way to kick a little stage fright, and that was to perform right through it.

He remained quiet, his expression intense, until the waitress brought his drink. Carly expected him to grimace at the taste, but instead, he threw it back as if it were the sweet tea he sometimes favored.

Okay, so maybe he hadn't always been the teetotaler she'd thought he might be. But if a stiff shot eased his nerves, that was fine with her.

Fortunately, they didn't have to wait long. Just before nine o'clock, Earl Tellis, the owner of the Stagecoach Inn, took the stage, following two cowboys who played the fiddle.

"Folks, we have a real treat for y'all tonight. Most of you know Rosabelle Rayburn, who owned the Leaning R Ranch and who was one of the finest women in these parts. Well, her great-granddaughter, Carly, and her foreman, Ian, will be singing for you now. Come on up here, you two."

"You ready?" Carly asked as she slid out from the booth.

Ian, who'd corralled his empty shot glass with both hands, grumbled like a bear coming out of his cave in the spring. But like he'd said, he'd given her his word that he'd sing with her tonight.

A rush of guilt and regret swept through her, sending her tummy on a roller-coaster ride. Okay, maybe she shouldn't have pushed him to do something that made him uncomfortable. But it was too late to back-pedal now. So she headed to the stage as Ian joined her, his guitar in hand.

Just as they'd done during their practice sessions on his porch at the ranch, they sang and played their hearts out. And when they were done, the honky-tonk crowd whooped and hollered and cheered.

This wasn't the kind of stage Carly had set her sights on, but it certainly was the audience appreciation she'd hoped for. She glanced at Ian, who simply nodded at the crowd, then returned to his seat at the table.

So much for wishing he'd be inspired by the crowd's reaction.

Carly had no more than reached the booth where they'd been sitting earlier when Earl Tellis joined her and Ian.

"That was amazing. I can't tell you how much I enjoyed hearing you two play and sing. What talent—and you seem to bring out the best in each other."

Carly brightened. She'd felt that same chemistry in Ian's arms as well as on his front porch when they'd sung together. So it was nice to know she wasn't the only one who'd sensed it. "Why, thank you, Earl."

"In fact, I'd like to offer you a job singing here on Friday and Saturday nights."

"That'd be great." Carly glanced at Ian, hoping he'd be as flattered as she was.

"Thanks for the offer," Ian said, "but I'm afraid I'm not interested."

His words slammed into her, and she struggled to get back on an even keel. "Mr. Tellis, why don't you let us talk this over. We'll get back to you."

"There's nothing to talk over," Ian said. "My mind was made up before I even walked in the door."

She'd known that, but she'd hoped he'd feel differently once they got on stage together, once he saw the reaction she'd expected. "Can't you please think about it for a few days? I mean, what would it hurt?"

"I'm a rancher, not a performer." Ian tipped his hat at Earl. "But thanks again for the offer, Mr. Tellis."

Carly crossed her arms. "Well, my mind isn't made up."

"Isn't it?" Ian's gaze grilled into her. "Nobody is stopping you from taking the gig. I wouldn't dream of trying to talk you into doing something you didn't want to do."

Her cheeks flamed with guilt, and she couldn't think of a response, other than another apology, but she doubted that would help at this point.

"I'll see you back at the ranch," he said.

As Ian strode across the floor, Carly turned to Earl. "Give me a day or two. But either way, I might just take the job, even if I have to find another guitarist."

Then she followed Ian outside. She didn't catch up to him until they reached the graveled parking lot.

"I'm sorry for pushing so hard," Carly said to his

back. "But what's the matter with you? I don't get it. You have more talent than anyone I've ever met. You could really go somewhere with that guitar and your voice. Do you know how many people would kill for talent like that?"

Ian slowed to a stop and turned. "I'm not interested in going anywhere. Remember?"

"Yes, but why not? Are you afraid of crowds? Everyone gets a little nervous before performing, but you'll get used to it. I promise."

"Just drop it, Carly. You might have set your sights on a singing career, but I haven't. Can't you get it through your pretty head and one-track brain that I'm perfectly content staying in Brighton Valley?"

"Yes, I know. You told me that. But I can't seem to wrap my mind around it. Not when you're so musically gifted. Have you ever heard yourself play and sing? You're every country girl's dream."

Ian lifted his hat and raked his fingers through his dark hair. "That life isn't for me, Carly. And nothing you can say is going to change my mind."

"You're as stubborn as a mule, Ian McAllister."

He blew out a heavy sigh and shook his head. "You might have been able to wrap your daddy and mama around your little finger—or guilt them into doing whatever you asked. But it won't work with me." Then he turned and headed for his truck.

"Darn it, Ian." She followed after him, speaking to his broad back. "You have no idea what it was like for me as a child. And just for the record, I was never able to guilt anyone into doing squat for me."

When he reached for the door handle, she grabbed his shirtsleeve and gave it a tug. "Would you please wait?"

He turned, and their gazes met. She stroked his muscular forearm, hoping to disarm his irritation. For a moment, passion flared between them, just as it always did whenever she touched him. But this time, her entire body began to buzz, too. Colors merged and Ian's face blurred before her eyes.

Her lips parted, but before she could tell him she felt lightheaded, everything went black.

Ian had never been so angry at a woman in his life. He was about to lay into Carly and tell her so, when her grip on his arm loosened and she uttered a weird sound before slumping to the ground in a dead faint.

What the hell? He stooped and caught her just before her head hit the gravel.

"Carly? Are you all right?" He knelt beside her, holding her close, his heart pounding like crazy. "Honey, talk to me. What's wrong?"

A couple of cowboys wandered past him, heading to the bar. As they spotted him holding a limp Carly, they changed their course and approached him.

"Is she okay?" one asked. "Do you need an ambulance?"

Ian had a cell phone in his pocket, but he'd rather have both hands available to hold her. "Yeah. Would you call 9-1-1?"

He had no idea what was wrong with her. He did know she'd come home from San Antonio with some kind of lingering virus. Or so her brother Jason had told him.

Was it something more serious? Something Carly hadn't wanted him to know?

Ian had no idea, but the thought of losing her, of seeing her hooked up to wires and tubes and…

Okay, slow down. Maybe she'd only fainted. Maybe it was something easily explained, like iron-poor blood.

"Do you know CPR?" the cowboy who wasn't talking on his cell phone asked.

Ian had taken a first-aid course in high school. And while he wasn't an expert, he remembered what he'd learned. But Carly's pulse was strong, her breathing slow but steady. "She doesn't need it."

Not yet, anyway.

The cowboy on his cell disconnected the line, then shoved his phone back in his pocket. "Paramedics are on the way."

By that time, a small crowd had gathered around them. Someone whispered, "That's the pretty little gal who was singing just a few minutes ago. I wonder what happened?"

"Was she hit by a car?" another bystander asked.

"She's probably had too much to drink," the guy next to him said.

Ian didn't bother to set either of them straight. His thoughts were centered on Carly.

When she moaned and lifted her hand to her forehead, he figured that was a good sign. "Honey, are you okay?"

Her eyes flickered opened. She looked at him and blinked a couple of times, as if trying to focus.

What had caused her to pass out? High blood pressure? Low blood sugar? At times like this, Ian wished he'd gone on to medical school like his grandma had hoped he'd do. But first aid, a human biology course in junior college and talking to every nurse or doctor he could corner while seated at his granddad's bedside in the cardiac unit ICU four years ago hadn't made him an expert.

After what seemed like ages, but was probably only a couple of minutes, an ambulance sounded in the distance, causing Carly to become even more aware of her surroundings.

"What…happened?" she asked.

"You passed out." Ian brushed the hair from her forehead and caressed her cheek.

She glanced at the crowd gathered around her, pressing into them.

"Give her some air," Ian told the bystanders.

Carly tried to sit up, but he stopped her. "Just lie here until the paramedics arrive. We'll get you checked out at the medical center, and you'll be fit as a fiddle in no time at all."

She slumped back in his arms. "I was going to call and make a doctor's appointment on Monday morning."

"Yeah, well, now you won't need to do that." Before he could say anything else, the ambulance pulled into the lot, red lights flashing.

The crowd slowly dispersed, giving paramedics room to move in. Ian knew he should give them space to work, too, so he asked one of the cowboys still standing nearby if he could borrow his jacket.

He rolled it up and placed it under Carly's head, then he eased back, but he remained on his knees beside her.

The paramedics, a red-haired man and a brunette woman, moved in to assess their patient. After taking Carly's vitals, the woman asked, "Any chance you could be pregnant?"

The question, the remote possibility, nearly knocked the wind right out of Ian, and while he waited for Carly's response, he thought he might pass out, too.

## Chapter Four

*P*regnant?

The very question threw Carly into a tailspin that had nothing to do with her becoming lightheaded before and everything to do with Ian, who was gazing at her, waiting for an answer.

Sure, the thought had crossed her mind a time or two, but she'd never had morning sickness. She'd only been nauseous in the evenings. She'd also had a couple of periods, although they'd been lighter than usual, which was normal for her, considering her gynecological problems. But what difference did that make? Her doctor had told her it was unlikely that she'd ever conceive.

Had that diagnosis been wrong? Could she have conceived a baby during her fling with Ian? Could that be the real cause of her bouts of nausea and not some strange virus?

They'd used protection, but there were nights when their passion had been so hot, when they'd been so desperate for sexual release that they'd become careless once or twice. But she couldn't admit that here—and now.

Still, she had to respond to the unsettling question. She should be completely honest with the paramedics, but she didn't want to deal with a life-altering possibility now. Not in front of a gaping crowd.

And certainly not in front of the man who'd be the baby's father.

So she said, "No, I don't think so."

While the paramedics took her vitals, Ian got to his feet and took a step back, allowing them room to work. But he remained beside her, waiting, watching. *Listening.*

The brunette medic kneeling beside Carly pulled the stethoscope from her ears. "Everything appears to be normal, but it might be a good idea for us to take you to the hospital just to be sure. The doctors may want to run some tests."

A pregnancy test would probably be the first one on the list, but Carly couldn't deal with that thought tonight.

"I'm feeling better now," she said. "I'd rather just go home and take it easy. I'll call my doctor first thing on Monday morning and make an appointment to see her."

Ian eased closer. "Carly, I'd rather you go to the ER tonight and get checked out."

Was he concerned about her health—or eager to hear if she was pregnant? She wanted to have that test, too, so she could rule it out.

Or wrap her mind around the possibility.

The more she thought about it, the more plausible it seemed—in spite of what her doctor had said. But if she was pregnant, she'd be…what? Four months along? Why, that was nearly halfway there…

She fought a flash of panic and the urge to place her hand on her tummy, where she'd noticed that she'd put on weight. She'd blamed it on her hormonal imbalance. But had she been wrong?

She scanned the faces of the strangers who'd gathered around her.

This couldn't be happening.

*Think, girl. Think.*

"I'm sure it isn't anything serious." She sat up, hoping her head didn't start spinning again. But shoot, just thinking about—

Oh, for Pete's sake. She was making way too much out of this. A doctor had given her every reason to believe that it was unlikely she would ever be able to have a baby. Besides, she and Ian had used contraceptives, so surely there wasn't a chance of pregnancy. At least, she hoped not.

Carly blew out a sigh and looked at Ian. "I'm fine. I didn't have much for lunch, so I probably just need to eat something."

He studied her, questioning her with a gaze so intense that she felt herself start to unravel.

To be honest, she wasn't sure about anything right

now, but she didn't want him to worry—or worse, have any doubts about the truth of her response.

"I'm sure a juicy hamburger will do the trick." She offered him a wobbly smile, although the thought of a greasy burger suddenly turned her stomach.

The crowd, no doubt realizing her fainting spell was minor and that there'd be more excitement inside the honky-tonk, began to disperse. And the paramedics packed up their gear.

The only one who didn't seem convinced that the crisis was over was Ian.

Concern and suspicion swirled in Ian's head, at odds with each other. Carly might say that she couldn't be pregnant, but why had she fainted? Was it just a troubling stomach bug?

If she was pregnant and the baby was Ian's, she'd have to be about four months along. But then again, she could have met someone else while she was away, someone who'd broken her heart and caused her to quit the show and run home to the Leaning R.

The realization that she might have found another guy so quickly didn't sit very well and gnawed at him for more reasons than one.

After he and Felicia Jamison had become lovers, things had been good between them for a while. But then Felicia had gotten pregnant. Ian had been stunned, yet pleased at the prospect of becoming a father. But she'd chosen to have an abortion rather than have their baby, saying that a child would sidetrack her booming career.

Ian had always wanted a family of his own, so he'd been crushed by her decision. And that's when the bright lights and glamour of touring and performing onstage began to fade.

His and Felicia's relationship had faded at that point, too. And she soon moved on to someone else.

Ian hadn't been all that bothered by their breakup, though. The fact that Felicia had cared so little about the baby they'd created told him how she felt about their relationship—and about him.

Splitting up had actually been for the best. He wanted more out of a lifetime partner, more out of a wife.

He reached out to Carly and helped her to her feet. "Then let's go home. We'll take my pickup. You can leave yours here, and I'll bring you back to get it in the morning."

He half expected her to object, since they didn't always see things eye to eye, but she said, "All right."

"And on the way home," he added, "I'll get you that juicy burger."

"Sounds good. Thanks." She followed him to his Dodge Ram. When he opened the passenger door, she slid onto the seat.

The drive to Burger Junction only took five minutes, yet neither of them spoke on the way.

Was Carly still feeling the effects of her fainting spell? Or was she thinking about what might really be wrong with her? His curiosity, as well as the silence in the cab, grew until he thought he'd go crazy.

"Do you want to order takeout or go inside and eat?" he asked.

"Actually, I'd rather eat at home—if you don't mind."

"Not at all."

They pulled into the drive-through and placed their orders. When they finally headed back to the ranch, Ian's suspicion had built to the point that it was all he could think of.

He stole a glance at her and watched as she stared out the window and into the night.

"So you don't think you could be pregnant?" he asked.

She bit down on her bottom lip, as though pondering the question—or even the possibility. Then she turned to him. "I don't see how. I mean, we used condoms."

Did that mean he was the only possible father?

"They aren't a hundred percent effective," he said.

"I know, but I doubt I'm pregnant." She offered him a breezy smile that didn't do much to reassure him.

"Maybe we should stop by the all-night drugstore in Wexler and pick up a pregnancy test."

"We don't need to do that. I'd rather wait and see what the doctor has to say on Monday."

She hadn't given him any reason to think that she'd been with someone else. Not that he could object since they'd ended things between them. It's just that he hadn't felt the need to find another lover.

Not yet, anyway.

Still, after what he and Felicia had gone through, Ian wasn't sure he wanted to face something similar again.

Damn. That's all he needed—Carly pregnant with his baby, yet hell-bent on being a star.

Then again, she'd said she didn't think it was possible. And at this point, he had no reason to doubt her.

True to his word, Ian took Carly to get her pickup at the Stagecoach Inn on Saturday morning. To ease the awkwardness and to avoid discussing her potential health issue, Carly focused their conversation on safe subjects like the weather and the long-forgotten items in Granny's attic that still needed to be sorted through and packed away.

As soon as they arrived at the honky-tonk, she slid out of the truck, grabbed her purse and thanked him for the ride.

"No problem." He studied her again, his left arm draped over the steering wheel, his expression unreadable. "I'll follow you back to the ranch."

And face his scrutiny again? She'd be a basket case within an hour. "You go on ahead. I have some errands to run in Wexler, so I'll see you later."

To be honest, even if she didn't have a single thing on her to-do list, she planned to make herself scarce today. She had to escape the intensity in his gaze, which reached deep inside of her, making her question every word she'd ever said, anything she'd ever done and each emotion she'd ever felt. So she would stay away from the ranch until late that evening.

But first she had a very important stop to make.

Ian had suggested it last night on the way home from the Stagecoach Inn, but she'd refused to even consider it then. He was the last person she wanted with her when she purchased a home pregnancy test. But now that she was on her own, she could hardly wait to buy one and see what it had to say.

Fifteen minutes later, she pulled into the parking lot of the largest drugstore in Wexler. Then she slipped on a pair of sunglasses, hoping to avoid being recognized by anyone who might possibly know her, and headed for the entrance.

She'd be darned if she was going to get into the checkout lane with only one item in her hand, particularly a pregnancy test, so she grabbed a small red basket, hung the handle over her arm, and walked up and down the aisles until she'd filled it with stuff she really didn't need.

Along the way, she picked up a box of chocolates, peach-scented lotion and a get-well card for Braden's grandpa. She added deodorant, toothpaste and tampons, which she thought was a clever way to throw off suspicion. Then she headed for the shelves that held her primary reason for the shopping venture and snatched the first box she spotted, not taking the time to read the claims or directions on the box.

As nonchalantly as she could, she made her way to the checkout lanes.

If the clerk at the register thought anything strange about her purchase, she didn't blink an eye. Instead, she tallied the total and waited for Carly to count out the cash.

Moments later, Carly was out the door and pondering her next step. She could wait until she was at home tonight and in the privacy of her own room to take the test, but she'd probably die of anticipation in the meantime.

But where should she go?

As she climbed into her truck, she noticed a fast food restaurant to the right—Billy Bob's Burgers. They'd have a public restroom inside, which made the ordeal feel pretty clandestine. But that seemed like the best option since she didn't want to wait another minute.

She parked near the entrance, went inside and placed an order for a breakfast burrito and an orange juice. Then she headed for the ladies' room and chose a stall.

Her fingers trembled as she took the box from her purse, tore into it and read the instructions. After following the directions, she placed the small, plastic apparatus on top of a folded paper towel, then set it on the shelf where she'd left her purse and waited. Apparently, it was supposed to take several minutes for a positive line to show up, but the answer formed almost immediately.

She blinked twice, hoping to get a better read, but there was no doubting the results.

*Pregnant.*

As the line brightened like a neon sign, her heart raced. That couldn't be right. Could it? Dr. Connor had told her it wasn't likely that she'd ever conceive. But the plastic apparatus on the shelf argued otherwise.

The doctor had been wrong.

Or was it the test? Maybe it was a false positive.

The door to the restroom opened and closed, indicating someone else had come in. Carly needed to get out of here, but she couldn't seem to make her feet work.

She was…*pregnant*? She wasn't sure if she should laugh or cry. She supposed she'd get used to the idea with time. But if she was actually going to have a baby, what in the world would she tell Ian?

Somehow Carly stumbled through the morning. She'd managed to drink her juice, but she'd yet to remove her breakfast burrito from the bag. Apparently, the results of the pregnancy test had stolen her appetite.

She was still determined to avoid going home so she didn't have to face Ian, who deserved to know the truth. But until she was able to wrap her own mind around the news and figure out some sort of game plan, she wasn't ready to tell him anything.

For that reason, she'd gone window shopping on Wexler Boulevard. She was studying a bright red dress on a blonde mannequin in the window of the new women's shop that opened recently when her cell phone rang. She pulled the iPhone from her purse and glanced at the display.

She didn't feel like talking to anyone, but her mother didn't call often, so she probably ought to take it. If Carly had a normal mom, she might be tempted to share her news—or rather, her confusion. But Carly and Raelynn had never had that kind of relationship.

"Hey, there," Carly said. "How's it going, Raelynn?"

The country singer turned oilman's wife paused for a beat. "You know, darlin', it's okay now for you to call me Mom or Mama."

Maybe so, but old habits were hard to break.

And relationships were what they were.

"How's David?" Carly asked. Her mother had fallen hard for her second husband, hard enough to give up her singing career. Or maybe she just yearned for another spotlight these days—the wife of a bigwig senator.

"He's doing fine—and gearing up for reelection. So we've had a slew of dinner parties and fundraisers to attend. Thankfully, we're flying to London later on this month, which will be a nice break. But I called to check on *you*."

That was nice—yet a little unexpected.

"I was in San Antonio last night with some friends," Raelynn added, "and we tried to attend your show."

That was an even bigger surprise. Raelynn usually hadn't found the time to attend any of Carly's performances before—even when she'd been a child in school.

"The director told me you'd gotten sick and quit," Raelynn added. "What happened? And where are you?"

Her mother's concern touched her, yet she wasn't about to go into detail. "I got a persistent case of the stomach flu and had to leave the show. I've been staying at the Leaning R."

"Are you feeling better now?"

"Yes, I am. Thanks." But the revelation of another diagnosis was on the horizon, one Carly doubted her mother could possibly be prepared for. She'd just given Carly permission to call her Mom, but how would she feel about someone calling her Grandma?

"You know," Raelynn said, her voice lacking the Southern twang that had been her trademark on the stage. "You're always welcome to come to Houston and stay with David and me. We have plenty of room. You can even housesit while we're gone."

While she appreciated the offer, that was out of the question. It wasn't that Carly didn't like Senator David Crowder. He was as charming as her father had been—maybe even more so. Nor had she held on to a childish wish that her parents had stayed together. They really hadn't been suited.

But Carly had never been comfortable staying at her stepfather's house. Not that she'd felt truly at home in Raelynn's elegant townhouse prior to their marriage, either.

"Thanks for the offer," Carly said, "but I'm helping Jason inventory Granny's belongings." That was true, of course. And the best reason to give her mother. She might not have ever been especially close to Raelynn, but there was no reason to hurt her feelings.

"How is your brother?" Raelynn asked. "I'll bet he's been busy since Charles died. He's in charge of the estate, isn't he?"

"Yes, and he's fine. He married Juliana Bailey, an old friend of mine, last weekend. They're on their honeymoon."

"I don't remember her."

Why would she? Raelynn had been on tour so often that she'd scarcely remembered she even had a daughter.

"Juliana grew up on a ranch here in Brighton Valley," Carly said. "She and I used to ride horses together whenever I stayed with Granny at the Leaning R."

"So where did Jason take his new bride?" Raelynn asked.

"To Mexico." Carly wasn't going to tell her mother about the family mystery or how Braden had learned their father had been looking for a woman named Camilla Cruz when he'd died down in that car accident six months ago.

When Braden learned this his grandfather was ill, he had to return home, but not before finding out Camilla had died and that her two young children had been placed in an orphanage. So Jason and his new bride had continued the search for the kids.

"You'd think Jason could be more imaginative and take his wife to Tahiti or to Paris—somewhere romantic. But then again, when it really mattered, your father wasn't very romantic, either."

Carly let the comment go unchallenged and tried to come up with another topic.

Raelynn gave a little snort. "I always feared that boy would grow up just like Charles. Now he's dragged his new wife on a business trip and he's masking it as a honeymoon."

That wasn't true. Jason told Carly he planned to take Juliana on a real honeymoon once they located Camilla's children. But there was no need to defend him at this point. The truth would come out one of these days.

Raelynn had falsely assumed that Charles had been in Mexico, working on some big business venture, when he'd had that accident. And it was just as well that she did. She had a tendency to repeat tales, but not before adding a little to them.

Besides, Raelynn had always had hard feelings toward Charles after their split. In fact, their divorce had taken several years to settle. Too bad their courtship hadn't lasted long enough for them to realize just how ill-suited they were and saved each other the trouble.

Carly had only been eight at the time, but she didn't remember being too affected by their breakup. She hadn't seen much of either parent when they'd been together. As a result, she'd grown up in their shadows. Was it any wonder she wanted to break free and do something on her own?

"Well, I suppose I'd better let you go," Raelynn said. "I have a hair appointment at eleven, then a lunch date with Claire, Senator Dobson's wife."

"Have fun."

"How about you?" Raelynn asked. "Do you have any special plans today?"

"No. Nothing out of the ordinary."

In fact, the only thing she had going on in the near future was figuring out a way to break the news to Ian that he was going to be a father.

And making an appointment on Monday with the woman who'd been Carly's gynecologist before opening a family medical practice. The doctor who'd told her it wasn't likely that she'd ever get pregnant.

Bright and early Monday morning, at least as far as Carly was concerned, she called Dr. Selena Connor's office. After she told the receptionist about the positive pregnancy test and her fainting spell, the woman asked when she'd had her last period.

"I'll have to check my calendar, since I've had a couple of light ones lately, but if you're trying to figure out how far along I am, I can't possibly be less than four months."

"Have you had any prenatal care?" the woman asked.

"I only learned that I was pregnant yesterday," Carly said. "Unless those home tests aren't accurate."

"You'd be more apt to get a false negative," the receptionist said. "Let's get you in here as soon as possible." After a slight pause, she added, "Dr. Connor is going on a short vacation, starting tomorrow, but we can squeeze you in at two o'clock this afternoon. Will that work?"

So soon? Everything seemed to be happening at record speed. And instead of waiting nine months for a baby, she'd only have to wait five.

"That'll be fine. I'll see you then."

With that call out of the way, Carly made a cup of herbal tea. She'd just buttered a toasted English muffin when Ian knocked at the back door.

"Come on in," she called to him.

He entered the kitchen through the mudroom, Cheyenne tagging along behind him, panting as her short legs tried to keep up. He stood with his hat in hand, a slight furrow in his brow. "Good morning. How are you feeling?"

She offered him a smile. "I'm fine." But then again, with the handsome cowboy's eyes caressing her, taunting her—and yes, questioning the truth of her answer—she was feeling all kinds of things that could make her lightheaded enough to swoon.

"Did you get that doctor's appointment?" he asked.

"Yes, I did. It's at two o'clock this afternoon."

"Would you like me to take you?"

No way. Not when she knew that he'd pressure her to find out what she'd already learned. When she told him, she wanted to be prepared for his reaction—and any questions he might have about the future.

"Thanks," she said, "but I'll drive myself."

When he cocked his head, as if doubting her decision, she added, "I'll be okay."

"I'm not so sure about that."

*Really.* Couldn't he just let it go? The last thing she needed was to have him sitting with her in the waiting room. Of course, she might be sorry she'd declined his offer, which actually had been sweet, if Dr. Connor gave her bad news or a startling, unexpected diagnosis.

Ian continued to study her, his gaze picking at loose threads in her heart.

Shaking his inspection, which was sure to unravel her, she asked, "Can I fix you coffee—or maybe an English muffin?"

"No, thanks. I ate a couple of hours ago."

Of course he had. His days always began at the crack of dawn, and she was a night owl. In fact, when they'd been a couple and sleeping together, he'd always slipped out of bed quietly, not wanting to wake her.

A mental picture of the two of them in bed began to form in her mind. But this time they weren't sleeping.

Ian had been a considerate lover. An amazingly good one, too. But there was more to life than sex.

Yet as his musk and leather scent taunted her and attraction sparked between them, she wasn't so sure about that.

Ian, on the other hand, merely slipped on his hat, turned for the door and strode out of the house with a sexy cowboy swagger, the little wannabe cattle dog bounding out behind him.

Okay, she had to admit that in the scheme of things great sex had its perks and should never be underrated. But she couldn't stew about that now. Not without complicating her life all over again.

For the next hour, Carly went over the inventory list Juliana had left behind. After realizing that it wasn't just the attic that was untouched, but that no one had even begun to pack the basement yet, she turned on the light and headed downstairs. Then she got busy assessing the various antiques and the boxes the Rayburn family had been storing for a couple of generations.

Only trouble was, she hadn't been able to focus on anything other than what the doctor might say this afternoon. So, rather than waste her energy, she returned upstairs, took a shower and headed into town early.

Since she had plenty of time to kill, she drove through Hamburger Junction and ordered a grilled chicken sandwich and a drink. Then she went to the office building next to the Brighton Valley Medical Center, parked under the shade of an elm and tried to force herself to eat something even though her tummy was jumbled.

At one thirty, she walked across the parking lot to the redbrick building that housed various doctors' offices. Once inside the lobby, she took the elevator to the second floor, where Selena Connor practiced family medicine in room 204.

As Carly stepped out the elevator doors, she spotted Shannon Miller, Braden's mother, standing outside another physician's office, next to a man wearing a light blue dress shirt and a stylish tie. The white lab coat he wore suggested he was a doctor.

She'd always liked Braden's mom, who'd gotten pregnant by Carly's dad right after she'd graduated from high school. The wealthy businessman had charmed the young woman into an affair while he was still married to Jason's mom.

Of course, Carly hadn't been born when it happened, but she'd heard the whispers ever since. Apparently it had been quite the town scandal.

When Shannon, whose eyes were red-rimmed, spotted Carly exiting the elevator, she waved her over and introduced her to Dr. Erik Chandler, saying he was an "old friend."

Carly greeted the doctor, then turned to Shannon. "I was sorry to hear that your father isn't doing well."

Shannon tucked a strand of brown hair behind her ear. "It's been tough. The hospice nurse said she couldn't be sure, but she thinks he only has a week or two left. But his affairs are in order. So at least that's one less thing for Braden and me to stress about."

Dr. Chandler placed a comforting hand on Shannon's back. "I need to get back to my patients, but I'll stop by the house this evening."

She offered the man a smile that made her look younger than her forty-six years. "Thank you, Erik. I don't know what I'd do without you."

The handsome doctor cupped her cheek. "You're one of the strongest women I know, Shannon. I'll see you later." Then he headed down the hall.

When a door shut behind them, Shannon said, "Erik and I dated for a while in high school, then he left for college. He's only recently come back to town, but he's been very supportive and helpful. A real blessing, actually."

Carly could understand that, even though the doctor had been right—Shannon was strong. She'd raised Braden on her own, in spite of the town-wide rumors calling her a home wrecker.

After Carly's parents had divorced, Carly had spent summers and holidays at the Leaning R with Granny. She couldn't remember how many times Shannon would invite her over to hang out with Braden. And at Christmas, she always bought presents for both Carly and Jason.

Looking back, Carly suspected that Shannon had felt sorry for her. And in a sense, maybe she'd had reason to. As a child, Carly had been lonely much of the time.

"Braden said you were back in town," Shannon said, "and that you'd gotten sick and had to quit that show in San Antonio. I hope it isn't serious."

It wasn't, at least not in the way Shannon was implying. But the diagnosis was pretty unsettling, especially when Carly had expected an entirely different future for herself.

"I'm just here for a checkup," she said.

"That's good. I know how badly you want to perform. It's all you used to talk about when you were younger."

As a child, Carly had taken music and dance lessons, finding that she had a talent that surpassed her mother's. She'd even gone to an impressive college of performing arts. Yet about the time her mother could have introduced her to the stage and given her a leg up, she'd married David Crowder, a state politician, and retired. Still, Carly had set out to become the country-western star her mother once was.

"I still have that dream," Carly said. "And I intend to make it happen."

"I'm sure you will." Shannon glanced at the elevator. "Well, I'd better go. I need to check on my dad, and I don't want you to be late for your appointment."

"Take care," Carly said. "And please call me if there's anything I can do."

"Thanks, honey. I will."

Then they each turned to go their own way.

Once inside the waiting room, Carly signed in and then took a seat. Thanks to her chat with Shannon, she wasn't nearly as early as she thought she'd be. Her name was called in just a few minutes.

After a stop at the scale, Carly was taken to an exam

room. She didn't have to wait long for Dr. Selena Connor to enter.

"What seems to be the problem?" the pretty brunette asked.

Carly told her about the fainting spell, the evening bouts of nausea and the positive pregnancy test. "I'm not the kind who would ignore those symptoms for so long, but I had some light periods and I wasn't nauseous in the mornings."

"All women are different, and the symptoms can vary. Some aren't even sick at all."

"I told myself there were a zillion reasons I couldn't be pregnant. For one thing, you told me it wasn't likely. Plus we used protection." She placed her hand on her stomach, felt the small bulge that she'd blamed on that dumb hormonal imbalance and bloating.

A small part of her—the little girl who'd once played with dollies and dreamed of being a mommy someday—perked up. But she did her best to shake it off.

After witnessing the disaster of her parents' marriage and divorce, she'd learned not to trust those happy-ever-after urges, and as a result, she'd focused on having a successful career instead.

Still, she'd imagined that she'd have a family someday, an adopted one. But not until her career was going strong.

"I can't believe this," Carly said. "And if you check your notes, you'll see that it wasn't supposed to happen."

The doctor didn't even look at the chart. "Yes, I remember saying it wasn't likely. But I also told you it wasn't impossible."

Carly's heart thumped in both fear and anticipation. That little girl rose up again, and she wondered what it might be like to have a child grow inside her womb, to feel it move and kick.

But could she do right by her son or daughter? Could she overcome her own limited mothering to become a good and loving one herself?

"Why don't you lie back and let me examine you," Dr. Connor said.

Carly complied, stretching out. She stared at the ceiling, afraid to speak, afraid to breathe.

The doctor had hardly palpated Carly's belly when she said, "Your uterus is definitely enlarged."

Carly draped a hand across her eyes. "So it's true. I'm pregnant."

After further examination, the doctor replied, "About four months, from what I can tell, although we'll need to do a sonogram to know for sure. I'm running a very tight schedule today, so I'd like to make an appointment for you to come back for that. I'll also have the nurse provide you with prenatal vitamins and some reading material to answer your questions. In the meantime, you will need some lab work, so we'll have your blood drawn today, too."

Carly nodded. "No problem."

But that wasn't true. It was a huge problem. One she'd have to figure out how to share with Ian.

## Chapter Five

Ian lifted his Stetson to cool his sweat-dampened hair. He glanced down the long, graveled driveway that led to the Leaning R, then wiped his brow. A light breeze had finally kicked up, providing a respite from the heat.

All afternoon, the summer sun had been beating down on him while he was hoeing weeds around the yard. But he kept a steady pace, determined not to let up. To his right, Cheyenne had curled up to sleep on a patch of grass in the shade of a maple tree, exhausted from chasing butterflies.

It hadn't been difficult to find chores to do that would keep him close to the house while Carly was in town at the doctor's office. She might have told him that she was feeling much better, but that didn't keep him from worrying about her and wondering what she'd found out.

He stretched out the kinks in his back. He'd gotten quite a workout from his labor and was just about to call it a day when he finally spotted her pickup heading down the drive. So he leaned on the hoe and waited for her to park.

As she climbed from the cab, he asked, "What did the doctor say?"

She reached across the seat for her purse. "It's nothing to worry about." She closed the driver's door, then tossed him an unconvincing smile.

When she didn't offer any more than that, he decided to prod her a bit.

"Are you pregnant?" he asked, focusing on her eyes instead of allowing his gaze to drop to her waistline.

She flushed, then glanced at her feet for a moment. When she looked back at him, she said, "I told you that wasn't likely. Remember?"

Yes, she'd mentioned that on Saturday night. Is that what the doctor had told her again today?

The breeze blew a strand of hair across her face, and she swiped it away.

"I'll tell you what," she said. "Give me time to make a phone call, whip up a salad and make a pot of spaghetti. Then come to the house and have dinner with me. I'll give you more details about my visit to the doctor then."

So what was that supposed to mean? That her diagnosis was long and complex?

Ian's mind swirled with all the possibilities, none of which were the least bit comforting.

"Okay," he said. "Spaghetti sounds good. How much time do you need? An hour?"

"Sure. That works." Then she headed for the back door.

As he watched her go, he continued to lean on the hoe. Her voice and tone had sounded normal. Yet her shoulders slumped.

In defeat? In worry?

Damn. He didn't like waiting. Didn't like stressing about what she might say.

Was she going to drop a bomb about her health? Or was she trying to concoct a believable story meant to not worry him, to not involve him?

Carly had never lied or deceived him before.

So why was he so skeptical now?

Carly had wanted to lie to Ian. And she'd nearly done so. Well, not outright. But the noncommittal response she'd given him was just as dishonest as if she'd come right out and told him she wasn't pregnant. And for that reason, she felt as guilty as sin.

But Dr. Connor had verified her positive test results, which had nearly blown her away. The news had her torn between feeling completely unbalanced and utterly delighted.

How could she share it with Ian when she could hardly fathom it herself?

She entered the kitchen, taking time to run her gaze over the scarred but familiar oak table and chairs, where she used to tell Granny her deepest troubles and secrets. Then she scanned the various plaques, pictures and cross-stitch hangings with upbeat sayings that adorned the walls.

This room had always been a haven for her. She only wished her great-grandma was still here to tell her everything would be fine, that things would work out just the way they were supposed to.

Why couldn't she grasp that reassuring thought now?

She set her purse on the countertop next to the old-style, wall-mounted telephone.

Braden had called her while she'd been at the clinic and had her cell turned off. She'd tried to return his call on the drive back to the ranch, but he hadn't been free to talk to her then. He did, however, say that their brother Jason had called him from Mexico. So she was eager to hear the latest news.

Last month, Braden uncovered the fact that their dad had been searching for a woman named Camilla Cruz, whose father had once been the foreman on the Leaning R. Camilla was an artist who'd died of breast cancer two years ago. No one knew much about her— or why she didn't go by her father's last name of Montoya. But they suspected she'd once been married.

Their father had gone so far as to hire a private investigator to help him find her. He had to have learned that Camilla had passed away, so Carly and her brothers couldn't understand why he'd continued to search for some of Camilla's shirttail relatives.

Then, a couple weeks ago, they'd had a small breakthrough. Jason had found some of her paintings and other artwork in a storage shed their father had rented, indicating their dad had gotten involved in an art import business of some kind. He also discovered some private letters that revealed their father and Camilla had been romantically involved at one time.

Braden had gone to Mexico to follow a lead, and right before he had to return home because of his grandfather's illness, he'd learned that Camilla had two children—a boy and a girl who'd been placed in an orphanage.

Carly wondered if the kids could be their father's, given his past, but it was unlikely. He'd never kept his relationships secret, and since neither of her brothers had a clue that he'd been involved with the artist, they suspected the whole thing must have blown over before it had a chance to take off.

During a family meeting, Carly and her brothers had agreed that the search for those kids should continue. They believed that their father, who'd been a big supporter of the Boys Club and various organizations that benefitted children, had probably been looking for Camilla's son and daughter so he could rescue them and find them a decent home.

Jason and his new bride had taken up the search at that point. In the meantime, Braden was trying to find someone who might be willing to adopt Camilla's children here in the States.

Carly blew out a sigh. She hoped Jason and Juliana would find them. And that they'd make sure the siblings were happy, healthy and safe.

Yet it was her own dilemma, her own burden that weighed her down now. And she felt as if she'd just chugged down a cocktail of surprise, delight and fear.

She was *pregnant*. With Ian's baby.

She'd like nothing better than to cling to her secret for a while longer, to allow it to settle over her so she could come up with a game plan. But Ian wasn't about to let his curiosity rest.

Besides, she'd have to tell him. She was four months along, and soon her baby bump would reveal the truth.

How would the news affect him?

She suspected that he still carried a torch for her. Not that she didn't care for him, too. The man was everything her father wasn't—honest, dependable, trustworthy. And Ian would undoubtedly make a good dad.

But what about her? Would she make a good mom?

Unlike her own mother, she would never go on tours and leave her child in the care of a nanny. She'd take the baby on the road with her.

But while she thought of Ian as a go-with-the-flow kind of guy, she had a feeling that he'd have some very strong opinions about that particular plan.

The unexpected news, the unsettling news, was sure to complicate her life.

And what about Ian? She suspected he would want to be a part of the baby's life. But he'd made it clear several times that he was determined to be a rancher.

And he'd be a good one.

Many years ago, Granny had hired Reuben Montoya as the Leaning R foreman, and he'd done a great job. But about three years ago, he'd been called home for a family emergency and returned to his hometown, a small village located somewhere near the coast in Baja California.

Granny had gone through several different foremen but none of them had worked out—nor had they been able to match the job Reuben had done.

Then she'd met Ian at Caroline's Diner, taken him home and given him a try. From what she'd said several times, Ian had worked out like a charm.

"That boy's got an inborn skill at ranching," Granny had said. "And he has a way with sick and injured critters that's pert near better than any vet I've ever seen."

So it was no surprise that Ian wanted to have his own spread one day. But there lay the biggest hurdle of all. Carly had dreams to reach the sky, and Ian had his boots firmly planted in the Brighton Valley soil.

So how would an unplanned pregnancy fit into either of their lives?

Once Ian learned about the baby, he might try to convince her to stay on the Leaning R and live the humble life of a cowboy's wife forever. And if Carly agreed to something like that, she feared she'd wither and die.

Okay, so he hadn't exactly given her reason to believe that he'd actually want to marry her. But it did seem like the kind of thing that noble Ian would offer.

And marriage was out of the question, especially if it meant giving up her dream.

Of course, she wasn't exactly sure how motherhood would play into her plans for the future. If she was entirely honest, she'd admit she actually could envision herself rocking a baby on the porch, taking a toddler to pick huckleberries in the hills and even baking and decorating sugar cookies from Granny's recipe box with her little one. But living a life of obscurity, like the one Ian had chosen, wasn't an option. There was no way she could possibly live both a vision and a dream.

Still unable to plot a course of action, she moved about the kitchen to fix the dinner Ian would soon come to eat, the dinner at which she'd have to tell him what she'd learned today.

She'd just put the pasta into boiling water when the house phone rang. She wiped her hands on the apron she wore and hurried to answer before the caller hung up.

It was Jason.

"Hey," she said. "How's it going?"

"Romantically speaking, I've never been happier."

"I'm glad to hear that," she said. Jason had been a lone wolf all his life—or for as long as she'd known him. So that was good news indeed. "What about Camilla's kids? Have you located them yet?"

"No, but we've learned that they're seven-year-old twins. After their mother died, they moved in with Reuben, their grandfather, but he passed away last summer. Since that's about the time Dad hired the private investigator, we think his death may have somehow triggered Dad's search."

"So what happened to the kids when their grandfather died?"

"That's where the orphanage comes in to play. We actually found it, but the kids were only there for a few months. They've been staying in the care of a nanny Dad hired."

"Wow." The whole story was growing more mysterious. "Where's the nanny? And what do you know about her?"

"Just her name. We're going to try to find her next. I hope it won't take too long. I really need to head back to the corporate office in Houston soon. Rayburn Energy has an important stockholders' meeting soon, and as CEO, I should attend."

"I understand." Her older brother not only had his own company to run, but he was in charge of their father's family trust and his corporate holdings, too.

She hoped Jason wouldn't expect her to take up the search next. She couldn't speak Spanish, so she'd be lost in Mexico.

No, she'd better stay here on the Leaning R until she figured out her next move.

After taking a long, hot shower to soak his aching muscles and giving himself a fresh shave, Ian turned Cheyenne out to do her doggy business, then left her in the cabin.

The pup whimpered in complaint, and he paused at the door and spoke to her. "Take it easy, girl. I'll be back later."

Cheyenne let out a howl, clearly not understanding that she could trust him to return. But that was something she'd have to learn.

He closed the door, then crossed the yard and arrived at the ranch house, braced to hear what Carly had to say. When he reached the back door, he stood on the porch for a moment, then lifted his hand and knocked.

"Come on in," she called out.

He made his way through the mudroom and into the kitchen, where the aroma of tomatoes, garlic and Italian spices filled the air.

"Dinner is ready," Carly said. "All I have to do is put it on the table."

"It smells great. Can I help?"

"Thanks, but I have everything under control."

Moments later, they were seated across from each other at Granny's antique oak table, preparing to eat.

Ian glanced at the large serving of sauce-covered pasta on his plate, his thoughts as tangled as the strands of spaghetti.

"So what's the deal?" he finally asked.

"Well, I..." Carly sucked in a deep breath, then slowly let it out. "I have a confession to make. I wasn't completely honest with you earlier. It's just that I'm having trouble believing it myself."

"You mean you're *not* fine?" He set down his fork, unable to eat in spite of his hunger, and merely stared at her. "What did the doctor say?"

"No, I'm okay. It's just that..." She worried her bottom lip. "I guess there's no easy way to say it. I'm pregnant, Ian."

He pushed his plate aside, no longer able to eat. "I asked you that an hour ago, and you said—"

"I know. I implied that it wasn't likely. But that's what I was told a couple years ago. Apparently, it wasn't impossible. Dr. Connor confirmed it today. I somehow got pregnant in spite of the odds. And I mis-read the symptoms, thinking that there was no way I could be."

Ian and Carly hadn't made love in ages—four or five months, to be precise. So he asked the logical question. "Who's the father?"

She stiffened. "You are, you big jerk."

He hadn't meant to offend her. "I'm sorry, Carly. It's just that you'd have to be pretty far along."

"According to Dr. Connor, I'm about four months."

He fought the urge to look at her belly, to see if he could detect a bump. Wouldn't she be showing?

Finally he said, "I'm at a loss for words."

"Imagine how I felt when the doctor confirmed it."

Had she been upset by the news? Shocked to learn she was confronting the same crisis Felicia had once faced?

When Felicia had announced that she was expect-ing Ian's child, he'd taken it in stride. In fact, he hadn't minded the idea of becoming a father. But it hadn't panned out that way. And he'd been left to grieve for the child he would never meet. But this was different.

*Carly* was different. And there was something about knowing they'd conceived a baby together that... delighted him.

But what if she decided that a child wasn't in her future, just as Felicia had done?

"So what do you plan to do?" he asked.

She tugged on a strand of hair, then twirled a curl around her finger. "I'm not sure."

He felt compelled to offer to marry her, to promise to be there for her and the baby for the rest of his life. It was, after all, the right thing to do. But, knowing Carly and the big dreams she had, he didn't think it was a good idea to put too much pressure on her when she was just getting used to the idea of expecting their child.

It was too late for an abortion, wasn't it? He hoped he didn't have to go through that again—the pleading, the bargaining…and then the eventual grief at not being able to stop Felicia from what she'd been so damned determined to do.

Yet, if Carly decided to have the baby, to keep it, she might want to take it on the road with her. And he'd hate that.

A baby needed regular hours, a loving home, a mom who was always there for it, a dad who—

Hey, now that was an idea. Maybe Carly would consider joint custody. Or maybe Ian could raise the baby himself.

He'd have to hire a housekeeper and a qualified nanny, though.

"What are you thinking?" Carly asked, drawing him from his thoughts and the plans he'd yet to think through.

The fact that his feelings, his choices, mattered to her eased his mind considerably and gave him… What? Hope?

"I'm actually okay with it," he said.

"I suspected you would be."

Then why wasn't her expression softening? Why wasn't she pleased by his support?

Hell, he'd marry her—if that would help, if it would make her feel better. And if he were to be honest with himself, he wouldn't mind having her live with him. He could see himself coming home to her each night, holding her in his arms, making love until they were both sated and smiling. But something told him she'd been so scarred by her parents' dysfunctional relationship and ultimate divorce that she would be opposed to the idea.

Of course, he could always try to convince her that some couples actually did make a go of it, that they could be happy together for fifty years or more. Take his grandparents, for example.

Yet maybe Ian had been scarred, too. His unhealthy relationship with Felicia had made him leery of trusting a woman to love him more than she loved her career. So now probably wasn't the time to make any serious decisions.

"Why don't we sleep on it?" he said.

Her brow arched as if he'd suggested they do so together—and in the same bed. He wouldn't be opposed to that. In fact, he'd like it. But that would take some courting, too—no matter how sexually compatible they'd been.

He told himself to exercise caution. After all, he had let his hormones convince him that he'd loved Felicia when they'd been in lust. Their relationship had ended badly, and he wasn't about to make that same mistake twice, especially when he and Carly had even more chemistry.

"We both have a lot to think about before we make any decisions," he added. "But I'm glad you told me."

"I figured you'd say that."

He wanted to add that he'd support her decision—no matter what it was—but that wasn't true. He wanted their baby. And he'd do whatever he could to be a big part of its life, even if he had to hire an attorney and fight Carly every step of the way.

Ian had taken the news well, Carly decided, although he'd remained quiet and introspective during dinner. He'd offered to help her with the dishes, but she'd sent him on his way, saying she needed time to think and would rather talk more in the morning.

He'd seemed relieved to have some time alone, too. He might have said that he was okay with the news, but it still must have taken him aback. Heck, she was okay with it, too, but that didn't mean the diagnosis hadn't thrown her for a loop.

After moving numbly through the kitchen, washing the dishes, putting the leftovers in the fridge and wiping down the countertops, Carly retreated to the guest room, where she'd left her purse and the paperwork the doctor's nurse had given her about pregnancy and what she could expect. She planned to look it over tonight.

But as she approached the doorway to her great-grandmother's bedroom, her steps slowed to a stop. She suddenly missed Granny more than ever and took a moment to walk inside, to surround herself with loving, comforting memories.

There was still a familiar hint of lavender lingering in the bedding, as well as in the Irish lace curtains. Other than the kitchen, it was the one place in the house in which Carly felt her great-grandmother's presence. But then again, maybe that had something to do with the dear old woman's portrait, which hung on the wall.

Camilla Cruz had painted it and captured something special in her expression—a knowing look that had put a twinkle in her eye, a warm smile. There was even the appearance of wisdom on her brow. She almost looked alive and ready to listen to Carly's hopes, joys and sorrows.

"Granny, I miss you so. And I wish you were really here." Carly took a seat in the antique rocker that rested near the bed, a hand-crocheted afghan draped over the wooden spindles in the back. She placed her hands on the slight swell of her stomach, where her baby grew, and looked at the portrait. "I'm pregnant. Imagine that."

She'd known about it for more than twenty-four hours now, yet it still seemed so surreal. The baby was real, though, and already its own person, yet Carly hadn't even been 100 percent sure of its existence until this afternoon.

As she set the rocker in motion, she envisioned holding her little one, rocking it. Singing lullabies.

She wasn't sure if it was a boy or girl, but that really didn't matter. Still, she wasn't sure how a baby would fit into her dream of performing. She'd planned to pursue her career for ten years or so, then retire and adopt children, creating a family of her own. Yet now, the timing had gone wrong, and her dreams had crisscrossed.

Did she care?

No, she already loved the life that grew inside of her. She'd just have to hire a nanny and take them both on tour. Somehow, she'd make it work. She just hoped Ian didn't make a fuss. For being an easygoing cowboy, he could sure get stubborn at times.

She just hoped this wasn't one of them.

## *Chapter Six*

The next morning, Ian left Cheyenne outside with one of the teenage hands who'd come to help out. Then he let himself into the ranch house through the back door, put on a pot of coffee and waited in the kitchen for Carly to wake up.

Last night, after eating dinner with her and then returning to his place, he'd called Todd Adams, a cowhand who'd been looking for work, and asked him to help out on the Leaning R. Carly's brother Jason hadn't authorized him to do any hiring, but Ian planned to buy the ranch himself as soon as it went on the market, so he would pay the man out of his own pocket.

He'd already lined up Todd for the day, so he was free to talk to Carly. He had no idea how long he'd have to wait, but he was determined to talk to her first thing.

Carly didn't usually get up before nine, so he figured he'd just keep himself busy doing one of several fix-it projects Jason's new wife had told him about. One of those was to check out a leaky valve under the sink.

Ian was just getting started on that when Carly entered the kitchen wearing a pair of white shorts and an oversize green T-shirt. Her feet were bare, and her hair was damp. She'd taken a morning shower, but she hadn't put on any makeup. She didn't need to fuss with any of that, though. Anytime of the day or night, she was just about the prettiest woman he'd ever met.

She paused in the doorway and blinked when she spotted him kneeling near the open cupboard below the sink, a wrench in hand. Apparently she was surprised that he'd let himself in, something he'd done often when they'd been lovers.

"Good morning," he said, as if it were the most natural thing in the world for him to greet her like this. "I'm going to fix a leak under the sink before it gets any worse."

Her brow furrowed, and she cocked her head slightly, as if not buying his explanation.

He pointed toward the electric percolator on the counter. "Want some coffee? It's fresh."

"No, thanks. I'm…avoiding caffeine."

"Then how about a glass of milk?" He didn't mention that it would be good for the baby, but she must have known what he was getting at.

"No, I've never been a big milk drinker. But I'll have some in my cereal."

She crossed her arms and shifted her weight to one

hip. "You could have fixed the leak yesterday—or the day before. What's going on, Ian?"

He set down the wrench, then stood and tucked his thumbs into his front pockets. "I slept on it, Carly. Did you?"

She unwrapped her arms and made her way into the kitchen. "Well, I *did* go to sleep. But I'm still not sure what I'm going to do. I'd like to keep this between us right now."

There went the phone call to his grandparents, but he couldn't very well make an announcement like that until he could tell them what his plans were—like an upcoming marriage, raising a child on his own or even the possibility that he was heading into a custody battle, although he hoped it wouldn't come to that.

"I won't say anything," he said. "I take it you don't want to tell your brothers."

"No, not yet." She glanced at the far wall, where a couple of cardboard boxes were stacked. "For the time being, I have work to do. After breakfast, I plan to take up where Juliana left off on the inventory. I hope to have it done by the time she and Jason get back from Mexico."

"But it's almost finished." He hoped she wasn't planning to pack up the bedroom and the kitchen, then skedaddle. "You shouldn't pack up the rooms you'll be living out of."

"I won't do that, but the basement is full of stuff. And the attic is, too."

"I'll help you," he said.

Her lips parted, and her brow crinkled. "That's not necessary."

He pulled his hands from his pockets. "You shouldn't be doing any heavy lifting. So I'll do it for you. Just let me know where you want to start."

"Seriously?" She waited a beat before adding, "Who's going to work on the ranch? You haven't had enough help as it is."

"Actually, I just hired a new hand who's experienced and knows what to do before I even point it out."

She didn't ask whether he'd gotten permission from her brother, which was just as well. Ian didn't want her thinking he'd done anything out of line, but the last time he talked to Jason about the sale of the ranch, Jason gave him every reason to believe that both Carly and Braden were close to agreeing to list it. If Carly was planning to help with the inventory, then she'd obviously made up her mind.

"I'm not so sure about this." She paused, then bit down on her lower lip. "I mean, working in close quarters and all."

So it wasn't his offer to help with the heavy work that bothered her. She was worried about being tempted by him.

A slow smile spread across his lips. "Aw. I get it. But I wasn't trying to take advantage of you."

She seemed to shake it off—her attraction or whatever had her perplexed. "I'm not worried about that."

When she bit down on her bottom lip, he realized she wasn't being entirely truthful. She might be more concerned about fighting off her own desire.

"Oh, what the heck," she said, brightening. "I'll accept your offer to help. Besides, I really didn't feel like lugging around those boxes anyway, even though it has to be done."

If they were going to sell the ranch, it did. Although Ian wouldn't mind buying some of the stuff they didn't plan to keep. He was going to need furniture, dishes and other odds and ends. And since the ranch house had always felt cozy and welcoming to him, he wouldn't mind buying it furnished.

Carly crossed the kitchen, opened the pantry and pulled out a box of cereal. He watched her fill her bowl, then add milk and sugar. When she finished, she turned to him. "Want some?"

"I already ate. Back at my place."

She nodded, then took a seat at the table. For some reason, he felt as though he'd made a major stride today. She was going to let him help her inventory the rest of the house. Maybe they could reach other compromises along the way, and he wouldn't have to take her to court after all.

Still, they had a long way to go before they could coparent—or whatever they decided to call their new relationship.

If Ian thought that helping Carly pack and stack boxes would make her job any easier, he was wrong.

Well, physically speaking, she was glad to have him handle the heavy stuff, but the job of inventorying Granny's belongings was beginning to take a toll on her emotionally.

She doubted he knew it, though. Not based on the way he kept whistling.

What was the name of that song anyway? She didn't recognize it, but she liked the snappy tune.

Apparently, he was in a good mood, although she wasn't sure why. Maybe he was just glad to be indoors instead of outside, although she suspected he might be happy about being a daddy. That was a good sign, wasn't it? He could have been upset by the news, which would only make things more difficult for her.

"Are you okay?" he asked. "Is the dust getting to you? Your eyes are watery."

Carly swiped at her tears. "Being surrounded by all these things, by the memories, is making me a little weepy."

"I'm sorry."

"Don't be." She pushed aside the doll buggy Granny had given her, which had been one of her favorite playthings.

"Did that little stroller make you feel sentimental?" he asked.

She gave a little shrug. "On my sixth birthday, both of my parents were out of town and completely forgot what day it was. So Granny took me into town, purchased that little buggy, a new doll and several other gifts she let me pick out for myself. Afterward, we went to Caroline's Diner for a slice of German chocolate cake and a bowl of vanilla ice cream."

"Sounds like Granny did her best to make it up to you."

"She used to pick up the slack and do things like that

all the time, but I hadn't realized what she was doing when I was a kid." Carly sniffled, then smiled. "Do you know what else she did that day? She had everyone in the restaurant sing 'Happy Birthday' to me."

Ian eased close and slipped his arm around her in a gesture meant to be comforting. But as his alluring scent, a manly mixture of soap and musk, enveloped her, her thoughts turned to more recent memories, more recent emotions.

In spite of her resolve to keep her distance from the handsome cowboy, she leaned into him. "I'll be okay. Really."

She sniffed again, then turned away from him. But if she thought she could escape the warmth of his touch, it didn't work out that way. His scent seemed to cling to her as she returned to her work, tempting her, taunting her.

"What are you going to do with the toys?" he asked.

She had no idea. She could save them for her baby—*their* baby—but since she was between homes as well as jobs, she had no place to store them. "I suppose we should donate them to charity."

"All right. I'll stack them with the other things you plan to give away."

Carly scanned the basement, spotting the old Singer sewing machine, a vintage treadle model that had belonged to Granny's mother-in-law as well as an antique settee covered with a sheet. Next to it was a card table stacked with books and a slew of odds and ends.

It was going to take a long time to go through all of this and inventory it. She glanced at the old Saratoga trunk in the corner and blew out a heavy sigh. "What do you suppose is in there?"

"That's anyone's guess," Ian said. "Want me to open it?"

"Sure."

The old hinges creaked as he lifted the trunk's lid. "Looks like quilts." He pulled out the one on top, a colorful patchwork design.

Carly eased closer to get a better look at the hand-made blanket. "It's beautiful. Look at all that intricate stitching. I wonder who made it."

"Granny, maybe." He continued to pull out several more, some of them stitched, but whose edges weren't finished. "I'm beginning to think these weren't hers. She never liked leaving things undone."

"She was also a better cook than a seamstress," Carly added. "Not that she couldn't hem a dress or darn socks. But she never used to sit around and sew for a hobby."

"There's something else in here." Ian handed a small cedar box to Carly.

As she accepted it, their hands brushed, and the warmth of his touch, as brief as it was, set off a spark that nearly singed her skin and sent her pulse rate into overdrive. She almost lost her grip on the box and dropped it, but she scrambled to gather her wits and her senses.

Still, her heart continued to pound as she peered inside the velvet-lined interior and spotted a man's ring, a filigreed cross on a silver chain and a gold pocket watch.

"Who do you think they belonged to?" Ian asked. It was a simple question, but his soft Southern twang did wacky things to her ability to think.

Her response came out in a near whisper as she set the box aside. "I have no idea."

The musty basement smelled of dust, but it was the scent of soap, leather and cowboy that stirred her hormones and her memories.

As her resolve weakened, she realized she would have to escape before she did something stupid—like fall into his arms.

Ian was sweet. And as sexy as sin. He was also charming when he put his mind to wooing her.

Of course, her father had been a charmer, too.

Not that Ian was anything like her dad. But still. She had to keep her wits about her until she could decide whether he was just being a thoughtful expectant father or trying to make her see things his way.

As she turned her back to him, a small puff of brown fur scurried across the top of her sandaled foot, and she let out a scream as though a cougar had just entered the basement. Without a conscious thought, she spun back to Ian and nearly climbed up his body. "Get it out of here!"

He laughed, but he scooped her into his arms, rescuing her from the tiny critter. "He's more afraid of you than you are of him."

"I don't care. Mice and rats give me the willies."

And clinging to Ian was giving her pause. But she couldn't fall back into a sexual relationship with him. So, with her cheeks glazing hot and her heart soaring, she unwrapped herself from his arms. "Will you please shoo that mouse outside? I'm going to call it a day."

"He's long gone by now—probably suffering from a cardiac arrest."

"Good," she said, as she hurried up the stairs to the main part of the house.

"We can always get a cat," he called out behind her. "That ought to keep the mice and rats at bay."

Maybe so. But who was going to keep Ian and temptation at bay?

As the days passed, the slight bulge in Carly's tummy seemed to practically double in size, and she soon found that a lot of her pants felt tight. So she took a break after inventorying the basement and before tarting on the attic and drove into town to find some looser clothing to wear.

She wasn't big enough to warrant a purchase at the maternity shop in Wexler, but she suspected she could find something to tide her over a month or two at the Mercantile in downtown Brighton Valley. And she'd been right.

After buying a couple pairs of pants and several tops that would work, she returned to her pickup. Well, almost.

A walk past Caroline's Diner triggered a craving for lemon meringue pie.

How about that? Once Carly had learned that she was pregnant, all the signs and symptoms had flared up, making the diagnosis real. Of course, she'd always craved something sweet to eat whenever she strolled past the diner.

For some reason, the local eatery, with its yellow walls, white café-style curtains and cozy booths, offered her comfort and a feeling of coming home— almost as much as the Leaning R did. Or rather, like it had when Granny had been there.

She'd no more than walked inside when she spotted the blackboard that advertised the daily special for $8.99. In yellow chalk, someone had written "What the Sheriff Ate," followed by "Fried Chicken, Mashed Potatoes and Gravy, Buttered Carrots and Cherry Pie à la mode."

As Carly turned to the refrigerated case that displayed yummy desserts, she spotted Stu Jeffries, the new mayor, sitting at the counter. When he recognized Carly, he pushed his plate aside, picked up his bill and got up from his seat.

Mayor Jeffries, a short, stout businessman in his mid to late fifties, snatched his Stetson from the chair next to where he'd been sitting and plopped it on his head, reminding Carly of a giant thumb tack.

"Why, Carly Rayburn! You're just the person I want to talk to."

She greeted him with a smile. "Hi, Stu. What's up?"

"First of all, I'd like to compliment you. Marcia and I were at the Stagecoach Inn last Friday night when you and the Leaning R foreman played. I'd meant to talk to you afterward, but you slipped out before I got a chance."

Carly had noticed that the mayor and his wife had

occupied one of the corner booths. But she wasn't about to tell him why she'd hightailed it out of the honky-tonk so quickly. "What can I do for you?"

"First of all, I wanted you to know how much we enjoyed that duet. You and Ian—that's his name, right?"

She nodded.

"Anyway, the two of you are very talented. A real hit. Marcia told me to ask you to perform at the Founder's Day Festival in a couple of weeks—and again at the dance that evening at the Grange Hall. How about it?"

Carly's heart leaped at the praise as well as the invitation. But when she imagined what Ian's reaction would be, her pulse hit a snag.

"We're charging admission at the dance," the smiling mayor added. "And the proceeds are going toward the new program for disabled children at the Brighton Valley Kids Club."

She hadn't known about the new program, but she certainly could support something like that. And while Ian had made it clear he'd never go on stage with her again, she wondered if he'd change his mind because it was for such a good cause.

It was hard to say, but if he still wouldn't budge, she couldn't let that screw up her own opportunity. So she went out on a limb and said, "I'd be delighted to perform that day. And I'm sure Ian will, too."

"I'm glad to hear that. Our PR committee has been working hard on this, so we'll get you on the schedule as soon as we can. And it just so happens that Jolene, one of the clerks down at City Hall, plans to drop it off at the print shop this afternoon—right before her softball game with the Hot Mamas League. So if I hurry back to the office, I should be able to add you to that brochure, too."

Carly wasn't sure what Ian would say when he realized she'd already made a commitment for them. But at least the proceeds of the evening dance were going to help disabled children. So how could he object?

Besides, she had two weeks to talk him into it. And a whole recipe box of tempting goodies to soften the blow.

Ian was at the ranch house painting the front porch railing when Carly drove up. Cheyenne, who'd kept getting in his way all morning—bless her ever-lovin' puppy heart—trotted toward the small pickup, the stump of her little tail wagging. She was no doubt hoping to find a more enthusiastic playmate than he'd been for the past hour.

Carly opened the driver's door, slid out of the truck, then stooped to pat the rascally pup. "Hey! What are you doing, girl?"

Cheyenne was so excited to get an ear rub that her little tail wagged her entire hind end from side to side.

"Uh-oh," Carly said. "You have white paint on your fur."

Ian laughed. "I'm not surprised. She wasn't content to nap or just watch."

Carly reached into the cab and withdrew a couple of shopping bags that bore the Mercantile branding.

"Did you find any bargains?" he asked.

"Not really. But I picked up some pants and blouses that I can wear for a while."

He glanced at her waistline, which seemed to have expanded since her arrival. Apparently, their baby was growing, which pleased him. But he figured he'd better bite back a proud-papa smile.

"What are you doing?" she asked as she approached the house.

"The railing was loose, so I fixed it. And now I'm giving it a coat of paint."

She nodded, then bit down on her bottom lip—a habit she had when she was pensive or stressed.

Ian didn't like seeing her troubled, so he set the paintbrush across the lid of the can and got to his feet. "What's wrong?"

"Nothing." She brightened momentarily, then went back to biting her lip. "I…uh…ran into Mayor Jeffries in town."

Ian lifted his arm, wiped the perspiration from his brow with his shirtsleeve and grinned. "You mean to tell me the new mayor shops at the only ladies' dress shop in town?"

She chuckled at his attempt to lighten her mood. "No, that's not where I saw him. He was at the diner."

Since Carly didn't usually find it newsworthy to tell him about the various people she ran into while in town, he waited for her to continue.

"You might not have noticed, but Stu and his wife were at the Stagecoach Inn last Friday night and saw our performance."

Again, Ian remained silent. He suspected that she

had something she was worried about telling him. And that she didn't expect him to be happy about it. If that was the case, he wasn't going to make it any easier for her to announce whatever it was. So he crossed his arms and stood tall.

"He'd like for us to perform at the Founder's Day Festival, which will be held in Town Square in two weeks. Then, that evening, we'd play at the community dance at the Grange Hall." Carly glanced down at her boots, then back to Ian and smiled, her blue eyes damn near sparkling. "I hope you don't mind, but it's for a really good cause—the new program at the Brighton Valley Kids Club for disabled children. So I told him we'd do it."

Ian stiffened. "You agreed for both of us?"

Tears welled in her eyes, and she swiped at them. "What's one more little singing gig? It's not like I'm trying to drag you to the Grand Ole Opry. It's just a small-town thing. Besides, all the money they make at the dance will go to a good cause. Surely you can't say no to that."

"You know good and well how I feel about performing."

Her eyes flooded with more emotion, and she sniffled, then wiped the moisture away again. "Damn these hormones."

Ian hated to see her cry, but he wasn't about to admit it. And he couldn't give in to her like her father had always done. The last thing he needed was for her to think she had him wrapped around her pinkie, too. "I'm not going to do it, Carly."

"Not even for those poor little kids?"

Sure, he'd do just about anything to benefit children in need. But Carly was working him, and he had to hold his ground. "If I thought you were only concerned about charity, that'd be one thing. But I know what you're really trying to do. You want me to eventually agree to go on the road with you, and I'm not going to do it."

She blew out an exasperated sigh. "You frustrate the heck out of me, Ian. And yes, I'll admit that I want to perform in the future—with you, if possible. But you don't seem to care about what's important to me. I need to make a name for myself, even if Brighton Valley is only a stepping stone."

"You're a *Rayburn*, Carly. You already have a name for yourself."

"That's *not* what I meant." She crossed her arms, the tears a thing of the past now as she dug in her boots for battle. "At first, I wanted you to perform with me because you're so talented. And also because we have good chemistry—and not *just* in bed. But now it's a matter of principle. We need to be able to work together and do what's right."

Ian clucked his tongue and shook his head. She was taking this way out of context. "Granted, it's a good cause. And I'd be happy to write a generous check to the charity itself. So don't lecture me about doing what's right."

"You don't get it, Ian. If we can't learn to compromise and respect each other's ideals and honor our dreams, how will we ever be able to coparent?"

Her last blow hit below the belt. There was nothing he'd like more in the world than parenting their child with her—even before the birth. He wanted to argue, to object, to flat-out refuse. But she'd argued him into a corner and there was no other way out than to agree.

"Okay, Carly. I'm not happy about this, but I'll do it—just this one last time."

Her anger melted into a breezy smile. "Thank you, Ian. You won't be sorry. I promise."

He wasn't sorry about performing, but he was already regretting the fact that she'd managed to talk him into doing something he'd been dead set against. Again.

But on the upside, if he could convince her to be happy performing in two-bit venues here in Brighton Valley, then maybe that would be enough for her and she'd agree to stick close to home, where they could actually create a family of their own.

Then maybe they could learn to parent their baby together. And Ian could be the husband and father he'd always wanted to be.

## Chapter Seven

Ian steered clear of Carly for the next couple of days—
at least, that's what he seemed to be doing. At first,
she'd made up her mind to leave him alone until his
mood improved. But it soon became apparent that he
was avoiding her and she would have to make the first
move.

While she hadn't meant to make him angry, she
should have realized that a man like Ian didn't like
being pressed to do something he didn't want to do.

And Carly had pushed him too hard. She not only
owed him an apology, but she ought to do something
to mend fences.

The only plan she could come up with was to tell
him how sorry she was over a home-cooked meal made
entirely from Granny's recipes.

So the next morning, after Ian and the ranch hands had ridden out together, she came up with the perfect menu and made a list of all the ingredients she needed to purchase at the market. Next, she slipped a note under Ian's cabin door, telling him she needed to talk to him and inviting him to dinner this evening.

When she returned home from her shopping trip, she took a shower, then shampooed and styled her hair. After slipping on a new pair of black stretch pants and an oversize mint-colored blouse, she stood in front of the bathroom mirror and primped a bit longer than she'd intended. After all, she and Ian weren't lovers anymore.

But they would be parents. So, for that reason, it was best for everyone involved if she put her best foot forward, apologized and did whatever she could to put them back on even ground.

Satisfied with her appearance and her game plan, she headed for the kitchen and made a meal sure to soften his heart.

While the meat loaf was in the oven, she set the table with Granny's best dishes, which she'd found packed in one of the stacked boxes in the dining room. She'd wanted everything to be perfect tonight, so while she was at the market, she'd also picked up some candles as well as a bouquet of flowers, which would add a nice touch.

A knock sounded at the front door, taking her by surprise. Ever since they'd first made love, Ian had let himself into the house through the mudroom. Obviously, things were different between them now, although she was determined to shake the awkwardness—as well as the mounting sexual tension that threatened to unravel her whenever he was near.

Still, she was ready for his arrival.

Or so she thought.

As she swung open the door and spotted the handsome cowboy on the porch, her heart took a tumble. He wore a Western shirt—a soft blue plaid she'd never seen before—and black jeans. He removed his hat, revealing damp hair—fresh from the shower.

"Am I too early?" he asked.

"No, you're right on time. Come on in." She stepped aside and waited for him to enter.

Instead, he glanced over his shoulder and called out, "Cheyenne, come on or I'll leave you outside."

Moments later, the black-and-white pup bounded up the steps wearing a red bandanna around her neck. Apparently, Carly and Ian weren't the only ones who'd spiffed up for their dinner.

"Aren't you cute," Carly said as she stooped to pat the puppy.

Ian continued to stand on the porch, his hat in hand. "So what's on your mind?"

"First of all," she said, stepping aside so Ian and Cheyenne could enter, "I want to apologize. I never should have agreed to perform as a duo when you'd made it clear how you felt about going on stage. It's just that I was so excited about being asked, that I said yes without a thought. But I was wrong, and I'm sorry. It won't happen again."

When he didn't say anything, she wondered if he

was going to accept her apology. But then, he'd come to dinner, hadn't he?

"To make matters worse," she added, "I pushed you until you agreed to sing with me, which wasn't fair. Will you forgive me?"

A slow smile spread across his face. "You promised not to agree to any more singing engagements on my behalf. But what about pushing me?"

She returned his grin. "I can try, but I don't want to make promises I might not be able to keep."

"That's what I figured." He placed his hat on the rack near the door. "You didn't need to invite me to dinner, though. Besides, I already agreed to perform with you."

She straightened. "I know, but this seemed like the best way to let you know I'm sincere. And while I admit that I'm glad you agreed, I'll respect your feelings about singing in public next time."

"I'd appreciate that." He took a whiff and broke into a broad smile. "I sure like the smell of your apologies. What's on the menu tonight?"

She grinned. "Granny's famous meat loaf, roasted red potatoes and buttered green beans with slivered almonds. I hope you'll like it."

"No doubt about that."

As Carly led Ian through the living room and into the kitchen, he said, "You sure went all out. You're even using Granny's good dishes."

"Like I said, I want to do this right."

Minutes later, they were seated at the table, enjoying a meal that Ian said was a good as any Granny had ever made. Carly was thrilled with the compliment.

"I know you don't want to hear this," Ian said, "but you belong on the Leaning R."

His words rang true. Granny had said the same thing to her, and at the time, she'd been right. But Carly had outgrown small-town life. And she wanted her child to have more opportunities than could be found on a ranch.

She took a sip of water from her goblet. "Maybe I did belong here once—when I was a kid. But not anymore."

"I'm not talking about a permanent residence here, but you're a part of this ranch, Carly. As much as or more than your great-grandmother was. And in case you haven't figured it out, this is the place you always come home to."

Carly wasn't so sure about being a part of the ranch. It did feel like home, but it should. Her best times had been spent on the Leaning R with Granny. "I have a lot of good memories here, but this isn't where my future lies."

"I understand that." He speared the last potato on his plate and put it in his mouth. Moments later, he added, "I take it that you've let Jason know you've agreed to the sale."

She nodded. "Yes, I have. And truthfully, I'll be sorry to see it go—especially to strangers. But it's not feasible for us to keep it in the family."

His lips parted as if he was going to say something—or maybe disagree—but he kept quiet.

"So what about you?" she asked. "Don't you have a place you call home?"

"I did, but my granddad sold it a few years back. And even though he and my grandma moved to Florida and are living in a condominium now, it still feels like home when I visit them."

"Really?" She found that hard to believe. "Why is that?"

"Because a home is more about the people who live there than the actual house itself."

She thought about that for a while. Granny had been more of a mother to her than the one who'd given her birth. And maybe that's why she always found herself returning to the Leaning R. Even now, after her great-grandmother's passing, it was still the only place where Granny seemed to be. At least the memories of her were here.

"You mentioned growing up on your granddad's ranch," Carly said. "What about your parents? Where did they live?"

"I don't remember my mom. She died in a car accident when I was three."

Carly had never really talked to him about his past because it hadn't seemed to matter. But for some reason, it mattered now.

"I'm sorry," she said. "What about your dad?"

Ian studied his empty plate for the longest time, and for a while, she wondered if he was even going to answer the question.

"When I was three, my parents left me with my grandparents while they took off to celebrate their anniversary in town. Apparently, they got into a heated argument, which led to the crash. At least, that's what it said in the police report. My father was sent to prison for vehicular manslaughter."

Carly had no idea what to say, especially when another "I'm sorry" seemed inadequate.

"While my dad was in jail, I lived with my grandparents at their cattle ranch near Dallas." Ian leaned back in his chair, his pose anything but relaxed. "When he was finally paroled, I moved to Fort Worth with him, but that didn't last very long."

She couldn't believe that they'd once been lovers, yet he'd never revealed anything about his early years. He seemed to know a lot about hers, though. Some she'd shared with him, and other things he might have learned from Granny.

But what about Ian? Not that she hadn't cared or been curious about his past before, but she'd been so convinced that they didn't have a future together that she'd once thought it wasn't any of her business. Yet now with the baby coming, learning more about him suddenly seemed important.

She leaned forward, her forearms resting on the table. "What do you mean? Why didn't you stay with your father?"

"He was an alcoholic, and whenever he went on a binge, he would miss work and get fired. Or he'd get in fights at bars or wherever. Each time he was arrested, I'd end up back at the ranch with my grandparents."

No wonder he was so close to them. "I'm sorry, Ian. I had no idea life was so difficult for you as a child."

"It wasn't so bad. At least, not at the ranch. I loved it there and learned how to rope and ride and work with cattle."

"So when they sold it, that's how you ended up here?"

He gave a simple shrug. "Actually, I was just passing through town and stopped at Caroline's Diner for lunch. I mentioned to Margie, the waitress, that I was a cowhand looking for work, and she introduced me to Granny, who was having a piece of peanut butter pie with a friend."

"Margie's a real sweetheart," Carly said, "but she has a way of asking questions and passing news along."

Ian laughed. "Yeah, I learned that quickly. But she did me a favor that day. Otherwise, I wouldn't have landed a job at the Leaning R. It was a win-win for Granny and me."

"In what way?" Carly asked.

"She needed a son as badly as I needed a family, so we looked after each other."

Carly was touched by his affection for her great-grandma, yet something niggled at her. "Why did you stick around, even after she passed away? I mean, I know my dad wasn't the easiest guy to work for."

"You're right about that." Ian took a chug of his iced tea. "No offense, Carly, but Charles Rayburn didn't give a rip about ranching."

Ian had that right. Her father had been put in charge of Granny's estate for a year before she died, but he was too caught up in his own company and his own life to even visit. But then, he hadn't ever had time for Carly, either. Why would it be any different for the woman who'd practically raised him?

"I guess you could say that I'm still looking out for Granny's best interests," Ian added.

Carly hadn't expected him to say that—or to stick around after Granny had died. Apparently Ian wasn't the tumbleweed she'd imagined him to be.

What else about him had she misread? It was going to take more than one intimate dinner for her to find out, she supposed.

"I appreciate all you've done around here," she told him. "And the fact that you're helping us sell a place you've considered a home."

Ian studied her for a moment. A long moment.

Again, she thought he might be pondering a comment, but if he had something to say, he kept it to himself.

Finally, he spoke. "Believe it or not, I'm happier than I've been in a long time. And that's why I plan to settle down in Brighton Valley for good."

He'd made that clear early on, so she wasn't surprised. But that was also the reason they'd never be happy together, at least not in the long run. Their dreams for the future were as different as their pasts.

Carly placed a hand on her baby bump, caressing it and wondering about the little one who grew there— and if he or she would inherit traits from both Ian and Carly.

Raising a baby together wasn't going to be easy. She just hoped they would be able to put aside their differences in order to become a better mom and dad than the ones who'd birthed them.

\* \* \*

Ian pushed back his chair, got up from the kitchen table and began to gather the dishes.

"Don't worry about cleaning up," Carly said. "I'll do it after you go."

"I don't mind helping. Besides, this is my way of showing my appreciation for dinner." Ian carried the stack of dishes to the counter. After reaching for the plastic bottle of soap from the cupboard under the sink, he turned on the hot water. "That was the best meal I've had in a long time."

"It was no big deal," Carly said. "I had fun cooking tonight."

He didn't doubt that for a minute. Carly was far more domestic than she realized. She also had a way of doing special little things for him—at least, she had when they'd been sleeping together.

One day, she'd picked wildflowers on her walk in the meadow. She'd brought them into his cabin and put them in water in the only vase she could find—a mason jar. Then she set them on the dinette table, brightening up his home as well as his day.

Another time, she'd purchased a cookie jar for him in town and filled it with candy because she knew he had a sweet tooth.

Was it any wonder he believed she had a domestic streak?

She'd insisted that she didn't, though. And he suspected that was because she feared acknowledging it would encourage him—or maybe it would hamper her dream of becoming a star.

"Oh, no! Cheyenne, give me that! Look what you've done."

Ian turned to see his rascally pup with Carly's black dress shoe in her mouth. She'd done a real number on the black spiked heel, chomping at it until she'd left little bite marks up and down. "I'm sorry, Carly. I owe you a shopping trip and a new pair of heels."

Carly, who now held the sexy shoe in her hand, slowly shook her head. "Don't worry about it. Something tells me I won't be wearing these for a while anyway."

She appeared to be resigned to the puppy's mischief as well as the change in her immediate plans for the future.

Did that mean she intended to have the baby and not give it up—or worse? He sure hoped so. He didn't want to lose another child before he had the opportunity to hold it, to love it. To protect it.

Ian shut off the water, dried his hands and crossed the room to where Cheyenne sat, perplexed that she'd lost her newfound toy. "I brought you to dinner, thinking that you'd remember your manners and stick close to me. You're not supposed to roam the house, looking for trouble."

"She was just being a puppy," Carly said. "I'll have to pick up some of those rawhide strips for her to chew on next time she comes to visit."

So there would be a next time. He was glad to hear it.

His life had taken a nice turn when he'd stopped in Brighton Valley that day and met Granny. Then it had really looked up when he'd met Carly. But as amazing as their short-lived time together had been, Carly only had eyes for the fame and glory Ian had left behind.

And he wasn't sure where that would leave him and their child.

Carly and Ian arrived early at the Founder's Day Festival with Ian in the driver's seat of his truck and his guitar resting between them. He lucked out when a car in front of Caroline's Diner pulled out of a space, allowing him to park along the tree-shaded main drag of Brighton Valley.

"I really appreciate this," Carly said again as she slid out the passenger door.

"I know. You've mentioned that a time or two." He reached for his guitar, then locked the truck.

They seemed to have reached a truce and an understanding, which was good.

As they headed toward Town Square, Carly nudged him with her elbow. "Can I ask you something?"

"Sure." He stole a glance at her, then continued to set his sights on the route ahead.

"What are you afraid of?"

He shot her a second glance, this one sharp and pointed. "What are you talking about?"

"I mean, I respect your wishes and all, and I'll keep my promise to let you be. But what's your real reason for not wanting to perform in front of an audience? You certainly don't seem to be the least bit nervous."

Nervous? No. But he was worried. Worried about being found out. He liked his peaceful existence and didn't want to jeopardize it by having anyone—especially Felicia—find out who he was, where he was and what he was doing.

As the soles of their boots crunched along the dusty sidewalk, he said, "Maybe I'm just afraid you'll try to drag me out on tour, and I'm happy here in Brighton Valley with the quiet life I've chosen."

If he did tell Carly who he really was, would she be content to let it go? Or would she hang on to his identity like a hungry Rottweiler with a meaty bone?

Even though she thought he was just a simple cowboy, she'd nearly pestered him to death.

He supposed he'd have to tell her—one of these days. But now didn't seem to be the time. If he knew Carly, she'd use her mother's contacts to look up Felicia, who hadn't had a platinum hit since Ian had written his last song for her.

"I don't really understand your refusal," Carly added, "but like I said, I'll respect it."

"Thanks."

They continued several blocks until they reached Town Square, with its park-like grounds and big clock tower in the center of the lawn.

The townsfolk who'd already gathered to wait for the festivities to start stood in intimate clusters or sat at the various rented tables and chairs that had been set up in the shade.

Near the courthouse, The Barbecue Pit, a local restaurant that catered parties and special events, had already brought in their old-style chuck wagon with its portable grill, setting off the aroma of wood smoke and sizzling beef, pork and chicken. The cooks, in their black cowboy hats and white aprons, turned the meat and brushed a spicy sauce over the top.

A stage had been set up, and several bands had begun to gather already.

"What time are we supposed to perform?" Ian asked Carly.

"I'm not sure, but there's the mayor." She pointed to Stu Jeffries, who was talking to Arthur Bellows, one of the town councilmen.

The mayor, who was dressed in his finest Western wear, looked especially short and squat next to the tall, slender councilman. But he seemed to puff up a wee bit taller when he spotted Ian and Carly approaching him.

"Excuse me," Stu told Arthur. Then he turned to welcome Carly with a broad smile and shake hands with Ian.

"You have no idea how happy I'll be to introduce you two when you get on stage today," he said. "Your performance at the Stagecoach Inn rocked the house. How long have you been singing together?"

"Not long," Ian said.

The mayor hooked his thumbs into the front pockets of his spankin' new jeans. "Well, kids, I'm here to tell you that the two of you are going to go far. My wife and I think you have what it takes to be stars."

Carly nudged Ian with her elbow. "What did I tell you?"

He arched a brow, reminding her of their agreement.

Whether Stu knew it or not, this performance, and the dance later at the Grange Hall, was their last hurrah. After tonight, Ian would go back to his life on the Leaning R.

"Did you see the posters we put up around the county?" Stu asked.

Ian stiffened. "What posters?"

"Advertisements for today's event." The short mayor seemed to rise up an inch or two taller. "My wife, Marcia, took a photo of you two when you were playing at the Stagecoach Inn the other night. You looked so natural together, and the shot we had was so clear, we used it to promote the dance tonight."

Ian flinched. His photo was being plastered all over the county?

He nearly took Carly aside and chewed her out for not telling him about the mayor's PR plan. But how clear could the picture be? The mayor and his wife had been seated in one of the booths, and the honky-tonk had been dark.

His initial concern eased and he began to relax. Besides, what were the chances that Felicia would see it— or get wind of it—and come looking for him?

## Chapter Eight

Ian and Carly's performance in Town Square went without a hitch. And by the time they wrapped up with the love song Ian had written about him and Carly, the crowd went wild, giving them a standing ovation.

As they took a final bow, Ian didn't dare glance Carly's way. He knew what he'd see in her expression. She had to be walking on clouds at the obvious appreciation and community validation. But the two of them had made a deal, and he expected her to honor it.

As they stepped off the stage, several people in the crowd swarmed around them, praising them and asking where they would perform next.

"Do you guys play for parties?" one man asked. "My wife and I are celebrating our twenty-fifth wedding anniversary next month, and I'd like to hire you."

"No, I'm afraid this is a onetime thing." Ian sensed Carly's disappointment, but he wasn't about to give in to her again.

A buxom, big-haired brunette dressed in tight jeans and a red silky blouse pressed a business card into Ian's hand. "I'm Molly Carmichael with Star-Studded Nights Entertainment. If you two are looking for a manager, I'd like to talk to you. Maybe we can step over to one of those tables and have a little chat."

"I'd be interested in talking to you," Carly said. "But Ian isn't looking for a manager."

"That's a shame." The attractive brunette focused her baby blues on Ian. "Are you already represented?"

In a way, yes. Ian had worked with Samuel R. Layton, one of the top managers in the country. So if he wanted to get back to work, one simple phone call to Sam was all it would take to fill his schedule of appearances for the next year.

Ian lifted his Stetson and raked a hand through his hair. "Thanks for the offer, Ms. Carmichael, but I'm not planning to perform publicly anymore."

"Now that's an even bigger shame," she said.

He supposed that depended upon how you looked at it. He'd had his fill of the fame and glamour…as well as the phoniness of people wanting to ride his coattails in order to make a name for themselves. And that was one reason he hadn't come clean with Carly.

She merely thought of him as a cowboy or a rancher, and she'd pressed him hard enough as it was. What would she do if she knew of his past success on the stage?

He watched Carly take the woman's card, wanting to object, to ask, what about the baby? But he had no right to interfere in her life.

Ian did have paternal rights, though. And he'd exercise them if he needed to. Surely Carly didn't plan to go out on the road while she was pregnant.

In spite of his resolve not to insist that she do things his way, he slipped his arm around her expanding waist, staking a claim he had no right to make.

"When do we need to head over to the Grange Hall?" he asked her.

Apparently, his boldness didn't surprise her, because she seemed to lean into him. "Before dark, but the sooner the better."

"Then we ought to go." He turned his focus to their wannabe manager. "Will you excuse us, Ms. Carmichael?"

"Of course." The woman smiled at Carly. "I'll be in my office on Monday morning, so I'll expect your call."

"All right." Carly tucked the business card into her pocket.

"Come on." Ian guided Carly through the crowd and across the street. As they headed for his truck, he said, "Thanks for not pushing me to meet with that woman."

"We made a deal. Besides, I've come to realize that I can't change your mind when it's made up."

He was glad she'd finally come to that conclusion, but could he change *her* mind? He'd let the baby questions pile up ever since he'd first learned she was pregnant. She hadn't wanted to discuss the future when she was still trying to get a perspective on the present. But he couldn't help bringing it up now.

"How does the baby fit into your career plans?" he asked.

"I'll figure out something."

Like what? Hiring a nanny to take on the road with her? He'd known performers who'd done that, but it hadn't worked out very well in some cases.

"Don't forget," he said, "I want to be a part of our child's life, so you won't be raising it on your own."

"I appreciate that, Ian. And just for the record, I know you'll be a good daddy."

It wouldn't take much to be an improvement on her old man's parenting. Or his own father's, for that matter. But come hell or high water, Ian was bound and determined to do right by his son or daughter—or to die trying.

He felt a rising compulsion to tell Carly he'd make a good husband, too. But sharing his feelings for her— which were complicated, to say the least—wasn't as easy as talking to her about their child.

As they approached his truck, Carly gave his shirt-sleeve a gentle tug. "Do you think the baby will inherit our musical talent?"

He smiled. "I imagine so. Maybe I should write a lullaby or something so we can encourage a love of music early on."

"That's sweet."

They continued on to where he'd left his pickup. When they arrived at the parking space, she asked, "Did your parents sing or play any instruments?"

"Not that I know of. But my grandma McAllister plays the organ at her church."

Carly seemed to ponder that as he opened the passenger door for her. After he got in and started the engine, she continued with her questions. "When did you learn to play the guitar?"

"My grandma insisted that I take piano lessons when I was seven, but once I laid hands on my first guitar, I was hooked. Before long, I was playing country music instead of old hymns."

"It's nice that she encouraged you. My mom always tried to talk me out of following in her footsteps."

Ian figured that's why she'd been so determined to make a name for herself. And while he believed she had talent and ambition, he wondered if at least a small part of that was rebellion.

"Actually," he said, "my grandma wasn't all that supportive of my switch to country music, so I taught myself to play the guitar."

"Now I'm really impressed."

As far as he was concerned, he hadn't had any other options. He'd been a quiet and introspective kid who'd often turned to his instrument for solace. And that was about the time he began writing tunes of his own.

"Did your grandmother forgive you for giving up gospel tunes?"

Ian couldn't help but chuckle. "Oh, yeah. She's a real sweetheart and would never hold anything against me—or anyone else. But we did strike a compromise. Whenever I'm in Sarasota, which is where she and my granddad retired, I play for her church's old gospel hour."

Carly turned in the seat, her eyes bright, her smile contagious. "That's very cool. So you really don't mind performing for an audience."

"I told you that was never an issue."

She studied him a moment, her smile waning ever so slightly. "You're an interesting man, Ian McAllister."

She didn't know the half of it.

Was now the time to tell her about his years of playing with Felicia?

The thought of confessing his past didn't last long. He'd finally convinced her that he didn't want to perform, and they seemed to be reestablishing a relationship— of one kind or another. So he bit his tongue and continued to drive to the Grange Hall. One more gig, and his performing days were over.

He just wished Carly would make that same decision— at least until their child was older. But when he glanced across the seat and saw the glimmer of anticipation in her pretty blue eyes, he had his doubts.

Carly and Ian were even better received at the Grange Hall than when they'd performed in Town Square. As he strummed the final chord of their last song, even the couples on the dance floor clapped and cheered. She felt a rush of elation she'd never expected. Still, she'd agreed this would be their final act together.

In fact, knowing how Ian had dug in his boot heels, she'd actually expected him to grab her hand and hightail it outside before the applause ended. But he surprised her stopping by the refreshment table and getting them each a glass of punch.

When Bud Mobley and his trio took the stage next and began to play a slow country love song, Ian reached for her hand. But instead of heading for the door, he led her onto the dance floor.

As he slipped his arms around her, he whispered in her ear, "Just for old times' sake."

For that very reason—and perhaps for another reason she didn't want to admit—she stepped into his familiar embrace. The musky scent of his woodsy aftershave snaked around her, holding her captive in its warmth and with the seductive sway of his body.

As they danced cheek to cheek, all the longing she'd ever felt for him rushed back full force, and she struggled to hold it in check.

Ian was an amazing lover, a good man—one of the finest she'd ever met. And she cared about him—far more than she'd ever let him know. More than she dared to even ponder, if she knew what was good for her.

Yet when Bud Mobley crooned on about a love that would never die and a man being the kind of lover a woman could build her dreams on, Carly almost believed it was possible.

Could she and Ian find a way to compromise about their future plans? Could they create a home in which to raise a family, while she pursued a singing career on her own?

He drew her near, his soft breath warm against her neck. She felt herself weakening. And for a moment, she wasn't nearly as eager to see her name in bright lights. Not that she'd given up the dream, but it just didn't feel so pressing.

She'd never thought that loving Ian and living in Brighton Valley for the rest of her life would be enough for her. But now, as she leaned into him, her heart swelling and desire building deep in her core, she wasn't so sure about that.

Did she dare give this up, give him up? Of course, that was assuming he wanted her. But if she'd ever had any doubts about his feelings for her, they eased when the song ended and he continued to hold her close.

She could have slipped out of his arms, but if truth be told, she'd missed his embrace.

And she'd missed *him*.

"Come on," he whispered against her ear. "Let's go home."

She couldn't have objected, even if she'd wanted to. She actually liked the sound of going home to the Leaning R with Ian, no matter how temporary that home might be.

The ride back to the ranch was quiet, yet the cab sparked with desire and pent-up emotion. She risked a glance at the handsome cowboy, at the intensity of his stare as he peered through the windshield at the road ahead. And she suspected he felt it, too.

Once they arrived home, they walked along the path that led to both the house and his cabin. A full moon glowed in the star-splattered sky overhead, making the evening seem almost magical. And even though Carly told herself to ignore it, to tell Ian good-night and go on her way, something much stronger overrode her common sense.

"Would you like to come in for a cup of coffee or tea?" she asked.

"Sure. That sounds good to me."

She led the way to the front porch, unlocked the door and let him inside. But once they entered the house, she didn't dart off to the kitchen. Instead, she turned to the man who'd fathered her baby and touched her heart.

Could she compromise her dream? Could she lay her hope on having a real home and family? A week or so ago, her answer to both questions would have been no. But now she wasn't so sure.

"I want to thank you again for performing with me tonight," she said.

"No problem. When I make a deal, I stick to it."

As their eyes met and their gazes locked, she eased closer to him. She might be sorry for this later, but she reached up, cupped his cheek with one hand, felt the light bristle of his beard.

He placed his palm over the top of her hand, holding her touch against his face, melding her to him as if they'd never been apart.

She didn't know why it was so difficult for her to speak, to tell him she'd like to make love with him again, but she couldn't find her voice. Still, her heart pounded in anticipation.

"I've missed you," he said. "And I've missed the closeness we once shared."

She'd missed him, too. She'd never known a man like Ian.

Without another word, she slipped her hand around to the back of his neck and drew his mouth to hers.

The moment Carly's lips touched his, Ian pulled her into his arms and kissed her with a longing he hadn't expected. He'd told himself it had been for the best when they'd split up, yet being around her again had him questioning that. Now more than ever.

As she leaned into him, he intensified the kiss, his tongue seeking hers, sweeping, dipping and tasting.

It had been so long since he'd felt this kind of fire, this urgency, and he couldn't seem to get enough of her.

As their bodies pressed together, their hands stroked, caressed, explored. When he sought her breast, his thumb skimmed across a taut nipple, and she whimpered. Making love with Carly had always been incredible, yet he'd almost forgotten just how good they were together. When she ended the kiss, he thought he might die if she told him she was having second thoughts. But she remained in his arms.

"I'm willing to take this to the bedroom," she said, "if you are."

"There's nothing I'd like more."

Carly led him to the guest room in which they'd made love in the past. She'd once laughed about it, telling him she didn't feel right about sleeping with him in Granny's bed, especially with the elderly woman's portrait looking on. But at this point, Ian would agree to make love anywhere, including the living room floor.

When they reached the double bed in the room that had become their love nest, Carly pulled down the spread. Then she turned to him and opened her arms, letting him know she was far from changing her mind.

This was the warm and willing woman he remembered, the one he'd nearly fallen heart over head for. He kissed her again, long and deep. As their tongues mated, a surge of desire shot through him, and he pulled her hips forward against his erection.

She moaned, then clutched at his shoulders, moving against him, making him wild with need. When he thought he might explode from the pent-up passion, he tore his mouth from hers. His breath came out in soft, ragged pants when he said, "You have no idea how badly I want you."

"Yes, I do. I want you, too. And even though—"

He placed his finger against her lips, stopping her from mentioning any second thoughts, any concerns. "Don't think about the past or worry about the future, honey. Just concentrate on the here and now. I want us to make love the way we used to."

Apparently, she did, too, because she began unbuttoning her blouse. Her breasts were much fuller than he remembered. Her pretty black lace bra could scarcely contain them.

He watched as she slid down the zipper of her jeans, and peeled the denim over her hips, revealing a pair of skimpy black lace panties. He'd never imagined that he could find a pregnant woman so damned sexy.

The swell of her baby bump was the sweetest and most amazing thing he'd ever seen. And when she stepped out of her black Wrangler jeans and kicked them aside, he placed his hand over the mound of her belly where their child grew. Then he looked into her eyes and smiled. "This is beautiful. *You're* beautiful. And it makes you more desirable than ever."

An "I love you" nearly rolled off his tongue, but he bit it back. The last thing he needed to do was to scare her away, even though he'd never actually realized the truth of those three little words until this very moment. He loved Carly. He wanted her. *Needed* her.

He removed his clothes, then slipped his arms around her waist. She skimmed her nails across his chest, sending a shiver through his veins and a rush of heat through his blood. Then she unsnapped her bra and freed her breasts, full and round, the dusky pink tips darker than he'd remembered, yet peaked and begging to be kissed.

He bent and took a nipple in his mouth, using his tongue and lips until she gasped in pleasure. Then he scooped her into his arms and placed her on top of the mattress. He wanted nothing more than to slip out of his boxers and feel her skin against his, but he paused for a beat and savored the angelic sight of the woman he was sorely tempted to offer marriage—if he thought she might agree.

He joined her on the bed, where they continued to kiss, to taste and to stroke each other until they were both wild and breathless and flinging their undergarments across the room.

When he rose up and over her naked body, she opened for him. He entered her slowly at first, this time without the need of a condom, relishing the feel of being inside her. But passion soon took over.

As her body responded to his, giving and taking, any reservations either of them ever had seemed to disappear. Nothing else mattered but this very moment and the pleasure they gave each other. When he felt her reach a peak and heard her cry out, he let himself go, releasing along with her in a sexual explosion.

As the last waves of their climax ebbed, Ian rolled to the side, taking Carly with him, holding her close. "It's like our bodies knew right where they'd left off."

"I know." She smiled and placed a hand on his chest. "We probably should talk about the future."

He wanted to object, to tell her to let it wait until morning—or next week. Or better yet, even after the baby came. But she was right. And he feared that making love had only complicated the issue.

As Carly lay in Ian's arms, fully sated, she realized how deeply she cared for him—and how hurt she'd be if he refused to give up his job at the Leaning R and support her quest to make a name for herself in the country music world.

She no longer expected him to sing with her, but if they were going to create a family together, they couldn't do it from the Leaning R, especially since the ranch might belong to someone else within a few months.

He drew her close and nuzzled her neck, a move that should have comforted her. Instead, it set off a sudden onslaught of bells and whistles.

This wasn't going to be easy. Where would they

live? How would they work things out so they could both fulfill their dreams?

Or would she be expected to give up hers?

She'd grown up as Charles Rayburn's daughter, a princess in many ways. But her life in the castle hadn't been very happy. Her father had rarely come to any school plays, award ceremonies or sporting events. He'd even missed her high school graduation. "I'm sorry, baby girl," he'd said over the telephone. "I have a critical business meeting I have to attend. But I'll add five thousand dollars to your trust account. Go shopping on me."

He hadn't always given her an excuse for his paternal absences, but when he did, they were always business related.

Then there'd been her mother—a country star who'd lit the stage with her dazzling smile and talent. But Carly had always remained in the shadows, watching her mother on TV or hearing her hits on the radio. She'd just nod when people said, "Aren't you a lucky girl." But she'd quit smiling by the time she was ten. It was hard enough to hold back the tears, let alone feign happiness.

Could Carly be content only to be known as Ian's wife or her child's mother?

She supposed she could if Ian didn't smother the dream of the little girl inside her.

Yet the longer she lay in bed with him, the harder it was to breathe. She couldn't foresee a future for them unless Ian was willing to compromise and give her the freedom she needed to be someone.

"Do you ever see yourself as a wife and mother?" he asked.

His words struck a chilling blow, and she realized she'd given him the wrong idea.

"Not the way you probably do."

Silence stretched across the mattress, creating a distance between them in spite of their embrace.

Making love, as good as it had been, as much as she'd needed to be in Ian's arms tonight, had been a mistake.

One she didn't dare make again.

## *Chapter Nine*

Not wanting to lose the afterglow of their lovemaking, Ian suggested they discuss the future in the morning, and Carly agreed. They spent the night together, as had been their routine before, but sometime during the wee hours of the morning, she'd rolled to the far side of the bed, hugging her pillow instead of him.

He'd told himself not to give it much thought, but he'd slept like hell. Before dawn, he got up, dressed quietly and slipped out of the room, taking care not to wake her. But this time he wasn't heading out to do his morning chores, although he'd need to tend to those, too. He was going to check on Cheyenne.

The puppy had plenty of food and water, but she'd undoubtedly missed his company. So there was no telling what she'd chewed up or how many puddles or piles she'd left on the floor.

But as he tiptoed through the quiet ranch house, snuck out the back door in the darkness and headed for his cabin, he realized there was actually another reason for his stealthy departure. He wanted to avoid Carly.

Sure, they needed to talk. And maybe he should even level with her and tell her that he'd fallen in love with her. But he doubted she felt the same way about him. And he wasn't about to settle for a relationship in which one partner wasn't fully committed to the other. On his grandparents' ranch, he'd grown up in a loving household and seen firsthand how a good marriage worked. His grandparents had honored their wedding vows for nearly fifty years, and Ian didn't want anything less.

But Carly hadn't had the same loving example when she'd been a child, and he was afraid that when they finally broached the future, she'd decide to end their relationship again. He couldn't do anything about it if she chose to leave, but he wasn't going to let the baby go as easily.

When he opened the front door to the cabin that had been his home for the past three years, Cheyenne charged him, jumping up on her hind legs, whining and wagging her little stump of a tail in greeting.

What Ian wouldn't give to have Carly and their child greet his arrival like this, but that wasn't likely.

He loved Carly—and he would adore their son or daughter—but she didn't appear to want to create a family with him. At least, not the kind he'd always envisioned for himself. He tried to understand that it wasn't her so much as the childhood she'd had that influenced her thinking, but it was getting more and more difficult to make excuses for her.

Still, it was going to kill him to see her go on tour— which she seemed hell-bent on doing. But what other option did he have?

None that he could see, because he was every bit as determined to chart his own future as Carly was. And the paths they'd chosen weren't likely to cross.

A telephone rang, waking Carly from a sound sleep. The morning sun peeked through the slats in the blinds, but other than that, she had no idea what time it was. Or where she was.

She opened one eye and scanned the surroundings, suddenly recognizing the guest room and realizing that she was tangled up in the sheets alone. Apparently Ian had slipped out of bed earlier, which had usually been his habit. But this time... Well, things weren't the same anymore.

The phone rang again. Not her cell, but the old-style house telephone.

She rolled out of bed, still naked from the night of lovemaking, then hurried to the living room and snatched the receiver off the cradle. She managed to answer before the fourth ring.

It was Shannon Miller, Braden's mother.

"How's it going?" Carly asked, wondering why she'd called so early.

"My...uh...dad passed away a few hours ago."

Carly's heart dropped to her stomach. "Oh, no. I'm so sorry to hear that. Is there anything I can do?"

"Not that I can think of. Erik is here and has been handling everything."

Carly combed her fingers through her tousled hair. "All right, but please let me know if you need anything."

"Thanks, honey. I appreciate that. Could you please tell your brother?"

"Of course." At least, she'd try to get a hold of Jason. His cell reception in Mexico was sometimes sketchy.

After she said goodbye to Shannon, she dialed Jason's number. While it rang, she bit back a yawn and wondered what time it actually was.

She glanced at the fireplace mantel, looking for the antique clock, but it had already been packed away in one of the sealed boxes that lined the far wall. The house, she realized, had never looked so empty. As a rush of grief and loneliness swept through her, she wished she'd gotten dressed before placing the call.

"Hey, Carly," her older brother said. "What's up?"

Rather than blurt out her news, she decided to ease into it. "Are you and Juliana still in Mexico?"

"Yes, we're staying in a motel in a small town that's about a hundred miles south of Guadalajara. I'm glad you called. We found the twins."

"That's good news." Now maybe her brother and his new bride could come back to the States and start their lives together.

"Juliana and I were relieved to find them with the

nanny, but we'll have to brush up on our high school Spanish. They don't speak English."

Carly could see where communicating would be tricky and smiled. "Then they're lucky I wasn't the one to find them. I took French in school."

He laughed. "Yeah, we've come up with our own kind of sign language, so we're getting by."

"Then they weren't living in an orphanage?"

"No, they've been staying with the nanny, an older woman dad had hired. But she isn't happy with the setup. Her English isn't very good, either, but she made herself clear. She doesn't want to keep them any longer."

"Oh, no. Those poor kids."

"Apparently Dad's private investigator paid her for two months in advance and told her Dad would either send for her and the kids or pick them up as soon as he could. But he never called or showed up."

"Did she know that he was killed in a car accident, probably on his way to get them?"

"She does now. Apparently she's upset about not being paid for her services, so I gave her five hundred in cash. But I'll need to find a bank to get the rest of the money she says he owes her, although I suspect she's not being completely honest about the amount."

Carly ran a hand through her hair again, her finger catching on a tangle. "What are you going to do with the kids?"

"I'll bring them back with us. Fortunately, their paperwork seems to be in order. At least Dad managed to get that squared away."

"Does that mean you won't have any problem crossing the border with them?"

"We shouldn't. And apparently we found the nanny just in time. She'd already had the kids packed and ready to return to the orphanage."

"That's so sad. And pretty cold. What kind of woman is she?"

"A businesswoman, it seems."

Carly slowly shook her head. If the children didn't have anyone to love and care for them, no wonder her father had felt sorry for them and wanted to bring them to the States. "I hope the nanny didn't abuse or neglect them."

"They seem to be well fed and healthy. And we haven't seen any cuts or bruises. So my guess is that she did all right by them."

That was a relief. Her father wasn't the only one who'd had a soft spot for disadvantaged children. Of course, he'd always put his wallet where his heart was, making large donations to charities that funded various programs for kids.

He hadn't actually gotten personally involved, though. And that had been true with his own children. She wondered what made Camilla's twins different.

Had he known that Camilla was a single mother and that there wouldn't be anyone to look after her kids? That seemed likely.

"Will you tell Braden that I found them?" Jason asked.

"Yes, of course. But just so you know, his mother

called me a few minutes ago. His grandfather passed away during the night, so I told her I'd let you know."

"Oh, no. I'm sorry to hear that."

"It was expected."

"I know it was, but Mr. Miller was a good man—and more of a father to Braden than our dad ever was."

Jason had that right. And while she and her brothers had been as different from each other as the three mothers who'd borne them, they'd been raised by the same dad who'd provided for every financial need they'd ever wanted, often neglecting the emotional ones.

The line went silent for a moment. Then Carly asked, "When are you coming home?"

"In a day or two. But I have a couple of business issues to take care of in Houston, so I'll have to stop by the corporate office first."

"At Rayburn Enterprises?"

"No, at Rayburn Energy Transport. There's talk of a strike, and I'd like to settle things before they get out of hand. But I may have to be there for a while. I just hope Braden was able to find someone to adopt the twins. I can't keep them forever. Besides, I have plans to take Juliana on a real honeymoon."

Carly doubted that Braden had found anyone yet, and with his grandfather's passing, he probably wouldn't be searching for a while.

Gosh, she hoped Jason didn't ask her to take on the twins, especially when she had a baby of her own on the way.

For the briefest moment, she considered sharing her

baby news with her older brother, but she opted to hold off a little while longer. They hadn't been especially close in the past, although that seemed to be changing now that their dad was gone. But Jason might not like the idea that she and Ian weren't married, or that they hadn't decided where a baby would leave the two of them.

"I'll let you know when we get back to the States," Jason said.

"Okay. Take care."

When the call ended, Carly returned to the bedroom, her hand resting on her bare tummy. As long as she didn't announce she was expecting, she didn't have to think about the future and how the baby would fit into her plans.

And the longer she could put off discussing her future plans with Ian.

As the day wore on, Ian knew he couldn't avoid Carly indefinitely. He'd already checked all of the pastures as well as the pump he and the boys had fixed earlier, so there wasn't any other reason for him to stay away from the house.

When he finally rode into the yard, Carly stepped out onto the front porch as if she'd been waiting for him. She was dressed in a loose-fitting white sundress, the skirt billowing. Her pretty legs were bare—and so were her feet.

The breeze kicked up a strand of her hair, whisking it across her face, and she brushed it aside. She looked as pretty as a picture. Whether she knew it or not, she was a living, breathing part of the Leaning R. And he couldn't help thinking how nice it would be to return home to her each day.

As he dismounted, she approached him and his bay gelding, as though eager to talk. Had he misread her last night? Had she not been drawing away from him?

"Shannon called," she said. "Gerald Miller passed away last night."

"That's too bad." Ian swung down from his horse. "But he was pretty sick and in pain."

"They said he passed peacefully." The wind picked up another strand of her hair, and this time, when she swiped it aside, she tucked it behind her ear. "I just got back from the Miller ranch. I fixed Braden and his mom a casserole and baked a cake. I also offered to help in any way I can."

"That was nice. I'm sure they won't feel like cooking for a while."

"That's what I thought." She placed her hands on her hips and blew out a sigh. "While I was there, Braden told me that he's going to sign the listing agreement. So it looks like the Leaning R will go on the market within the next week."

"You're still going to sign, right?" Ian asked.

She nodded. "I can't run this place on my own. Besides, I'm not planning to stay in Brighton Valley forever." She studied him as though she was waiting for him to object or to bring up the baby, but he didn't do either.

"I'm sorry your family isn't going to keep the place," he said, lifting his hat and readjusting it over his mussed, sweat-dampened hair. "But I'm glad you all agreed to sell."

"Why? I'd think you'd be worried about losing your job or having to work for someone new."

Ian proceeded to remove the saddle from his bay gelding. "Did Jason tell you that Ralph Nettles had a buyer interested in purchasing the ranch?"

"Yes, he mentioned it. If that's true, then it should sell quickly, which I suppose is good."

Ian placed the saddle and blankets over the top rung of the corral. "Well, I'm the buyer Ralph Nettles was talking about."

Her brow furrowed, the news clearly taking her by surprise. "You?"

Apparently she still saw him as a simple cowboy, which ought to bother him, but how could it? He'd never revealed his life in Nashville. "Believe it or not, I've already got the offer ready to go."

Disbelief—or maybe distrust—twisted her expression. "Can you pull it off? I mean, my brothers are going to want top dollar, and I don't think they'll be willing to carry paper."

He didn't need them to extend him any kind of credit. He'd made some sound investments and still had plenty of royalties rolling in. "It just so happens that I have a little nest egg put aside."

Her brow furrowed deeper still, as she no doubt pondered what "little" meant to him.

What she didn't realize was that he could probably pay cash for the place—unless they were actually asking a lot more than it was worth. But he'd already gone over the figures with Mr. Nettles, and he figured it would work out okay.

"Well, then," she said, giving a little shrug, "I guess that's good news. I'd rather see the ranch go to you than to a stranger."

"You're still welcome to come home anytime you want. I'll keep the guest room ready for you." He offered her a smile, an olive branch of sorts.

"Thanks. I might take you up on that." Then she slowly turned and made her way back to the porch. As she placed her hand on the railing and her foot on the first step, she paused and turned around. "I forgot to mention that I talked to Jason and got an update from him."

That wasn't what he'd expected her to say, but apparently she had some news to share. "How's the search going?"

Carly told him about the twins, the money-minded nanny and the plan to return with the twins soon. After bringing him up to speed, she turned and continued into the house.

The fact that she hadn't mentioned eating dinner together didn't go unnoticed. But he wasn't going to make any speculations when it came to Carly. She had to do what she thought was right.

And so did he.

Carly felt a little dumbfounded as she returned to the house. Ian planned to buy the ranch?

The idea had blindsided her because she hadn't expected him to have saved up enough money for a sizable down payment. He seemed to think he had it all figured out, though.

She hoped he was right. Because even though his game plan seemed to come out of the blue, she actually preferred to have him take ownership rather than someone she didn't know.

But now he would be even more tied to Brighton Valley and the Leaning R than ever. So where did that leave her and the baby?

She'd hardly given her thoughts room to breathe when she heard her cell phone ring. The customized ringtone told her it was her mother.

After reaching her cell, which had been charging on the maple bureau in the bedroom, she answered the call. "Hi…" *Raelynn* nearly rolled off her mouth, but she opted for a belated "Mom."

Raelynn's voice came out in a rush. "Are you doing all right, honey? I had the weirdest dream last night. You know I never give that stuff much thought, but on the outside chance that something was wrong, I thought I'd better call."

"I'm fine. So whatever dream you had wasn't a premonition."

"That's good. I'd dreamt that you went for a ride on a pretty little pinto pony. But when it reared up, it turned out to be one of those rodeo horses your brother Braden raises on the Bar M. The crazy, snorting, red-eyed beast bucked you off, and you broke your neck. It was so real that I woke up in a cold sweat."

"Everything is okay here, but oddly enough, Braden's grandfather passed away last night."

Raelynn's breath caught. "Oh, that's too bad. What happened? Don't tell me he was thrown from a bronco and killed."

"No, he had cancer. He'd been fighting it for a while."

"What a shame. He seemed like such a nice man. I'd like to send flowers or something. When are the services?"

"On Wednesday. According to what Shannon said earlier today, it'll be a celebration of his life. They plan to hold it on the ranch."

"I'll make sure to order a nice spray of roses and have them delivered. I'm afraid David and I will be leaving for London the next day, and I'll be busy packing and having my hair and nails done."

"I'll tell Shannon you're sorry you had to miss it."

"Thank you, honey."

"I do have something to tell you, though." Carly bit down on her bottom lip, wondering how her mother would take the news, but she couldn't keep it a secret forever.

"What is it?"

"I'm pregnant." The line went still, and Carly sensed her mother's shock.

After several beats, she found her voice, "Oh, dear." Her tone indicated she'd just been given some disturbing news. Had she connected the dots to realize that meant she was going to be a grandmother? That ought to send her over the edge.

"I take it you didn't elope without telling me," Raelynn said. "Are you going to marry the baby's father?"

"I'm not sure. We haven't discussed it yet."

Raelynn blew out an exasperated sigh. "I suppose we can keep it quiet."

"We won't be able to keep it under wraps too long. I'm already nearly five months pregnant."

Raelynn clucked her tongue. "I can't believe you're just telling me now. David is up for reelection, and I'd hate to have it get out that my daughter is unwed and pregnant. It might put a real damper on his standing with conservative voters."

*Great, Raelynn. Why don't we make this all about you?* Carly didn't say what she was thinking, but then again, every hope, every dream she'd ever had, everything she'd ever done, had revolved around her mother's career and her convenience.

But Carly would be darned if she'd get married just to please Raelynn and the senator's potential voters. And she was rebellious enough these days to refuse to marry Ian, even if he asked her.

"I'm not sure what I plan to do about the baby's father," she said. "We can talk more about it when you get back from Europe."

"All right. But I hope you won't tell anyone in the meantime."

Like who? The paparazzi? The *Brighton Valley Gazette*? Or was she afraid Carly would announce it on Facebook, where the news networks might catch wind of it?

"For Pete's sake, Mom. Can't you be just a little supportive? My pregnancy might seem like a scandal to you, but I'm actually happy about having a baby."

As the words rolled off her lips, she realized they held some truth. "I just wish you'd be happy, too."

"I'm not unhappy," Raelynn said. "And I'm not a prude. Lord knows I've made mistakes, too."

Somehow, Carly didn't see her baby as a "mistake." And it grated upon her to think her mother did.

"It's just that the timing could be better," Raelynn added.

Granted, that was true. Carly would have preferred to have gotten married before she got pregnant. And it would be nice if she'd had a chance to establish her career before starting a family. That way, she would feel good about taking time off to be a real mother to her son or daughter.

"I'll tell you what," Carly said, "I'll do everything I can to save you and the senator from any undue embarrassment, even if that means staying out of your life until the baby reaches adulthood."

"Now, that's not what I meant, Carly. You don't have to be so testy."

Didn't she? This entire conversation only reminded her how lousy her childhood had been. And how little she'd actually mattered in her mother's world. Raelynn may have given up singing and performing, but she still lived on a stage of sorts.

But none of that mattered anymore. Carly was going to have a baby—one who was loved. And she'd be a much better mother than Raelynn had been.

"Let's talk more about this later, after we both have a chance to let the news set in. In the meantime, have a good trip. I'll talk to you when you get back." Then they said their goodbyes and disconnected the line.

Carly wasn't so sure that she actually would call her mother after the London trip. But she did need to talk to Ian. And there was no point in putting it off any longer. They had some planning and compromises to make. After all, the baby would be here in a little more than four months.

Carly went outside, determined to find Ian and have the discussion she'd meant to have this morning. It took nearly ten minutes, but she finally heard Cheyenne yipping at something or other. So she followed the sound to the back of the barn.

Ian was leaning against the corral, studying one of the mares, while the little cattle dog tried to herd a couple of butterflies that hovered near a patch of bluebonnets. He turned when he heard her approach.

"Got a minute?" she asked.

"Sure." He pushed away from the wooden rail and slid his hands into the front pockets of his jeans. He was a handsome yet formidable sight as he stood there, all muscle and sinew and…cowboy strong.

"I've been putting off talking about the baby," she said, "mostly because I've been trying to wrap my mind around the news. But don't get me wrong. I'm not unhappy about it."

"I'm glad to hear it. And for the record, I'm actually looking forward to being a father."

"That's good to know."

The gelding moved to the side, and Ian gave it a pat

on the rump. "I want you to know that you can live here while the baby is young."

She'd suspected he would offer that. But did he think she'd be content to be a rancher for the rest of her life?

"Are you suggesting I give up my dream?" she asked.

"No, I'm just throwing out the idea that you could postpone it a bit. At least, the big-time aspects. Keep in mind that Earl Tellis would let you perform anytime you want at the Stagecoach Inn. I know it's not your idea of stardom, but you'd be doing what you want to do until you moved on to something more glamorous."

Would performing in a local honky-tonk be enough for her?

"And Stu Jeffries loves your voice," Ian added. "He'd have you singing at all the community events."

He was probably right about that, but would she grow to resent the small-town life in time?

She feared that she might. But instead of speaking her fears, she lifted her foot and brushed her big toe against a clump of dandelions on the ground.

"I'd marry you in a heartbeat," Ian added. "Just so you know."

Her own heartbeat fluttered at the thought, even though it wasn't a real proposal. Still, a wedding would certainly please Raelynn, but Carly couldn't marry a man who'd only proposed to provide his child with a name and to make an honest woman out of her. She needed to know that she was loved unconditionally.

She struggled with the urge to admit that she loved him, that his offer, while sweet, hadn't been enough.

But she knew admitting those words would only lead to heartbreak, so she kept them to herself.

"The way I see it," Ian said, "we have a lot of options. I'd be happy to watch the baby while you go on the road."

She ought to be thankful to have his support, but she didn't like the idea of going anywhere and leaving the baby behind. Yet she also hated the thought of remaining on the ranch with him indefinitely. The dilemma was killing her.

"Why can't you just go on the road with me?" she asked. "You don't have to perform. You could watch the baby."

"I can't do that," he said. "You're asking me to be Mr. Carly Rayburn."

"No, I'm not."

"Either way, a baby doesn't belong on the road with a singing act. It isn't a good environment—the long hours, the touring, the various hotel rooms. And that's just the logistics. There are other factors, too."

"How do you know what it would be like on the road?"

Ian opened his mouth to speak, then shut it and slowly shook his head.

Maybe he realized any argument he came up with wouldn't hold water.

"I'll tell you what," Carly said. "Why don't we give ourselves time to think about the options?"

"All right. But don't toss out the marriage idea."

She'd remember his offer. But she couldn't marry a man who didn't love her to the moon and back.

# Chapter Ten

Shannon and Braden planned a celebration of life for Gerald Miller at their ranch on Wednesday afternoon, where many of the longtime Brighton Valley residents could pay their respects to a man who'd been their friend and neighbor.

Carly had driven over to the Bar M earlier that morning so she could help them set up. She'd asked Ian if he wanted to go with her, but he said he'd meet her there later.

So far they hadn't talked any more about the baby or the future, but they would have to do so soon. Her blind determination to pursue her dream at all costs seemed to be weakening. In fact, she still held Molly Carmichael's card in her purse and had yet to call her about representing her. How could she, when she'd just learned she was pregnant? She had no idea what the future might bring and hadn't wanted to make any kind of commitment until she figured it out.

Surprisingly, she found herself actually wanting to stay on the Leaning R until the baby came. After that, she'd just have to take each day as it came.

The more Carly thought about that plan, the better she actually liked it. Last night while she'd watched TV, she'd seen a commercial about a new baby store that had opened in Wexler. It seemed only natural for her to think about cribs and rockers—and to wonder which bedroom she should fix up for the nursery.

And as she'd continued to nest in her mind, she hadn't thought once about singing on stage. Instead she'd found herself humming lullabies and wondering if Ian had been serious about writing one of his own. If he was, maybe he'd let her come up with the lyrics for whatever tune he created.

Now, however, she would have to focus on the work at hand—and on the tribute to Gerald Miller, the gruff but kindly man everyone had liked and respected.

Gerald Miller had been a champion bronc rider who'd competed in rodeos all over the country. After his retirement, he'd turned his sights on breeding and training cutting horses. He was a successful businessman in his own right, honest and fair.

Folks around these parts looked up to cowboys. They seemed to have a code of honor unique to them. And Gerald was no different. He had a strong work ethic and a love of family and community.

Ian, too, was the epitome of the honorable cowboy.

And she'd found herself considering more than once over the past few days that he'd make a good husband and father. But at this point, she wouldn't entertain any thoughts other than that.

When the doorbell rang, Carly left the caterers in the kitchen and volunteered to answer it. "I'll bet it's the florist with another delivery."

And she'd been right. The driver held a plant garden in one hand and a large bouquet in the other. "Where do you want these?"

Carly scanned the living room, which was already adorned with several arrangements. Then she reached for the potted plant. "I'll set this on the hearth. You can put the bouquet on the coffee table."

"You got it." The delivery boy did as she instructed, then added, "There's one more still in my van."

He went outside and returned carrying a large spray of roses that had been arranged in the shape of a cowboy boot.

Carly gazed at the flowers and the stand that came with it. Something like that must have cost a pretty penny, and she wondered who'd sent it.

She reached for the small card and read, "With deepest sympathy. Senator David Crowder and Raelynn Fallon."

"Where would you like this to go?" the young man asked.

The stand-up display was too large for the living room, especially with all the other arrangements set out. "It should go in the backyard, near the horse arena, where the celebration will take place. But I'll take it."

"Thanks." He set the stand on the floor, then reached for the clipboard he'd tucked under his arm. "Can I get you to sign for this?"

After scratching out her name, Carly carried the spray outside, where several other large arrangements had been placed already. She found a spot for her mother's flowers, but before placing them, she took one last look at the large, colorful floral boot. It was a fitting arrangement for a man who'd been a true cowboy in every sense of the word.

As Carly started back to the house, Braden came out of the barn. He was dressed in black jeans, a white cotton shirt and a bolo tie. Talk about real cowboys—her brother also fit the image to a tee.

She hadn't had a chance to speak to him yet, so she crossed the yard and met him near the vegetable garden his grandpa had planted each spring.

"How are you holding up?" she asked.

"I'm doing okay. We were expecting it—and Grandpa had taken care of all the financial issues. Having his affairs in order has made everything easier."

"He was a good man," Carly said. "I'm sorry you lost him so soon."

"I guess we're never ready for a loved one to pass on." Braden blew out a sigh. "Thanks for coming early to help out today. My mom and I really appreciate it."

She offered him a smile. "That's what sisters are for."

A crooked grin tugged at his lips. "Yeah, maybe so."

"That reminds me," Carly said, "Jason and Juliana

will be coming back with the twins soon. Have you had any luck finding them a home?"

"No, not yet. I talked to Pastor Steuben at the Brighton Valley Community Church last week. He was going to look into it for us, but as far as I know, he hasn't found anyone yet."

"I guess it won't be easy to find someone willing to take on two kids, especially when they don't speak English."

"You're probably right. But I've got my fingers crossed."

Carly did, too. The poor kids had been through a lot already—losing their mother and their grandfather, spending time in an orphanage and then with a nanny who seemed to care more about finances than children. Now they were being uprooted again and moved to a different country where they would have to learn a new language. They'd also have to adjust to family life with strangers.

"On the upside," Braden said, "I stopped by Nettles Realty and signed the paperwork to list the Leaning R yesterday. From what I understand, Ralph still needs your and Jason's signatures, but he seems to think it's already as good as sold."

"I'll see Ralph and sign on Monday. I have a doctor's appointment that afternoon, so I'll be in town."

Braden furrowed his brow. "Is something wrong? I know you were sick while you were in San Antonio. You're not still dealing with that, are you?"

She was tempted to skate around the issue by telling him it was just a checkup, which it was. But there really was no use in keeping the news from him. "Actually, it's nothing to worry about. I'm just pregnant."

Braden flinched. "Boy, I didn't see that coming."

"Neither did I."

He glanced at her waistline, which was hidden behind the loose beige top she wore over a pair of black stretch pants. Then he asked, "Who's the father?"

She couldn't very well hold back that information, either. "Granny's foreman—Ian McAllister."

Braden seemed to give that some thought, then asked, "Does he know?"

She nodded. "He seems to be happy about it, but we're still trying to figure out how we're going to co-parent. He offered to marry me, but I'm not so sure that's a good idea. I think he just made the offer because he's an honorable guy."

"Don't you want to get married?" Braden asked.

Not if they weren't crazy in love with each other. And although she had come to the conclusion that she might feel that way, it had to be a two-way street, and she wouldn't settle for less.

"Like I said, the future is still up in the air." She tucked a strand of hair behind her ear. "And you may as well know, Ian is the one who's interested in purchasing the Leaning R."

"That's what Ralph told me. And to be honest, I like the guy and have no problem with him buying the ranch. But where would a cowboy get that kind of money?"

"Ian said he's got it. Heck, maybe he has a trust fund like us." Even as she said it, she doubted that was the case—it didn't fit with what he'd told her about his family.

"The down payment alone is pretty hefty," Braden said. "And then he'll need the money to buy more cattle as well as to hire extra hands."

Carly hadn't thought about the startup funds Ian would need. "He mentioned having a small nest egg, but maybe he does have an inheritance of some kind."

"He seems pretty levelheaded," Braden said. "But I hope he isn't just dreaming about being able to make a purchase like this."

"No, I think he's serious."

Yet she couldn't help wondering the same thing. Could Ian actually come up with enough money to buy the ranch? Or was he chumming her?

He knew how she felt about selling the place. Was he trying to tempt her to stay with him?

"With the baby coming," Braden said, "maybe he's hoping you'll throw in your third from the proceeds, which would allow him the start-up funds he'll need."

Braden had a point. If Carly threw in her third, he'd only need to purchase the other 66 percent.

But Ian had never given her reason to believe he was using her for any reason. So she slowly shook her head. "No, he wouldn't expect me to do that."

Still, as the seeds of suspicion had sprouted, she cut them off at the root. There was no reason to believe Ian was pulling a fast one and trying to rope her into a situation she didn't want to be in. Her father might have pulled a stunt like that, but Ian wouldn't.

"I guess we'll find out soon enough," Braden said. "Once you and Jason sign the listing agreement, the ranch will be on the market. And then we can see what kind of an offer Ian makes."

And what kind of man he really was, she supposed.

"How soon do you think Jason will be able to sign the paperwork?" Braden asked.

"Within the next couple of days, I would guess."

Braden stroked his chin. "Do you think he and Juliana would consider keeping the twins—at least for a while?"

"That's a lot of responsibility for newlyweds to take on," Carly said.

"Maybe you can take them until we find a permanent home."

*"Me?"* Carly raised her hand, palm out. "Oh, no. Don't even go there. I wouldn't be any good with kids."

"Who says?" Braden smiled, then added, "Besides, you'd better get some practice if you'll be having one of your own."

That was true. She placed her hand on her tummy, which seemed to be growing bigger each day. She was just beginning to wrap her heart and mind around the changes taking place in her life. But she wasn't ready to add non-English-speaking twins to the list.

At the sound of an approaching vehicle, Braden said, "Speak of the devil. Here comes your baby daddy now."

Devil?

Again, Carly shook off her suspicion. Ian had been nothing but sweet and supportive. How could she possibly think he had any ulterior motives?

\* \* \*

Ian arrived at the Bar M early. As he pulled into the drive, he spotted Carly and Braden talking in the yard.

He'd barely climbed from his truck when Braden's mother walked outside with a well-dressed man in his mid to late forties and joined them.

Ian was struck by how pretty Shannon Miller was. He'd never seen her fixed up before, with makeup on and with her brown hair soft and loose around her shoulders. If he didn't know better, he'd think she was Braden's older sister.

When Ian approached and offered his condolences, Shannon introduced her friend Dr. Erik Chandler. "He's been incredibly supportive these past few weeks. I don't know what I'd do without him."

The doctor slipped his arm around her waist, making a show of solidarity.

Ian liked seeing that. His grandparents leaned on each other through the good times and the bad. He'd noticed them talking in soft whispers, eyes glimmering and lips quirked in a smile. And he'd seen them cry together when their dog Buddy had died. To this day, they held hands when they took their afternoon walk.

He hoped Carly would learn that she could lean on him as the months wore on—or even the years. With a baby on the way, their lives would be entwined forever.

"Erik hired a caterer to fix the food, to set it out and to clean up afterward," Shannon said. "So there isn't much for us to do now except wait for people to arrive."

Dr. Chandler gave her a gentle squeeze. "You've been through enough already. And you've carried a heavy load for a long time. You don't need to worry about making sure everyone else is taken care of on a day like this."

Their smiles and his gentle touch implied they were more than just friends. If so, Ian was happy for her. From what Granny had told him, she really hadn't dated after Braden was born. And he'd found that to be sad.

"When things settle down," Shannon said, "Erik is going to take me to Hawaii for a vacation."

At that, Braden brightened. "I'm glad, Mom. You've spent your entire life looking out for me, Grandpa and the ranch. And that's not to mention all the time you poured into the church. You've always focused on others, so it's time you took a vacation and enjoyed yourself."

"Thanks for understanding, honey." Shannon placed a loving hand on Braden's sleeve. "For the time being, we'd better focus on getting through today."

A car sounded in the distance, and they turned to see who would be the first to arrive.

Ian took the opportunity to steal a glance at Carly, but instead of looking at the approaching vehicle, she was studying the older couple as intently as he'd been. Their friendship—or whatever they might call their particular relationship—was warm and loving as well as enviable.

In fact, their bond appeared to be the kind a couple made after supporting each other through life's ups and downs. Could she see that some relationships could be loving and strong?

As Carly continued to watch Shannon and Erik, Ian could have sworn he spotted a longing in her eyes. He wanted to assure her, to tell her to give him and her time and a chance to become a couple and a family.

But now wasn't the time, and this wasn't the place.

On Monday morning, Carly told Ian she was going to shop for baby furniture so she could fix up a nursery in what had once been Granny's sewing room.

He was relieved to hear of her decision and as much as he wanted to go with her, he didn't want to crowd her, especially since she planned to stick around for a while. So he was content to let her go alone.

Besides, he had plenty lined up to do today. Todd and the boys were going to start on the new fence he wanted to build in the south forty, and he figured it was best if he rode out with them.

By noon, they'd measured the field he planned to enclose, and he'd lined the teens up to start digging post holes. He probably should have waited until the property was officially his, but he wanted a place to keep the new calves he planned to buy.

While the hands took a lunch break, he rode back to the house to order the lumber and material they would need. He'd no more than entered the yard when he spotted a sleek, black limousine parked near the house.

He swore under his breath. There was only one person who could have arrived in a luxury car like that, and he braced himself for a strained reception as the chauffeur opened the door for Felicia Jamison.

"Just look at you," the red-haired country music star

said as she exited the limo. "I never would have believed it if I hadn't seen it for myself. Mac McAllister—in all his dusty, cowboy glory."

Ian rested a hand on the pommel, but he remained in the saddle. "I might have shaken off the dirt from my boots and cleaned up if I'd known you were stopping by."

"I certainly would have given you fair warning—if you would have left me a phone number or a forwarding address." She splayed her manicured hands on her hips. "If I didn't know better, I'd think you had been trying to avoid me for the past three years."

Damn. Why couldn't she have just let him be?

He bit back his frustration as well as his disappointment at seeing her. "Why would I do that? You're the prettiest stalker I've ever met. And the most famous."

"Actually," Felicia said as she approached him and the bay gelding he rode, "I let you slip off my radar for a while. But I need another big hit, and you're the only one who's ever been able to write with my voice and style in mind."

That was a fact. It had been his music and lyrics that had sent her to the top of the charts time and again. And she hadn't had an album go platinum since he ended their relationships—both personal and professional.

"I didn't think you were serious when you said you didn't want to perform anymore. But I realize now that you meant it back then."

He still meant it.

"But, Mac," she implored, "you don't have to go on

tour with me anymore. You can write songs here. And just to make the offer more tempting, I'll pay you twice the going rate if you'll come up with something special for me to sing in Los Angeles next month."

"I'm sorry, Felicia, but I'm not interested in furthering your career."

She stiffened. "You certainly hold a grudge."

"You're wrong. I let the past go years ago, but that doesn't mean I didn't learn a lesson along the way."

She offered him that little pout that used to work its charm on him. "Performing with me wasn't that bad, and you know it."

The hell it wasn't. He'd had to down several shots of tequila just to get through each day—a bad habit that might have become much worse, if he'd let it. But he bit back his objection.

"You can play rancher all you want," she added. "All you need to do is write one or two songs a year for me. With your talent and my voice, we'll go platinum again. I know it as sure as I'm standing here looking at you."

The anger and resentment he'd held toward her had disappeared a long time ago, but not his mistrust. And that alone had been enough for him to bow out of the public eye forever.

Felicia eased closer and placed her hand on the gelding's neck. "Come on, Mac. Climb down from there and let's talk about this on even ground."

There'd never been a level playing field between them, and it had taken Ian a while to learn that the fun-loving country girl on stage wasn't the real Felicia.

He didn't like being pressured, as had become Felicia's habit. It had only worked on him at first—until he knew the real woman behind the glossy red hair and big blue eyes. He soon got sick and tired of the energy it took to deal with all her demands, so he'd dug in his boots, which had frustrated her to distraction.

About the time he decided to cut bait and find a new band, she'd gotten pregnant. He hadn't been able to leave then. And for a couple of weeks, he'd thought they'd have to see a counselor so they could work things out. At least, that had been the idea until she'd chosen to abort the baby.

"Mac, honey." Her Southern twang deepened. "I know you haven't quit singing or playing. Or writing music, for that matter. It's in your blood. And strumming your guitar is how you wind down at night. You probably have a slew of new songs all ready to go."

He merely stared at her, yet he didn't swing down from his horse. He knew where this was going. She'd cozy up to him and make it sound as if they were long lost lovers who'd just stumbled upon each other. But this wasn't a chance meeting. She'd sought him out—probably thanks to the performances Carly had insisted they take part in recently. But he wouldn't give her the satisfaction of dismounting and meeting her at her level.

"You plannin' to make that little blonde a star?" she asked.

So he was right. She'd seen photos of him and Carly, probably on those damned posters the mayor had printed and stuck up all over the county.

"Nope. I'm not making anyone a star—nor am I helping anyone remain on top of the charts."

"I see." Felicia took a couple steps back. "You must be sleeping with her."

The assumption, which came out as an accusation, raked over him, but he wouldn't give her the pleasure of a reaction. "That's none of your business, Felicia. You moved on a long time ago."

"A girl can make a mistake, can't she?"

"Didn't you hear me? I'm *not* interested. I'm not about to repeat the past or work you into my future."

She crossed her arms again and shifted her weight to one hip. "That's a shame. You're wasting your talent."

Ian remained in his saddle, looking down at her. He'd seen her snub other musicians and singers on occasion, and it served her right to be on the other side of a brush-off.

"Don't you miss it?" she asked, her twang nearly nonexistent now. "The excitement, the glamour, the bright lights, the roar of the fans?"

"Nope. I don't miss it a bit." That wasn't exactly true. He still felt the magic of creating a brand-new tune and finding just the right words to go with it. But it had been nice to watch a crowd's reaction when his words and music struck something deep in their hearts.

"That blonde girl," Felicia almost spit out. "What's her name? Carly something? She probably thinks she's hit the big time now that she's met you."

"She knows better."

But Carly didn't really know who Ian was. The other day she'd asked him how he knew what it was like on the road. He could have revealed himself then, but he'd decided to wait until they came up with a satisfactory game plan for raising a child together.

At the time, he'd been afraid that, if Carly knew his true identity, she'd really pressure him. And he hadn't been about to let her force his hand. But it was time to tell her now.

In the meantime, he had to get rid of Felicia.

"I'm sorry, but I've gotta go. I'm meeting some hands out in the south forty. So you'll have to forgive me for leaving. I'm sure your driver can get this vehicle turned around on his own."

Then he jabbed his heels into the gelding's flanks and rode off, hoping Felicia would leave just as quickly.

## *Chapter Eleven*

On her drive back to the ranch, Carly turned the radio up and sang a duet with Martina McBride. She hadn't been in this good of a mood for a long time.

She was pleased with her baby furniture purchase, which would be delivered to the ranch next week. Yet a single shopping spree hadn't appeased her desire to nest. If anything, it only made her want to start turning the old sewing room into a nursery as soon as possible.

If she'd had more time before her doctor's appointment this afternoon, she would've swung by the hardware store to look at paint samples as well as the fabric shop so she could choose the perfect print for the new curtains she planned to sew herself.

Imagine that. She was actually getting excited about having a baby. And in just an hour or so, she hoped to learn whether she would have a boy or a girl. The doctor hadn't had time for the ultrasound at her last visit, but it was scheduled for today.

She probably should have driven straight to the clinic, but she decided to stop by the ranch first so she could tell Ian what she'd done. She knew he'd be glad to hear that she was looking forward to getting a nursery ready for their child. And that she was even considering the possibility of making a home together.

Of course, she wouldn't agree to marriage unless he could convince her that he truly loved her. But who knew what time would bring?

While at the house, she planned to freshen up and maybe change into one of her new tops and a pair of comfy, loose-fitting jeans before heading to her appointment. The slacks she had on today were too snug and so was the blouse, even though she'd left the last button undone.

If Ian was around, she would invite him to go with her to the doctor's office. He'd probably like to see the ultrasound of their baby.

Since things had been up in the air before, she hadn't mentioned the test or the appointment to him. But now that they were… Well, not that they'd made any major decisions about their future, but they seemed to be falling into their Mommy and Daddy roles. And learning the sex of their baby together seemed like the right thing to do.

As she drove down the long, graveled drive to the Leaning R, she spotted a black limousine parked near the front porch, and her grip on the steering wheel tightened.

Had her mother come to visit? Raelynn would be the type to drive up in a limo. But she was supposed to be in London, so it couldn't be her.

The limo was turning around, as if leaving the house, but as Carly arrived, the driver pulled over. So she parked her pickup next to it.

Her dad used to own a limousine, which was a corporate vehicle now. Maybe Jason and Juliana had arrived in it. However, the Rayburn car had personalized license plates, so it couldn't be them. Well, not unless Jason had rented a limo after he arrived at the airport.

There was only one way to find out who it was. So she climbed from the pickup, leaving her shopping bag in the cab. She grabbed her purse and shut the door, just as the chauffeur exited the limo and proceeded to let his passenger out.

Carly watched an attractive redhead step out wearing snazzy cowboy boots, designer jeans and a denim jacket with a load of fancy sparkles. Dressed like that and riding in style meant she had big bucks.

As the redhead turned and faced the pickup, recognition dawned, and Carly's breath caught. What in the world was Felicia Jamison doing here?

Had Raelynn set up some kind of surprise for Carly? Had her mother actually used her connections to give her daughter's career a boost?

Carly had told Raelynn that she didn't need her help, but she wouldn't have objected if her mother had been insistent.

"Hi there," Carly said as she closed the pickup door and smiled. "What can I do for you?"

Felicia crossed her arms and, wearing a slight grin, gave Carly a once-over. "So you're the singer Mac hooked up with."

"Mac? I'm afraid I don't know who you're talking about."

"Mac McAllister, my old guitarist and song writer."

Carly blinked, hoping to catch up quickly and to connect the dots. "Do you mean *Ian* McAllister?"

"That's his given name, but he goes by Mac in music circles."

Music circles? Carly's head began to spin as if she were going to have another fainting spell, but it was just her thoughts swirling in her head.

"I…uh…" Carly nodded toward the barn. "His truck is here, so I suspect he's out in the south pasture. He said something about digging post holes and building a fence."

Felicia unfolded her arms and placed her hands on her denim-clad hips—her tight jeans a size two, no doubt. She wore gold bangles and a diamond bracelet on her wrist, and her fingernails sported a French manicure with square tips.

"I haven't heard you sing," Felicia said, "but rumor has it you're good. And that you might be trying to keep it a secret that you're Raelynn Fallon's daughter."

Rumor had it? And how had this woman known about Carly's connection to Raelynn? It's not like Carly threw her mother's name around.

But Ian knew. And right now, Carly would like to

throttle the quiet cowboy who'd failed to tell her he had music industry contacts of his own.

"I can see by the look in your eye that it's true," Felicia said. "How is your mama, now that she's retired and jet-setting with the senator?"

Carly knew she'd have to wipe the dumbfounded look off her face or she'd feel even more foolish than she did already. "What do you want with... Ian?"

"Well, apparently, he's already involved with... someone else, so I'll settle for just a musical reunion."

The story kept getting worse. Ian not only used to sing with Felicia, but he'd slept with her, too?

A flood of betrayal threatened to knock Carly off her feet, but she stood as tall as her five-foot-two frame would allow. "I guess you'll just have to talk to Ian— or rather, Mac—about that."

He'd had a hundred chances to level with her, but he'd never said a word. Wasn't that the same as lying?

"Actually," Felicia said, "I've already talked to him. He rode off a few minutes ago."

Apparently Felicia hadn't just arrived. She'd been about to leave. Carly wanted to tell her to climb back in that limo and hit the road because right now she wanted to be alone so she could have a good cry. Or maybe so she could kick something—or some*one*.

"Well, I'd better go," Felicia said. "It was nice meeting you."

Was it? Carly wasn't so sure, but she feigned a smile. "Same here."

"I'll leave you with one bit of advice, though," Felicia said.

Carly stiffened, and her stomach knotted. "What's that?"

"Be careful, hon. It's all fun and games with Mac until he gets you pregnant. Then he'll expect you to give it all up and settle down."

Felicia's parting shot struck Carly like a wallop to the chest. Sure, she'd started nesting and had considered settling down, at least a bit. But she'd thought that had been her idea.

Had Ian gotten her pregnant on purpose? They'd used protection, but had he known those condoms might fail? Had he planned to have her move in with him on the Leaning R all along?

Worse yet, maybe he expected her to use her share from the ranch proceeds to help him buy cattle and hire more hands.

Ian had often accused Carly of "working" him, but had it been the other way around all along?

As Felicia turned and headed back to the limousine, emotion clogged Carly's throat. She couldn't utter a goodbye or—what seemed even more fitting—a good riddance.

Ian had no more than reached the section of land that bordered the county road when he spotted Carly driving back to the ranch. If Felicia hadn't left yet, she'd probably stick around a bit longer now.

Damn. He didn't want those two talking without him present. Who knew what tale Felicia might concoct in an effort to get back at him? He'd seen her in action before and knew how she could morph from country sweetheart to jealous vamp in no time at all. He had to get back to the ranch. And fast.

He rode into the yard, just as the limo driver was opening the passenger door for Felicia to get back inside. But Carly was parked and standing outside her truck. Obviously the two had already had words.

When Felicia noticed that Ian had returned, she paused in midstep, then turned to face him, grinning as smugly as a fat-cheeked cat with yellow tail feathers poking out from its clenched lips.

Carly, on the other hand, appeared ready to bolt.

"I see you two have already met," he said as he dismounted.

Carly didn't utter a response, but she didn't have to. Her wounded gaze gave her emotions away. And why wouldn't she be hurt? He should have told her about his past earlier. There was no telling what kind of a spin Felicia had put on things.

"You're back," Felicia said. "That's nice. I'd love to stay and chat, but I have a business meeting in Houston, then I'm flying back to Nashville."

That was good news, assuming she was being honest. But the damage had already been done, and the smirk on her face told him she knew it. Now he'd have to do his best to rectify whatever havoc she'd created. But first he needed to make a point, especially with Carly looking on. "Just for the record, Felicia, you and I were done years ago. And I'm not up for a reunion of any kind."

"It's a shame you feel that way, Mac. But you know me. I've never been one to take no for an answer. Who knows what the future might bring." Felicia motioned to her driver. "Let's go." Then she climbed into the back of the limousine.

Mac led the horse to the corral, opened the gate and let him in. By the time he'd secured the latch, Felicia was well on her way down the drive.

On the other hand, Carly was still standing in the yard, her arms crossed, waiting for an explanation.

"I'm sorry," he said. "I should have been more up-front with you."

"You *think*?" Her sarcasm rang in the air. "Holding back information like having a music career and working with Felicia Jamison was just as dishonest as a flat-out lie."

He had that coming. And the fact that he valued honesty above all else sent his regret and guilt reeling.

"I'm not sure what Felicia told you," he said, "but just so you know, she's not the sweet little Southern gal she projects on the stage and in the media. She has a mean and vindictive streak she's good at hiding."

Carly placed her hands on her hips. "And just what kind of persona did *you* project on stage, *Mac*?"

He gave a half shrug. "I only wanted to play the guitar."

She swept her hand across the yard. "And now you do, except you're entertaining a puppy and a bunch of cows."

"I entertained you a time or two."

"Ain't that the truth." She clucked her tongue and slowly shook her head. "Do you have any idea how badly it hurts to know that you couldn't trust me enough to level with me?"

"I can only imagine—and I apologize yet again. But just so you know where I'm coming from, Felicia wasn't content to let me be myself. She tried to manage every minute of my life, and I got tired of it. I needed a complete break."

"You were so tired of it that you couldn't share the truth with me? We were lovers, Ian. And you're the father of my baby. Didn't I deserve to know?"

"Yes, you did. But the more you pushed me to perform with you, the more I held back. I figured you'd only press me harder."

He waited for her to soften, for her to give him some kind of clue that she might forgive him. But she glanced at her bangle wristwatch, then shook her head. "I can't do this." She walked to her pickup and opened the door. "I *won't* do it."

"What do you mean?" he asked. "Where are you going?"

"To see Dr. Connor." Then she slid behind the wheel, started the ignition and sped off, blowing gravel and dust behind her.

Why was she going to the doctor again? Was she sick? Or was she having a pregnancy complication?

A shudder of apprehension shook him to the bone. All he could think about was the day Felicia had gone to the clinic to end her pregnancy.

Surely that's not what Carly had in mind. She wasn't anything like Felicia. But she was hurt and angry. And he felt compelled to chase after her and make sure she didn't do something they'd both regret.

Carly was in tears before she pulled onto the county road and headed for the clinic. What in the world was she going to do now?

Ian wasn't the man he'd led her to believe he was. Besides that, all along he'd had the connections to open doors for her. Not that she would have wanted him to, but why hadn't he trusted her with the truth about his past?

Her cell phone rang, and she glanced at the number display on her dashboard. It was Ian, but she wasn't up to talking to him now. She let his call go to voice mail.

Moments later, another call came in. Assuming it was Ian again, she was about to shut off the phone completely when she spotted the incoming number and realized it was her brother.

She sniffled, then answered. "Hi, Jason. How's it going?"

"Just fine. But I have some news for you. *Big* news."

Not as big—or as messy—as hers was going to be. "What's up?"

"You know Camilla's twins?"

"What about them?"

"Are you sitting down?"

She rolled her eyes. "Come on. Don't keep me hanging."

"I told you that their paperwork was in order," he began. "But I hadn't looked it over until Juliana and I were getting ready to head to the airport with them."

"Was something wrong with their passports?"

"That depends on how you look at it."

"Okay, cut to the chase, Jason. I have an appointment in about ten minutes, and I don't have time for guessing games."

"Do you remember telling me that you always wished you'd had a sister?" He chuckled softly. "Well, you have one. And she's seven years old. You have a little brother, too."

Carly was so stunned she could barely find her voice. He had to be pulling her leg. Or else there was some mistake. "Are you kidding me?"

"Nope. It's true."

Jason had never lied to her before, but she still had trouble believing this. "Did Dad adopt them?"

"I don't think so. He's listed as their father on the birth certificates."

"Maybe they were forged or something. Dad could have paid to have someone create phony paperwork so he could bring them across the border more easily."

"That's not likely. The kids were born in San Diego, and those certificates aren't copies. They're legit. It's all there in black and white. Their parents are Camilla Cruz de Montoya and Charles Rayburn."

A horn tooted behind Carly, and when she glanced in the rearview mirror, she spotted a Ford sedan on her tail. The driver honked again, then sped up and passed her. When she looked at her speedometer, she realized she'd slowed almost to a stop.

She accelerated, then said, "So you're saying that Dad had another family in Mexico."

"Apparently so. That has to be why he was so determined to get those kids back to the States."

"Wow. I don't know what to say. I'm speechless."

"So are we. But we'll be heading back to Houston with them later today. I'll have some work to take care of at the office, but we need to schedule another family meeting. In the meantime, Juliana and I will keep them with us in my condo in Houston."

"Have you told Braden yet?" she asked.

"No, I called you first, but he's next on the list."

Carly glanced in the rearview mirror and noted that there weren't any more impatient drivers behind her. Then she blew out a sigh. "I'm still having a hard time believing this."

"While you try to figure it out, you might want to take a speed course in conversational Spanish."

Great. She'd finally gotten the little sister she'd always wanted, only nearly twenty years too late. And to make matters worse, they wouldn't be able to communicate.

"But now we have another problem," Jason said. "Since we know who the kids are, finding someone to adopt them isn't going to be the answer. Not when they're our blood kin."

He meant they'd have to figure out which sibling was going to step up and raise them. But that wasn't going to be easy. It had taken them months to agree to sell the Leaning R, mostly because they'd never been close—thanks to their father's two marriages and various affairs that left the half siblings feeling more like strangers than kin.

And while she had to admit that things had gotten better between her, Braden and Jason after their father died, and that the family dynamics had suddenly changed—big-time—they were still getting to know and respect each other.

And speaking of the Rayburns multiplying like bunnies... "Hey, listen. I have a doctor's appointment. I have to hang up or I'll be late. Call me when you get to Houston. I have some news for you, too."

"You can't tell me now?"

She'd rather have some time to let her thoughts settle after that blowup with Ian. "No. I'll talk to you later this evening or tomorrow morning."

Then she ended the call, just as she pulled into the clinic's parking lot. Maybe she'd better sit in the car and listen to some calming music. If the nurse took her blood pressure right now, it would probably be sky-high.

## *Chapter Twelve*

Ian had just brushed down the gelding—the fastest cool down he could allow the horse. Then he went to the cabin and grabbed the keys to his truck, hoping he wouldn't be too late to catch up with Carly.

He'd no more than opened the door of his vehicle when Todd rode in with the boys. He was leading Jesse Ramirez's mare, while the seventeen-year-old sat in the saddle and held on to his left hand.

"What happened?" Ian asked.

"Jess had a run-in with a hammer and a stubborn nail," Todd said. "I think he might have busted his hand."

Jesse appeared more disappointed and angry at himself than hurt. "It was my fault. I can't believe I was so stupid. I sure hope it isn't broken."

"These things happen," Ian said.

"I know," Jesse said. "I just wish it hadn't happened to me. Maybe, if I put some ice on it, the swelling will go down and I'll be good as new tomorrow."

Jason Rayburn had hired the kids, all football players for Brighton Valley High School, and Ian hadn't liked the idea. But they all had busted their butts to do a good job, saying that ranching during the summer gave them a harder workout than the gym.

They'd all bulked up in the past month or so, which had been their plan, along with earning some spending money.

"I didn't mean to let you down," Jesse said. "I know how much work you have to do around here."

"Don't worry about me. I have to cut out now anyway." In truth, Ian was more concerned about the kid than a day's work. He didn't want to see Jesse miss the opening football game. This was his senior year, and he was hoping to earn a college scholarship.

"Let's call it a day," Ian told Todd. "Can you take Jesse to the ER to have an X-ray?"

Todd lifted his hat, then readjusted it on his head. "Sure thing, boss."

Ian was grateful for that. Normally, he'd be the one taking an injured employee for medical treatment. But having Todd do it would allow him to follow Carly to the clinic and make peace with her. "I've got to run into town," he told Todd. "Call me and let me know what the doctor has to say about Jesse's hand. I'll see you tomorrow."

Then he climbed into his truck and took off. All the while, he planned what he'd say to Carly.

He'd swear that he would never lie to her again—or withhold information. But there was one thing he'd neglected to confess.

He loved her with all his heart. And he was willing to lay his dreams on the line if that's what it took to create the family he'd always wanted.

He just hoped he wasn't too late—in more ways than one. God willing, he'd catch up with her before she made any foolish decisions.

And before she decided he wasn't the kind of man she could trust.

As he drove, he whipped out his cell phone. He dialed 411 and requested the number to Dr. Connor's office. When the receptionist answered, he asked for the address and directions. Apparently, the doctor's practice was located near the Brighton Valley Medical Center.

Twenty minutes later, he pulled into the parking lot and spotted Carly's pickup.

He entered the redbrick building that housed various medical offices and made his way to Dr. Connor's waiting room, which was nearly full. He noticed several mothers with children as well as a middle-aged man reading *Sports Illustrated*. But Carly was nowhere in sight.

"Excuse me," he said to the receptionist, prepared to stretch the truth. "I'm late. I'm supposed to meet Carly Rayburn here. I'm the father of her baby."

The matronly blonde smiled. "She was just called back to see the doctor. But I can take you to her."

"That would be great. Thanks." Ian had no idea how Carly would react when he crashed her visit with the doctor, but he wouldn't think about that now. He had to see her, to convince her to talk to him, and it couldn't wait a minute longer.

"She's right back here," the receptionist said as she led Ian to exam room three. She knocked lightly on the door. "Dr. Connor?"

"Yes?" another female voice said.

"The baby's father is here."

"Send him in. He's just in time."

Just in time for what? Ian was hesitant to enter the room, but Carly hadn't uttered an objection.

As he stepped inside, he spotted Carly stretched out on the exam table, her belly exposed. Something slick and wet was smeared on her skin, and the doctor was running some thingamajig over the swell of her belly. Apparently she was so transfixed by the image on a small screen that he practically slipped into the room unnoticed.

"That's the heartbeat," the doctor said. "It's strong and steady. Can you hear it?"

All Ian could hear was a *whoosh-whoosh-whoosh* sound, but he zeroed in on the black-and-white screen Carly was studying intently.

And then he saw it. Arms and legs. It was their baby. His heart lurched.

"Everything looks great," the doctor said.

As Ian watched the screen, the little feet kicked.

And one hand moved toward its mouth, providing a thumb to suck on.

Ian was awestruck and eased closer to watch his and Carly's baby. The image was grainy, but it was still clear enough for him to make out every finger on its hands.

Carly must've been caught up in the miracle of it all because she still hadn't objected to his presence. And he was glad. This was the most amazing thing he'd ever seen.

"Do you want to know if it's a boy or a girl?" the doctor asked. "Some parents want to be surprised."

Not Ian. He wanted to know. It would make the baby even more real for them. Maybe that would help them reach some kind of compromise that would leave them both happy.

And if truth be told, he didn't care one way or the other if they were having a son or daughter. He just wanted a healthy baby.

"Yes," Carly said. "I'd like to know." And then she glanced at Ian, her expression solemn—more like a grimace, actually.

He offered her a smile as an olive branch, but she didn't return it. At least she wasn't going to lay into him in front of the doctor and insist that he leave.

"In that case," the doctor said, "it's a girl."

At the revelation, a smile finally stretched across Carly's face. "Are you sure?"

The doctor chuckled. "Yes, I am. Congratulations." Then she paused the machine and introduced herself to Ian.

"It's nice to meet you," he said. "I didn't mean to interrupt."

"No problem. I'm glad you were able to join Carly." Then she went back to work, continuing the scan.

"That's amazing," Ian said as he continued to study the screen. "Look at that, Carly. She's sucking her thumb."

Carly swiped at the tears that had pooled in her eyes. "I can't believe that. We're having a little girl."

*We.* Ian was glad that she'd included him. And for a few magical moments, their conflict disappeared, and the wonder of new life took center stage.

He hoped the amazing feeling would last, but he suspected it was bound to end as soon as the exam was over.

Dr. Connor shut down the ultrasound, then reached for Carly's hand and helped her sit up. "I'll see you in three weeks."

Carly thanked her and stepped down from the table. As the doctor wheeled the machine out of the room, leaving her alone with Ian, she could finally let loose on him without embarrassing herself in front of her physician.

"What are you doing here?" she asked, her tone sharp.

"I came to see you. We need to talk."

Carly adjusted her blouse and grabbed her purse from the chair. "We definitely have a lot to discuss, but it could have waited until I got home."

"No, it couldn't. Besides, I'm glad I'm here. Seeing

our daughter on that screen was amazing. We're going to have a little girl, Carly. Can you believe it?"

She was thrilled, of course, but her anger at Ian and her sense of betrayal hadn't eased, and she wasn't sure it ever would.

How in the world could they ever be lovers again, or even coparent their daughter, if Carly couldn't trust him to be honest with her?

"We have some issues that might be insurmountable," she said.

He opened the exam room door for her. "I understand that, but give me a chance to explain myself."

Carly paused in the hallway. As she studied his remorseful expression, she was overwhelmed with emotion. She loved this man in spite of her anger and frustration. But she could only see heartbreak in their future.

As much as she'd like to tell him to take a permanent hike, he was right. They needed to talk, and it had been put off way too long.

"Okay," she said. "Let's find a quiet place where we can have some privacy."

Ten minutes later, after Carly made her next appointment, they left the parking lot in Ian's truck and drove to the community park a few blocks off Main Street.

As Ian pulled into a shady parking space, he asked, "Does this spot work for you?"

Carly scanned the stretch of grass, where a man threw a Frisbee to his golden retriever. Across the way, two young women sat on a bench near the playground, where several preschoolers climbed on a big, colorful jungle gym that had been set up in the sand.

"Sure," she said. "This is a good place to talk."

They exited his truck and made their way to a bench that was located away from everyone else.

"First of all," Ian said, "I was wrong for not being up-front with you, and I apologize. It won't ever happen again."

She wanted to believe him, but she wasn't sure she could.

"Why don't I start off by telling you everything?" he added. "How I met Felicia, why I quit singing with her and why I was so determined to have a quiet, peaceful life as a rancher."

"I'd like to hear it."

"Ask me anything you want to know, and I won't hold anything back."

"Okay. I know that you taught yourself to play the guitar, but when did you start playing professionally?"

"When I was seventeen. I was living in Fort Worth with my dad at the time. Most teenagers my age got fake IDs so they could drink and smoke. But I got mine so I could perform in a seedy neighborhood bar. A musician passing through heard me play one night and asked me to try out with his group. Before long, I traveled with the band to Nashville, where I eventually earned a name for myself."

"As Mac McAllister?"

"Yeah. One of the guys started calling me Mac, and the nickname caught on."

"When did you meet Felicia?"

"One day, when she was just starting out, she heard me play and hired me to be her lead guitarist. She could really rock the house with her voice, but she's always realized that a part of her success and popularity was due to my music and the songs I wrote. Trouble was, I'd always been an introvert and didn't like being forced into the limelight."

A light summer breeze whipped a strand of hair across her face, and she swiped it away. "But you said you didn't mind being on stage."

"Performing wasn't the problem. But Felicia began to place more and more demands on the band, our manager and on the people who hired us to perform. She thrived on the attention and fame, and it didn't take long for it to go to her head."

Carly asked, "Were you lovers at the time?"

Ian glanced at the man playing with his dog. "Yes, and both our personal and professional relationships soon became strained."

"So you broke up with her, quit the band and decided to live in obscurity for the rest of your life?"

"Not exactly. I joined another band, and Felicia flipped out. She set about having my new group's contracts cancelled."

"That's pretty vindictive. I'm surprised she had that much clout."

"I agree. She isn't a nice person and she exploits her fame at times."

Carly turned to the handsome cowboy, watched him as he studied the children on the playground. "How did you ever get involved with a woman like her in the first place? I'm not talking about performing with her. But as lovers. The two of you don't seem very well suited."

"It turned out that we weren't. But at first, our fit was magical on the stage. A romance seemed like a natural next step, but it didn't last very long. I soon found out how self-centered she could be."

"Did you end things then?"

"I wanted to, but I'd just found out that she was pregnant. I couldn't just leave her then. But she chose to have an abortion because a child would sidetrack her booming career. She didn't give it a second thought. On the other hand, I was crushed by the choice she made. I'd always wanted a family, and she knew it. But she made a unilateral decision that took the opportunity to be a father away from me. That's when I finally saw the real woman behind the fancy clothes and makeup."

"So you broke up?"

"The bright lights and glamour had really faded by then. So had the romance, especially when Felicia moved on to someone else."

"I'm sorry."

"Don't be. I really wasn't all that bothered by the breakup. The fact that Felicia cared so little about the child we created told me how she felt about me. And I realized that I wanted more from a lover or a lifetime partner." Ian turned to face her, his knee brushing hers. "That's why I didn't like you pressuring me to perform with you. It brought back too many bad memories."

She suspected the pregnancy had brought back bad memories, too, although he'd seemed happy about it. Delighted, actually.

"I'm sorry, Ian. I didn't mean to push you."

"Maybe not, but you ignored my feelings. I'm not trying to throw you under the bus, Carly, but I was afraid to level with you. I figured you'd work even harder to convince me to let you have your way. So, in truth, I wasn't the only one who created problems in our relationship."

Carly wanted to object, to say she hadn't tried to force his hand, but she had. "I'm sorry, Ian. I'll try not to push you anymore. You once mentioned that you'd seen me work my parents, and even though I hadn't wanted to admit it, you were right. I knew my dad's first reaction was to throw money at a problem, so I would use that to my advantage. And my mother would get so caught up in her own life that she sometimes forgot I existed, until I did something to remind her."

"I have a question for you," he said. "You're a beautiful and talented woman. There's no doubt in my mind that you'll hit the top of the charts. But are you determined to have a musical career because you truly want it? Or is it a way to show your parents—or rather, your mom—that you're someone special and important?"

Carly wanted to deny it, but she was afraid Ian had seen right through her. "I do want to sing and perform. I love being on stage. But you're probably right, at least partially. I do have a desire to show people that I count."

"You count to me."

She smiled. "Thanks. But to be honest, after meeting Felicia in the flesh today, I can see why I should think long and hard about what I want out of life."

"I'm glad to hear it. Not that I think you should change your mind. But I do hope you'll give your decision a lot of thought."

She studied the children on the playground, watched one of the moms push her daughter in a swing and listened to the child's squeal of laughter.

The person who'd taken Carly to the park when she'd been a child had been either Granny or one of the au pairs who'd watched her when her dad had been working and her mom had been on tour.

No way did Carly want that kind of life for her daughter.

A man and a boy walked out onto the lawn, carrying two mitts and a baseball. Her father hadn't spent any time with her brothers, either.

Carly turned to Ian. "I wish I'd had a chance to know the man you used to be—before Felicia."

"I'm still the same man, Carly. I'm just more guarded after what she put me through. You may not have seen it, but like I told you before, Felicia can be pretty selfish and vindictive."

"I saw that in her today," Carly admitted. The woman had a much different demeanor than the country-girl-next-door image she projected on stage.

"Well, I didn't see through her right away. I think that's because I wanted her to be the sweet, effervescent woman she pretended to be. I was young and naive, so I was caught up in it all."

"The fame?" she asked.

"No, it was never that. I just loved music and musicians. And I only wanted to play the guitar."

"And she wanted more from you?"

"Let's just say we never wanted the same things. And like she admitted earlier, she isn't one to take no for an answer."

Carly placed her hand on Ian's thigh, felt his warmth and strength. "I'm glad you realized what you wanted out of life. And I'm sorry that I pushed you so hard. I didn't realize what you were avoiding or why."

Ian reached for her hand, and she let his fingers curl around hers. "I love you, Carly. And if your career means that much to you, I'll let someone else buy the Leaning R and I'll go on the road with you. I'll be Mr. Mom while you perform."

Tears filled her eyes, and a rush of emotion built to an ache in her chest. "I love you, too. And I can't believe that you'd sacrifice your dream and happiness for me. No one has ever offered me that much before."

"You're every bit a star to me, Carly. I'm looking forward to seeing our little girl—and I'm hoping she'll be just like you."

Carly wiped her eyes. Seeing their little one on the screen had made her so real, so special, that she wasn't sure what she wanted anymore. Maybe she did want to spend time rocking her baby on a porch swing, picking huckleberries and baking one of Granny's yummy pies or even teaching her daughter to ride a pony.

"How can we make it work for all of us?" she asked him.

"When a man and woman love each other, anything is possible. Maybe we can become a songwriting team and try out the music and lyrics in front of an audience at the Stagecoach Inn."

"Then maybe it will work, Ian." She kissed him long and hard. When they came up for air, she smiled and said, "We'd better not get carried away here. Let's go home."

He stood and reached for her hand, drawing her to her feet. As they started toward his truck, she said, "Oh, I forgot to tell you. Jason called with some big news."

"What's that?"

"You know those twins he's bringing home to the States? He finally found out why our father was so intent on finding them. They're Rayburns, too."

"No kidding?" Ian asked as he opened the passenger door for her.

"I'm still trying to take it all in myself, but Jason is convinced. And I have no reason to doubt him. Just think. I have two more half siblings."

Ian cupped her cheek, his eyes glistening. "When it comes to family, I say the more the merrier."

"Something tells me you just might be right." She tossed him a happy smile. "Let's go home. I'm eager to unpack some of Granny's things and put the house back to rights."

*Back to rights.* Ian liked the sound of that, especially coming from Carly. They hadn't come up with a firm plan for the future, but they loved each other and wanted the best for their daughter.

On the drive back to the ranch, they talked about her

visions for the nursery as well as the way he wanted to fix up the house once the sale was final.

They'd no more than arrived at the Leaning R when Carly turned to him. "I'm glad we've agreed to be completely honest with each other and to come clean with everything."

"So am I."

"That's good, because talking about creating a nursery and refurbishing the ranch house got me to thinking. I owe you another apology."

Ian shut off the ignition, but he didn't even consider getting out of the truck. "What are you sorry for?"

"For assuming that you might not be able to come up with the money to buy this place. Now I realize that your 'little nest egg' is probably sizable."

"So what's wrong with coming to that conclusion?" he asked. "I never gave you any reason to think I had the kind of money to pull off a purchase like that."

"I know. But I should have trusted you when you told me that the purchase wouldn't be a problem. And I'm sorry I didn't."

He reached across the seat and took her hand. He rubbed his thumb against her wrist, felt the soft throb of her pulse. "You don't need to apologize for that. But from now on, we're both going to have to be completely honest and trust each other about everything."

She gave his hand an affectionate squeeze. "You're right. Why don't I go inside and fix dinner for us."

"Sounds good."

"Maybe you should bring a change of clothes and

your shaving kit when you come to eat. I'm looking forward to spending the night with you."

He flashed her a smile and winked. "That sounds even better. But just to make my intentions clear, I plan to spend every night together for the rest of our lives."

Fifteen minutes later, Ian had taken a shower and packed an overnight bag. But before leaving his cabin, he called Todd's cell number to check on Jesse Ramirez.

Todd answered on the second ring.

"What did you find out at the hospital?" Ian asked without preamble.

"Jesse has a bruised and swollen hand, but no broken bones, torn ligaments or tendons. I'm on my way right now to drop him off at his house."

"That's great news. Tell Jesse to take the rest of the week off, or even longer if that injury is still bothering him. I want that hand to heal completely—and before that first football game. I plan to be there, cheering him and the other boys on when Brighton Valley beats Wexler."

Todd laughed. "You and me both. Have a good evening, boss."

"Thanks. I intend to."

After disconnecting the line, Ian grabbed his overnight bag and took a sack of dog food out of the pantry. Then he went to the door and called Cheyenne. "Come on, girl. We're all going to have to learn how our family life is going to work. Let's go spend the night with Carly."

Cheyenne gave a little yip and wagged her entire hind end as if she knew exactly what he'd told her.

Then she dashed out the door and across the yard to the ranch house. She was waiting at the back door by the time his strides caught up with her.

They entered through the mudroom and caught the spicy aroma of sizzling meat, onions and peppers.

"Dinner smells good." He was going to like coming home each night.

Carly, who stood at the stove, flashed him a pretty smile. Then she lowered the flame on the burner.

Ian set Cheyenne's dog food on the table, and when Carly turned to face him, he swept her into his arms and placed his lips on hers. The kiss deepened, and their hearts beat in sync.

He wasn't sure how long the kiss lasted—long enough to catch the scent of scorching meat and veggies. Carly was the first to break away, as she removed the skillet from the flame.

Then she laughed. "I'd better focus on dinner, or we won't have anything to eat tonight."

"Right now, I'm only hungry for you. So a peanut butter sandwich a little later wouldn't bother me a bit."

"I have no problem postponing dinner, but I think I can salvage the chicken fajitas. Just give me a minute to put them into another pan."

As she took a spatula and scooped their meal out of Granny's cast-iron skillet, Ian eased behind her and brushed a kiss on her neck. "What's your calendar look like over the next few weeks?"

"Other than my doctor's appointment in three weeks, it's clear. Why?"

"I'd like to take you to Sarasota next weekend. My

grandparents are celebrating their fiftieth wedding anniversary with a big party."

"Seriously?" she asked. "That's awesome. I'd really like to meet them. I've never known a couple who've stayed married that long."

"And happily, too." Ian watched as she carried the skillet to the sink. "You might have to change the date of your next doctor's appointment."

"Why?"

"Because two weeks after their anniversary, I'm taking the family on a Mediterranean cruise."

Carly turned to him, her eyes lighting up. "I'd love to go with you. Whenever my parents went on a cruise, I had to stay home."

"Well, now it's your turn. I'll make the arrangements in the morning." He slipped his hand into hers, then led her out of the kitchen. "And as for Sarasota… I was planning to leave on Friday, but why don't we make a quick trip to Las Vegas first?"

She gave his hand a little tug. "For a cowboy who never wanted to leave the ranch, you certainly have a travel bug. Or are you a closet gambler?"

"I've never seen the fun in throwing money away. But I'd like us to get married before going to Florida, and that's the quickest way I can think of."

"Is that a proposal?"

He laughed. "If you plan to say yes and throw your arms around me, it is."

She tossed him an impish grin. "And if I don't give you that kind of reaction?"

"Then maybe we should take things day by day. But

it would be in our best interest to arrive in Sarasota as a married couple, especially since we'll be announcing that we're expecting a baby."

"Oh, now I remember. You mentioned that your grandparents were conservative churchgoers. I take it that a pair of wedding rings will put their minds at ease." She put her hands on her baby bump.

"That's not why I'm making the suggestion. They're not that stuffy. They'll accept you and our baby with open arms no matter what the circumstances."

"So the proposal has nothing to do with making me an honest woman?"

Ian pulled her into his arms. "Carly, you swept me off my boots the first day I laid eyes on you, and if I'd known how much I was going to love you, I would have proposed right then and there. But we had a few things to learn and get behind us first."

"You've got that right."

He smiled. "You know what? I once thought you had it all because of your parents and the Rayburn wealth. But I've realized that isn't true. You never had a real family."

"I have one now," she said.

"That you do." He brushed his lips across hers. "And I don't want to wait another day to make you my wife."

Carly raised up on tiptoe and slipped her arms around his neck. "Neither do I. Besides, I don't want our daughter to think we only got married because of her."

Ian chuckled.

"What's so funny?"

"I just thought of another good reason to tie the knot before we go. It'll make our sleeping arrangements better in Sarasota," Ian said.

"What do you mean?"

"My grandma is as sweet and gracious as can be, and you're going to hit it off immediately. But she's old-fashioned. She'll insist upon separate bedrooms if we're not married."

"She reminds me of Granny. I can't wait to meet her and your grandfather."

"I can't wait to introduce you."

As Ian led Carly to the bedroom, she asked, "You know what I think?"

"What's that?"

"The best limelights are those lit in the hearth at home."

A smile stretched across his face. "I couldn't agree more."

Then he proceeded to show her just how much he loved her, lighting a permanent flame in their hearts and souls.

## *Epilogue*

Carly had been nervous about meeting Ian's family from the moment she boarded the flight in Houston, but she had no reason to be. Sean and Dottie McAllister were the sweetest and kindest couple she'd ever met.

The two had picked her and Ian up at the airport in Sarasota, then they'd driven them to their comfortable two-bedroom apartment in a seniors' complex not far from the home of their son and daughter-in-law, Roy and Helen.

Sean McAllister was a tall, slender man with silver hair, a twinkle in his blue eyes and an easy smile. He had a dry wit, which Carly could appreciate, and she warmed to him immediately.

The same went for Dottie. Ian's grandma wore her gray hair in an elegant French twist, but she was as

down-to-earth as could be. She wasn't much taller than
Carly, but she had a strong presence—and a loving
heart.

The moment Ian introduced his new wife to his
family, Dottie welcomed Carly into the fold with open
arms. And news of the baby tickled her no end.

The woman who'd raised Ian truly was a lot like
Granny, and Carly suspected the two would have become fast friends if they'd ever had the opportunity
to meet.

The only down side was when Dottie mentioned
her disappointment at not being invited to Carly and
Ian's wedding.

"I hope you took plenty of pictures," she said.

Just one, actually. And Carly didn't have the heart
to tell her that they'd said their vows at a chapel in
Las Vegas with two strangers standing up with them
as their witnesses.

"I'll tell you what," Ian said, "Carly and I will renew
our vows after the baby is born, and you'll be at the top
of our invitation list."

"Oh, good," Dottie said. "I'll make the cake."

For the first time in her life, Carly finally felt a part
of something bigger than herself. And she was determined to provide that sense of love, acceptance and
belonging for her child.

In fact, she intended to make sure that her brothers found the same thing, too. Jason appeared to have
found it now that he had Juliana, but Braden deserved
someone special, too.

Fortunately, the brothers' relationship had improved

considerably with their solving of the Camilla mystery. And they'd become closer than they'd been before, although Carly hoped they'd grow closer still, especially since they'd all have to figure out how to create a home and family for the twins. But that was something she'd deal with when she went home. In the meantime, she was enjoying every moment with Ian's family.

The anniversary celebration was held on Saturday afternoon in the rec room at the seniors' complex. Aunt Helen and Uncle Roy, who'd hoped to spring a surprise on the older couple, had decorated the room with balloons and various floral bouquets. But the secret was blown when one of the neighbors spilled the beans, telling Dottie and Sean she'd see them at their party on Saturday.

Nevertheless, the older couple was thrilled to know their new friends and neighbors had come together to share the day with them.

While the celebration was in full swing, Ian reached for his guitar, then took Carly's hand and led her to the front of the room, where a microphone awaited them.

"Are you ready?" he asked.

She smiled and nodded.

"While we're singing," Ian told her, "I want you to remember that, while I wrote the lyrics for them, every single word rings true for you and me. In fifty years, I want us to sing this at our own golden wedding anniversary."

Her heart soared with love for her new husband and the promise of a life together.

Ian stepped in front of the microphone. "On behalf of Sean and Dottie and their family, my wife and I would like to thank you all for coming out today to help them celebrate their anniversary. I've had the pleasure of knowing and loving this special couple all my life. And they were instrumental in making me the man I've become."

As the guests took their seats, Ian continued, turning to the celebrating couple. "Granddad and Grandma, I wrote this song just for you. And now my beautiful bride and I will sing it—as our gift to you."

As Ian began to strum the chords, Carly sang from the heart about a love that would last for all time. When they finished, everyone in attendance cheered and clapped in delight.

Ian slipped an arm around Carly and drew her close. "See, honey, I told you there would be plenty of opportunities for us to perform."

"I know. And I want you to know that I'm okay with being a local celebrity. As long as I can be a wife and mother, that's good enough for me."

He brushed a kiss on her lips. "You won't have to ever settle. Todd is proving to be a good ranch hand. I'm going to make him a foreman. Once the ranch is going strong again, I'd like to cut a record with you and even go on tour."

His offer surprised her—in part because it had come from his heart. She hadn't had to prod him, which was something she'd vowed not to do anymore.

"I'd love that, Ian. And I love you, too. You're the best thing that's ever happened to me."

"I'm the lucky one, honey."

She was glad he felt that way, but she still couldn't help thinking she was the one who'd gotten the better deal. If there's one thing Ian and his family had taught her, it was that the best gift in life was the heart of a cowboy.

\* \* \* \* \*

'I—I wish—' Carrie began to chew at her thumbnail. After a bit, she said, 'I wish I could remember meeting you. How did it happen? Did our eyes meet across a crowded room? Or did you chase me?'

She dropped her gaze to the gnawed thumbnail.

'Did I flirt with you?'

Max recalled the amazing chemistry of that night. The glittering harbourside venue and that first heart-zapping moment of eye contact with Carrie. Her shining dark eyes and dazzling bright smiles… the electric shock of their bodies touching the first time they danced.

He couldn't suppress a wry grin. 'I reckon we could safely claim all of the above.'

# THE HUSBAND
# SHE'D NEVER MET

BY
BARBARA HANNAY

First Published in Great Britain 2016
By Mills & Boon, an imprint of HarperCollins*Publishers*
1 London Bridge Street, London, SE1 9GF

© 2016 Barbara Hannay

ISBN: 978-0-263-91953-0

23-0116

Our policy is to use papers that are natural, renewable and recyclable products and made from wood grown in sustainable forests.The logging and manufacturing processes conform to the legal environmental regulations of the country of origin.

Printed and bound in Spain
by CPI, Barcelona

**Barbara Hannay** has written over forty romance novels and has won the RITA® award, the Romantic Times Reviewer's Choice award, as well as Australia's Romantic Book of the Year.

A city-bred girl, with a yen for country life, Barbara lives with her husband on a misty hillside in beautiful Far North Queensland, where they raise pigs and chickens and enjoy an untidy but productive garden.

Thank you to all the wonderful readers who have helped me to turn a hobby into the happiest of careers.

# CHAPTER ONE

THE SUITCASE WAS almost full. Carrie stared at it in a horrified daze. It seemed wrong that she could pack up her life so quickly and efficiently.

Three years of marriage, all her hopes and dreams, were folded and neatly layered into one silver hard-shell suitcase. Her hands were shaking as she smoothed a rumpled sweater, and her eyes were blurred with tears.

She had known this was going to be hard, but this final step of closing the suitcase and walking away from Max felt as impossible and terrifying as leaping off a mountain into thin air. And yet she had no choice. She had to leave Riverslea Downs. Today. Before she weakened.

Miserably, Carrie surveyed the depleted contents of her wardrobe. She'd packed haphazardly, knowing she couldn't take everything now and choosing at random a selection of city clothes, as well as a few pairs of jeans and T-shirts. It wasn't as if she really cared what she wore.

It was difficult to care about anything in the future. The only way to get through this was to stay emotionally numb.

She checked the drawers again, wondering if she

should squeeze in a few more items. And then she saw it, at the back of the bottom drawer: a small parcel wrapped in white tissue paper.

Her heart stumbled, then began to race. She mustn't leave this behind.

Fighting tears, she held the thin package in her hands. It was almost weightless. For a moment she pressed it against her chest as she battled painful, heartbreaking memories. Then, drawing on the steely inner strength she'd forced herself to find in recent months, she delved into the depths of the suitcase and made a space for the little white parcel at the very bottom.

There. She pressed the clothes back into place and snapped the locks on the case.

She was ready. Nothing to do now but to leave the carefully composed letter for her husband propped against the teapot on the kitchen table.

It was cruel, but it was the only way she could do this. If she tried to offer Max an explanation face to face he would see how hard this was for her and she would never convince him. She'd thought this through countless times, and from every angle, and she knew this was the fairest and cleanest way. The only way.

At the bedroom window, Carrie looked out across paddocks that were glowing and golden in the bright Outback sun. She smelled a hint of eucalyptus on the drifting breeze and heard the warbling notes of a magpie. A hot, hard lump filled her throat. She loved this place.

*Go now. Don't think. Just do it.*

Picking up the envelope and the suitcase, she took one last look around the lovely room she'd shared with Max for the past three years. With a deliberate lift of her chin, she squared her shoulders and walked out.

\* \* \*

When the phone rang, Max Kincaid ignored it. He didn't want to talk, no matter how well-meaning the caller. He was nursing a pain too deep for words.

The phone pealed on, each note drilling into Max. With an angry shrug he turned his back on the piercing summons and strode through the homestead to the front veranda, which had once been a favourite haunt. From here there was a view of paddocks and bush and distant hills that he'd loved all his life.

Today Max paid the view scant attention. He was simply grateful that the phone had finally rung out.

In the silence he heard a soft whimper and looked down to see Carrie's dog, Clover, gazing up at him with sad, bewildered eyes.

'I know how exactly you feel, old girl.' Reaching down, Max gave the Labrador's head a good rub. 'I can't believe she left you, too. But I s'pose you won't fit in a city apartment.'

This thought brought a sharp slice of the pain that had tortured Max since the previous evening, when he'd arrived from the stockyards to find Carrie gone, leaving nothing but a letter.

In the letter she'd explained her reasons for leaving him, outlining her growing disenchantment with life in the bush and with her role as a cattleman's wife.

On paper, it wasn't convincing. Max might not have believed a word of it if he hadn't also been witness to his wife's increasingly jaded attitude in recent months.

It still made no sense. He was blowed if he knew how a woman could appear perfectly happy for two and a half years and then change almost overnight. He had a few theories about Carrie's last trip to Sydney, but—

The phone rang again, interrupting his wretched thoughts.

*Damn.*

Unfortunately he couldn't switch off the landline the way he could his cell phone. And now his conscience nagged. He supposed he should at least check to see who was trying to reach him. If the caller was serious, they would leave messages.

He took his time going back through the house to the kitchen, where the phone hung on the wall. There were two messages.

The most recent was from his neighbour, Doug Peterson.

*'Max, pick up the damn phone.'*

Then, an earlier message.

*'Max, it's Doug. I'm ringing from the Jilljinda Hospital. I'm afraid Carrie's had an accident. Can you give me a call?'*

## CHAPTER TWO

'GOOD MORNING, MRS KINCAID.'

Carrie sighed as the nurse sailed into her room. She'd told the hospital staff several times now that her name was Barnes, not Kincaid. More importantly she was Ms, or at a pinch Miss, but she had certainly never been Mrs.

Now this new nurse, fresh on the morning shift, removed Carrie's breakfast tray and set it aside, then slipped a blood pressure cuff on her arm. 'How are we this morning?'

'I'm fine,' Carrie told her honestly. Already the headache was fading.

'Wonderful.' The nurse beamed at her. 'As soon as I'm finished here you can see your visitor.'

A visitor? Thank heavens. Carrie was so relieved she smiled. It was probably her mum. She would set this hospital straight, sort out the mistake, and tell the staff that her daughter was Carrie Barnes of Chesterfield Crescent, Surry Hills, Sydney. And most definitely *not*, as everyone here at this hospital mistakenly believed, Mrs Kincaid of the Riverslea Downs station in far western Queensland.

The blood pressure cuff tightened around Carrie's arm and she resigned herself to being patient, concentrating on the view through the window. It was a view of gum trees and acres of pale grass, flat as football fields, spreading all the way to low purple hills in the distance. There was also a barbed wire fence and she could hear a crow calling…

Carrie experienced an uncomfortable moment of self-doubt.

The scene was so unmistakably rural, so completely different in every way from her home in the busy Sydney suburb of Surry Hills. She was used to trendy cafés, bars and restaurants, small independent bookstores and funky antique shops. She had no idea why she was here. How had she got all the way out *here*?

'Hmm, your blood pressure's up a bit.' The nurse was frowning as she released the cuff and made notes on the chart at the end of Carrie's bed.

'That's probably because I'm stressed,' Carrie told her.

'Yes.' The nurse sent her a knowing smile. 'But you're sure to feel *much* happier when you see your husband.'

*Husband?*

Carrie flashed hot and cold.

'But my visitor…' she began, and then had to swallow to ease her suddenly dry mouth. 'It's my mother, isn't it?'

'No, dear. Your husband, Mr Kincaid, is here.' The nurse, a plump woman of around fifty, arched one eyebrow and almost smirked. 'I can guarantee you'll cheer up when you see him.'

Carrie felt as if she'd woken up, but was still inside a nightmare. Fear and confusion rushed back and she wanted to pull the bedclothes over her head and simply disappear.

Last night the doctor had told her a crazy story: She'd fallen from a horse, which was laughable—the closest she'd ever been to a horse was on a merry-go-round. A couple called Doug and Meredith Peterson had brought her to the hospital after this fall, apparently, but she'd never heard of them, either. Then the doctor told her that she'd hit her head and had amnesia.

None of it made sense.

How could she have amnesia when she knew exactly who she was? She had no trouble rattling off her name and her phone number and her address, so how could she possibly have forgotten something as obvious as the doctor's other preposterous claim—that she had a husband?

'I'm sure I'm not married,' she told the nurse now, just as she'd told the other white coats last night. 'I've never been married.' But even as she'd said this, hot panic swirled through her. She'd seen the pale mark on the ring finger of her left hand.

When had that happened?

How?

Why?

When she'd tried to ask questions the medical staff had merely frowned and made all sorts of notes. Then there'd been phone calls to specialists. Eventually Carrie had been told that she needed CT scans, which were not available here in this tiny Outback hospital. She would have to be transported to a bigger centre.

It had all been so crazy. So frightening. To Carrie's shame she'd burst into tears and the doctor had prescribed something to calm her.

Obviously the small white pill had also sent her to sleep, for now it was already morning. And the man who claimed to be her husband had apparently driven some distance from his cattle property.

Any minute now he would be walking into her room. What should she expect?

What would *her husband* expect?

Carrie wondered what she looked like this morning. She should probably hunt for the comb in the toiletries pack the hospital had provided and tidy her hair. Then again, why should she bother to look presentable for a man she didn't know? A man who made such discomfiting claims?

Curiosity about her appearance got the better of her. She reached for the bag and found the comb and mirror inside.

The mirror was quite small, so she could only examine her appearance a section at a time. She saw a graze on her forehead and a bluish-black bruise, but otherwise she looked much the same as usual. Except…when she dragged a comb through her hair it was much longer than it should have been. Not a neat bob, but almost reaching her shoulders.

When had *that* happened? And her hair's colour was a plain brown. But she'd always gone to Gavin, the trendiest hairdresser in Crown Street, to get blonde and copper streaks, with the occasional touch of aqua or cerise.

Carrie was still puzzling over this lack of colour when footsteps sounded outside in the corridor.

Firm, no nonsense, *masculine* footsteps.

Her heart picked up pace. She shoved the comb and mirror back in the bag and felt suddenly sweaty. Was this her supposed husband, Max Kincaid?

When she saw him would she remember him?

Remember something?

*Anything?*

She held her breath as the footsteps came closer. Into her room.

Just inside the doorway, her visitor stopped.

He was tall. Sun-tanned. His hair was thick and dark brown and cut short, and despite his height he had the build of a footballer, with impressively broad shoulders, his torso tapering to slim hips and solid thighs.

His eyes were an astonishing piercing blue. Carrie had never seen eyes quite like them. She wanted to stare and stare.

He was dressed in well-worn jeans and a light blue checked shirt that was open at the neck with the long sleeves rolled back. The whole effect was distinctly rural, but most definitely, eye-catching.

Max Kincaid was, in fact, quite ridiculously handsome.

But Carrie had never, most emphatically, *never* seen him before.

Which was crazy. *So* crazy. Surely this man would be impossible to forget.

'Hello, Carrie.' His voice was deep and pleasant and he set a brown leather hold-all on the floor beside her bed.

Carrie didn't return his greeting. She couldn't. It would be like admitting to something she didn't believe. Instead, she gave the faintest shake of her head.

He watched her with a fleeting worried smile. 'I'm Max.'

'Yes.' She couldn't help speaking coolly. 'So I've been told.'

Frowning, he stared frankly at her now, his bright blue eyes searching her face. 'You really don't remember me?'

'No. I'm so—' Carrie almost apologised, but she stopped herself just in time. Max Kincaid didn't seem too immediately threatening, but she certainly wasn't ready to trust him. She couldn't shake off feeling that he had to be an impostor.

She sat very stiffly against the propped pillows as he moved to the small table beside her.

She watched him, studying his face, searching for even the tiniest clue to trigger her memory—the shape of his eyebrows, the remarkable blue of his eyes, the crease lines at their corners. The strong, lightly stubbled angle of his jaw.

Nothing was familiar.

'Are your belongings in here?' he asked politely as he lightly touched the door to a cupboard in the bedside table.

Carrie found herself noticing his hands. They were squarish and strong, and slightly scarred and rough, no doubt from working in the outdoors and cracking whips, or branding unfortunate cows, or whatever it was that cattlemen did. She saw that his forearms were strong, too, tanned, and covered in a light scattering of sun-bleached hair.

He was unsettlingly sexy and she scowled at him. 'You want to search my belongings?'

'I thought perhaps…if you saw your driver's licence it might help.'

Carrie had no idea if her driver's licence was in that cupboard, but even if it was… 'How will I know the licence hasn't been faked?'

This time Max's frown was reproachful. 'Carrie, give me a break. All I want is to help you.'

Which was dead easy for him to say. So hard for her to accept.

But she supposed there was nothing to be gained by stopping him. 'Go on, open it,' she said ungraciously.

Max did this with a light touch of his fingertips.

*If he really is my husband, his fingertips—those very*

*fingertips—must have skimmed beneath my clothing and trailed over my skin.*

The thought sent a thrilling shiver zinging through her.

There was something rather fascinating about those rough, workmanlike hands, so different from the pale, smooth hands of Dave the accountant...the last guy she could remember dating.

She quickly squashed such thoughts and concentrated on the contents of the cupboard—a small, rather plain brown leather handbag with a plaited leather strap, more conservative than Carrie's usual style. She certainly didn't recognise it.

Max, with a polite smile, handed the bag to her, and she caught a sharp flash of emotion in his bright blue eyes. It might have been sadness or hope. For a split second, she felt another zap.

Quickly she dropped her gaze, took a deep breath and slid the bag's zip open. Inside were sunglasses—neat and tasteful sunglasses, with tortoiseshell frames—again much more conservative than the funky glasses she usually wore. Also a small pack of tissues, an emery board, a couple of raffle tickets and a phone with a neat silver cover. Sunk to the bottom was a bright pink and yellow spotted money purse.

*Oh.* Carrie stared at the purse. *This* she definitely remembered. She'd bought it in that little shop around the corner from her flat. She'd been bored on a rainy Saturday morning and had gone window shopping. She'd been attracted by the cheery colours and had bought it on impulse.

But she had no memory of ever buying the plain brown handbag or the neat silver phone. Then again, if the phone really *was* hers it could be her lifeline. She could ring her mother and find out for sure if this man standing beside her bed in jeans and riding boots truly was her husband.

Or not.

'I need to ring my mother,' she said.

'Sure—by all means.' Max Kincaid's big shoulders lifted in a casual shrug. 'I've already rung her to explain about the accident, so she'll be pleased to hear from you.'

This did not bode well. He sounded far too relaxed and confident.

Carrie's stomach was tight as she scrolled to her mum's number and pressed the button. The phone rang, but went straight through to the voicemail message.

At least her mother's voice sounded just as Carrie remembered.

'Mum, it's me,' she said, trying to keep her own voice calm. 'Carrie. I'm in hospital. I'm OK, or at least I *feel* OK, but can you ring me back, please?'

As she left this message Max waited patiently, with his big hands resting lightly on his hips. He nodded when she was finished. 'I'm sure Sylvia will ring back.'

*Sylvia.* Max Kincaid knew that her mother's name was Sylvia.

Feeling more nervous than ever now, Carrie picked up the familiar purse. While she was waiting for her mother's call she might as well check the driver's licence.

*Please let it say that I'm Carrie Barnes.*

The usual spread of cards were slotted into the purse's plastic sleeves, and right up front was the driver's licence. Carrie saw immediately that, while the photo was typically unflattering, the picture was definitely of *her* face. There could be no doubt about that.

And then her gaze flashed to the details...

*Name: Carrie Susannah Kincaid.*
*Sex: Female.*
*Height: 165 cm.*
*Date of birth: July 8th 1985.*
*Address: Riverslea Downs station,*
*Jilljinda, Queensland.*

Her heart took off like a startled bird.
*Thud-thud-thud-thud.*
Her headache returned. She sank back against the pillows and closed her eyes. This was either a huge hoax or the hospital staff were right. She had amnesia and had forgotten that she was married to Max Kincaid.

'I don't understand,' she said.

'You've had an accident, Carrie.' He spoke gently. 'A fall from a horse. A head injury.'

'But if I can remember my name, and my mother's name, why can't I remember anything else… Why can't I remember *you*?'

Max Kincaid gave an uncomfortable shrug. 'The doctor is confident you'll get your memory back.'

The problem was that right now Carrie wasn't sure that she *wanted* her memory to come back. Did she really want to know that it was all true? That she wasn't a city girl any more? That she lived on a cattle property and was married to this strange man?

It was far too confronting.

She wanted the reassuring comfort of the life she knew and remembered—as a single girl in Sydney, with a reasonably interesting and well-paid job at an advertising agency and a trendy little flat in Surry Hills. Plus her friends. Friday nights at Hillier's Bar. Saturday afternoons watching football or going to the beach at Bondi or Coogee. Every second Sunday evening at her mother's.

It was so weird to be able to recall all these details so vividly and yet have no memory of ever meeting Max Kincaid. Even weirder and more daunting was the suggestion that they hadn't merely met, but were married.

Did she really live with this strange man in the Outback?

Surely that was impossible. She'd never had a hankering for the Outback. She knew how hard that life was, with heat and dust and flies, not to mention drought and famine, or bushfires and floods. She was quite sure she wasn't tough enough for it.

But perhaps more importantly, if she was married to this man…she must have slept with him. Probably many times.

Involuntarily Carrie flashed her gaze again to his big shoulders and hands. His solid thighs encased in denim. She imagined him touching her intimately. Touching her breasts, her thighs. Heat rushed over her skin, flaring and leaping like a bushfire in a wind gust.

For a second, almost as if he'd guessed her thoughts, his blue eyes blazed. Carrie found herself mesmerised. Max's eyes were sensational. Movie star sensational. For a giddy moment she thought he was going to try to lean in, to kiss her.

On a knife-edge of expectation, she held her breath.

But Max made no move. Instead, he said, matter-of-factly, 'I'm told that you can check out of the hospital now. I'm to take you to Townsville. For tests—more X-rays.'

Carrie sighed.

He picked up the holdall he'd brought with him and

set it on the chair beside her bed. 'I brought clean clothes for you.'

'*My* clothes?'

His mouth tilted in a crooked smile. 'Yes, Carrie. *Your* clothes.'

He must have gone through her wardrobe and her underwear drawer, making a selection. Invading her privacy. Or was he simply being a thoughtful husband?

If only she knew the truth. 'Thank you,' she said.

'Do you need a hand?'

Instinctively her gaze dropped to his hands. *Again.* Dear heaven, she was hopeless. 'How do you mean?'

'With getting out of bed? Or getting dressed?'

She was quite sure she blushed. 'No, thanks. I'll be fine.'

'I'll be outside, then.' With the most fleeting of smiles, Max left.

In the hospital hallway, Max dragged in a deep breath and let it out slowly as he tried to ease the gnawing anxiety that had stayed with him since his initial panic yesterday, when he'd heard about Carrie's accident. He'd never experienced such gut-wrenching dread.

In that moment he'd known the true agony of loving someone, of knowing his loved one was in trouble and feeling helpless. He'd wanted to jump in his vehicle and race straight to the hospital, but Doug had warned him to hold off. Carrie was sleeping and probably wouldn't wake before morning.

Now, Max felt only marginally calmer. Carrie was out of danger, but he was left facing the bald facts. Two days ago his wife had walked out on him. Today she had no memory of ever meeting him.

It was a hell of a situation.

One thing was certain: he had no hope of sorting anything out with Carrie if she didn't even know who he was. But by the same token, there was no question that he wouldn't look after her until she was well again. He was still her husband, after all. He still loved her. Deeply.

And he couldn't shake off the feeling that Carrie still loved him, that she hadn't been totally honest about her reasons for leaving. But perhaps that was just wishful thinking. There was a strong possibility that when Carrie's memory returned she would also recall all her grievances in vivid detail.

The very thought ate at Max's innards, but he would worry about that when the time came. Till then, his role was clear.

Carrie edged carefully out of bed. Her feet reached the floor and as she stood she felt a bit dizzy, but the sensation quickly passed. The bump on her head throbbed faintly, but it wasn't too bad.

She took out the clothes Max had brought—a pair of jeans and a white T shirt, a white bra and matching panties. There was also a plastic bag holding a pair of shoes—simple navy blue flats. Everything was good quality, and very tasteful, but Carrie found it hard to believe they were hers.

Where were the happy, dizzy colours she'd always worn?

Conscious of the man waiting mere metres away, just outside her door, she slipped off the hospital nightgown and put on the underwear. The bra fitted her perfectly, as did the pants, the jeans and the T-shirt.

She was surprised but rather pleased to realise that she

was quite slim now. In the past she'd always had a bit of a struggle with her weight.

She combed her hair again and then checked the bedside cupboard and found a plastic hospital bag with more clothes—presumably the clothes she'd worn when she arrived here. Another pair of denim jeans and a blue and white striped shirt, white undies and brown riding boots. *Crikey.*

She felt as if her whole life and personality had been transplanted. These clothes should belong to a girl in a country style magazine. Which was weird and unsettling. How had this happened? Why had she changed?

Anxiety returned, re-tightening the knots in her stomach as she stuffed the bag of clothes and the brown handbag into the holdall. She checked her phone again. Still no reply from her mum.

*Mum, ring me, please.*

She needed the comfort of her mum's voice. Needed her reassurance, too. At the moment Carrie felt as if she was in a crazy sci-fi movie. Aliens had wiped a section of her memory and Max Kincaid was part of their evil plan to abduct her.

She knew this was silly, but she still felt uneasy as she went to the door and found Max waiting just outside.

His smile was cautious. 'All set?'

Unwilling to commit herself, she gave a shrug, but when Max held out his hand for the holdall she gave it to him.

They made their way down a long hospital corridor to the office, where all the paperwork was ready and waiting for her.

'You just have to sign here…and here,' the girl at the counter said as she spread the forms in front of Carrie.

Carrie wished she could delay this process. Wished she could demand some kind of proof that this man was her husband.

'Will I see the doctor again before I leave?' she hedged.

The girl frowned and looked again at the papers. 'Dr Byrne's been treating you, but I'm sorry, he's in Theatre right now. Everything's here on your sheet, though, and you're fit to travel.'

'Carrie has an appointment in Townsville,' Max said.

The girl smiled at him, batting her eyelashes as if he was a rock star offering his autograph.

Ignoring her, he said to Carrie, 'The appointment's for two o'clock, so we'd better get on our way.'

Carrie went to the doorway with him and looked out at the landscape beyond the hospital. There was a scattering of tin-roofed timber buildings that comprised the tiny Outback town. A bitumen road stretched like a dull blue ribbon, rolling out across pale grassland plains dotted with gum trees and grazing cattle. Above this, the sun was ablaze in an endless powder-blue sky.

She looked again at her phone. Still no new message.

'Carrie,' Max said. 'You can trust me, I promise. You'll be OK.'

To her surprise she believed him. There was something rather honest and open about his face. Perhaps it was country boy charm, or perhaps she just needed to believe him. The sad truth was she had little choice… she was in the Outback and she had to drive off with a total stranger.

Max opened the door of a dusty four-wheel drive.

He was nervous, too, she realised. Above the open neck of his shirt she could see the way the muscles in his throat worked, but his hand was warm and firm as he took her arm. Her skin reacted stupidly, flashing heat where he touched her as he helped her up into the passenger's seat.

A moment later, having dumped the holdall beside another pack in the back, he climbed into the driver's seat beside her. Suddenly those wide shoulders and solid thighs and all that Outback guy toughness were mere inches away from her.

'Just try to relax,' he said as he started up the engine and backed out of the parking space. 'Close your eyes. Go to sleep, if you like.'

If only it was that easy.

## CHAPTER THREE

THEY WERE ABOUT twenty kilometres down the road, with the small town of Jilljinda well and truly behind them when Carrie's mother rang back.

'It was such a relief to find your message and to hear your voice,' her mum said.

'It's great to hear you, too, Mum.' *You. Have. No. Idea.*

'How are you, darling? Have you really lost your memory?'

'Well, yes. Some of it, at least. The more recent things, apparently. I can remember all about Sydney, and about you and my friends, but I have no memory of meeting M-Max, or coming to Queensland.'

'How very strange. It must be extremely upsetting, dear.'

Carrie's stomach took a dive. She'd been hoping her mother would tell her this was all a terrible mistake.

Now, clearly, the impossible was not only possible, it was true. She was married to Max, an Outback cattleman.

'Yeah, it's *very* upsetting,' she said. 'It's weird.'

'And Max said this happened when you fell from a horse?'

'Apparently.' Carrie didn't add that she had absolutely no memory of ever learning to ride a horse. The situation was bizarre enough, without giving her mum too much to worry about.

Just the same, she heard her mother's heavy sigh. 'I always knew something dreadful like this would happen to you out there. I warned you right from the start that you should never marry a cattleman. The lifestyle is just too hard and dangerous, and now this accident proves it.'

A cold wave of disappointment washed over Carrie. She'd been hanging out for maternal reassurance, or at the very least a few motherly words of comfort.

'I don't feel too bad,' she felt compelled to add. 'My headache's just about gone. But I have to go to Townsville for more tests.'

'Oh, dear.'

Carrie sent a sideways glance to Max. Clearly her husband wasn't in her mother's good books and she wished she knew why. Was it something he'd done? Or was it merely because he lived in the Outback? She wondered if he'd guessed her parent's negative response.

'Are you in an ambulance?' her mother asked next.

'No.' Carrie felt cautious now as she explained, 'I'm with Max. He's driving me to Townsville.'

'Oh.'

Carrie didn't like the sound of that. *Oh.* It reinforced all the fears and doubts she'd been battling ever since Max had walked into her hospital room. Now she'd virtually handed herself over to a complete stranger, who was also apparently her life partner, her *lover*.

In the car park he'd given his word. *'Carrie, you can trust me, I promise. You'll be OK.'*

She wanted to trust Max. All evidence pointed to the fact that he truly was her husband, so she needed to trust him. And as far as she could judge he had a very direct and honest face, although right now he shot her a sharp, frowning glance, almost as if he'd guessed the tenor of her mother's message…

'I suppose Max hasn't said anything about—?' Frustratingly, her mum stopped in mid-sentence.

Carrie frowned. 'Said anything about what?'

'Oh…I—I—I'm sorry. Don't worry, dear. I—I spoke without thinking.'

*Mum, for heaven's sake.*

Beside Carrie, Max was very still, his eyes focused on the road ahead, his strong tanned hands steady on the steering wheel.

'Is there's something I should know, Mum? Just tell me.'

'No, no, darling. Not now. You shouldn't be stressed at a time like this. You should be trying to relax. Ring me again after you're safely in Townsville. After you've finished with the tests.'

Carrie hated being fobbed off. Her mum had been on the brink of telling her something important. 'But what did you mean? What don't I know?'

Her mother, however, would not be coerced.

'I'll say goodbye for now. Take care, Carrie. I'll be thinking of you and sending my love.'

Then silence. She'd disconnected.

Carrie gave a soft groan, dropped the phone back into her lap, and felt her uneasiness tighten another notch.

*Here we go*, thought Max. *The Dragon has fired her first flare.*

He kept the thought to himself, clenching his teeth to hold back a comment. Carrie had enough to deal with right now.

Beside him, she sighed. 'Am I right in thinking that I *often* feel angry or frustrated after a phone conversation with my mother?'

He sent her a sympathetic smile, but she looked so tired and confused he wanted to do a hell of a lot more than smile. His instincts urged him to pull over to the side of the road and take her in his arms. He wanted to ease that furrow between her fine brows, press a gentle kiss to her forehead, then another on the tip of her neat pointy nose, before finally settling on her sweet lush lips.

*Yeah, right. Like* that *would solve anything.*

Instead, he gave a shrug. 'I guess you realise I'm not Sylvia's dream son-in-law?'

'Mum claims she warned me about life in the bush.'

Max nodded. 'That started from the moment we met.' He'd never meant to think of his mother-in-law as The Dragon, but three years of poorly veiled hostility could stuff with a man's good intentions.

Carrie's eyes were wide. 'So my mum was against it, but I married you anyway?'

He chanced a quick grin. 'You were stubborn.'

Then he quickly sobered. He'd only told Carrie half the story, of course. Right now she innocently assumed that all was rosy in Max-and-Carrie Land—the nickname they'd given their marriage in happier times. And this morning he'd assured her she could trust him. Which was true, but her accident had left him walking a fine line between the truth and the way he wished things could be. The way they *should* be.

Now, as he drove on over wide rolling grasslands, he wondered how much he should tell Carrie. It would be weird to try to explain that she'd walked out on their marriage. He didn't want to confuse her. Given her memory loss, it was hard to gauge how much she could take in.

And yet they had two hours of driving before they reached the coast… Two hours of tiptoeing through a conversational minefield.

'How did we meet?' Carrie asked suddenly.

Max swallowed to ease the sudden brick in his throat. This was the last question he'd expected. It was hard to accept that she remembered nothing of an occasion that was enshrined in his mind for ever and lit up with flashing neon lights.

He told her the simple truth. 'We met at a wedding.'

Carrie's lovely chocolate-brown eyes widened. 'Really? Was the wedding in Sydney?'

'Yes. A work colleague of yours—Cleo Marsh—married one of my mates.'

'Gosh, I remember Cleo. She was great fun. Quite a party girl. And she married a cattleman?'

Max nodded. 'Grant grew up on a cattle property, but he studied medicine and now he's a rural GP based in Longreach. He met Cleo when they were both holidaying on Hayman Island.'

'How romantic.'

'Quite,' he said softly.

'I—I wish—' Carrie began to chew at her thumbnail. After a bit, she said, 'I wish I could remember meeting you.'

The question slugged him like a physical blow. Perhaps he should just tell her the truth and stop this conversation now.

'How did it happen, Max? Did our eyes meet across a crowded room? Or did you chase me?' Carrie dropped her gaze to the gnawed thumbnail. 'Did I flirt with you?'

Against his better judgement Max allowed himself to relive the amazing chemistry of that night, the glittering, harbourside venue and that first, heart-zapping moment of eye contact with Carrie. Her shining dark eyes and dazzling bright smile, the electric shock of their bodies touching the first time they danced…

Quietly, he said, 'I reckon we could safely claim all of the above.'

'Wow,' she said, but she didn't sound very happy.

She let out a heavy sigh, gave a toss of her long brown hair and flopped back in her seat, with her arms crossed over her chest and her eyes closed, as if even this tiny slice of information was more than she could handle.

Carrie wished she could go to sleep. She just wanted the next few hours—the tedious journey over endless sweeping plains, the Townsville hospital and the medical tests—to be over and done with. Along with that fantasy she wanted a miraculous mind-clearing drug that would restore her memory and bring her instantly back to normal.

Or did she?

Was she ready for reality?

Did she really want to wake up and find herself reliving every minute detail of her life as an Outback wife?

She slid another glance Max's way. She had to admit she couldn't fault her husband's looks. Yes, he had a distinctly outdoorsy aura, but she was rather partial to well-developed muscles and piercing blue eyes.

She wished she could remember meeting him at Cleo's wedding. For that matter she wished she could remember their own wedding. She looked again at her left hand and the faint mark on the ring finger and contemplated asking him about her wedding ring and why she wasn't wearing it, but she wasn't sure she was ready to hear his answer.

Of course the reason might be simple—she'd taken the ring off as a practical safety precaution—but the answer also might be complex and awkward, and right now Carrie was quite sure she had as many complications as she could handle. So, although her curiosity about Max was off the scale, she decided it was wisest to choose her questions carefully. Best to stick to the past. The straightforward simplicity of their first meeting.

'Were you wearing a tux?' she asked. 'On the night we met?'

Max looked surprised, and then mildly amused. 'I suppose I was.' He thought for a moment. 'Yes, of course I was. It was an evening wedding. Quite formal.'

'And what was I wearing?' She wondered if it was a dress she could remember. 'What colour?'

He shot her a twinkling sideways glance. 'The female mind never ceases to amaze me.'

'Why?'

'All the questions you could ask and you want to know what colour you were wearing more than three years ago.'

She narrowed her eyes at him, feeling almost playful. 'You don't remember, do you?'

'Of course I do.'

'Tell me, then.'

'It was a slinky almost backless number in a fetching coppery shade. And you had matching streaks of copper in your hair.'

Carrie smiled. She couldn't remember the dress, but it sounded like the sort of thing she might have chosen, and she'd loved having her hair streaked to match an outfit.

Suddenly emboldened, she asked, 'Did we sleep together on that first night?'

To her surprise, she saw the muscles jerk in Max's neck as he swallowed, and then he took his time answering. 'What do you think?' he asked finally.

Carrie blushed, caught out by her own cheeky question. As far as she could remember she wasn't in the habit of jumping into bed with men on a first date. Then again, she couldn't remember ever dating anyone quite as disturbingly sexy as Max.

'Well,' she said carefully. 'We did end up getting married, so I guess there might have been sparks.'

Max didn't shift his gaze from the road in front of them, but his hands tightened around the steering wheel and a dark stain rose like a tide up his neck. 'Oh, yeah,' he said quietly. 'There were sparks.'

Something in his voice, half rumble, half threat, sent Carrie's imagination running wild. Without warning she was picturing Max in his tux, shedding his jacket and wrenching off his bow tie, then peeling away her slinky copper dress. She saw him bending to touch his lips to her bared shoulder, to cup her breasts in his strong hands and—

*Oh, for heaven's sake.* She knew very well that this wasn't a memory. It was pure fantasy. But it was a fantasy complete with sparks that lit flashpoints, burning all over her skin, and firing way deep inside.

Silenced and stunned by her body's reaction, she slunk back in her seat, crossed her legs demurely once more and folded her arms. It was time to stop asking questions. Any kind of conversation with this man was dangerous.

* * *

At last the tests were over and Carrie had seen the Townsville specialist. As far as her head injury was concerned there were no serious complications and she had been told that her memory should return, although the doctor couldn't tell her exactly when this would happen. For the time being Carrie was to follow the normal precautions.

She shouldn't be left alone for the next twenty-four hours and she should have plenty of rest and avoid stressful situations. She should not drink alcohol or take non-prescription drugs, and there was to be no more horse riding for at least three weeks, when she was to return for another appointment.

'I'm sure your memory will be restored by then,' the doctor told her confidently as they left.

It was good news, or as good as she could expect, and Carrie knew she should be grateful. To a certain extent she *was* grateful. She could expect a full recovery, and she had a husband who seemed willing to help her in every way possible.

But the problem of her lost memory felt huge, like an invisible force field between her and Max. He was a constant physical and highly visible masculine presence at her side, and yet she didn't know him. He knew everything about her, but she didn't know him. *At all*.

Apparently the memories were there, locked inside her brain, but she couldn't reach them. It was like living with a blindfold that she couldn't remove.

She was ignorant of basic things—Max's favourite food and his most loved movies. She didn't know what footie team he followed, or whether he shaved with an electric razor. And she knew nothing about his character. His heart. Was he a good man? Was he even-tempered or prone to anger? Was he kind to old ladies and kittens? Did he love being a cattleman?

Did he love *her*?

And the biggest question that dominated her thoughts right at this moment—where did he plan to sleep tonight?

# CHAPTER FOUR

'I'VE BOOKED AN APARTMENT,' Max said as their vehicle crested a hill and a vista of sparkling blue sea and a distant green island suddenly lay before them. 'I made the booking for a few days, in case you need time to adjust before we head back to Riverslea Downs.'

'Thanks,' said Carrie. 'That's thoughtful.' Already, as they'd travelled from the hospital through the city, she'd noticed large shopping centres, several restaurants and cafés, and a movie theatre or two.

'If you can't be in Sydney, a big city like Townsville is at least better than a remote Outback cattle station,' her mother said when she rang to find out how Carrie was.

'Yes, I guess so.' Carrie was actually more interested in finding out what it was that her mother had been going to tell her during their previous phone conversation.

'I can't remember,' her mother said now, quite bluntly. And then, in more soothing tones, 'Honestly, darling, I've forgotten. It can't have been important.'

Carrie was certain she was lying, but it seemed pointless to push the matter.

Now, having rung off, she asked Max, 'If we stay here for a few days who will look after your cattle?'

This brought a smile. 'The cattle can look after themselves for the time being. We've had a good wet season, so the dams are full and there's plenty of pasture. But anyway Barney's there.'

Carrie frowned. 'Who's Barney?'

Max looked momentarily surprised, as if he considered this person entirely unforgettable, but then he said quickly, 'He's an old retired ringer. He lives on the property. He worked there for nearly sixty years. Worked for my father before me. And when it was time to retire he couldn't bear the thought of leaving the Outback, so he has his own little cottage and does odd jobs around the place.'

'A kind of caretaker?'

Max grinned. 'Better than a guard dog.'

So it seemed Max was kind to old family employees. Carrie approved, and wondered if she should make a list of things she was learning about her husband.

She soon discovered he'd chosen an impressive apartment. It was on the fourth floor of a building built right beside the sea, very modern and gleaming, with white walls and white floor tiles and a neat kitchen with pretty, pale granite bench tops. The living area was furnished with attractive cane furniture with deep blue cushions. A wall of white shutters opened on to a balcony with a view over palm trees to the dazzling tropical sea.

'How lovely,' she said. 'I'm sure this must be the perfect spot for my recovery.'

Max's blue eyes were warm as he smiled. 'That's what I was hoping.'

Tentatively, Carrie returned his smile. 'We haven't stayed here before, have we?'

'Yes,' he admitted. 'We usually come to Townsville a few times a year for a city break.'

Really? It sounded like a pretty nice lifestyle. But right now Carrie had one rather big and worrying question—how many bedrooms were there?

She looked around nervously, counting the doorways that led from the main living area, somewhat relieved to see there was more than one.

'This is the main bedroom,' Max said smoothly as he watched the direction of her gaze. And then he crossed to an open doorway. 'Come and look—it's not bad.'

Still clutching the small leather holdall with her few possessions, Carrie followed him. The room was huge, with what seemed like acres of pale cream carpet and an enormous white and aqua bed. And there were floor-to-ceiling windows giving an incredible view to the sea on one side and to a pretty marina filled with sleek, beautiful yachts on the other. Another doorway led to an en-suite bathroom that was equally huge and white and luxurious.

'It's lovely,' she said, and heat spread under her skin as she wondered, again, if Max planned to share this room with her.

He was standing just a few feet away and his wide-shouldered presence seemed to make the bedroom shrink. Her imagination flashed forward—she was lying in that enormous bed, the sheets smooth and silky against her skin. Max was emerging from the bathroom, coming straight from the shower, naked, his powerful body gleaming in the lamplight. And then he was lifting the sheet and sliding in beside her…

To her dismay, she realised he was watching her and she sucked in a shaky breath. The play of emotions on his face suggested that he was remembering something from their past. She wished she knew what it was. Wished she knew how many nights they'd spent in rooms like this.

Max was so earthy and masculine... She was sure, deep in her bones, that those nights had been wild.

'Were—were you planning to sleep in here, too?' she asked, and her voice was ridiculously breathless.

'You're supposed to stay relaxed, so I was assuming you'd want your own bed, but it's entirely your call.' His expression was cool now, as if he was deliberately clearing it of emotion. 'I don't need to sleep here. There's another room. Whatever you prefer.'

Carrie gulped. 'Right.' Flustered, she looked around at this room which, in reality, was big enough to house a small village. She looked anywhere except at Max, who was waiting for her decision.

'I'll take the other room,' he said quietly.

She must have taken too long. She blinked and exhaled the breath she'd been holding, letting it go with an embarrassingly noisy *whoosh*. Foolishly, she felt a moment's disappointment.

Then she caught Max's stern gaze, still fixed on her, and she couldn't think what to say so she nodded. Almost immediately she marched back to the living room, curiosity driving her to check out the other bedroom.

It was obviously designed for children, and was much smaller than the main room, without any of the views and with two single beds that looked ridiculously small for such a big man.

She turned to Max, who had followed her. 'You won't be comfortable in here. We should swap. I'll be perfectly fine in one of these beds, and I'm tired, so I don't need the views and I wouldn't—'

'Carrie, calm down.' Now Max looked almost amused. 'It's OK. I'll be fine in here.' The skin around his eyes creased as he smiled. 'You're convalescing. You'll be better with a room to yourself, and the main bedroom has an en-suite.'

'Well, yes,' she said, still flustered. 'Of course.'

'Now, you should go on to the balcony and enjoy the view,' he said. 'I'll make you a cup of tea.'

Max looked more like a cowboy than a waiter or a chef, but he made a surprisingly good cuppa and, without asking, knew exactly how Carrie liked her tea—with just a dash of milk and no sugar. The evidence that he really was her husband was growing, and she accepted it with a mix of dismay and bewildering excitement.

Perhaps when she got her memory back her life would be suddenly wonderful. Perfect. Far better than she could possibly imagine…in spite of their marriage's Outback setting.

For now, at least, it was very pleasant to sit on the balcony with a cool breeze blowing in from the sea. She caught the scent of frangipani in the air, and the sky was tinged with pink from the setting sun. Down by the water cockatoos squabbled in treetops. Out on the still, silvery bay, kayakers paddled.

The setting was idyllic. Carrie's companion—her *husband*—was handsome and charming. She wanted to enjoy the moment and not to worry.

If only the situation didn't feel so unreal—like a pretence, as if she'd slipped through a time warp and was living someone else's life.

Max organised dinner, ordering takeaway food from a nearby Chinese restaurant, which he collected and then served using the apartment's pretty aqua blue dinner service.

The night was deliciously balmy, so they lit candles with glass shades and ate on the balcony. Moonlight shone on the water and lights on the black shape of Magnetic Island twinkled in the distance. A yacht left the marina and glided smoothly and silently over the dark bay, heading out to sea.

For Carrie, the combination of the meal and the moonlight was quite magical, and she could feel her body relaxing, the nervous knots in her belly easing, even while her curiosity about Max and their marriage mounted.

'Do you know what I've done with my wedding ring?' The question, just one out of the hundreds of questions circling in her head, spilled from her before she quite realised what she was saying.

She felt a bit foolish as soon as it was out—especially when she saw surprise and then a flash of pain in Max's eyes.

He took a moment to answer and she was nervous again, her heart fluttering in her chest like a trapped bird. *What's wrong?* she wanted to ask him.

But when he answered he spoke quite calmly. 'Your rings are at home on the dressing table.'

*At home on the dressing table.* It sounded so incredibly ordinary and sensible. Why had she been worried? 'I suppose when you're living in the Outback it makes sense not to wear them all the time?'

'Yes, that's what you decided.'

But there was something in Max's eyes that still bothered her.

'What's my engagement ring like?'

'It has two diamonds.'

'Two? Lucky me.'

Max smiled at this. 'It was my grandmother's ring. She died not long after we met, but she wanted you to have it.'

'Oh…'

'You were happy to wear it. You liked her.'

Carrie felt a bit better, hearing this. It was reassuring to know that she'd got on well with Max's grandmother. But it hinted at an emotional health that she didn't feel.

*Are we happy?* Carrie wanted to ask next, but she wasn't brave enough. For one thing she was haunted by her mother's confusing question—the one she'd cut off and left dangling with no further explanation. As well, Carrie had the sense that both Max and her mother were carefully avoiding anything that might upset her.

Perhaps she should stop asking questions for now. But it was so hard to be patient and simply wait for her memory to return.

As they ate in silence, enjoying the delicious food and the pleasant evening, the questions kept circling in Carrie's head.

It wasn't long before she had to ask, 'Did we have a honeymoon? Did we go somewhere exotic and tropical like this?'

Max smiled. 'We most certainly had a honeymoon. We went to Paris.'

'Paris?'

Stunned, Carrie let her fork drop to her plate as she stared at him. Paris was the last destination she'd expected. Max was an Outback cattleman, a rugged cowboy who loved the outdoors. He rounded up cattle and battled the elements, and no doubt rode huge rodeo bulls or wrestled crocodiles in his spare time.

She found it hard to match that image with a sophisticated and cultured city like Paris.

'Did—did *I* choose Paris?'

He lifted a dark eyebrow. 'We chose it together. We were tossing up between New York, Paris and Rome, and we couldn't choose, so we ended up throwing the three names in a hat.'

'And then, when we drew the winner, we went for best of three?'

'Yes.' He frowned, then leaned forward, his elbows on the table and his gaze suddenly serious and searching. 'How did you know that, Carrie? Can you remember?'

She shook her head. 'No, sorry. I can't remember anything about Paris, but I've always gone for the best out of three. Ever since I was little, if I was tossing up, trying to make any kind of decision, I've always tried three times.' She gave an embarrassed little shrug. 'Just to make sure.'

'Of course.' His smile was wry, and Carrie felt somehow that she'd disappointed him.

She took a sip of her drink, lemon and lime and bitters, with clinking ice cubes. 'I know this will probably sound weird, but I'd love to hear about it,' she said. 'I've always wanted to go to Paris and I'd really like to know what you thought of it. Not—not the honeymoon bit,' she added quickly.

The sudden knowing shimmer in Max's blue eyes made her blush.

'I mean the city itself,' she said. 'Did you like it?'

At first Max didn't answer…and there was an unsettling, faraway look in his eyes.

What was he thinking about?

'Paris was wonderful, of course,' he said suddenly. 'Amazing. Or at least I found it amazing once we'd survived the hair-raising taxi ride from the airport to our hotel.'

'Is the traffic in Paris crazy?'

'Mad.'

'Where did we stay?'

'In a small hotel in St-Germain-des-Prés.'

'Wow.'

'It was a brilliant position. We could walk to the Seine, or to the Louvre, or Nôtre Dame. The café Les Deux Magots was just around the corner and we had lunch there several times. It was Ernest Hemingway's favourite place to hang out, along with Pablo Picasso and a mob of intellectuals.'

Max's face broke into a warm grin.

'We drank amazing red wine and French champagne, and we ate enough *foie gras* to give ourselves heart attacks.'

'It sounds wonderful.' Carrie closed her eyes, willing herself to remember. But nothing came. 'And what about the sights?'

'The sights?' Max repeated, then lifted his hands in a helpless gesture as he shrugged. 'How do you do Paris justice? It was all so beautiful, Carrie—the Seine and the bridges, the parks with their spring flowers and avenues of trees. The skyline. All those rooftops and church spires. The whole place was just dripping with history.'

'So you really liked it?' Carrie's voice was little more than a whisper.

'Yeah, I loved it,' Max said simply.

Goose bumps were breaking out all over her skin. Their honeymoon sounded so perfect, *so-o-o* romantic, so exactly what she'd always dreamed of.

'And it was Paris in the springtime?' she said. 'It wasn't May, was it?'

'Yes, you were dead-set to go there in May.'

'It's always been my favourite month.'

'I know.'

They shared a tentative smile.

'You're not making this up, are you?' she asked. 'About Paris?'

Max frowned. 'Of course not. Why would I?'

She gave a sad shrug. 'I don't know. It's just so hard, not being able to remember any of it. To be honest I feel cheated that I had a honeymoon in Paris and can't remember a single thing.'

'Well, everything must be weird at the moment.'

In the candlelight, she saw his sympathetic smile.

'Your memory will come back, Carrie.'

'Yes.' She knew she shouldn't give up hope. After all, she'd had amnesia for less than a day. She thought about her memory's eventual return and wondered how it would happen. Would everything come in a rush, like switching on a light? Or would it dribble into her consciousness in little bits and pieces, slowly coming together like a jigsaw puzzle?

*Patience, Carrie.*

'Tell me more,' she said. 'Did we have coffee in those little pavement cafés with the striped awnings?'

'Every day. And you developed a fondness for Parisian hot chocolate.'

She tried to imagine how the hot chocolate had tasted. For a moment the rich flavour was almost there on her tongue, but she was sure the real thing had surpassed her imagination. Giving up, she said, 'And were we served by handsome waiters with starched white napkins over their arms?'

'We were, indeed, and they spoke surprisingly good English.'

'But with charming French accents?'

'Yes to that, too.' Max narrowed his eyes at her and his smile was teasing. 'You were very taken by their accents.'

'Were you jealous?'

He gave a small huffing laugh. 'Hardly. We were on our honeymoon, after all.'

*Their honeymoon.* Her mind flashed up an image of the two of them in bed. She could almost imagine it... their naked bodies, the exquisite anticipation...

But then the barriers came up.

She had no idea what it was like to touch Max, to kiss him, to know the shape of his muscles and the texture of his skin, to have his big hands gliding over her, making love to her.

She let out another heavy sigh.

'It's time you were in bed,' he said.

'Now you're talking like you're my parent.'

'Not your parent—your nurse.'

'Yes.' That put her in her place. She *was* a patient, after all, and Max was being sensible, responsible, following the doctor's orders and making sure she had plenty of rest.

They gathered up their plates and cutlery and took everything inside. While Max stacked the dishwasher Carrie had a shower in the gorgeous big bathroom. Max had packed a nightgown for her—pale blue cotton with a white broderie anglaise frill and shoestring straps. It seemed all her clothes these days were either very pretty or very tasteful. Nothing funky, like the oversize purple and green T-shirt that she remembered being her favourite sleepwear.

She found a fluffy white bathrobe in the cupboard and pulled it on, tying it modestly at the waist before she went back to the living area to bid Max goodnight.

He was relaxed on the sofa, scrolling through TV

shows with the sound turned down, but he stood when she came into the room.

'Thanks for dinner, and for looking after me today,' Carrie said.

'My pleasure.' A confusing sadness shadowed his eyes as he said this.

Carrie's throat tightened over a sudden painful lump. Was Max upset because she wasn't acting like his wife? What did he expect now? A goodnight kiss?

He came towards her across the square of cane matting and her insides fluttered as she imagined lifting her face to him and their lips meeting. Would his lips be warm? Would he take her in his arms and hold her close to that hard, big body?

'I hope you sleep well,' he said, lifting a hand to her shoulder.

Through the towelling robe she felt the pressure of his fingers, warm and strong on her shoulder.

'Goodnight, Carrie.' He gave her shoulder a friendly squeeze and then stepped back.

That was it.

Not even a peck on the cheek. He was being so careful, and she knew she should be grateful. It was what she needed, what she wanted.

So why did she feel disappointed?

'Goodnight, Max.' She gave a tiny smile, a wave of her hand, and then turned and walked back into her room.

Max let out the breath he'd been holding, aimed the remote at the TV and turned it off, then went quietly outside to the balcony. Standing at the railing, he felt the sea breeze on his face, slightly damp and cool, as he looked out across the dark satiny water. His throat was tight and his eyes stung.

*Damn it.*

Carrie had nearly killed him in there. She'd looked so vulnerable, standing in the middle of the room in her dressing gown and bare feet, a nervous sort of smile playing at the corners of her mouth. So beautiful.

He'd sensed that he could have taken her in his arms and she wouldn't have put up a fight. In a moment of weakness he'd almost hoodwinked himself into believing that Fate had given him the old Carrie back, the girl who'd once loved him without reservation.

All that talk of their honeymoon had been agony. So many poignant, passionate memories. He'd been so tempted to take advantage of her innocence, to draw her in and kiss her, to have her once more in his arms, so soft and womanly and sensuous. To rekindle the uninhibited wildness and rapture of happier days.

To show her everything she'd missed.

But how could he take advantage of her now, too late? And why bother, when he knew her memory would return, and along with it her bitterness and resentment?

His hands tightened around the railing as he pictured the chilling moment when Carrie's memory came back. He could almost see the curiosity and the light fading from her warm brown eyes to be replaced by dawning knowledge and cynicism, and quite possibly anger.

A soft groan escaped him. This was a crazy situation—having Carrie back with him, helpless and needing him. It was tearing his guts out.

He had no choice, though. He had to see this through. While his wife needed him he had to do everything he could for her, and then, with grim, unhappy resignation, he would weather the storms that inevitably followed.

Eventually Carrie slept, and when she woke the room was filled with pale light, filtered by the shutters. She heard sounds coming from the kitchen. The kettle humming to the boil. The chink of mugs being set on the granite bench.

She should get up and join Max. Throwing off the bedclothes, she sat up.

At the same moment there was a knock at the door.

'Yes?' she called, snatching at the sheets.

Max appeared. He was bringing her a cup of tea, and Carrie found herself mesmerised by the sight of him in black silk boxer shorts and a white T-shirt, spellbound by his muscular chest so clearly defined by the snug-fitting shirt.

Stupidly, she completely forgot to cover herself with the sheet, and now his intense blue gaze settled on her, taking in her dishevelled hair, her bare shoulders, the thin fabric of her nightgown. To her dismay her nipples tightened, and she was quite sure that he noticed.

Her pulse took off at a giddy gallop.

'I thought you'd like a cuppa,' he said.

'It's all right.' Carrie knew she sounded nervous. Out of her depth. She had no idea how to deal with this. Quickly, she swung her legs over the side of the bed and reached for the bathrobe that she'd left on a nearby chair. 'I'll come out.'

'As you wish,' he said politely. 'I'll be in the kitchen.'

She could tell by the mix of amusement and sympathy in his eyes that he knew exactly why she was nervous.

She was sure he'd guessed at her lustful interest in him. It was almost as if her body remembered...*everything*...

They went out for breakfast. Max suggested that Carrie should choose a venue, and without hesitation she selected at a café with a deck built over the waterfront.

A friendly young waiter with a shaved head and a gold earring welcomed them with a beaming smile. 'Haven't seen you guys in a while.'

To Carrie's astonishment, he stepped forward and smacked kisses on both her cheeks.

'Hey, Jacko,' Max responded, giving the waiter a hearty handshake and back-slap. 'Good to see you.'

'And it's great to see you two. How are you both?'

Carrie gulped, wondering how well she knew this fellow and how much she should tell him.

'We're really well, thanks,' Max said smoothly. 'It's been a good wet season, which always helps.'

Jacko nodded, then shot a quick glance to a table right next to the water. 'Must have known you two were coming. Your favourite table's free.'

'How's that for timing?' Max was grinning as they took their seats.

Carrie hoped that her smile didn't look too surprised as Jacko flicked out a starched napkin and deftly placed it, unfolded, on her lap.

'Shall I fetch menus?' he asked with a knowing smile. 'Or would you just like your usual?'

*Their usual?* Carrie knew she must look stunned and confused. She shot a quick look to Max, who sent her a reassuring smile.

'Our usual, of course. We can't break with tradition,' he told Jacko.

Carrie was shaking her head as Jacko left. 'Don't tell me I picked our favourite restaurant?'

Max smiled again, and his blue eyes shone in a way that set off another starburst inside her. 'It was uncanny,' he said. 'There are half a dozen places along this strand, but you zeroed straight in on this place, like it was the only possible option.'

'I have no memory of ever coming here.'

'Perhaps your taste buds remember?'

And there it was again…the disturbing possibility that her body remembered the secrets her mind withheld.

Carrie took a deep breath. 'So, what's my usual breakfast order when I'm here?'

'Pancakes.'

'Really?' She gaped at him. 'But I—I thought…I've always been so careful with carbs.'

'Paris cured you of that,' Max assured her. 'Whenever you eat here you always have blueberry pancakes and whipped cream.'

Walking back along the foreshore, on a path that wove between lush tropical gardens, Max had an urge to take Carrie's hand or to slip his arm around her shoulders, just as he always had in the past.

It was tempting to ignore the letter she'd written, claiming she'd grown tired of life in the bush. Damn tempting to take advantage of this situation. To simply carry on as if their marriage was fine.

He knew the chemistry was still there. More than once he'd caught Carrie checking him out, and he'd seen the familiar flash of interest and awareness in her eyes.

'Max?' She turned to him now, and her lovely dark

brown eyes held a hint of excitement. 'How long does it take to drive to your place?'

Caught out, he frowned. 'My place?'

'Your property. Riverslea Downs.'

'About six hours. Why?'

'There's still time to go, then, if we got away quickly?'

'You want to go there today?'

She smiled uncertainly. 'I think so—yes.'

Max held his breath. This didn't make sense. Yesterday Carrie had been dead unhappy to find herself in the Outback, and she'd seemed so relieved to arrive in this city. 'But I thought you liked the idea of staying here?' he hedged. 'Didn't you want to go shopping? Perhaps see a movie?'

It would be like dating all over again, he'd decided. A chance to gain some ground before her memory returned.

Carrie shrugged. 'I'm sure shopping and movies would be lovely. I admit that did seem like a good idea yesterday.' Her mouth twisted in a shy, lopsided smile. 'But it's not going to help me, is it? If I stay here in the city I'll have a pleasant time, but I won't learn anything about the important things—about our life together in the Outback.'

'No, I don't suppose so…' he said, reluctantly.

'I thought it might help my memory if I'm surrounded by familiar, everyday sights—or at least by things that *should* be familiar.'

Max suppressed a sigh, suspecting that she was right, but knowing also that those same familiar things she was so keen to see would almost certainly displease her when her memory returned. If not before.

'As I said, I'm willing to stay or to leave,' he told

her. 'The apartment booking's flexible, so whatever you prefer.'

'Thank you, Max. I think I'd like to go…home.' The word *home* was added shyly.

Max swallowed. 'Right.'

The look she gave him now held a shimmer of amusement. 'Are you always this obliging?'

'Hell, no.' It was a poor attempt at a joke, so he tempered the retort with an answering smile. 'Make the most of my good mood while you can.'

# CHAPTER FIVE

It was late in the afternoon when they arrived at Riverslea Downs. Max steered the vehicle off the highway and onto a dirt bush track and suddenly gumtrees crowded on either side, throwing striped shadows over the ground in front of them.

Carrie felt quite exhausted, even though she'd dozed off and on for a great deal of the journey, but now she sat forward, suddenly awake and keen to see everything. This was Max's land. Her land, too, if she was his wife.

It was hard to believe that she potentially owned such a big slice of country. While she was growing up in Sydney their yard had comprised a pocket-handkerchief-sized front lawn and a small courtyard at the back. Now, the twists and turns in the track showed her glimpses of endless paddocks dotted with silvery hump-backed cattle. She had a vague idea they were Brahmans.

Every so often she also caught sight of a stretch of river, wide and sleepy and gently curving, with sandy beaches and banks lined with bottlebrush and paperbark trees that trailed weeping branches low to the water.

'I imagine it would be fun to canoe down a beautiful river like that,' she told Max.

'Yeah, it is.'

His wry smile prompted her to ask, 'Have we done that? Have we canoed down there?'

'It was one of the first things you wanted to do after you arrived here. We paddled all the way to the junction at Whitehorse Creek and we camped overnight at Big Bend.'

'Goodness.' Carrie couldn't remember having ever been canoeing or camping in her life—not even when she was in high school. And yet, as a child, she *had* been fascinated by the stories of Pocahontas and Hiawatha. She'd adored the idea of having her own canoe and paddling silently down beautiful rivers, stealthily gliding beneath overhanging trees or boldly discovering what lay around the next bend. 'Did I enjoy it?'

This brought another wryly crooked smile from Max. 'You loved it.'

She had no trouble imagining herself in a canoe, but the picture blurred when she thought about camping out in the bush and lying on the ground in a sleeping bag. She wondered if it had been a double sleeping bag that she had shared with Max.

*Damn.* Almost every time she thought about her life with this man her mind seemed to zap straight to sex. The more time she spent with him the worse it got. Already her curiosity about their love life was driving her crazy.

She was so aware—almost *desperately* aware—of Max's physical presence. He was so very big and masculine. She found it impossible to ignore his size and strength, not to think about him as a lover. As *her* lover. She couldn't help wondering about the secrets they'd shared in the bedroom.

But she wished she could switch off these pestering thoughts. Until her memory returned it would be much more sensible to forget that Max was her husband. She should think of him as a polite stranger who was hosting her on his property for a day or two.

Unfortunately the knowledge that this man really was her lover was like an electric current that couldn't be turned off. It ran through Carrie, keeping her constantly feverish and aware of his broad shoulders and strong hands, of the way his hair sat against the back of his suntanned neck. Everything about him held her attention—the sensual curve of his mouth, the smoulder in his compelling blue eyes that hinted at private knowledge, at the secrets her memory had blocked out.

It was all very distressing, and she was grateful now to be distracted when the track opened out of the dense bush into open grassland again. Ahead of them stood the homestead, surrounded by lawns and shrubbery and big old shade trees, and then paddocks of pale grass.

Carrie tried to remember if she'd ever seen it before, but she could only recall photographs of Outback homesteads in magazines.

As far as she could tell this one seemed pretty typical. It was low-set and sprawling, with timber walls painted white, an iron roof and deep, shady verandas on three sides. Hanging baskets of ferns made the verandas look cool and inviting, and she could see a table and chairs set outside on the grass under one of the shade trees.

Beyond the house were weathered timber stockyards and an iconic Outback windmill, silhouetted against the orange afternoon sky, its sails circling slowly. There was also a cluster of sheds housing tractors and other farm machinery, and a cottage or two.

As they drew closer to the house a dog—a golden Labrador—rose from the front veranda, gave a vigorous wag of its tail, then came racing down the steps and across the lawn towards them.

'What a gorgeous dog,' Carrie said.

'She's yours,' Max told her. 'Her name's Clover.'

'I called a dog *Clover*?'

He shot her a quick grin. 'You insisted.'

She'd had a favourite book when she was very small, about a golden puppy called Clover. How she'd loved that book, and how amazing, now, that she was not only married to a man she didn't know, but she owned a real-life Clover.

Max pulled the car up on to a gravel drive in front of the homestead and Clover danced in happy circles, eager for Carrie to get out.

Max was there first. 'Take it easy,' he ordered, reaching for Clover's collar and holding her at his heel. 'We've had a long journey and Carrie's tired. We don't want you bowling her over.'

Grateful for his intervention, Carrie took a deep breath. She had never been a 'dog person', and Clover was large and seemed very determined to jump at her. Max opened the door for her and took her hand as she stepped down.

The dog stood obediently still now, looking up at Carrie with eager brown eyes, panting excitedly, her tail waving madly like an over-wound metronome.

'Should I pat her?' Carrie asked.

An emotion that might have been pain flashed in Max's eyes. 'Of course,' he said. 'She's not a working dog. She's your pet—your companion. She's been yours since she was six weeks old.' With a grimacing smile, he added, 'She loves a scruff between her ears.'

'Right…' Carrie knew it was foolish to be nervous.

Clover had a very non-threatening, friendly face. In fact she was almost grinning. 'Hey there, girl,' she said, tentatively touching her hand to the top of the dog's head. The hair there was short, not especially soft or silky. She gave a little scratch and managed not to flinch when Clover thanked her with a wet lick on her wrist.

'She's missed you,' Max said, and he looked incredibly sad.

'That's…nice.' Carrie couldn't think of anything else to say.

The dog stayed close, her warm body pressed against Carrie's legs, as Max mounted the three short steps and crossed the veranda to open the front door.

After a bit, Carrie followed him. 'Is Clover a house dog? Does she come inside?'

'Sure—especially when there's a thunderstorm. She's terrified of the noise. Particularly the lightning.'

'Poor girl.' Carrie offered her another comforting pat. *I think I'm going to like you.*

'Mostly she's happy to loll about here on the veranda,' said Max. 'Or she loves running out on the lawn, chasing crows.'

Carrie turned her attention to the verandas. There were several chairs, with blue and white striped canvas seats and extended arms and, in the corner, a cane dining setting. She thought how nice it would be to eat there, with the view of the paddocks and the distant hills.

Beside the front door there was a pair of riding boots, dusty and well creased with wear. She imagined Max coming in from riding his horse and taking those boots off before he entered the house. On the wall was a row of heavy hooks, where battered and dusty Akubra hats hung, along with a dark brown oilskin coat and a bright yellow raincoat. She wondered if the raincoat was hers.

The front door was painted white, with panels of red and blue glass. Max pushed the door open and Carrie saw a long hallway running deep into the house, giving a glimpse of a modern lemon and white kitchen at the far end. The tongue-and-groove walls of the hall were painted white, and the floor was polished timber.

There was a large mirror on the wall, and beneath it a narrow table which housed a blue pottery bowl filled with water-washed stones and an elegant, tall glass vase holding lovely white lilies. Carrie had to look carefully to see that the lilies were artificial.

Everything was very tasteful, very clean and tidy.

*This is my home*, she thought. *I've probably vacuumed and mopped this floor a hundred times. Max and I have eaten on this veranda, and no doubt I've prepared meals in that kitchen.*

But it was all so disappointingly strange and foreign. She remembered nothing.

Not a thing.

Despair washed over her like a drenching of cold water. It was such a huge let-down.

She had been hoping that familiar surroundings would jog at least a spark of memory. Now, entering this unknown homestead, she could feel an anxious knot tightening in the centre of her chest. Surely somewhere in this house she would find things from her past? Things she recognised?

'Go on in and make yourself at home,' Max said, but his smile couldn't quite hide the worried shadow in his eyes. 'I'll get our bags.'

Carrie went down the hallway, looking into the rooms

that opened off it. Most of the furniture in the lounge room and dining room was old. Antique, really. It looked as if it had been in the house for generations, but it was well cared for and quite beautiful, giving an air of timeless graciousness.

At the main bedroom, Carrie stopped. This room was the room she'd shared with Max. Here they'd made love, and the very thought stole her breath.

The room was especially lovely, with fresh white walls and gauzy floor-length, white curtains at the deep windows. The timber floor glowed a warm honey colour in the afternoon sunlight. The bed was covered by a white quilt, and the decorative touches in the cushions and rugs were in various shades of lime and green.

The tastefulness of the decor no longer surprised her. She'd obviously grown up, moved on from the gaudy array of colours she'd loved in her teens and early twenties.

As she stepped into the room Max appeared behind her with the luggage. He set the holdall with her things on the floor, just inside the door, and Carrie couldn't bring herself to ask him where he planned to sleep. She couldn't bear to go through all that silly stress and indecision again. It was easier to assume they would remain sleeping apart until her memory returned.

'Thanks,' she said simply.

'Can I get you anything? Would you like a cuppa?'

'I'd love one, Max, but I can get it. You don't have to keep waiting on me. I'm sure I'll be able to find my way around the kitchen. There are probably things you want to see to.'

He nodded. 'If you're OK here, I'll duck down to Barney's cottage and explain how the land lies.'

'How the land lies?'

He looked embarrassed and gave a shrug. 'About your memory loss and—and everything.'

'Oh, yes—of course.'

'His house is just beyond the machinery shed. I won't be gone long.'

Carrie nodded, but she felt ridiculously alone when Max left.

The old stockman was sitting on the veranda, making the most of the fading daylight as he mended a saddle, his aged blue cattle dog sprawled at his feet.

'Hey, there,' he called as Max approached. 'Saw you drive in.' He set the saddle on the floor and then looked up at Max, his grey eyes sombre and narrowed, as if he was trying to suss out the situation. 'How's Carrie?'

'Actually, she's pretty good,' Max told him. 'I had to take her into Townsville for tests, but there's no sign of serious head injury. She doesn't feel too bad, just a bit headachy and tired.'

'That's lucky.'

'Yeah.' They both knew plenty of horror stories about falls from horses. 'The only problem is her memory,' Max said. 'At the moment she seems to have amnesia.'

'Her memory's gone?'

Max nodded. 'She shouldn't be left alone. I've brought her back here with me.'

The old guy's eyes widened. 'Here? To the homestead?'

'She just needs to rest and wait, basically.' Mac caught the look in Barney's eyes and let out a sigh. 'I know it's a weird situation. It's going to be tricky for a day or two. Carrie doesn't remember anything about this place.'

'Nothing?'

'Zilch.'

'Blow me down. So she doesn't know about—?' Barney stopped and gave a slow, disbelieving shake of his head. His mouth twisted in an embarrassed attempt at a smile. 'So she doesn't know how things are between the two of you?'

'No.' The admission brought a dark grimace from Max. 'She doesn't remember me at all. Can't even remember how we met.'

Tipping his hat back, Barney scratched at his head, a sure sign that he was flummoxed. 'That's a turn-up for the books.'

He opened his mouth, as if he was going to say something else, but then seemed to think better of it. Instead, he stood with a worried little frown, letting his gnarled hands rest on his skinny hips as he stared off into the distant sunset.

'So how are things here?' Max asked. 'Everything OK?'

Barney blinked at the change of subject. 'Yeah, sure. No problem, Max. I checked all the bores and the dams and took some molasses out to that mob in the western paddock.'

'Good man. We should probably wean those calves in the next week or so.' Shooting a quick glance over his shoulder to the homestead, Max said, 'Anyway, I'd better be getting back now, to see if Carrie needs anything. I just wanted to let you know—to warn you about the situation.'

'Yeah...thanks, mate.' The grave expression in Barney's grey eyes lingered for a moment, then abruptly disappeared. Next moment he was grinning. 'You never know, Max, this accident of Carrie's could have a really good outcome.'

'You reckon?' Max made no attempt to hide his doubt.

'Why not? Carrie could be—I don't know—like Sleeping Beauty or something. This could turn out all right.'

'I wouldn't bank on it, old fella.'

'Don't be a pessimist. I reckon it could be a godsend, and we'll have you and Carrie back together like a flamin' fairytale.'

Max couldn't hold back a bitter clipped laugh. 'You mean she'll wake up and realise I'm her prince?'

'Why not?'

Barney's naive optimism was like a knife twisting in Max's gut. 'This is real life,' he said grimly, and he turned abruptly, to escape the disappointment in his old friend's eyes.

Carrie was tired, and she knew she should probably lie down. The doctor had told her to get plenty of rest. She was too uneasy, though, too anxious to explore the mystery that was her new home.

Nursing her mug of tea, she wandered around the house, studying the unfamiliar everyday items—the cooking utensils in the kitchen cupboards, the things in the bathroom, including a woman's dressing gown hanging on a hook behind the door, and the dirty clothes basket overflowing with Max's jeans and blue shirts. There were twin washbasins—one with a mug of shaving gear beside it and the other with a pretty bottles of creamy pink liquid soap and moisturiser.

It was all so 'settled' and so strangely normal.

In the hallway again, she stopped to study the paintings on the walls. There was nothing remarkable, but they were very pleasant—several landscapes, a bowl of tropical fruit and a vase of wildflowers set by an open window. Looking a little closer, Carrie saw that most of the paintings carried the same signature. *Marnie Rossiter.* She wondered if Marnie was one of Max's relatives.

In the lounge room she found a large portrait, also painted by Marnie, of a man who bore a surprising resemblance to Max. His father? Grandfather?

So far she could find nothing that hinted strongly at her own presence in this house. She felt invisible—a generic wife.

A small cyclone of panic started inside her. Perhaps this *was* a terrible hoax, after all. Max had kidnapped her.

The silly thought had barely formed when she moved into the next room, the dining room, and saw a collection of silver-framed photographs on the old-fashioned sideboard.

*Oh, my God.*

Carrie hurried closer and there she was. Dressed as a bride, she was coming down a church aisle, arm in arm with Max Kincaid.

Her hands were shaking as she carefully set her mug down on a mat and picked up the photo to study it more closely. Her dress was gorgeous, soft and floaty and romantic, with a sweet off-the-shoulder neckline. And Max looked heart-stoppingly handsome in a black tuxedo.

But it wasn't the clothes that grabbed her attention and held it. It was the shining happiness in her face. In Max's face, too.

*Radiant* was the only word to describe how they looked. Radiant and triumphant. Glowing with unmistakable joy.

The ache in Carrie's chest bloomed, pressing under

her ribs and making her feel sick as she stared miserably at the photo, wishing she could remember, wishing she could experience again the obvious truth it showed her.

As she set the photo down, however, she felt a reassuring warmth begin to spread slowly through her as she realised that her feelings for Max were valid. It was OK that she'd liked him from the moment he'd appeared in her hospital room. It was fine that her initial liking was growing deeper with every hour she spent in his company.

She didn't have to fight the emotions and longing he roused in her. He was her husband. He loved her. They loved each other.

Wonderfully reassured, she looked at the other photos. Her good friends Joanne and Heidi had been her bridesmaids. They were dressed alike, in charcoal-grey silk, and carried pink and white bouquets.

Then her attention was caught by another photo, and in this one she was arriving at the wedding, leaving a sleek black car decorated with white satin ribbons and walking into the church on the arm of a tall and rather striking silver-haired older man. He must have given her away, but although he looked ever so vaguely familiar Carrie couldn't place him. He certainly wasn't an uncle or an old family friend, and she'd never known her father. He'd died when she was a baby.

She was still puzzling over the man's identity when she heard the fly-screen door in the kitchen swing open, then shut, followed by Max's footsteps. He came into the hall and stopped at the doorway.

Carrie turned.

'Hi, there,' he said quietly.

Just looking at him, she felt her heart-rate kick up a notch. 'How's Barney?' she remembered to ask.

'Fine. I explained how things are. He's looking forward to catching up with you at some stage.'

'Right.' Feeling awkward about any future conversation with the unknown Barney, Carrie pointed to the photos. 'I've just found these. I guess they're the final proof that we tied the knot.' She tried to sound lighthearted and amused as she said this, knowing that Max must be tired of her looking worried all the time.

A dark stain coloured his neck. 'You were a beautiful bride, Carrie.'

'You scrubbed up pretty well yourself.'

A brief smile flickered, but he didn't look happy.

*Why?* Carrie felt a new niggle of alarm. Was she behaving so very differently from usual? She wondered what kind of wife she'd been. Affectionate? Given to passionate impulses? Right now she wished Max would take her in his arms and kiss any doubts away.

It wasn't going to happen. He was being too careful.

She picked up the photograph of herself with the strange silver-haired older man. 'Who's this fellow? Did he give me away?'

'Yes.' Max came closer and his gaze was serious now as he fixed on the photo she held. 'He's a neighbour.'

'One of *your* neighbours?' she asked, feeling more puzzled than ever.

'Yes.'

'What's his name?'

'Doug Peterson.'

'Why on earth would *he* give me away?'

Max's eyes shimmered with sympathy. 'Carrie, he's your father.'

# CHAPTER SIX

'MY FATHER?' SHOCK EXPLODED through Carrie, zapping and bursting in a white-hot blast.

'Yes,' Max said gently, but with inescapable certainty.
*But I don't have a father. My father's dead.*

Her emotions were rioting—a panicky mix of anger, confusion and doubt.

All through her childhood she'd longed for a father. So many times she'd tried to imagine him, conjuring up her perfect fantasy. A strong, kind, loving man who was inclined to spoil her...

She'd been so conscious of the lack of a father figure. It had made her noticeably different from the other kids. Her parents weren't merely divorced. Her father wasn't a man to be visited on weekends or during school holidays. He was dead. Gone for ever.

Now... This news...

A wave of dizziness swept over her and her legs felt as weak as water. She might have slumped to the floor if Max hadn't caught her.

'Hey, take it easy.' His rock-solid arms held her safe and she felt so helpless she let her head rest on his shoulder, grateful for his strength.

'You should be lying down,' he said.

'But you have to tell me what you meant. How can that man be my father?'

'One thing at a time.'

Before she quite knew what was happening Max had slipped one arm around her shoulders, the other beneath her knees, and with breathtaking ease swung her feet from the ground. He carried her as if she weighed no more than a kitten. Without further comment, he took her to the bedroom.

For a brief few moments she enjoyed the heady luxury of being carried by her strong, hunky husband before he laid gently her on the big white bed.

'Thanks,' she said as she sank into the pillows. 'I'm OK, though, Max. It was just such a shock about my father. I—I don't understand.'

'I know. I'll explain.' Carefully, he stepped a discreet distance from the bed, his expression both concerned and sympathetic. 'But first let me get you a drink of water.'

'No, I don't need water. I've just had a cup of tea.' Impatient now, Carrie rose up on one elbow. The loss of her father had always been a black hole in her life. She *had* to know more. 'Tell me about this Doug Peterson.'

After a moment's hesitation Max moved closer again. To her surprise, and secret delight, he sat on the edge of the bed, his thigh almost touching her leg, leaving her excruciatingly aware of the minuscule gap between them.

'You've already been through the shock of discovering your father once before,' he said. 'I'm sorry you have to go through it again. It was hard enough the first time.'

Carrie frowned. 'So when did it happen? How did I meet him?'

'Doug and Meredith were at Grant and Cleo's wedding—the same wedding in Sydney where we met.'

'Is Meredith Doug's wife?'

'Yes, his new wife. Well, not so new now. They've been married for about ten years. She's also Grant's aunt.'

'OK…' Carrie was only just managing to follow the links between these strangers she'd never met. 'So I met you *and* this man who claims to be my father on the same night?'

It sounded incredible.

'He *is* your father, Carrie.' Max's voice was warm with sympathy. 'Your mother married Doug when she was just twenty-one. She's admitted to—er—let's say "fudging the truth" when she told you that he'd died.'

*Whack.*

It was like stumbling and falling into the black hole that had always haunted her. Carrie felt disorientated again—as if she could barely tell which way was up. All these years she'd had a father.

How could her mother have lied about something so terribly important?

'Why would she do that?'

'I'm not exactly sure.' Max frowned at a spot on the floor. 'As I understand it, Sylvia realised she'd made a mistake soon after she married Doug. She couldn't stand living in the Outback. The isolation really got to her.'

That was certainly believable. Her mum had always been a city woman. No doubt about that. She thrived on getting together with her girlfriends and going for coffee and to art galleries and the theatre.

'Sylvia didn't want you to know about Doug,' Max added. 'She was afraid you'd insist on visiting him. I think she was terrified of sending you away for holidays on his property. I've always thought—'

Max broke off and his mouth tightened. He seemed

to be thinking through the best way to word what he needed to tell her.

'I think your mother might have been scared she'd lose you,' he said gently. 'Anyway, for whatever reason, she persuaded Doug to keep his distance.'

'But to say he was dead was so *extreme*.'

It was cruel.

Knowing her mother, though, Carrie thought it was also highly credible. She could remember the way her mother used to carry on whenever there was a story on the news about graziers, or the Outback, or drought.

'Mum used to say that anyone who lived in the bush was mad. Reckoned they shouldn't complain and ask for government assistance because they'd chosen to live out there.'

'Yes, I know.' Max was scowling now and his mouth was a grim downward curving line.

Carrie wondered if she'd offended him. 'Obviously I didn't agree with her,' she said.

He didn't respond to this. He didn't meet her gaze either, and she wondered what this meant. Had she become like her mother? Had she also found the Outback lifestyle too hard? It was a disappointing thought, but it was also quite possible, she supposed—perhaps even likely. She was a city girl at heart, like her mum.

Or was she?

If only she knew.

She thought how incredibly emotional the discovery of her father must have been for everyone involved— herself, her mother *and* her father. But it was hard to feel those emotions now, when she had no memory of that meeting.

Carrie was more interested in the man in front of her.

'Tell me about *us*,' she said, driven by a sudden burning need to know.

Max's blue eyes widened with something close to shock. 'Us?'

'I love how happy we look in those wedding photos. Is—is it still like that for us?'

Max swallowed. and for a terrible moment he looked upset. A hint of silver shimmered in his gorgeous blue eyes.

Fear clutched at Carrie's heart. What was the matter? Was their marriage in trouble?

'I'll be honest,' he said eventually, and his gaze was once again steady and warm, making her wonder if she'd imagined his earlier distress. 'I still love you as much as I did on our wedding day, Carrie.'

She shivered. They were lovely words to hear, but why didn't Max look happier? Was it simply because he was worried about her amnesia? Or was there something else?

'What about me?' she had to ask. 'Have I been a good wife?' Good grief, that sounded so pathetic. Hastily, she amended her question. 'Have I made you happy?'

With a heartbreakingly crooked smile Max reached out and traced a gentle line down her cheek with his thumb. 'You've made me happier than I ever dared to hope,' he said.

But his smile was so sad that Carrie felt inexplicably depressed. And completely confused.

A heavy sigh escaped her.

Max must have read this as a signal and he stood.

'You should try not to worry about any of this for now,' he said. 'You need to rest.'

She supposed he was right, but she'd rest more easily

if she didn't sense that there was something vitally important he hadn't told her.

'Take it easy in here and I'll fix you something to eat,' he said.

In an instant Carrie was sitting up. 'I don't expect you to wait on me.'

'It will only be something simple. How does grilled cheese on toast sound?'

'Oh…' Grilled cheese on toast was her favourite comfort snack, and right now she couldn't think of anything she would like better. Max must have known that. She could very easily have kissed him. 'That would be perfect,' she said with a smile. 'Thank you.'

His mouth tilted in a funny little answering smile and he sent her a comical salute before he left the room. She wondered if this was an old joke between them.

When would she know? When would any of this make sense?

When the phone rang in the kitchen, Max answered it quickly.

'Oh, it's you, Max.' His mother-in-law made no attempt to hide her disappointment. 'I was hoping to speak to Carrie.'

'She's resting, Sylvia. I'm afraid the long journey has tired her.'

'Of *course* it will have tired her. I can't believe you dragged the poor girl all the way out there in her condition.'

Max grimaced. 'It was Carrie's decision to come home.'

'*Home?*' There was no missing the scoffing tone in Sylvia's voice now. 'I'm quite sure Carrie doesn't think of Riverslea as her home any more.'

Just in time, Max bit back a four-letter word. He was at the end of his patience.

'But the more important question,' his mother-in-law continued, 'is whether my daughter is in any condition to make wise choices.'

This was a question Max had asked himself, but he wasn't prepared to concede a major point to The Dragon. 'Carrie seems perfectly lucid.'

Sylvia sniffed. 'Well, I'll make no bones about it. I'm not happy about this situation.'

That was hardly the surprise of the century. Sylvia hadn't been happy from the moment she'd met Max. When their meeting had been closely followed by Doug Peterson's revelations, Sylvia had put on such a turn that she'd had to spend a night in hospital. Max had felt sorry for her at the time, but his sympathy had been sorely tested over the years that had followed.

'Sylvia, can I suggest you *don't* tell Carrie how you feel about this when you speak to her? It wouldn't be helpful.'

There was a distinct gasp on the end of the line. 'I'll thank you not to lecture me on how to speak to my own daughter.'

With no polite response at the ready, Max held his tongue.

'I believe in speaking my mind,' Sylvia continued. 'And there's something I need to say to you, Max. I'll be upfront.'

'I'm all ears.'

'Don't be facetious. I'm worried about Carrie. I'm concerned that you plan to take advantage of this situation.'

This time Max gritted his teeth so tightly it was a wonder his jaw didn't crack. 'What the hell are you implying, Sylvia? That I'll seduce Carrie while her memory's gone?'

'Well…yes. That *is* my concern. Carrie's vulnerable right now.'

'I'm aware of that,' he said coldly. 'And I'll ask you to give me some credit for acting in my wife's best interests.'

'Well, yes, but I happen to know…'

Sylvia paused and Max was gripped by a new tension. Did his mother-in-law know that Carrie had planned to leave him?

There was a heavy sigh on the end of the line. 'I trust you'll keep your word, then,' Sylvia said, although she didn't sound satisfied.

'I'll tell Carrie you called and that you send her your love.'

'Thank you. I'll call again in the morning.'

Max's thoughts were grim as he set the phone back in its cradle. Sylvia had always resented him for luring her daughter away from the bright lights and into the depths of the Outback.

Not that Carrie had needed much luring. She'd been dead keen to leave the city when they'd first met. With her lovely dark eyes gleaming with excitement, she'd declared she would follow him to the Antarctic, to the top of Everest or to Timbuktu, as long as they could be together. Much to her mother's despair.

Max remembered again the one and only time Sylvia had come to Riverslea Downs to stay with them. She'd barely ventured outside, even to sit on the veranda. She'd spent most of the five-day visit ensconced in the lounge room, dressed as if she was expecting a visit from the Queen.

With her hair just so, her nails carefully painted and

pearls at her throat and ears, she'd worn a petulant frown as she'd filled in the time when Carrie had been too busy to entertain her by doing cross-stitch.

There had been all-round relief when she left. Her parting gift had been a cross-stitched cushion bearing the message *Families are For Ever*.

Max had read this as a threat.

But tonight he had a deeper worry than his mother-in-law. He was haunted by the inescapable fact that Carrie had followed in her mother's footsteps and walked away from her marriage. And yet this evening she'd asked that heartbreaking question.

*Have I made you happy?*

He'd told her the truth. She *had* made him happier than he'd ever dared to hope. For two and a half years they'd worked in harmony together on the property, they'd been good mates and passionate lovers.

He was unwilling to tell Carrie the rest of it—that she'd lost her love of the land and left him. That mere days ago she'd trampled on his heart with hob-nailed boots.

A soft dawn filtered through the white curtains. In the vague state between dreaming and waking properly, Carrie lay staring about her at the room—at the painting of a misty hillside, at the white dressing table and pretty green glass bowl that held a jumble of her earrings. Everything felt familiar, and for a moment she felt as if she remembered it all…remembered it from a time before yesterday when Max had brought her home.

But as soon as she tried to pin down those memories they drifted away like cobwebs in a breeze, leaving her with nothing. Not a single sense of ever having seen this room before her accident, or the house, or the man who shared it with her.

She wondered where Max had spent the night. And then she couldn't help wondering what it had been like when he'd slept in here with her. Not the sex—she got far too hot and bothered whenever she thought about their naked bodies joined in passion. But she allowed herself to wonder about other intimacies.

Did she sometimes reach out and touch her husband during the night? Just because she could and because she liked to reassure herself that he was there, warm and breathing by her side? Did she sleep in his arms? Or snuggle into the solid warmth of his back?

Or did they lie unromantically far apart, with as much distance between them as possible?

Sobered by this last possibility, Carrie got up. She found clean clothes in the wall of built-in cupboards and got dressed. She chose jeans and a lavender polo shirt. She'd always associated lavender with old ladies, but when she checked herself in the dressing table mirror she was surprised to see how well the colour suited her. She sorted through the earrings in the green glass bowl and was contemplating trying on a pair of gold hoops when she saw the little glass ring-stand behind the bowl.

It held a plain gold wedding band and a pretty, old-fashioned style engagement ring with two diamonds and a very thin, worn band.

This must be Max's grandmother's ring. She liked it immediately.

Carrie tried the rings on. They fitted her perfectly and she held her hand out, admiring them. Again she wondered why she'd left them behind when she went riding.

Max had said she'd made him happy, but he'd looked so sad when he'd said that. She couldn't shake off the feeling that there was something else—some kind of mystery connected to her marriage.

She was distracted from this worry by Clover coming through the bedroom doorway, greeting her with a madly waving tail.

'Oh, good morning, gorgeous golden girl.' Carrie gave the dog a pat and her heart melted when she saw the joy in Clover's eyes. 'Have you missed me?' she asked, rubbing her silky back and then her ears.

A moment later she was kneeling, looking into the dog's face as she patted her.

'You must know the truth, Clover. Are Max and I really happy? I wish you could tell me.'

Clover simply rolled onto her back, wanting her tummy scratched.

Carrie laughed. 'I'll take you for a walk later. Would you like that?'

It was quite clear from her sudden excitement that the dog understood this. And that the answer was yes.

With a final scruff for Clover's ears, Carrie went to the kitchen, where she found a handwritten note propped against the tea caddy beside the stove.

*Hi Carrie,*

*I had to leave early to do a few jobs. Back soon, but help yourself to breakfast. Everything's in the pantry or fridge.*

*I've taken my sat phone and will ring at eight-thirty. If you need me before then, the number is beside the phone.*

*Oh, and your father rang. He's invited us to lunch on Sunday.*

*M x*

It was silly, the way her spirits suddenly plummeted. But Carrie realised she'd been quite buoyed up, expecting to find Max ready to greet her.

Her disappointment was a good sign, she told herself. And those odd moments when she'd worried that something wasn't quite right about their marriage might be totally unnecessary. All in her head.

Given her amnesia, this last thought was ironic. She was smiling as she selected a teabag, and while the kettle was coming to the boil she opened the doors to the pantry to consider her breakfast options.

It was a dream of a pantry—almost a small room, lined with shelves and well ventilated, thanks to a small louvred window at the back. Large bags of flour and sugar stood on the floor, and the shelves were loaded with all kinds of tins and cartons, which Carrie supposed was necessary, given their vast distance from supermarkets.

There was also a surprising number of shelves with neatly labelled jars filled with what looked like home-made preserves—chutney, pickles, fruit and jam.

Carrie picked up a jar. The label seemed to have been printed on a computer. *'Carrie K's Spicy Tomato Chutney'*. It was rather professional, with a small black and white drawing of a gum tree at the bottom of the label and then the Riverslea Downs address and phone number in tiny print.

'Goodness.'

So now she was Carrie K? And what a surprise that she'd learned how to make chutneys and jams. In the past, if she'd thought about bottling and preserving at all, she would have considered it an ancient black art.

*Don't tell me I've turned into a domestic goddess.*

Intrigued, she chose a jar of mango jam and decided to try some on her breakfast toast. It was delicious, accompanied by a hot cup of tea, and she was spreading more jam on a second slice when the phone rang.

She jumped as the shrill sound broke into the silent house, then quickly hurried to answer it.

'Hello?' she said tentatively, wondering how she would cope if the caller expected her to know them.

'Carrie.' Max's deep voice reverberated down the line.

'Oh, hi.' She sounded suddenly breathless, no doubt due to the buzz that his deep baritone stirred in her.

'How are you this morning?' he asked.

'I'm fine, thanks.' But she knew there was almost certainly a subtext to his query. 'No new memories I'm afraid.'

'OK. Right… I've a few jobs to do out here. If it's OK with you, I might be another hour or so.'

'That's perfectly OK, Max. I'm quite happy to potter around here. Oh, one thing. Have you already fed Clover?'

'Yes.'

She thought he sounded pleased by her question.

'She shouldn't need anything else till tonight.'

'Right. Thanks.'

As soon as Carrie had hung up she dialled her mother's number. After initial pleasantries, she got straight to the point. 'Max told me about Doug Peterson, Mum.'

'Oh.'

'We're going to his place for lunch on Sunday.'

Her mother didn't respond to this.

'I can't *believe* you told me he was dead.'

'Carrie, now's not a good time.'

'Not a good time?' Surely she was justified?

'It's complicated and too painful for me. You'll know the whole story when you get your memory back.'

'Is that all you can say? Wait till I get my memory back?'

'I'm sorry, love. I don't think it's worth rehashing. You and Doug are getting along fine these days, and that's all that matters for the moment.'

Deflated, Carrie rang off. She wondered if Doug Peterson was the reason her mother had been so flustered and vague in her earlier phone calls.

She looked about her, wondering what she should do now. What would she have normally done? It was a very strange situation to find herself in her own home but feeling like a stranger, a guest.

She washed the mug and plate she'd used and put them away, then made her bed and decided to take Clover for the promised walk.

Grabbing a hat from the hooks by the front door, she set off with the dog at her heels along a track that circled a couple of paddocks and a stockyard. Magpies called from the trees that lined the creek and a flock of budgerigars swept overhead in a pretty flash of green and yellow.

She drew a deep breath of crisp, eucalypt-scented air and felt an unexpected rush of good-to-be-alive happiness.

'Hello, there!'

Carrie whirled around as an unexpected voice came from across the paddock. She saw an elderly man, balding, with a fringe of white hair, dressed in typical Outback clothes—jeans and a long-sleeved cotton shirt—and waving his Akubra hat to catch her attention.

This had to be Barney, the old stockman. As he set his hat back on his head and came hurrying towards her on slightly bandy legs, Carrie retraced her steps and met him halfway.

'Good morning,' she said, politely holding out her hand.

'Morning, Carrie. I'm Barney Ledger.'

'I thought you must be.'

He had the wiry toughness of a man who'd spent his life in the bush, but his eyes were twinkling and his smile was gentle.

'It's good to have you back home, safe and sound,' he said as they shook hands.

'Thanks. I'm pleased to be back, I think. It's a bit weird to not remember anything.'

'Yeah, I bet it is.' Barney's face was a mass of creases as his smile deepened. 'Still, you know what they say about clouds and silver linings.'

'I guess…' Carrie supposed she sounded less enthusiastic than Barney would have liked, but she wasn't sure what particular silver linings Barney meant. 'At least the headache's gone now.'

'That's good news.' The old stockman fixed her with a steady gaze that she couldn't really avoid. 'I know you're at sixes and sevens right now, Carrie, but I don't think I'm speaking out of turn when I tell you that your husband, Max, is a really good bloke. He's as fine a man as you could hope to find anywhere.'

The sincerity of his praise for Max moved Carrie deeply. She wasn't sure how to respond. She nodded.

'He'll look after you,' Barney added, and there was

a heartfelt earnestness in his hazel eyes, almost as if he was willing her to pick up on a deeper, more significant message. Something more than the fact that Barney really loved and admired Max.

She sensed that he might also be worried about Max, and she wondered why. Was he concerned that she might say or do something to hurt her husband?

It was an unsettling possibility, hinting *again* at something not quite right about their relationship.

'Max has been looking after me beautifully,' she told Barney now, in a bid to reassure both herself and the old man. 'I'm very grateful.'

'That's the ticket.' He was smiling again, making deep creases from his eyes to the corners of his mouth. 'And if you ever need anything while Max is out on a job just give me a hoy. Pick up the phone and dial six. It's the extension to my place.'

'Yes, I will—thanks. Max left a note beside the phone explaining that.'

'Good.' Barney pointed to a small silver-roofed cottage behind them. 'I'm over there. Feel free to call in for a cuppa any time.'

'Thanks, Barney.' Carrie wondered if she should respond with a similar invitation for him to come up to the homestead, but she wasn't sure how the protocols worked in the bush. She looked down at Clover, sitting patiently at her side. 'I promised Clover a walk.'

Barney looked pleased about this. 'Great idea,' he said, and lifted a hand as if to wave them off. 'I'll see you around, then, and you know where to find me if you need me.'

'That's great. Thanks again for making me welcome.'

'Of course you're welcome, love. This is your *home*.'

'Yes, but it'll take a bit of getting used to.'

Carrie watched for a bit as he ambled off. She knew she should be grateful for the way things were turning out. Her situation could have been a lot worse. She might have been seriously injured when she fell from the horse. She might have woken up and become lost, wandering in the Outback completely disorientated.

Instead, she was here, in a comfortable house, with a husband who was keen to take care of her and now this old fellow, full of the open-hearted friendliness that people in the bush were famous for.

On top of that she was having lunch with her father on Sunday. It was time to stop feeling sorry for herself.

'Let's go down to the creek,' she said to Clover. 'I'm in a mood to explore.'

The dog happily followed her.

Carrie wasn't in the homestead when Max returned. He checked every room, just to make sure, his concern mounting with the sight of each empty space. He couldn't help fearing the worst—that she'd remembered. *Everything.*

His gut tightened at the thought. As he went through the entire house he steeled himself for her withdrawal, the sudden coolness in his wife's eyes as she reverted to the way she'd been before the accident.

But Carrie wasn't in any of the rooms.

He told himself there was no need to panic. She would be fine. But despite his resolve to stay cool, he felt unwanted fear snake coldly down his spine. The doctors might have been wrong about Carrie's head injury. She might have collapsed somewhere.

He rushed to the front veranda.

The dog was gone, but at least that meant Carrie wasn't alone. And there were no missing vehicles, so that was another good thing. She couldn't have gone too far. Even if she'd rung her father and asked him to come and collect her Doug Peterson wouldn't have had time to drive over here from Whitehorse Creek, so Carrie had to be on the property.

Standing at the top of the front steps, Max cupped his hands to either side of his mouth and called, 'Cooee!'

Almost immediately he heard an answering bark from Clover. The sound came from the creek, and Max's gut tightened another notch. What was Carrie doing down there? Was she lost? Had she slipped and fallen?

He cleared the steps in one jump and began to run.

But he was only halfway to the creek when he came to a skidding halt. Two figures were emerging from the scrub.

Carrie and Clover.

Max stood watching them as his heartbeats slowed. As his throat constricted. They looked so happy together, the woman in jeans and a shady Akubra and her dog deliriously joyous at her heels. It was a picture from the past, from the way things had once been. A picture to hold close.

But he had to remember it was only a mirage. It would melt when the truth came out.

Carrie drew nearer and waved to him. 'Hello!' she called.

He lifted his hand in response.

She was grinning. Glowing. Her dark eyes shining. His Carrie of old. He felt his heart crack.

'I hope you weren't worried about us,' she said as she reached him.

He managed a nonchalant shrug and wondered if she'd seen him racing like a mad man in a panic. 'I knew you couldn't be too far away.'

'We've had such a lovely walk—haven't we, Clover?' She bent down to rub the dog behind the ears, no longer tentative, as she'd been yesterday. He couldn't help watching the neat shape of her behind in close-fitting blue jeans.

Then she straightened again, still smiling. 'Isn't it beautiful down by the creek? And it's going to be even lovelier in a month or so, when all the wattle is flowering.'

Max wanted to kiss her. Wanted to taste those lovely smiling lips, to run his hands over the delicious curve of her butt, to haul her hard against him.

'It's looking good.' His voice was almost a growl. 'We've had a good wet season.'

Carrie laughed. 'And now I think I know why I'm so slim. It's all the healthy outdoor exercise.' She looked at him expectantly, as if she was waiting for him to confirm this.

'Sure,' he said quickly. He didn't want to tell her the truth—that her enchantment with the outdoors and everything about this lifestyle had diminished over the past six months.

'I met Barney,' she said next.

Barney. *Hell*. That showed what a state he was in. He should have spoken to the old guy before he panicked.

'He's a big fan of yours,' Carrie added.

Max frowned. He should have warned Barney to stay quiet. Last thing he needed was the old ringer turning into a high-pressure salesman, hoping to save his boss's marriage.

Together they turned back to the homestead, and Carrie asked companionably, 'So what have you been up to, Max?'

For a moment he thought she was going to tuck her arm through his, walk close, their bodies brushing, connecting, shooting sparks, the way they had as a matter of course before everything had gone wrong.

But there was no touching, and he forced his attention to Carrie's question. It was hard to remember that she knew nothing about his daily routine. 'I took molasses out to the cattle on the more marginal pasture. Then I mended a fence, and checked the dams and water troughs.'

He waited for her smile to fade, for her to sigh with her customary boredom.

Instead, she turned to him with another warm smile. 'I'd love to come out with you some time and see you at work with the cattle.'

*Oh, Carrie.*

# CHAPTER SEVEN

MAX CAME IN from the stockyards just on dusk, looking far sexier than any man had a right to look in dusty jeans and a torn and faded shirt. Carrie was smiling broadly as she produced a packed picnic basket.

'I was hit by an urge to have a camp fire,' she said. 'I thought we could cook our dinner down by the creek. Just sausages,' she added, when she saw his surprised frown.

She'd been fantasising about how crisp and crunchy the sausages would be—like on a barbecue, only better.

'I thought Clover could come, too.'

She could see that the suggestion had caught Max out. He looked quite shocked.

'Bad idea?' she asked.

'No.' He gave a quick shrug. 'Why not? Sounds great.' And then his lips tilted in a slow smile.

Carrie had been about to suggest that they invite Barney as well, but the utter sexiness of Max's smile prompted a quick change of heart. After all, her task here was to get to know her husband better.

She had found the perfect picnic spot on her morning walk, and she was pleased when Max approved of her choice—a low sandy bank in a deep bend of the river. Together, with Clover eagerly darting at their heels, they

gathered wood and kindling. While Carrie threw sticks
for Clover to fetch Max soon had a fire assembled and
crackling brightly.

It was a gorgeous evening to be outdoors, with the last
of the lavender and rose tints lingering in the sky and
the scents of smoke and burning gum leaves hanging on
the still, dusky air.

Carrie handed Max a beer. 'I'm sure you've earned
one.'

'Thanks.' He grinned as he snapped off the lid. 'Are
you having one?'

'I'm not supposed to at the moment.'

'Of course. Sorry. For a moment there I forgot.' Then
he grimaced. 'Ouch. Bad pun.'

They both smiled at this, and strangely, for a fleeting
second, Carrie fancied she could remember enjoying a
laugh and a camp fire meal in almost this exact spot.
But the feeling was a mere flash—gone so quickly she
couldn't hang on to it.

She wondered if this was the beginning—if her memory would return with little bursts of *déjà vu*.

But she didn't want to ponder too long…didn't want
to spoil the pleasant mood. The setting was magical. The
water was so still she could see the white trunks of the
paperbarks reflected in its surface. The dusk was so quiet
the only sounds were the faint crackle of the fire and the
far-off squawks of cockatoos calling to each other as they
headed for home.

Soon the sausages and sliced onions were sizzling in
the pan, and enticing smells added to the magic mood.

Sitting comfortably on a smooth rock, still warm from
the day's sun, she let the peace of the scene seep into

her. It was true, that old saying about the simplest things being the best.

She found herself watching Max, enjoying the easy athleticism of his movements as he crouched by the fire, then leapt up to grab another piece of wood from the pile they'd collected.

She was still watching as he kicked at a fallen coal with the toe of his boot, then leaned down to flip the sausages in the pan. 'Snags are almost done,' he said.

'Great,' Carrie said. 'I've made a salad.'

'Salad?' His expression was both amused and shocked. 'Green stuff?'

'Don't you like salad?'

He chuckled. 'Sure. But you can't beat a sausage with fried onions and tomato sauce wrapped in bread.'

When he grinned like that Carrie was in no mind to argue.

They stayed on the riverbank, enjoying the flickering firelight and the silvery path of the almost full moon as it rose majestically above the treetops.

Carrie, replete with crispy sausages, was glad that Max didn't want to rush back to the house. With Clover happily sprawled beside her, she sat hugging her knees and sneaking glimpses of Max's profile in the firelight.

'I proposed to you down here,' he said suddenly.

Carrie gasped, and almost immediately stupid tears sprang in her eyes as she tried desperately to imagine what must have been the most romantic moment of her life.

'How d-did it happen?' she stammered. 'Wh—what did you say?'

Max turned to her and his eyes flashed blue fire. Then

he smiled and pulled out a stick from the coals. There was a glowing ember at one end.

'It wasn't anything fancy,' he said. 'But there was a little sky-writing involved.'

He began to write in the air with the stick and the fiery ember glowed bright red and gold against the night sky. The movement caused sparks that hung in the air just long enough for Carrie to make out the words he was writing.

*MARRY ME*

She gave a delighted laugh. 'That's so cool! Simple and straight to the point. Did I write my reply?'

'You did,' he said quietly.

'I'm assuming I wrote *YES*?'

Max nodded and dropped the stick back into the fire. Then he gave a shrug and sighed.

Carrie supposed he felt frustrated. It was all so one-sided when he was the only one with memories. She wished that he would flirt a little, the way he must have when they first met. She wondered why he was holding back and began to worry again.

'How long have your family lived here?' she asked, feeling a need to steer the conversation in a safer direction.

'Almost a hundred and twenty years,' he said. 'There've been Kincaids on Riverslea for five generations.'

'Wow.' She was silent for a moment as she let this sink in. Clearly there was a huge family tradition associated with Riverslea Downs. The lovely old furniture in the homestead and the family portraits on the walls were just a part of it. There had been over a century of hard work put into managing the vast hectares. One family had served as ongoing custodians of a large slice of Australia. That was quite a legacy.

'So has the family name here always been Kincaid?' she asked. 'They never ran out of sons?'

Max poked a stick into the fire's embers, raising sparks. 'Not so far.'

A lump filled Carrie's throat as she registered the implications of this news. No doubt it was *her* job to produce the next generation of Kincaids. The thought of performing this duty with Max's help sent a bright flush rippling over her skin.

It wasn't long before curiosity nudged her to ask, 'How did I feel about the pressure to produce a son and heir?'

She gripped her knees tightly as she waited for Max's answer. In the firelight's glow she could see the blue of his eyes, the strong planes and angles of his cheekbones, his nose and his jaw.

He stared into the fire as he spoke. 'Last time we discussed it you were looking forward to the challenge.'

*Last time we discussed it.* It was a comment that opened up more questions than it answered. Deeply intimate questions about their marriage. But Carrie felt suddenly shy. It was too soon to try and go there.

'So, do you have brothers?' she asked instead.

'Two sisters.' Max's face relaxed and he smiled. 'Jane's a physiotherapist, married to a lawyer in Brisbane. Sally's a journalist, working in the UK.'

'How nice.' Carrie wished she could remember them. Being an only child, she liked the idea of sisters-in-law.

'And your parents?'

'Both alive and well. They've retired to the Sunshine Coast. Moved there shortly before our wedding.'

She had to ask. 'Did I get on well with them?'

'Sure,' Max said, but his face was in shadow now, so she couldn't see his expression. 'They're both very fond of you, Carrie.'

His voice sounded a little choked as he said this, making fine hairs lift on Carrie's arms. 'That's nice to know.'

'My parents were ready to retire,' Max said next. 'And they wanted to give me—to give *us*—a free rein here. So we could make our own decisions about running the property. They still visit quite regularly, though. They were here at Easter.'

'Oh.'

Her memory loss was like a brick wall that she kept running into. Perhaps she'd asked enough questions for tonight.

Conversation lapsed as Carrie repacked the picnic basket while Max stomped out the fire and poured water on the coals for good measure.

For him, this evening had been an excruciating test of willpower.

Carrie looked so happy tonight—like the Carrie he'd married. She'd eaten her charred sausages with the gleeful enthusiasm of a child, tipping her head back to catch dripping sauce and innocently showing off her white throat and the pale skin in the V of her blouse.

She was exactly like the starry-eyed happy bride he'd brought to Riverslea three years ago, doggedly determined to become the perfect Outback wife despite her mother's doleful warnings.

It was probably a mistake to have talked about the proposal, though. And it was unhelpful now for Max to recall the several times that he and Carrie had made love down here on the riverbank, spreading a picnic rug on the sand and stripping naked in the glow of the fire, falling onto the rug together and driving each other to ecstasy.

Tonight it had taken every ounce of his self-restraint to keep his distance. The memories had run hot and his body had throbbed with wanting. It hadn't helped that Carrie had been flirting. Her lovely dark eyes had shone with that special excitement and anticipation he knew so well, stirring memories of how eagerly she'd made love.

His imagination raced ahead. He tasted the sweetness of her lips, felt the silky smoothness of her skin, the soft swell of her breasts beneath his hands. It would have been all too easy to take liberties tonight. Delicious, tempting, glorious liberties.

The longing had nearly killed him, but he'd given his word to Sylvia. And even if he hadn't there was every chance that Carrie would be furious when she regained her memory and realised he'd taken advantage of her.

It had been a cruel irony, though, to watch his wife's unrestrained enjoyment of the campfire and the bush. Carrie had no idea that she'd changed so completely in recent months—that she'd lost interest in lovemaking and had scorned outdoor activities, claiming that all aspects of the bush life were boring.

Any day now she would remember, and Max knew he shouldn't be bewitched by her current happy mood. His task was to watch and wait, and to steel himself for the eventual fallout.

By the time they left for Whitehorse Creek on Sunday nothing had really changed.

Carrie's memory still hadn't returned. Max was still sleeping in the spare guest bedroom. Carrie was still as desperately curious about their relationship as ever, but she and Max were still treating each other more like polite acquaintances than husband and wife.

For Carrie, the tension of waiting for normality to resume was becoming unbearable.

On Saturday she'd done her best to discover as much as she could about life at Riverslea Downs. She'd risen at dawn with Max and had watched the sun rise majestically golden over the treetops. She'd travelled with him to the outer paddocks and had enjoyed watching the cattle tussle for molasses at the feed troughs.

She'd enjoyed even more watching Max do his cowboy thing—scaling stockyard fences and hefting heavy barrels with ease, moving fearlessly among all those hooves and horns.

Back at the homestead, she'd trawled through emails, had found a large file on her laptop crammed with recipes for preserves. She'd had also found, behind the orchard, an abandoned vegetable garden which Max told her had once been her pride and joy.

'You lost interest and I didn't have time to keep it going,' he'd said, when she'd asked him about the beds filled with ugly weeds.

It was a sobering discovery to learn that she'd once had a thriving garden. Now only a few shrivelled and withered chilli and tomato plants hung sadly from their stakes, their bright red fruit rotting on the stems.

For Carrie it only deepened the mystery and raised another host of questions. And now, as Max turned off the highway onto the track that led to the Whitehorse Creek homestead, she faced even more uncertainty. She was about to meet her father and his wife, but she felt more vulnerable and ignorant than ever.

'Max,' she said suddenly, unable to hold back. 'Before we get to the homestead I have to ask—is there something not quite right with us?'

He shot her a sharp frown. 'How do you mean?'

'I have this growing sense that we have a problem. I don't know whether it's you or me. I suspect I'm the problem, but it might be both of us. Anyway, I'm sure there's *something*.'

Max stared fiercely ahead and didn't answer.

'That's why you're being so cautious with me, isn't it?' Carrie persisted. 'And Barney is, too. I really get the feeling he's worried about us—and it's not simply because I've lost my memory.'

She couldn't hear Max's sigh over the noise of the motor, but she saw the way his chest rose and fell heavily.

'Now's not a good time for this, Carrie. You're about to meet your father…again.'

It was a reasonable excuse. Carrie was sure she should feel more keyed up about the impending meeting with her mystery father, but at this point Doug Peterson was still an unknown quantity—a vague possibility… The state of her marriage was a more pressing concern, hijacking her emotions.

Ever since she'd first seen Max in the hospital she'd felt a strong tug of attraction, and since then she'd discovered that she really liked him. She knew he really liked her, too. It was there in the way he looked at her, in the way he took care of her, as if she was someone he loved.

With every minute she spent in his company her feelings for him deepened. It was even possible that she was falling in love with him. Again.

If there was a problem between them, she was desperate to know what it was.

'I'm betting my father knows all about our situation,' she said. 'That means you and my father and his wife will *all* know about it—and I'll be sitting there at lunch like a dumb bunny, feeling—'

Without warning, the mounting tension inside Carrie threatened to burst. To her horror, she felt her throat tighten and her eyes fill with tears.

*Not now.* She couldn't arrive at Whitehorse Creek in tears.

She drew a deep breath, trying desperately to calm down. As she did so Max stopped the vehicle.

They were in the middle of a dirt track, with gumtrees and scrub closing in all around them.

Max turned to her. 'I know this is hard,' he said gently. 'But you have to believe that we all care. We want the best for you, Carrie. You should try to relax and enjoy this lunch. No one's going to be judging you. We understand.'

'But I don't!' she cried, her voice high-pitched and tight with tension. 'I don't understand *anything.*'

It was all very well for Max to preach to her about relaxing. He had no idea what she was going through. She glared at him, fuming with righteous anger.

But then she saw his handsome face, saw his beautiful blue eyes glistening with a suspicious sheen, and her heart slammed against her ribs. In the very next breath her body whispered the truth that her memory still withheld. There could be no doubt. She was in love with this man.

Without any knowledge of the whys or wherefores, she knew at some visceral, bone-deep level that she loved him. And with that knowledge came longing—crashing over her body like surf breaking on a sea cliff.

With a soft cry, she flipped the buckle of her seatbelt.

'Carrie…'

She heard Max groan, but she had no idea whether it was a warning or an invitation. She couldn't really see him through her tears.

It didn't matter. She was heedless to common sense as she melted towards him and there was only one thing that mattered now. To her relief, Max knew what that was. He met her halfway, hauling her roughly into his arms.

*Oh*… It was so good to feel him at last, to have the warmth and strength of him surround her, to have his mouth on hers, his tongue slipping past her lips, seeking, demanding, needing her.

*This* was how he tasted. *This* was how his kisses felt. Soothing and thrilling at once. Awakening her senses. Driving arrows of desire into the deepest part of her.

Carrie pressed closer, winding her arms around his neck, and he took her mouth in a hungry, desperate kiss, holding nothing back. Her face was damp with her tears as she matched his passion with a wildness of her own. It was so good to finally give in to the need that had been churning and burning inside her for days, to feel her longing build and burst as she poured her heart into their kiss.

All sense of time and place vanished as she surrendered to Max and to this storm-burst of longing. Heaven knew what might have happened if her elbow hadn't inadvertently bumped the car horn.

The sudden blast filled the cabin, startling them. Instinctively, as if an axe had fallen, they pulled apart.

Breathless and slightly panting, they stared at each other. Carrie knew Max was as surprised as she was. She stared in amazement at his crumpled shirt, at the buttons that she'd clawed undone, revealing his broad, brown now heaving chest.

She had no idea what to say as she edged back into her seat. After all, they had every right to be passionate. They were husband and wife.

And yet…

There were a thousand *and yets*…

As if he was remembering every one of them, Max stared ahead through the windscreen, his jaw tight. 'I'm sorry,' he said stiffly.

'Don't apologise.'

He slid her a frowning, questioning glance.

'It was my fault,' Carrie said, blushing. 'I guess my curiosity got the better of me.'

Max smiled sadly. 'Is that what it was? Idle curiosity?'

'Not exactly idle…' This time Carrie offered a shy smile of her own.

He gave a soft laugh. 'You're a hussy, Carrie Kincaid.'

She almost giggled with nervous relief.

'We'd better get going,' he said next, and he did up his shirt buttons while Carrie found a tissue and lipstick and a comb. Thank heavens she hadn't worn mascara. She'd left it off in case she became teary when she met her father, but it was her feelings for her gorgeous husband that had made her cry.

'All set?' he asked after a bit.

'Yes.'

'You sure you're OK?'

*OK* wasn't *quite* how Carrie would have described her emotional state. Not with the power of her husband's kiss still reverberating through her. Thunderstruck was possibly more apt.

But on another level she felt calmer. Reassured that there couldn't be too much wrong with their marriage when their chemistry was so explosive.

She nodded and managed to smile. 'I'm fine, Max.'

She glanced again at his shirt, which still looked a bit rumpled, at his face which was once again stern, as if he might already be regretting their impulsiveness.

But they weren't teenagers, stopping off for a quick fumble on their way to meet the parents.

Something deeply significant, perhaps life-changing, had happened. Carrie was sure of it.

# CHAPTER EIGHT

DOUG PETERSON LOOKED as distinguished as he had in the wedding photos as he waited with his wife on the homestead veranda.

Max got out, opened the door for Carrie and collected a cake that she'd baked from the back seat. Together they crossed the lawn. With the kiss still reverberating through her like the lingering notes of a song Carrie was almost floating as she walked beside Max, her feet not quite touching the ground.

Doug came down the steps. He had the lean, athletic figure of a man of the land and his silver hair glinted in the sunlight. His eyes were dark brown, like Carrie's eyes, and his arms were outstretched in greeting.

'Carrie, sweetheart.'

She hadn't expected to be called sweetheart, and she wondered if this man—*her father*—was going to hug her. But Doug was clearly sensitive to her uncertainty, and he merely kissed her cheek before shaking Max's hand.

'Good to see you both,' he said, and Carrie thought she read a special significance in the glance he sent Max.

His wife, Meredith, was close behind him. 'Carrie!' She was smiling as she took Carrie's hands in her own.

'It's wonderful to see you looking like your old self. You poor thing—we've been so worried.'

Meredith had fading red hair which she hadn't bothered to tint, sparkling grey eyes and fine wrinkles in an open, friendly face.

'Thanks,' Carrie told her, liking her on sight. 'But actually I feel perfectly fine.'

'You gave us such a scare,' Meredith said.

'I guess I must have. I'm sorry.' Somewhat guiltily, Carrie realised that she'd given very little thought to the worry she'd caused this couple.

'Oh, it wasn't your fault,' said Doug. 'If only that silly horse hadn't pigrooted...'

Carrie had no idea what pigrooting was. 'I brought a cake,' she said, pointing to the container Max held. 'Lime and coconut syrup.'

'How lovely!' Meredith was beaming, her eyes wide with evident pleasure. 'That's Doug's favourite.'

'Yes, Max told me.'

'Oh.' The other woman's face sobered. 'For a moment I thought you might have got your memory back.'

'Not yet, I'm afraid.' Doug's wife looked sympathetic, and Carrie found herself saying, 'It's really weird to know nothing about the past few years. I'm afraid I still think of myself as a city girl. I'm stunned to know that I was riding a horse at all, let alone riding here at your place. Why was I here?'

She sensed a sudden stiffening in the others, and a quick, furtive glance passed between them.

Doug made a deft recovery. 'You were just visiting your old man,' he said with a smile. And then, with a gesture to the house, 'Now, come on inside. Everything's ready.'

* * *

The lunch was very pleasant. Meredith had prepared Tandoori chicken and a delicious salad from freshly picked, home-grown ingredients.

Doug was a relaxed and charming host, and Carrie found herself often stealing glances in his direction. She fancied that she caught little glimpses of herself in his smile, or in the tilt of his head, or his laugh. She kept waiting to be hit by the emotional slug of a deeper connection. This man was her long-lost father, after all. She knew she should be feeling incredibly emotional.

But her lost memory was like a barrier, blocking her emotions. She and this man had a history she knew nothing about. No doubt when she remembered the past few years she would relive the impact of meeting him as her father for the very first time, as well as the pain of her mother's deceit. For now, though, their relationship didn't quite feel real.

Her father was a stranger—just as her husband was. Or rather as her husband had been. Before that kiss…

Throughout the meal Carrie couldn't help thinking about the kiss, still marvelling at the heat and the heart-stopping power of it. She'd never experienced anything like that before. Well, not that she could remember…

Now she was intoxicated by the possibility that she and Max had enjoyed a truly fantastic sex life, and it was only with great difficulty that she managed to pay attention to the conversation over lunch.

Max and Doug were talking about the coming mustering season. Apparently they helped each other to round up their cattle, as well as employing a contract mustering team. The men spent nights out in the bush and slept under the stars, and Carrie found it all rather fascinating.

'Max and I had a camp fire dinner down by the creek the other night,' she said.

Doug's eyebrows rose high. 'Did you *enjoy* it?'

She thought this was a strange question. 'Yes,' she said stoutly. 'It was wonderful.'

He looked mildly amused at this. Meredith, on the other hand, was frowning and looked confused, while Max kept his eyes on the plate in front of him.

Their reactions were puzzling. Why wouldn't she have enjoyed such a pleasant experience? She couldn't have rejected everything about the bush life before her accident, could she? Surely she hadn't turned into her mother?

Despite the occasional puzzling moment, the afternoon continued without a major hitch—which was probably a relief for everyone. At least everything went smoothly until Max and Carrie were on the veranda and about to leave.

'Oh, I should get your suitcase for you, Carrie,' Meredith said. 'You'll probably be wanting some of those things.'

Carrie frowned. 'My suitcase?'

Once again she was conscious of tension in the other three. Doug looked awkwardly from his wife to Max. For a split second Meredith looked pained, as if she regretted raising the subject, but she quickly covered this with one of her warm smiles.

'It's just a few things you brought over here,' she said lightly. 'I won't be a tick.'

She left quickly, disappearing down the hall to a bedroom. Doug turned his attention to their dogs, giving their ears a scruff and promising them a walk before dinner, while Max stood with his hands jammed in his jeans pockets, not meeting Carrie's curious gaze.

'Here it is,' Meredith said, returning with quite a size-able silver hard-shell suitcase.

Carrie stared at it, wondering why on earth she'd brought such a large piece of luggage to her father's place. But she sensed that to ask the question now would be like dropping a hand grenade on their pleasant gathering.

Max carried the suitcase to the car and everyone else followed. Once it was safely stowed in the back of the vehicle it wasn't mentioned again. They said their good-byes, exchanging kisses and hugs and promises to catch up again soon.

'Hopefully I'll have my memory back by the next time I see you,' Carrie said.

Doug and Meredith murmured that they certainly hoped so. But Carrie had the unsettling feeling that they might not have meant it.

She had a lot to think about during the journey home. The mystery of the suitcase. Her growing sense that in the months leading up to the accident something had gone terribly wrong with her life and possibly with her marriage.

The kiss. And the deep yearning it had stirred in her.

It was all very unsettling.

Of course she wanted to question Max, but when it came to the crunch she was afraid to ask. She'd enjoyed the past few days. Very much. She'd discovered that she liked and respected her husband, and—she might as well admit it—she was lusting after him. She'd been turned on before he'd kissed her, but now she was borderline obsessive.

And her feelings weren't only centred on Max. She liked the Riverslea homestead, too, and she loved going for walks with Clover. She had enjoyed trying some of the *Carrie K* recipes, and she'd even started weeding the vegetable garden.

Life had been good, really, but she was beginning to suspect that her amnesia was little more than an inter-mission—like a truce in the midst of some kind of war. In all likelihood hostilities would resume as soon as her memory returned.

Carrie hoped this wasn't the case. She didn't want to be told that her marriage was in trouble. So for now it was easier and safer to refrain from asking questions that might force Max to tell her an unpalatable truth. Perhaps it was cowardly, but she decided to keep quiet, to simply close her eyes and sink back against the headrest.

Max drove in silence and Carrie actually nodded off. It was almost dusk when they pulled up at Riverslea Downs. Long purple shadows stretched across the lawn. Clover greeted Carrie with her customary joy and Max retrieved the suitcase without comment, carrying it inside and set-ting it in a corner of their bedroom.

The hens had already returned to their roosts for the night so, as had become her habit, Carrie collected any remaining eggs, checked that they had water, and closed the door to their pen.

When she spoke to Max about supper he agreed that something light would be fine. She suggested scrambled eggs, and he declared this perfect, but despite the super-ficial air of normality Carrie sensed that something had changed. There was a new tension in the air.

She suspected that the suitcase was involved, and she knew she couldn't hold off indefinitely from asking Max about it. But she also felt a strong urge to ignore all the common sense arguments clamouring in her head and to follow her heart—forget the suitcase and explore the deeper ramifications of her husband's kiss.

Max stayed up late. It was mostly a matter of self-preservation. If he spent too much time in Carrie's company he would want to follow up on that kiss. He'd been barely able to think of anything else.

But with each passing hour the point when Carrie's memory would return drew closer. Any day now, any hour, any minute, everything could change…

He was in his office, checking the records he'd kept on his computer from the previous year's muster, when Carrie appeared at the doorway, instantly depriving him of oxygen.

Her face was freshly scrubbed, her glossy hair hung in loose curls, bouncing around her shoulders She was wearing a demure, long-sleeved nightgown that covered her from neck to ankle. The gown should not have been sexy.

It was sexy as hell.

This was Carrie, after all, and Max had intimate knowledge of every sweet dip and curve hidden beneath that soft fabric.

'You're saying goodnight?' he asked, in as offhand a tone as he could manage.

'Perhaps,' she responded enigmatically, and then she came into the room. 'But I've been wondering…'

She paused, standing a short distance from his desk and rubbing one bare foot against the other.

Pink bloomed in her cheeks. 'I was wondering how long you're going to stay sleeping in the other room.'

*Zap.* Every cell in Max's body caught fire. Carrie had no idea how hard this was for him. 'I thought we'd agreed it was best to stay apart—until you get your memory back.'

'But there's no real need for it, is there?' She looked perfectly innocent as she said this, but the colour in her cheeks deepened to match the rosy trim on her nightgown.

'Carrie, when you woke up in hospital you didn't even know I was your husband.'

'But I know it now.' She met his gaze bravely, but her lovely dark eyes shimmered and her teeth worried at her soft lower lip. 'Max, that kiss today—'

'Was a mistake,' he retorted, more gruffly than he'd meant to.

Of course it had been a mistake. He should never have given in to such passion. Yes, he'd adored every second of that mistake. It had been heaven to have Carrie in his arms again, so soft and womanly and willing. But it would only make the inevitable revelations so much harder to face.

'The emotions felt very real,' Carrie persisted.

Having no immediate answer for this, Max rose from his seat. 'Carrie, I don't think—'

'Oh, I *know* you're being cautious,' she interrupted, giving an impatient toss of her head. 'But we're *married*, Max. We've been husband and wife for the past three years and we must have slept together.' Her lustrous dark eyes were wide. Anxious. Pleading. 'We did, didn't we?'

He nodded, his throat suddenly too tight and raw for speech.

'I've been trying to imagine it,' she said next, dropping her gaze and blushing even more deeply. 'Imagination doesn't help. I just drive myself mad.'

And he'd been driving himself mad by remembering.

He gripped the back of the chair so tightly it was a wonder it didn't snap. Surely, having made her point, Carrie would leave now.

She stayed.

'If today's kiss was anything to go by,' she said next, 'we had something pretty special, Max. Something amazing.'

*Damn right. Hell, yes.* But the emphasis should be on *had.* Past tense.

Max knew he should tell Carrie the truth now. Get it out in the open and send her scurrying back to her room. It was time she understood that her interest in lovemaking had taken a downward plunge, along with her interest in every other aspect of life out here.

But she looked so vulnerable, standing there now in her nightdress, more or less offering herself.

Offering herself *to him.*

She moved closer and a lamp in the corner backlit her silhouette, revealing her shape through the thin fabric of her nightgown. He could see the lovely curve of her breasts, the exquisite dip to her waist, the feminine lushness of her hips and thighs. His mind filled in the other details, recalling how smooth and pale and soft her skin was. How responsive she was to his touch. He knew her body as intimately as he knew the back of his own hand.

And, damn it, he'd never felt so torn, wanting both to protect her and to take her, to recapture what they'd lost.

He'd promised himself that he wouldn't let this happen. He'd given Sylvia his word that he wouldn't seduce her daughter.

But clearly her daughter had other ideas.

Unwisely, he said, 'So you're still curious about us?'

'Desperately.'

Carrie's answer was a breathless whisper and she took another two steps closer, bringing with her a wafting scent of the soap she'd used. She smelled of midnight and roses.

'You know curiosity killed the cat,' he said now, allowing her a final chance to back away before he gave in to his burning need to touch her, to kiss her, to make wild, mad love to her.

Carrie smiled, and she stepped closer still. 'Then it's lucky I'm not a cat.'

# CHAPTER NINE

CARRIE HAD BEEN nervous about brazenly sailing into Max's office, bearding the lion in his den, so to speak. But now, as his blue eyes smouldered with heat, as he reached for her…as he framed her face with his hands and sealed his lips to hers…she felt a rush of relief, swiftly followed by pure elation.

This devastatingly sexy man was her husband. Her husband, yet also a stranger.

The combination was heady. Intoxicating. Especially when he pulled her even more closely to him and took the kiss deeper.

Tonight she sensed an even greater urgency to Max's kiss, as if he was claiming her, branding her as his own. And leaving her in no doubt about his intentions.

It was going to happen. This night, at last, would be theirs. A gift from the Fates.

Another chance for their marriage?

She had no answer for that, but it hardly mattered now, when she tasted the yearning he could no longer disguise, when his tongue delved deep, sending heat spreading through her belly, making her ache with wanting him.

Soon their intense and needy kisses were no longer enough. Holding hands, they hurried through the dark-

ened house to Carrie's bedroom—*their* bedroom, by
rights—now softly lit by shaded lamps.

The suitcase no longer stood in the corner like a stern
reprimand, a symbol of impending doom. Carrie had
shoved it, unopened, into the bottom of one of the capa-
cious built-in wardrobes.

Now the huge king-size bed commanded their attention, luxurious and inviting with its smooth white cover
softened by lamplight. Carrie's heart beat wildly. For a
scary moment she wondered if she'd been crazy to take
this risk, but her doubts were whisked away when Max
pulled her to him once again, melting all chance of ra-
tional thought with another deep and soul-searing kiss.

They didn't speak. It was almost as if they'd both
agreed that words could be dangerous…might break the
spell.

With no memory of how this had been in the past, Carrie was happy to follow her instincts. Winding her arms
around Max's neck, she pressed close with her breasts
against his chest, her hips against his.

He kissed her eyelids, her brow and then her mouth,
ravaging her wonderfully, turning her loose-limbed and
wanton. At some point he began to shed his shirt—with
a little eager help from her—and a soft gasp broke from
her as the shirt slipped away to reveal his big bare shoulders and chest, tapering tantalisingly to lean hips.

With trembling fingers she reached to touch him. So
hard and muscular. So intensely male.

And he wanted her. *Oh, yes.*

Now he kissed her face again, kissed her temple, her
cheek, her chin. With an almost lazy lack of haste he
opened the top buttons of her nightgown, pulling the
neckline slowly apart. Her knees almost gave way as he

dipped his head, brushing his warm lips over her bare skin, lavishing intimate kisses on her throat, her neck, her shoulders, sending exquisite thrills trembling through her.

'Carrie…' His voice was little more than a hoarse whisper.

She looked up to find him watching her, searching her face intently, his blue gaze fierce.

Her only thought was to beg him not to stop now, but she wasn't quite brave enough to plead.

'Yes?' she whispered back.

For answer he lifted her hand to his lips and pressed a light kiss to each knuckle. Such a sweet, touching gesture. Her heart rocked in her chest.

'You're quite sure you're OK with this?' he asked.

Looking clear into his eyes, Carrie smiled, loving that he cared enough to ask. 'I've never been surer.'

He gave a shaky laugh. 'As far as you can remember.'

Too true.

'What about contraception?' he asked.

*Oh, Lord. Good question.* She should have thought about that. 'Am I supposed to be taking the pill?'

'Yes, but don't worry. I can take care of things.'

Before she could respond he slipped his arms around her bare waist and then he was kissing her again, kissing her and walking her towards the bed. *Their* bed, Where, together, they tumbled into heaven.

In the lamplight they lay in a tangle of sheets as their breathing and heartbeats slowed.

'Wow…' Carrie couldn't keep the surprise from her voice. She'd never experienced such amazing lovemaking—or at least she certainly couldn't remember an occasion that came even close. She was brimming with happiness and wonder and a deeper emotion—an emotion akin to the way she'd felt after that morning's kiss.

And she'd fallen in love with her husband.

But, given all the mystery that still surrounded their past, it might be imprudent to admit her feelings to Max.

'I can't believe I don't remember *that*,' she said instead, lacing her voice with humour. 'I'm surprised it didn't bring my memory back. I'm sure Prince Charming didn't wake Sleeping Beauty with just a kiss.'

She'd half expected to hear Max chuckle, but he remained silent.

Turning to him in the subdued light, she saw that he was lying with his hands stacked under his head, staring up at the ceiling. No hint of a smile.

Fear trembled at the edges of her happiness. Fear and guilt as she recalled the question he'd asked her seconds before they'd tumbled so eagerly into bed.

*'You're quite sure you're OK with this?'*

At the time she'd thought Max was being considerate, because of her memory loss and general confusion. Now, after another glance at his solemn profile, she couldn't help wondering if his question had been prompted by something deeper.

Perhaps she should have shown a little more courtesy by asking him the same question.

If they'd had problems before her accident, as she was starting to suspect was the case, this tryst might have been totally out of line. But their passion had felt so honest. What could have gone wrong in their marriage?

Worried, Carrie struggled again to remember something, *anything* from her life with Max. But once again the effort was futile.

She rolled onto her side, looking at him. 'Max?'

When he turned, his face was in shadow.

'Is something the matter?' she asked.

He made a soft sound, a half-hearted chuckle. 'That's a strange question, Carrie…under the circumstances.'

'Well, yes, I know there's something the matter with *me*—but is there also something wrong with *us*? With our marriage?'

When he didn't answer, she dared to ask, 'How—how long is it since we've made love?'

His chest rose and fell as he sighed. 'Quite a while.'

'*Quite* a while? As in…months?'

'Yeah.'

'Oh.' Her new-found happiness deserted her, like air rushing from a deflated balloon. Here was the evidence she'd dreaded. 'Did we—?' She was scared to ask more questions, but she felt she had to get to the bottom of this. 'So obviously we've had problems?'

Now his Adam's apple slid in his throat as he swallowed and she felt her fear cause a cold shiver inside. She knew it was probably wisest to let things be, to wait for the full picture to become clear when her memory returned, but she had no idea when that might be and the waiting was nerve-racking.

'Can't you tell me, Max?' She couldn't stop herself from persisting. 'What's the problem? Is one of us having an affair?'

This brought another sigh. 'Give me a break, Carrie. I can only give you my version of things, and I'm not sure that's helpful. You'll know everything soon enough.'

He sounded tired, bored, but she was sure this was a front.

'But if you were having an affair with another woman I deserve to—'

'I wasn't having an affair. There's no one else.'

She supposed she should have been reassured by this, but she winced at the implications. Surely *she* hadn't been the unfaithful partner? 'It wasn't me, was it?'

'There were no affairs,' he said wearily. 'Not as far as I'm aware.'

That was something, at least. But now Carrie thought about the suitcase again, and felt another shiver…deeper and colder.

'Well, if it wasn't an affair…' Her voice trailed off as she thought about the withered and weedy vegetable patch that she'd apparently lost interest in. 'I didn't lose interest in sex, did I?'

'Would you believe me if I said yes?'

Silenced, finally, Carrie stared in dismay at his darkened profile. How could she have lost interest in making love with this gorgeous man? After all, sex was hardly in the same league as growing and bottling vegetables. And sex with Max was as good as it got.

'That doesn't make sense,' she said unhappily.

'Tell me about it.'

Flopping back onto the pillow, she lay beside him, joining him in staring up at the ceiling. She was more bewildered than ever. But not for the first time she realised how difficult this situation must be for her husband.

First she'd lost interest in her marriage, and then she'd lost her memory, and now she was pestering him. And her provocative behaviour this evening might have made things worse.

'I'm sorry,' she said after a bit. 'I more or less threw myself at you tonight.'

'I could have sent you away.'

'I'm glad you didn't.'

She reached for his hand and gave it a shy squeeze. 'I wish I understood what's gone wrong. Right now, it doesn't make any kind of sense to me.'

'It will in time.' He rose onto one elbow, giving her a fabulous close-up view of his massive shoulders. 'I should go.'

'To sleep in the other room?'

'Yeah.'

Now it was Carrie who sighed. She didn't want him to leave, to walk away, abandoning her as if this was nothing more than a casual one-night stand.

'Do you have to go?'

Her question was met by silence.

'I'd like you to stay, Max.'

She couldn't help feeling that her amnesia was giving her a chance—possibly an important chance—to set things right again. No doubt this was a shaky theory, but it felt right tonight to have her husband lying beside her. And with no reliable memories to draw from all she had to go on were her feelings.

To her relief, he settled back in the bed.

'If I stay you should try to sleep,' he said. 'Doctor's orders. Remember?'

'Sure.' She was happy to obey if it kept him near. 'Goodnight.'

'Night, Carrie.'

She felt the brief pressure of his lips on her brow, felt the movement of the mattress as he settled more comfortably beside her. With his warm, muscular body mere inches away, touching close, she smiled and closed her eyes.

* * *

From habit, Max woke at dawn. In the pearly grey light he saw his wife lying beside him. Her face was soft with sleep and her eyelashes were sweet dusky smudges against her cheeks. Her lips, pale with sleep, were soft and full and inviting.

While he watched, those lips curved with the hint of a drowsy smile and he felt happiness roll through him in a hot wave, enticing his mind to play with the crazy fantasy that their life from now on would always be like this.

Last night she'd been his Carrie of old—his eager, responsive, passionate wife. Chances were if he woke her now she would greet him again with the same unmistakable delight. His body grew hot and hard at the thought.

*I love you, Carrie.*

If only he could tell her. The need to remind her of his love burned in him. It was so tempting to simply forget the past, as she had, to carry on as if the slate had been wiped clean and they were able to start over.

He tortured himself by recalling the sweet early days of their marriage when they'd hardly been able to keep their hands off each other, when life had felt like one long honeymoon and everything about his lifestyle had fascinated and intrigued Carrie.

'I'm going to be a perfect cattleman's wife,' she'd told him when she'd arrived at Riverslea Downs, full of bright dreams. 'Now that I can ride a horse I'll go out mustering with you. I'll learn how to grow fruit and vegetables. And when our kids arrive I'll teach them at home till they're ready for boarding school. I know I'm going to love it. I'll never be bored.'

Those rosy dreams had been fine at first. Carrie had joined him and the other stockmen on the mustering camps. She'd made beef stew and golden syrup damper on an open fire and she'd slept in a swag on the ground with him at night.

She'd even helped in the stockyards, and she'd been full of enthusiasm for every aspect of life in the bush. She'd talked about starting a family, wanting to add to the generations of Kincaids who'd lived and worked at Riverslea Downs. It was a proud tradition that they'd both been keen to continue and they'd agreed that three children would be perfect.

Then, after one of Carrie's trips to Sydney, her dreams had faded. It seemed that almost overnight they'd turned to dust. The only answer Max had been able to find was that she'd finally accepted her mother's litany of reasons why life in the Outback was a disastrous mistake.

He knew it had been hard for an only daughter to be such a huge disappointment to her mother. But now, recalling the changes in his wife on her return, Max rose swiftly from the bed. It would be foolish to linger, to allow Carrie to wake beside him, to roll towards him with an expectant smile.

His body leapt at the thought, but he kept walking. Out of the room. It was a crazy fantasy to try to pretend even for a few days that the wheels hadn't fallen off their marriage. It was tempting to sweep the nasty truth under the carpet for now, but that would only make the return of Carrie's memory so much harder to bear.

Carrie wasn't too worried when she woke to find Max gone. She knew he was an early riser, and it was fairly common knowledge that this was a common trait for most men of the land. Besides, after last night's out-of-this-world passion she was feeling confident that all would be well.

There'd been an honesty about their lovemaking that couldn't be faked. It had hinted at deeper, more important emotions that went beyond the physical, and Carrie couldn't help feeling optimistic.

Whatever their problems had been in the past, she'd been granted this reprieve, and with luck it would provide a fresh new insight into her marriage.

Perhaps if she was at fault she would be able to find a way to make amends. She would give anything to see that worried light leave Max's eyes permanently.

Pleased by this positive prospect, she got dressed, then went to greet Clover and to plan her day.

Max joined her for lunch and she served homemade tomato and basil soup—another *Carrie K* recipe she'd found on the file. And as she knew Max would be hungry, she added toasted ham and cheese sandwiches.

'Great tucker,' Max said with a warm smile as he reached for another toasted sandwich. 'I always love the way you make these.'

She felt unexpectedly pleased. 'I know,' she said. Then gasped when she realised what she'd said.

Max frowned, watching her intently. 'You remember?' he asked quietly.

Carrie frowned. 'I don't know. I don't think so. The sandwiches just seemed…like a good idea. But it's weird. As soon as you said you love how I make them, I was quite sure I already knew that. It's to do with the way I butter the outsides.'

'Yes…'

Across the table they stared at each other. Watching. Wondering. Waiting for another clue to drop.

'Do you remember anything else?' Max asked cautiously.

It was hard for Carrie to concentrate, trapped in the beam of his searching blue gaze.

'I—I don't think so. But there may be other stuff. I didn't even know I remembered that.'

'Have a go,' he urged, and there was a new tension in his voice. 'When's your birthday?

'Well, I already knew that. It's the fourth of May.'

'What about mine?'

Carrie opened her mouth, hoping the date would just pop out. But once again trying to dredge up the forgotten past was like trying to wade through wet concrete. 'Sorry,' she said. 'I have no idea.'

'Our wedding anniversary?'

'You told me our honeymoon was in May, so I guess the wedding must have been some time around my birthday.'

'Fair enough.' He gave a brief shrug. 'I guess there's no use in forcing these things.'

'Are you in a hurry for me to remember, Max?'

He took a moment to answer, and then his mouth tilted in a hard-to-read smile. 'That's a loaded question.'

'Well, I won't push you to answer it.'

She supposed he was thinking about their problems—whatever they were. It was a depressing thought. Right now it was hard to believe there was anything wrong.

Lifting the teapot, she changed the subject. 'Would you like a refill?'

At the end of lunch Max announced that he was heading off to a distant corner of the property to mend the windmill pump.

'It's a tricky job,' he said. 'Barney's going to help me, but it might take most of the afternoon.'

Carrie walked with him to the kitchen door. 'If you'll be gone for hours, perhaps you need a kiss goodbye.'

He stopped in the doorway, his expression so stern and forbidding Carrie was sure he was going to refuse her suggestion, but then his blue eyes warmed, betraying the hint of a lurking smile.

'You're a minx,' he murmured, reaching easily to snag her waist and reel her in till she was hard against him, with her mouth inches from his.

Now, as he looked straight into her eyes, he challenged, 'OK—kiss me, Carrie.'

After last night she shouldn't have been shocked by the blaze that leapt within her. But Max didn't move. He simply stood completely still, and her heart hammered hard against her ribs while her face turned to flames.

She could scarcely breathe as she tilted her chin ever so slightly upwards. Now, with a hair's breadth separating their lips, she wondered if she should simply give him a quick peck on the cheek. But the thought died almost as soon as it was born. The temptation to taste him again was too fierce.

Another tiny lift of her face brought her lips brushing against his. She felt the first sweet *zap* of contact. Felt him stiffen, heard him breathe her name…an almost soundless whisper. Then she sipped at his lower lip, marvelling at its softness in stark contrast to the hard masculinity of the rest of his body.

As she moved to taste his upper lip a soft groan seemed to tear loose from inside him. A heartbeat later his arms were around her, taking charge, settling her hips against his, exactly where he wanted her. Then he kissed her slowly and lazily, but with utter devastation, taking his own sweet time as her knees threatened to give way…

'You there, Max?'

Dazed, Carrie turned in Max's arms to see Barney on the back steps, his eyes bulging in his flaming red face.

'Aw, hell. Sorry, boss.' The poor man backed down the steps so quickly he almost tripped.

'I'll be right with you, Barney,' Max called to him calmly.

Max was holding Carrie by the elbows now, looking down at her, his eyes glittering blue slits beneath half-lowered lids.

'Now I'll cop an earful,' he murmured.

'Sorry,' she whispered back.

'I'm not.' He smiled then, his expression changing from reproach to smouldering amusement. 'Catch you later.'

With a swing of the fly-screen door he was down the steps and gone, long legs striding, hurrying to catch up with Barney.

Carrie leaned against the doorframe and let out her breath in a shaky huff, then she smiled as she touched her fingers to her lips, remembering the tantalising moment when her lips had met her husband's. That first touch had been as light as thistledown, and yet as powerful as an earthquake.

She could still feel the aftershocks of Max's kiss now, as she gathered up the crockery and cutlery they'd used for lunch and stacked it in the dishwasher.

Outside, she heard the ute start up. Max and Barney were driving off to repair the windmill pump. She wondered how she would spend *her* afternoon and decided, on a sudden brave impulse, that it was time to tackle the one task she'd been so assiduously avoiding.

Afternoon sunlight streamed through the bedroom windows and pooled on the honey-gold timber floor where Carrie knelt to unlock the suitcase they'd brought back from Whitehorse Creek. She felt strangely nervous as she opened the lid and eyed the neatly folded clothes. It was still hard to believe these were *her* belongings.

Predictably, there was a pair of blue jeans, as well as several of the long-sleeved cotton shirts that were *de rigueur* for women in the bush. But there were other clothes too—both summer and winter things. And dresses…rather lovely dresses—a halter-necked dress in moss-green, a glamorous off-the-shoulder white pencil dress and a divine little black swing affair with a silver trim around the short hemline.

As Carrie stood before the mirror, holding the dresses in front of her, she wondered when she'd worn these outfits. Had her social life in the bush been busier and more varied than she'd imagined? Or had she been on her way to the city when she'd taken these things to Whitehorse Creek?

If so, why?

*Surely I wasn't leaving Max?*

She felt a cold shiver at the thought. Surely their relationship hadn't deteriorated to that chilling point?

Sickened by this disturbing possibility, Carrie hastily turned her attention to unpacking, stowing the dresses on hangers in the wardrobe and setting the jeans and folded shirts, shorts and sweaters on the appropriate shelves.

It was a strange experience. She felt like an intruder

into someone else's life as she unpacked frothy under-wear, a zipped bag filled with expensive toiletries, a couple of paperback novels by unfamiliar authors, a bottle of perfume, a drawstring bag of jewellery.

At the bottom of the case she found two pairs of carefully wrapped and rather swish high-heeled shoes—one pair was silver, the other black patent. Then, alone at the bottom of the case, another small bundle wrapped in white tissue paper.

For a moment, as Carrie stared at it, wondering what it might be, she felt a weird tingle—almost like a zap of electricity. Then she was gripped by a really strong sense of *déjà vu*.

She knew she'd seen this parcel before.

Goose bumps broke out on her arms. Her heart began to pump at a frightening pace. Scared, she closed her eyes and took a deep, hopefully calming breath.

When she opened her eyes the white tissue-wrapped parcel was still there in the bottom of the suitcase, and it was still inescapably familiar. With shaking hands she lifted it out. It was light as a feather.

Kneeling in the golden pool of afternoon sunlight, she felt her throat tighten and her pulses race frantically as she laid the little white package in her lap.

She wasn't sure how long she knelt there, too afraid to undo the tissue wrapping. It was only when a tear fell, making a soft splash on the fragile paper, that she realised the moment she'd both longed for and feared had arrived.

She knew exactly what she would find when she opened this parcel.

Now, without any warning, she remembered it.

She remembered it all. Every tiny, heartbreaking detail.

# CHAPTER TEN

*Five months earlier, in Sydney.*

'I'M SORRY THAT I can't give you better news, Carrie.'

The doctor sitting on the other side of the desk gave a slight adjustment to his bow tie before he finished delivering his bombshell. After conducting CT scans and X-rays he had discovered a malformation of Carrie's uterus. It was so severe that she would never be able to have children.

Unfortunately her particular problem could not be corrected by surgery, and while her ovaries were healthy. and she had a perfectly good egg supply, her womb would never sustain a pregnancy. For this reason IVF was not an option.

She would never give birth.

There was no chance of a baby.

None.

*Ever.*

It was too much to take in. Carrie could hear the doctor's words, and in theory she understood, but shock had numbed her from head to toe. The fateful message bounced off her like rubber bullets. Nothing made sense—not the kind of sense that sank in.

In a grey fog of confusion she thanked the doctor for his trouble.

He seemed a little shocked. 'You look pale, my dear.' Leaning forward, he pressed a button on the phone on his desk. 'Suzy, could you bring Mrs Kincaid a cup of tea?'

'I don't need tea,' Carrie told him.

'Er… Suzy, cancel the tea.' Behind gold-rimmed glasses, his grey eyes were sympathetic. 'A glass of water, perhaps?'

'No, I don't need anything to drink, thanks. I'm fine.'

The doctor looked concerned. 'This news has come as a shock, I'm sure. You'll want to talk it over with your husband. And perhaps the two of you might consider also talking to a counsellor? There are several good people I could put you in touch with.'

'Thank you,' Carrie said automatically. 'I'll think about that.'

The doctor accepted her assurance and showed her to the door. Outside in the reception area Carrie handed over her credit card and her Medicare card to the smiling girl behind the desk.

'Do you need another appointment?' the girl asked.

Carrie told her no. There would be no more appointments. She was working on auto pilot as she folded the printed receipt and slipped it into her neat leather handbag, then slotted the cards back into her brightly coloured purse.

Without looking to right or left, she walked out through the congregation of expectant mothers seated in the waiting area. Glass sliding doors opened at her approach and she stepped out into sunshine onto a Sydney footpath.

It was a hot, late spring day, blinding bright. Traffic

streamed past. From this point Carrie had a view of red rooftops, baking in the sun. In nearby gardens sprinklers sprayed softly, and New South Wales Christmas bushes bloomed with dainty red flowers.

The world looked exactly as it had an hour earlier, when she'd arrived for her appointment. But the doctor had just told her that *her* world had changed completely. Nothing about her future would be the way she and Max had planned.

It was still hard to believe. Still didn't feel real.

Slipping the strap of her handbag over her shoulder, she walked along the footpath to the station. The swish of tyres on bitumen and the tap-tap of her heels on the concrete were city sounds, so different from the laughing call of a kookaburra or the drum of horses' hooves on hard earth.

Carrie almost smiled when she realised what a country chick she was these days.

She'd been trying not to think about Max, her gorgeous, sun-tanned cattleman husband, but suddenly he was there, filling her head and her heart. And with thoughts of him the numbness in her body vanished, giving way to a pain so piercing that she almost stumbled.

Max would never be a father.

After five generations there would be no more Kincaids at Riverslea Downs.

*Oh, Max darling, I'm so sorry.*

Without warning, tears arrived, burning down Carrie's cheeks, and she had to fumble in her bag for a tissue and sunglasses before she could continue. When she reached the station she knew that she couldn't go home to her mother. She hadn't told anyone about her appointment—not Max nor either of her parents—and she certainly wasn't ready to talk to them about this.

She was still in shock. She needed time to adjust, if that was possible. Needed space to think.

It made sense to catch the next train into the city, and Carrie kept her sunglasses on even though most of the journey was underground. At Circular Quay she left the train and managed to board a Manly ferry scant moments before it pulled away from the wharf. The ferry was crowded, but she found a seat on the upper deck with a good view of the glittering harbour.

There, with a stiff breeze in her face and her hair flying, her arms tightly folded and hugged to her chest, she let her mind replay every terrifying detail of what the doctor had told her.

She had suspected there might be a problem, which was why she'd decided to see the city specialist, but she'd been confident the doctor would supply a solution. There was so much help for fertility issues these days. She'd expected to be told about treatment for endometriosis, or about IVF options. She'd even been prepared to have surgery.

It was so hard to believe that nothing could be done. *Nothing*.

How could she bear it?

How could she find the strength to tell Max?

Now she felt wretched about buying that baby dress yesterday. When she'd seen it in the shop window she'd feared that she might be tempting fate if she bought it before her doctor's appointment. But it had been so beautiful and sweetly old-fashioned, with delicate smocking across the front. She hadn't been able to resist it. It would make the perfect Christening dress, she'd decided. It was white, and so beautifully simple it would be suitable for either a boy or a girl.

Carrie had even allowed herself to fantasise about the Christening. The service would be held in the little white wooden church in Jilljinda. Max's parents would come from the Sunshine Coast, along with her mother and Doug and Meredith, and she would probably ask Max's sister Jane and her husband to be godparents. After the church service there'd be a celebration at Riverslea, with friends from surrounding properties.

Carrie had even pictured the party—a long trestle table on the veranda, or possibly out on the lawn under the tamarind tree. She'd imagined spreading white tablecloths, setting out rows of shiny crystal glasses to be filled with champagne. And there would be a beautiful Christening cake, standing ready to cut. She and Max would cut it together, holding their dear little baby between them.

It would all be so perfect. Lunch would be simple, but delicious. Max would man the barbecue while Carrie produced fresh garden salads, complete with her *Carrie K* dressings and chutneys.

*Oh, dear God.* Such a fool she'd been to let her imagination run wild. Just thinking about those silly plans now brought an agonising rush of tears.

With a sob of despair Carrie lurched out of her seat and hurried to stand at the ferry's railing, hoping to hide her face from the other passengers. Desperate to stem her tears, she stared hard at the seagulls wheeling overhead, at the pretty yachts zig-zagging across the water, at the stately Harbour Bridge, at the forest of skyscrapers that lined the shore.

But although she managed to staunch her tears, she couldn't stop the tumultuous flow of her thoughts.

So many plans she'd had for their family.

Such happy dreams.

She remembered the bassinet in the storage shed. It was the one she'd slept in as a baby on her father's property. Meredith had given it to her and Max to use when they were ready to start their family.

They'd wanted three children, and Carrie had known exactly which rooms in the homestead those little people would occupy. In her imagination she'd decorated the room closest to their bedroom as a nursery, with white furniture and yellow and white striped curtains, a brightly coloured mobile hanging above the cot. There would be shelves for books and toys, and a rocking chair. She'd also planned to renovate an old chest of drawers. She would paint it green, perhaps. Or bright red.

Now…

*Oh, help.* How could she bear it? How could she take this sad, heartbreaking news home to her husband?

*I'm barren, Max.*

*Barren.* Such a terrible word—especially for the wife of a grazier. For well over a century the Kincaids had worked hard to keep Riverslea Downs fertile and productive. And the women in the family had done their part by bearing sons.

Max would be a wonderful father. He was so steady and calm and loving. Carrie had always believed that together they would be fabulous parents. They had so much to offer their children—so much love as well as a healthy, adventurous lifestyle.

She knew she should try not to think about this now. It only made the pain in her heart cut deeper and sharper. At any moment it would break into bleeding chunks.

Even so, she couldn't stop torturing herself.

She found herself fixated by the generations of Kincaids who'd lived at Riverslea Downs. She kept recalling the magnificent trees planted by Max's great-grandmother, the family portraits painted by his grandmother, the vegetable gardens that Max's mother had built using railway sleepers—a tradition that Carrie had happily continued.

Now she had to bring Max and his family the devastating news that there would be no more Kincaids at Riverslea. And, given the weight of family tradition and expectations, she was sure it would be much harder for them to bear than for most families.

These tormenting thoughts continued writhing and circling through Carrie's head while she paced endlessly up and down the Manly foreshore.

Looking back, she could never pinpoint the precise moment that she'd finally hatched her plan. It had been a painful plan, but she'd been sunk in the pits of grief that day, mourning the loss of her dreams of motherhood. Utterly bereft.

Given her misery, and the tortured nature of her thoughts, it wasn't so surprising that her new plan had seemed to make perfect sense. By the time she'd caught a return ferry and another train, and had finally reached her mother's place, Carrie had been firmly convinced it was her only option.

*Riverslea Downs. Present day.*

To Max's relief, Barney said nothing about the kiss he'd witnessed as they worked on the windmill pump. Max knew the old bloke was practically bursting with the effort of keeping quiet, but he was grateful for his silence.

His own thoughts were disturbing enough as he wrestled with a rusted bolt. He was remembering Carrie's question: *'Are you in a hurry for me to get my memory back?'*

He was rather ashamed of the fact that his honest answer would have been *no*. Not that he wasn't justified in preferring a wife who found him attractive and desirable, but he supposed it would only be a matter of time before this new, keen Carrie grew jaded and uninterested, just as she had before.

It wasn't till the job was done and Max and Barney were stowing the tools in the back of the ute that Barney finally had to say something.

Hooking his elbows over the ute's tray back, the old ringer sent Max a shy, lopsided grin. 'So things are maybe working out, mate?'

Max knew exactly what Barney was talking about, but he pretended to misunderstand. 'Yeah, Barney. I just need to fix that leaky pipe now, and then we'll have the bore back and running.'

Barney looked at him as if he was a halfwit. 'I'm not talking about the bleeding windmill. I meant things are working out—' He swallowed and looked embarrassed. 'You know—for you and Carrie.'

Max sent him a warning glance. 'I wouldn't read too much into one little kiss.'

Barney's response was a cheeky, knowing grin. 'Yeah, *right*. Didn't look so little from where I was standing. And what about the way she looks at you—like you're chocolate mousse with cream and cherries and she hasn't eaten in a week?'

Max gritted his teeth. 'I'm not joking, Barney. Carrie still doesn't remember anything. Everything will change when she does.'

This stumped the old bloke. He lifted his hat and scratched at his bald patch—a sure sign that he was worried. 'You still think she'll take off again?'

The very thought made Max's innards drop like a leg-roped steer, but there was no point in fostering false hope. 'Yes, mate. That's exactly what I think.'

Barney gave a rueful shake of his head and his shoulders drooped dejectedly as he stood gazing into the distance. In the gumtrees behind them a crow called. *Ark, ark, ark, ark!*

Max added the shifting spanner to the tool bag. 'OK—let's go.'

The men climbed into the ute. As Barney slammed his door shut he turned to Max, fresh determination blazing. 'You're not going to let that happen, are you? You won't let Carrie just clear out without putting up a fight?'

Max didn't answer as he started up the ute. He was as surprised as Barney was by Carrie's recently renewed ardour. He welcomed it, of course. There was no way he could refuse Carrie when she looked at him as if he was the sexiest guy alive. A man would have to be nine-tenths glacier to ignore that. And yet Max knew he was setting himself up for a big fall.

The problem was he couldn't really *prepare* for the return of Carrie's memory. If the doctors were right it could happen any day now, at any moment, but he was as confused as anyone about the changes in Carrie before her accident.

He didn't know why she'd fallen out of love with him, and there wasn't a hell of a lot a man could do when a woman stopped fancying him. He certainly wasn't going to beg or plead.

On the other hand, he decided now, as the ute rattled over the dirt track that skirted the creek, if Carrie wanted to leave him again he'd be damned if he was going to meekly show her the door.

Carrie was in the bedroom when Max returned to the homestead. He found her sitting on the bedroom floor beside the empty suitcase they'd brought back from White-horse Creek. A small white parcel lay in her lap, and at the sound of his footsteps she looked up.

Her face was swollen and flushed, her eyes and nose pink from crying. When she looked at him he saw a flash of fear in her eyes and his heart gave a heavy thud.

He knew straight away.

She'd remembered.

His first impulse was to rush and take her in his arms, to find a way to protect her from the pain he read in her eyes. But he didn't dare. He had no idea if she would welcome him or repel him.

'Hey,' he said gently. 'What's wrong?'

'It's happened,' she said in a choked voice.

'Your memory?'

'Yes.' The single syllable was almost a wail of despair. 'Total recall.'

Max swallowed, hating to see her like this. What the hell had upset her so badly? What had triggered this pain?

He looked around the room. The suitcase was empty. There was only the white parcel in her lap.

Could that be the culprit? The heart of her distress? Could it even hold a clue to the cause of their break-up?

He had no idea what the parcel held. He'd never seen

it before. But the possibility that *he* might not be the sole cause of Carrie's distress brought a brief ripple of relief. He'd been blaming himself for so long. He was very aware, though, that it was far too soon to get his hopes up.

'How long have you been sitting here?' he asked, moving closer.

'I don't know. Ages, I guess.'

'Can I help you up?'

'Yes, please. I'm so stiff I can barely move.'

He offered a hand and then reached for her waist to support her as she got stiffly to her feet. With her free hand she kept the tissue-wrapped parcel close to her chest.

He tried not to stare too hard at the parcel, hazarding a guess at its contents.

Some item of clothing?

How could that cause so much distress?

'You look like you could do with a cuppa,' he said.

Carrie nodded, but she didn't look at him. 'Thanks.'

Max stood for a moment, stalled by uncertainty.

'I'm fine now, Max.' Carrie waved towards the doorway. 'I'll wash my face and join you in the kitchen in a moment.'

Clearly dismissed, he retreated. As he headed down the hallway he heard the snap of the suitcase's locks and a wardrobe door sliding open. No doubt the mystery parcel was being stowed away.

Despite having washed her face, Carrie still had the blotchy, drawn look of someone who'd done too much crying when she came into the kitchen.

Max had made a pot of tea and he filled a mug for her, added a little milk and sugar, the way she liked it.

'Thanks,' she said, leaning her hip against a cupboard as she took a sip. 'That's great. Just what I needed.' She took another sip. 'How's the windmill pump? Did you manage to fix it?'

To hell with the pump. It was hardly relevant now.

But Max kept the tension from his voice as he replied. 'Sure, the pump's fine.' His heart thudded again. 'More importantly, how are *you*?'

Carrie dropped her gaze to her tea mug. 'Right now I'm pretty messed up, I'm afraid.'

'That's...rough.'

She sighed. 'It's very hard to remember *everything*—both the way I was before the accident and—' Her brown eyes met his in a sideways glance filled with guilt. 'And the way I've been lately.'

He swallowed, hardly daring to hope, but unwilling to push her to explain.

'I know it must be messing with your head, too,' she said next. 'But I can't really talk about it at the moment, Max. It—it's still spinning me out.'

What could he say? He was desperate for answers, but Carrie looked so exhausted and strained. To force her to explain how she felt about everything wouldn't help, and yet it would kill him to remain patient.

'Oh!' Carrie groaned and tapped at her forehead with the heel of her hand. 'I haven't given a thought to dinner.'

Dinner was the last thing Max cared about, but he hastened to reassure her.

'There's bound to be something in the freezer we can throw in the microwave.'

Dinner was fine—a reheated beef stroganoff. And afterwards, Carrie went to bed early, pleading a headache, which was more than likely, given how exhausted she looked.

Max checked his emails and watched a little TV, mainly flipping channels without any real interest. He was too restless for light entertainment, too distracted to concentrate on anything serious. Eventually he knew it was pointless, sitting up, staring unseeingly at the flickering screen. He should turn in, too. But that involved a delicate decision—to join Carrie or head to the spare room again.

He didn't wrestle with this for long. He had no intention of letting Carrie withdraw from him. After the closeness of the past few days he was determined to hang on to the ground they'd regained.

As he moved quietly into their darkened bedroom there was just enough moonlight to show Carrie lying on her side with her eyes closed. He stopped, his chest tightening at the sight. The spill of her shiny hair across the pillow, the soft curve of her cheek, her lips softly parted…

He'd left his clothes in the bathroom and now, clad only in boxer shorts, he lifted the bedcovers and climbed in beside her. He held his breath as he listened for the regular rhythm of Carrie's breathing that signalled she was asleep.

She was silent, and utterly still, so there was a very good chance that she was probably awake.

A new tension gripped Max. Carrie was unlikely to fall into his arms with the eagerness she'd shown last night, but would she stir? Would she turn to him? Say goodnight?

Was there a chance of them talking quietly and calmly

now, under the protection of darkness? Or was she still too tense, still battling with her memories?

Or, worse, was she already planning her escape?

Carrie couldn't sleep. Despite her exhaustion she was as tense as a bowstring when Max came to bed. She'd half expected him to stay in the spare room this evening, but she'd hoped he wouldn't. She didn't want to be alone.

In a perfect world they would make love again. But her world was far from perfect. And, given the mess she'd created by her recent behaviour, she had no idea how to respond to Max now.

She'd been foolishly reckless these past few days—flinging herself at him when she'd had no idea of their past or their true situation. Now she was painfully aware of the real picture.

A week ago she'd walked out on her husband, declaring that their marriage was over, and she'd taken that suitcase with as much gear as she could fit into it to her father's place. It had been the first leg of her return trip to Sydney.

A couple of days later Max had collected her from the hospital and she'd requested to come back here, to Riverslea, and promptly set about seducing him.

How appalling was that?

The poor guy mustn't have known what had hit him.

She had to admit Max had handled the situation manfully. Her heart trembled when she thought about the way he'd made love to her, with such touching tenderness and passion. For just a short time their relationship had been fabulous, lit by the fire that had brought them together at the start. There'd been an extra dimension, too—a deeper layer of heart and soul that had left Carrie in no doubt about her husband's love.

*Oh, good Lord.* If only she hadn't thrown herself at him. She'd been unwittingly cruel, and she almost groaned aloud when she thought about the havoc she'd created.

Now she was super-aware of Max lying so close beside her. She could sense the warmth of his body, could smell the scent of soap on his skin, but she knew—no matter how tempted she was—she couldn't snuggle close. She'd forfeited that right.

There was no point in turning his way, wishing him goodnight like a normal wife. Now she had no choice but to accept the grim and terrible lesson that her returned memory had delivered.

Consumed by fresh misery, Carrie lay stiffly on her side, careful to keep a safe distance, but she couldn't stop her mind from trailing through the years of retrieved memories. The happiness and the heartbreak.

Against her better judgement she was remembering right back to the night she'd met Max at Grant and Cleo's wedding.

# CHAPTER ELEVEN

IN THE CHURCH, Max was sitting three rows in front of Carrie, and she found herself fascinated by the back view of him—by the breadth of his shoulders, the fit of his beautifully cut evening suit and the neat line his dark hair made across the back of his suntanned neck.

Then he turned around and she encountered her first flash of his amazing blue eyes. She was smitten. But she had to make discreet enquiries via several of the other wedding guests before she wangled an introduction.

At the reception, the bride's mother came to her rescue when she invited Max to meet her daughter's workmates. Max gave everyone warm smiles and nods, repeating their names as they were introduced, but when it was Carrie's turn she could have sworn there was an extra sparkle in his stunning blue eyes, a deeper warmth to his charming grin.

She fell fast and hard, and by some lucky alignment of the planets the attraction was mutual.

Max engineered a little sly rearrangement of the place card settings, so they could sit together throughout the reception. In the breaks between the wedding speeches they chatted animatedly like speed daters, collecting as much information about each other as they could, and no doubt grinning like love-struck fools the whole time.

Max seemed genuinely interested in Carrie, which made a nice change from the guys she usually dated, who were so intent on impressing her they only talked about themselves.

'You'll dance with me, won't you?' Max said after the speeches were over and they had watched and applauded as Cleo and Grant had given a beautiful rendition of the bridal waltz.

'Of course.' Carrie knew she shouldn't sound quite so eager, but she couldn't help herself.

Even before the sizzling magic of that first physical contact she was already abuzz. Then she placed her left hand on Max's shoulder and felt the rock-hard muscles beneath his expensive suiting. He placed his hand at her small of her back and took her right hand in his…and the impact of his touch tingled and zapped through her, clear to the soles of her feet.

She was floating as they danced, almost giddy with excitement and with building heat, swept away by the sparkle in Max's eyes and smile.

When the band took a short break they returned to their table, and one of Carrie's workmates leaned close to her ear. 'Crikey, girlfriend, I reckon you two might self-combust before the night's over.'

Carrie hadn't realised their chemistry was quite so obvious, and she found herself blushing, but she didn't want anything about this night to slow down.

Max obviously felt the same way. The bride had only just thrown her bouquet, and she and her groom were still completing a final circuit, farewelling their guests, when he whispered to Carrie, 'You think anyone will notice if we slip away now?'

Carrie gulped. 'Slip away?'

'I'm staying in this hotel.' His smile held just the right balance between country boy shyness and sexy intent.

Carrie had never been so reckless and wanton, had never had sex on a first date, but they had already said goodbye to Cleo and Grant and they'd thanked Cleo's parents.

Another smile from Max and she was willing to throw caution to the wind. She'd sensed that beneath his sexy good looks there was a steadiness she could trust.

They took the elevator up to Max's hotel room, and the door was barely closed before he drew Carrie in and kissed her.

And, oh, what a hot and steamy kiss it was. *Incendiary.*

They were both so burning for each other they stripped off in a frenzy, their clothes falling to the floor. It was only as they shamelessly slid naked between the sheets that Carrie felt a flash of fear. Was she being totally foolish, leaping into bed with a stranger?

Then, almost as if he knew how she felt, Max kissed her gently…tenderly…such a sweet, comforting kiss that it melted her fear as easily as the sun melted mist…

How on earth could she ever have forgotten it?

Everything about meeting Max had been perfect.

Until the next day, when her mother had called.

'Something terrible has happened, Carrie.' Her voice had been shaky and high-pitched, as if she was crying. 'I—I can't possibly talk about it on the phone. You'll have to come to my place. Please? It's important.'

Carrie had never heard her mum sounding so shaken.

Reluctantly, she'd said goodbye to Max. Told him if she was free she would ring him later in the day and possibly see him that evening. He'd been spending one more night in Sydney before returning home to Outback Queensland. In case another meeting wasn't possible, they'd both promised fervently that they would keep in contact—no matter what.

Then Carrie had hurried home to her flat to change before going to her mother's. It had been like riding a rollercoaster, to go from the heady glory of her night with Max to her mother's apartment.

Sylvia had looked deathly pale and about ten years older.

'Mum, what is it?' She looked so terrible she had to be ill. 'Have you called a doctor?'

Tears spilled from her mother's eyes and she stabbed at them with a tissue. 'There's someone here, Carrie. He—he needs to speak to you.'

Carrie was more worried than ever. Why would a visitor make her mum look so distressed? 'Who is it? He's not threatening you, is he, Mum?' She was beginning to wish she'd asked Max to come with her.

Her mother gave an impatient shake of her head. 'Don't ask questions, Carrie. Just come in.'

Bewildered, and more than a little worried, Carrie followed her mother into the open-plan living area. There was a tall, silver-haired man standing the far end of the room. He was at the window, looking out at a view of suburban rooftops. He turned as they entered.

'Oh,' Carrie said with surprise as she recognised one of the wedding guests. She couldn't remember his name, though. She'd been too busy falling for Max. 'We met last night, didn't we? You're Max's neighbour.'

His tanned outdoorsy aura reminded her of Max.

'Yes, Carrie. My name's Doug Peterson.'

He was smiling as he came forward, but Carrie fancied the smile was strained.

She glanced to her mother, who was twisting the tissue in her hands and looking as scared as someone about to be executed. What on earth was going on?

'I know this is completely out of the blue,' Doug Peterson said. 'And I'm sorry you haven't had more warning, but your mother and I have something to tell you.'

'*Your mother and I.*' Why did this sound so ominous?

'Perhaps we should all sit down?' he said.

Completely bewildered, Carrie sat on the sofa with her mother, while Doug Peterson took the armchair opposite them.

Across the coffee table her mother and Doug exchanged nervous glances, and then, in bits and pieces, they told Carrie their story. Doug, despite the silver sheen of tears in his eyes, spoke relatively calmly and reasonably, while her mother sobbed as she made her halting confession.

Such a disturbing story they told, of falling in love too quickly and marrying in haste, only to regret it when her mother came face to face with the realities of living in the Outback. Then the unconvincing decision that Carrie had been better off not knowing about Doug.

Throughout this recounting Carrie said nothing. She couldn't speak. She was too shocked. Too upset. Too angry. For as long as she could remember she'd understood that her father was dead. She couldn't believe her mother had kept him a secret all these years. And she couldn't believe Doug had been prepared to stay out of her life.

'Doug was reluctant,' her mother admitted. 'But I was sure it was best for you.'

'Why?' Carrie demanded. 'How could it be best to tell me my father was dead?'

'It was a mistake, Carrie,' Doug said. 'A bad mistake. I should never have agreed. I knew that as soon as I met you last night.'

It would have been nice if this had been like a scene from a movie, but Carrie knew that wasn't going to happen. Not yet. She wasn't going to simply fall into her father's arms for a fond hug, making up for lost time. And the two of them wouldn't be hugging her mother either, with everything forgiven.

Carrie had only so recently met her own Outback cattleman, and she was too upset by her parents' story—too angry with her mum, with both them. She was remembering, too, all the derogatory remarks Sylvia had made about the Outback, always downplaying life on the land throughout her childhood.

She wasn't ready for any kind of hugging.

But the situation only got worse when Doug made the mistake of mentioning his neighbour, Max, and the fact that Max and Carrie had hit it off so well last night.

'A *cattleman*?' her mother whimpered, going white as a sheet. 'Carrie, you don't want to make my mistake.'

Sylvia became even more distressed when she learned that Carrie planned to see Max again.

'Oh, please…no. Don't tell me it's happening all over again.'

Then she fell back against the sofa, with her head hanging at an awkward angle.

For an appalled moment Carrie and Doug could only

stare at each other, then Doug rushed to kneel at her mum's side while Carrie whipped out her phone.

'I'm calling the doctor,' she said.

It was late in the day when Carrie rang Max from the hospital and told him that her mother had been admitted.

'She's being kept in overnight for observation, and they'll also run some tests,' she told him. 'At this stage it doesn't appear to be anything really serious. Mainly stress, they believe. She's being treated for hypertension as the first step.' A small sigh escaped her. 'I don't think I can come out with you tonight, Max.'

'No,' he agreed. 'I'm sure your mother needs to have you close by.'

Which deepened her belief that he was a really nice guy. She didn't tell him about Doug Peterson. It was too soon to admit that her family was like something out of a soap opera.

They talked about when they could see each other again.

'I'm going to be busy mustering over the next few weeks,' Max said. 'But after that's done I'll try to get down to Sydney again. Or perhaps your mother will be better by then and you might be able to make a trip up to Queensland.'

Carrie smiled. 'That sounds like a plan. I'll text you my email address and we can keep in touch.'

*Perhaps it should have ended then*, Carrie thought now, lying uneasily in bed beside Max and remembering. *I would have saved everyone a great deal of heartache.*

But of course ending her relationship with Max had been the last thing on her mind. When the mustering was over she had taken leave and travelled to Riverslea

Downs. There she'd met Max's parents and Barney, who had welcomed her with open arms.

By then Max had been fully informed about her parents, and he'd taken her to Whitehorse Creek, where she'd met Meredith and deepened her connection with Doug. She'd enjoyed seeing her father in his own environment, and it had been at Whitehorse Creek that she'd had her first horse riding lesson. She'd sensed that in time she and Doug could become close.

The very best part about that first trip to Riverslea Downs, however, had been when Max had taken Carrie on a tour of his property. With a canoe tied to the ute's roof rack and swags stowed in the back, along with an ice cooler, a camp oven and cooking gear, they'd set off on the adventure of Carrie's lifetime.

They had canoed down the river, fulfilling her girlhood dream of a Pocahontas or Hiawatha experience. At night they'd camped on the riverbank and cooked on an open fire. They'd made love under the starry heavens and again in the mornings, when mist had drifted up from the river as white and pretty as a bridal veil.

Of course the more had Carrie got to know about Max the more deeply she'd fallen in love with him. She'd discovered his quiet sense of humour and been awed by his knowledge of the bush. He'd seemed to have a botanist's knowledge of native trees and plants, and an impressive understanding of the birds and animals.

He had told Carrie about the storm birds that migrated from Indonesia and New Guinea each summer and returned north at the end of March. On the river, he'd pointed out Burdekin ducks, ibises and white-breasted sea eagles.

'OK, David Attenborough,' she'd joked. 'I expect you to be able to name every bird we see.'

And of course he had. There had been whistling ducks, kites, goshawks, brolgas, pelicans. Way more than she could remember.

She had also learned that Max was surprisingly well travelled, having spent six months on a rural scholarship in South America, then backpacking around Europe, as well as hiking in the foothills of the Himalayas.

By the end of her stay at Riverslea Downs there had been no doubt. Max Kincaid was the man of her dreams. She'd adored him and she'd adored his Outback lifestyle, and nothing her mother could say would change her mind.

Not that her mother hadn't tried. Many times.

Even just a week before their wedding, she'd warned Carrie again. 'You'll live to regret the day you met Max.'

Carrie had been certain this prediction could never come true, and she'd been angry with her mother for trying to pass on her own prejudices and hang-ups.

Sylvia had never been reconciled, though. Carrie could still remember the strain on her face at their wedding—the tears in her eyes when she'd watched Carrie coming down the aisle on Doug Peterson's arm.

*I was too in love to let her spoil our joy.*

But now, fighting the sobs that welled in her throat, Carrie lay in the dark, clinging to her side of the mattress so that she didn't inadvertently make contact with Max, and knew that she should have listened.

The sickening truth was that her mother's warning had come true. Carrie *had* lived to regret the day she'd met Max.

After hearing the doctor's terrible news about her infertility she'd sunk into an awful, creeping sense of gloom. Perhaps it had been delayed shock, or a kind of depression, but whatever her mental state had been she'd arrived at the painful conclusion that she was the wrong woman for Max Kincaid and his vast rural inheritance.

Her mum's aversion to the bush had become handy when Carrie had found it necessary to walk away from her marriage.

Max soon realised his mistake. It was impossible to sleep next to Carrie. They were both as tense as trapped animals, but they weren't even able to toss and turn for fear of touching.

It was a ridiculous turnaround. Just twenty-four hours ago, in this very bed, they hadn't been able to keep their hands off each other.

Around midnight he gave up and went back to the spare room, hoping that Carrie, at least, would be able to sleep if she was alone. He had no expectations of sleeping, and was surprised to wake a few hours later, just on dawn.

Unwilling to lie there, with his desperate thoughts clawing through the mess of his life, he got up quickly and dressed. A glance through the bedroom doorway showed that Carrie was asleep at last, lying on her back now, with one arm thrown out like an exhausted swimmer, collapsed on the shore at the end of a marathon swim.

The sight was almost too sweet to bear.

He left the house and whistled up Phoenix, his favourite stock horse from the home paddock. In the past Max had always been able to rely on a long, hard ride to calm his heart and clear his head.

This morning wasn't one of those times, unfortunately.

Despite the crisp autumn air, the clear blue sky and the thundering pace of the stallion beneath him, Max couldn't throw off the gut-tearing reality that his marriage was circling the drain.

Tension still nagged at his innards as he returned, unsaddled his horse and gave him a good rub down. The problem was these past few days since Carrie's accident had been bittersweet, inescapable reminders of how good their relationship could be. How good it *had* been until Carrie's fateful trip to Sydney last November.

Max knew Carrie must be aware of this, too, and as he gave Phoenix a friendly farewell slap on the rump and strode back to the homestead he could only hope that she hadn't reverted to her former uninterested behaviour.

One good thing—he was prepared for it this time and he had no plans to back away. He was determined to get their relationship back on the rails.

'That smells great,' Carrie said as she came into the kitchen looking pale and tired, as if she hadn't slept well.

'Are you hungry?' Max turned from the stove.

He'd decided to rustle up a full breakfast of coffee, bacon and eggs, fried tomatoes and toast. He was hungry after the ride and he'd hoped the smells might entice Carrie out.

'I'm starving, actually. I'll do the toast.'

The toaster popped up two slices just then and she was already at the fridge, fetching butter, which she spread while Max served up the contents of the sizzling pan.

Despite the veneer of normality, however, he soon realised that things weren't entirely peachy as they sat down to breakfast. He knew Carrie well—when she was happy she was quite a chatterer, but this morning she had nothing to say except to comment that the coffee was good and the bacon crisp.

Max tried a couple of times to start a conversation. He made a comment about an item on the news, and another about the football team they both followed. But Carrie had the glazed-eyed look of someone whose mind was somewhere else entirely.

As Max finished his meal he poured himself another cup of coffee and sat back in the chair, trying to look a hell of a lot more relaxed than he felt.

'I guess we need to talk,' he said.

Carrie's face tightened and she looked distinctly uneasy as she shook her head. 'I don't think I'm ready, Max. I still feel really confused.'

'What are you confused about?' He had a fair idea, but he needed confirmation.

Carrie closed her eyes, as if the question was far too difficult to answer. 'Everything,' she said at last.

'Carrie.' With an effort, Max reined in his decreasing patience. 'I'm not going to let you withdraw from me. Not again. Not after these past few days. It doesn't make sense.'

At this, Carrie opened her lovely eyes, and the message in their chocolate-brown depths was all about guilt. 'I know,' she admitted softly. 'Right now it doesn't really make sense to me either.'

Dropping her gaze again, she fiddled with the handle of her coffee cup. 'I'm sorry, Max. I am—truly. I'm really sorry about the way I've carried on…especially the way I threw myself at you.'

'But why should you be sorry?'

She'd certainly seemed to enjoy herself. Max was sure that level of passion couldn't be faked. But he also knew that fantastic sex alone couldn't save a marriage. Even so, it surely had to help.

'It was wrong,' Carrie said. 'I—I wasn't myself. I'd forgotten how I feel.'

'Feel?' She wasn't making sense.

'About this place.'

His innards turned to ice. 'So,' he said, more coldly than he'd intended. 'We're back to this, are we? One minute you're carrying on about how much you love the bush, and begging for a campfire by the river. And the next you can't wait to get away from Riverslea. Is that what you're saying? Are you going to tell me the sex was a mistake as well? You only *thought* you wanted to make love with me? You only *thought* you enjoyed it?'

Looking as unhappy as Max had ever seen her, Carrie drew a deep breath and appeared to hold it as she stared hard at a spot on the floor. It was pretty clear she was struggling to come up with a reasonable answer.

Then the phone rang, cutting through the bristling silence like a sword.

Max cursed. It was the worst possible moment to be interrupted.

Carrie, on the other hand, seemed to welcome it. Jumping at the chance to escape their awkward conversation, she hurried to answer the phone.

'Hello?' she said, standing with her back to Max.

The caller seemed to have a great deal to say. It was probably Sylvia, Max realised, and he grimaced at the thought of everything his mother-in-law would want to tell her daughter. He began to collect their plates, knowing this was, almost certainly the end of this attempt at a deep and meaningful conversation with Carrie.

He would have to bide his time and try again later.

'I see,' Carrie was saying. 'That's terrible. Yes, I'll come straight away. Yes, of course.'

*Come straight away?*

Fine hairs rose on the back of Max's neck. What evil scheme had The Dragon come up with this time? There was no way he was letting Carrie leave this place until they'd had a proper, in-depth, no-holds-barred discussion.

This time he wasn't going to be fobbed off with vague excuses. He loved Carrie too much. If she had problems with their relationship he wanted her to spell them out. With luck, if he at least understood he might be able to negotiate a strategy.

He was so busy getting this straight in his head that he hadn't noticed the expression on Carrie's face as she hung up the phone. It was only when she flopped back down onto a kitchen chair that he saw how upset she was.

'What's happened?' he said. 'Who was on the phone? Your mother?'

She shook her head. 'No, it was Jean—Mum's neighbour.' Tears welled in her eyes and her lips trembled. 'Mum's in hospital. She's had a heart attack.'

'Oh, sweetheart.'

In two strides Max was beside Carrie. She felt his fingers stroking her hair and she longed to reach out to him, to have him wrap her in a big, warm, comforting hug. But she'd just spent an entire night lecturing herself that she mustn't weaken like that again.

'Do you know how bad Sylvia is?' he asked gently.

'Not really. But Jean said she's on the cardiac ward, not intensive care, so I guess that's a good thing.'

'I imagine you'll want to get to Sydney as soon as you can.'

'Yes.'

She was grateful that he understood—especially as she knew her mum had never endeared herself to Max. She also knew he would be sick at the thought of her leaving in the midst of their marital mess. And she would feel guilty about taking off when things were so up in the air.

But it was typical of her husband that he put her needs before his.

'Pity you unpacked your suitcase,' he said.

She managed a weak smile.

'I'll come with you, Carrie.'

Her smile faded. 'You can't. You're too busy getting ready for the muster. Max, you don't have to come.'

He shook his head. 'The mustering won't start for another couple of weeks, and Barney can look after things here. I want to come.'

*Oh, Max.*

After her erratic behaviour following her last trip to Sydney there was every chance that he didn't want her out of his sight. But despite the amnesia, and their recent closeness, their big problem had not disappeared. She was still infertile. She still needed to give Max his freedom. She was supposed to be distancing herself from him so their separation could ease into divorce.

But the news about her mother had scared Carrie. For all she knew her mum's life might be teetering on a knife-edge. And deep down she knew that she would love to have Max with her in Sydney.

She needed his calming strength, his ever-reliable love and support. But how could she ask that of him if she was still planning to leave him?

# CHAPTER TWELVE

As ALWAYS, MAX was magnificent. While Carrie dragged her suitcase out again and began to pack he organised their flights to Sydney and made bookings for a hotel close to the hospital.

The nearest big airport was in Townsville, and as they made the familiar journey Max refrained from asking any more difficult questions.

He and Carrie had listened to an interesting hour-long interview with one of their favourite crime authors on the radio, but Carrie leaned forward and changed the station when a programme about depression among rural and isolated people started.

Max frowned at her, but said nothing.

At the airport, Carrie bought a couple of magazines to distract her during the two-and-a-half-hour flight.

After her sleepless night she found the journey exhausting, but they went straight to the hospital and she was relieved to be there at last. Max suggested he should stay in the waiting room, which was sensible. His presence might only distress her mother.

Carrie, carrying a bunch of her mum's favourite pink roses, ventured somewhat nervously into the cardiac ward. She found Sylvia awake and apparently well, despite looking pale and tired and being attached to an alarming bank of monitors.

'Darling,' Sylvia said when she saw Carrie. 'What a lovely surprise. I didn't expect to see you so soon.'

The news was good, Carrie soon learned, or at least much better than she'd feared. There was to be a new medication regime, but the doctors had assured her mother that she should be fine.

Her mum pointed to the chair beside her bed. 'Take a seat, Carrie. Tell me your news.'

Carrie wished she had pleasant, uplifting news.

She explained that her memory had returned. She didn't add that in her current state of mind her memory was her worst enemy—that it had presented her with a reality she didn't want to face.

'I found it very stressful, worrying about you all on your own way out there in the Outback, with no memory,' her mother said. 'Poor thing—you didn't even know that you weren't supposed to be there.'

'No,' Carrie agreed, grateful that her mother had no knowledge of the messy details of this past week at Riverslea Downs.

'I suppose you'll stay on in Sydney now you're here?' her mother said next.

'Well…' Carrie dropped her gaze, wishing she had a quick and easy answer, wishing she didn't feel so confused and torn about her previous decision to leave Max. 'I'll certainly stay while you need me.'

'But you're not going back to Max? You told me you wanted to leave him. What's going on?'

Again, Carrie hesitated. The easy option would be to reassure her mum that her marriage and her life in the Outback were over, but she was wasn't ready to commit to any clear course of action. She still felt terribly confused.

'I'm still coming to terms with everything,' she admitted.

And then, to change the subject, she reached into her handbag for the magazines she'd been reading on the plane.

'Here's a little light reading. You'll love the house and home section, and there are even some yummy recipes designed by a heart specialist.'

Carrie stayed for another five minutes and managed to steer the conversation to her mother's interests and friends.

'I should leave you to rest now, Mum,' she said, leaning in to kiss her mother's cheek. 'I was told that I shouldn't stay too long.' She gave her mum's hand a gentle squeeze. 'I'll see you tonight.'

'I'll look forward that.' Her mother's eyes were shining with unexpected fondness, and Carrie felt the sting of tears as she left.

She found Max in the waiting room. As soon as he saw her he stood, inadvertently drawing her attention to his height and his strapping physique, his healthy outdoors tan. Such a handsome, vigorous contrast to the pale, listless patients on the ward she'd just left.

A painful rush of longing caught Carrie square in the chest. She blinked hard, terrified that she'd burst into tears.

Perhaps Max sensed this. He frowned and looked concerned, clearly fearing bad news.

'Mum's OK,' she quickly reassured him.

He let out a huff of relief. 'That's good news. You looked so upset you had me worried.'

'Sorry. I guess I'm tired.' She could hardly admit that the sight of him looking so hot and handsome had brought her to the brink of tears. 'But, honestly, Mum seems to be in pretty good shape. Much better than I expected.'

'That's great.' Max nodded towards the exit at the far end of a corridor. 'You want to get out of this place?'

'Yes, please. I'd kill for a really good coffee.'

'Let's find one, then.'

They were halfway down the corridor when Carrie recognised the man coming towards them. He was wearing a white coat and a bow tie and carrying a pile of folders tucked under one arm.

Unfortunately Dr Bligh also recognised Carrie. 'Mrs Kincaid,' he said, stopping to greet her. 'How are you?'

Carrie felt a bright flush spread over her skin. She'd never told Max about her visits to this hospital for scans and X-rays, or her subsequent consultations with the gynaecologist. Before she'd come to Sydney last November she'd been confident that everything would be sorted easily—that she would be able to tell Max about it afterwards, reporting that she'd had a minor 'feminine' problem and all was well.

Now, she could hardly pretend she didn't know this man. 'Hello, Dr Bligh.'

'Is everything OK?' he asked, as if he was worried to find her back in the hospital.

'Oh, yes,' Carrie assured him nervously. 'I've been visiting my mother.' She nodded towards the cardiac ward.

'Ah, good. I hope she's doing well?'

'Yes, she is, thanks.'

The doctor directed a warm smile towards Max. 'Hello. I don't think we've met…'

'Sorry.' Carrie jumped in, badly flustered. 'Dr Bligh, this is my husband, Max.'

She knew Max was wondering what the heck was going on, but he held out his hand. 'Pleased to meet you, Doctor.' Max's smile was polite, but also a little stiff.

'And I'm very pleased to meet *you*, Max.' Dr Bligh bestowed another warm smile upon them, but within a heartbeat his expression became serious. 'So, tell me, how are you both? Are you coming to terms with everything?'

*Everything.*

The doctor was talking about her infertility, of course.

Carrie's mind froze. She couldn't possibly think of an appropriate answer. She could only think of how messy her attempts to handle 'everything' had been. Her heart was thumping hard enough to land her in the cardiac unit right next to her mother.

'We're fine,' she managed at last, knowing how inadequate this must sound.

Concern glimmered in the doctor's eyes, but with another glance at Max, who remained silent, he nodded. 'That's good to hear. All the best, then. I'm running late. As always.'

With a wave he was off, hurrying down the corridor.

*Oh, dear Lord.*

Carrie was shaking as she slid a glance Max's way.

He made no attempt to hide his shock. 'What the hell was that about?'

To hide her nerves she kept walking, shooting a reply over her shoulder. 'I used to be a patient of his.'

'What kind of doctor is he?'

'A gynaecologist.'

Max frowned and reached for her elbow, forcing her

to stop. 'How long ago was this, Carrie?' He looked puzzled. 'Before we met?'

Carrie wished she could lie, but over the past five months she'd told enough half-truths to last her a lifetime. Besides, she'd heard the doubt in Max's voice. She knew he'd find it hard to believe that a doctor would bother to stop to speak to a patient after a gap of four years.

'I saw him last year,' she mumbled, turning and heading down the corridor once more.

Max quickly caught her up. 'Last year?' His expression was fierce. 'You saw a gynaecologist here in Sydney *last year*?'

'Yes,' she said, without looking at him.

'Last November?'

Her heart thumped harder than ever as she kept walking.

'Carrie!' Once again Max caught her arm, bringing her to a halt. 'Don't play games,' he warned through gritted teeth. 'We both know what happened after you came home from Sydney last November.'

They were standing near a nurses' station and Carrie was sure the nurses had overheard Max's outburst.

Max hadn't noticed, though. He was too worried, too shocked.

'Oh, God,' he said, taking both Carrie's arms and gripping her elbows tightly. His face was twisted with pain and fear. 'That doctor didn't give you bad news, did he? You're not—?' He gulped, and his face paled despite his tan. 'It—it's not serious? Terminal?'

Carrie gasped. The poor man looked terrified. 'No, Max, *no*,' she hastened to assure him. 'Nothing like that.'

She saw sliding glass doors indicating an exit.

'Let's get out of here.'

'OK,' Max said as he kept pace with her. 'But you're going to tell me everything.'

They found a conveniently empty courtyard, shaded by a large shady maple tree, with seats set around a large square goldfish pond.

There was no sign of a coffee shop, but Carrie's stomach was churning so badly she knew coffee would have made her sick.

'Right,' Max said, almost as soon as they were seated. 'What's this all about?'

His gaze was fierce, his blue eyes dark—the colour of a stormy sea.

'Why would you see a Sydney gynaecologist and not tell your husband a thing about it?'

'I didn't want to bother you.'

Carrie winced, wondering why the excuse sounded so weak now, when it had made good sense at the time.

'As you know, we'd been trying for a baby without any luck, and I was worried—I had this *feeling* that something wasn't quite right. But I was so fit and well I thought it had to be a little thing…easily fixed. I thought I wouldn't worry you. Just get it sorted.'

'But it wasn't just a little thing?' Max guessed.

'No.'

Carrie could feel the tears burning in her throat and behind her eyes. For so long she'd kept this to herself, and now she was afraid she wouldn't be able to get it out without breaking down.

Taking a deep breath, she forced herself to go on. 'Dr Bligh told me that I can't have a baby. Not ever. There's a problem with my uterus—a malformation—and it's not something that can be corrected by surgery.'

'Oh, Carrie…'

The flash of pain in Max's eyes was heartbreaking, but then he switched his gaze to the pond, staring hard at it as his white-knuckled hands gripped the edge of the bench seat.

If he'd turned back to her then—if he'd shown her even a glimmer of the sympathy he'd always shown in the past—she would have succumbed almost certainly. She would have fallen into his arms and cried her heart out. She might have asked for his forgiveness. She might even have received it.

But Max didn't move, and Carrie was too worried about what he was thinking to give in to her tears.

'You came home with important and life-changing news—something relevant to our marriage at a deeply personal level—and you saw fit not to tell me.' His face was stony, his voice hard, as he continued to stare at the pond, where fish darted in gold and silver shimmers between the slender green reeds.

'I'm sorry,' Carrie said. 'I thought it was for the best.'

She'd known how it would be if she'd gone home and told Max about her infertility. He would have been disappointed. He would have grieved for the children they would never have. But he would also have hugged her close, murmured soothing words and told her that it didn't matter. He loved her. They loved each other. That was enough.

He would have nobly accepted that he was the last of the Kincaids at Riverslea.

But she hadn't wanted him to make that sacrifice. It was *her* fault, *her* problem—not his.

She'd known he would never understand, so she'd found her own solution.

Now, however, he was glaring at her.

'Instead of telling me the truth you came home and lost interest in me. What was *that* about, Carrie? Was it because we couldn't have a family? Were children all you wanted from our marriage?'

'No!' she cried, aghast. 'You've got it wrong, Max. It wasn't about what *I* wanted. I did it for *you*. I—I knew how important is was for you to have children. You've had five generations of Kincaids on Riverslea. Your family's property is an important inheritance. There's such a long tradition, and I didn't want you to be the end of the line.'

'You've got to be joking.'

Max's eyes were wild now, his voice so angry it was almost unrecognisable. He leapt to his feet and turned to her, his hands raised in clenched fists. But then, with a groan, he let them fall to his sides.

'I can't believe you thought so little of me. Did you really believe I would cast you out if you couldn't produce a child?'

'No,' Carrie protested. 'I knew you wouldn't do that. That was the problem. I knew you'd tell me that it didn't matter. I knew you'd try to be noble about it.'

*'Noble?'* He looked at her as if she'd lost her mind. 'So your solution was to spend the months afterwards making out that you were tired of me and of Riverslea?' He lifted his hands in a gesture of helplessness. 'That's the craziest thing I've ever heard.'

The terrible thing was that it *did* sound crazy, coming from him. But what choice had she had back then? If she'd tried to leave Max straight after her return from Sydney he would have been suspicious. He would have pushed for answers till he got to the truth.

As it was, she'd found it relatively easy to build up her

criticisms of the Outback and sound convincing. After all, she'd had a lifetime of listening to her mother's objections to cattlemen and their way of life. She'd had a host of complaints at her fingertips.

She tried to explain. 'It was the only way I could think of to set you free.'

'Set me *free*?'

Once again Max looked incredulous, and Carrie knew she was digging a deeper hole for herself. Then, with a groan of frustration, Max whirled on his heel and strode away.

'You're not going to leave me?' Carrie called, but almost immediately wondered why she'd asked that. It was exactly what she deserved, after all.

'Why not?' Max was scowling as he turned back. 'Isn't that what you want?'

*No!*

She couldn't give voice to the protest, but he stopped and half turned to her, every muscle in his body tense, and pinned her with a cold, hard glare.

'OK, Carrie. Just so you're clear about my side of this. If you *had* told me that you couldn't have a child I *would* have told you that it didn't matter. Not because I'm noble. This has nothing to do with nobility. This is about the fact that I loved you.'

*Loved.* Past tense.

His mouth tightened formidably. 'Why couldn't you have trusted me? Why couldn't you have trusted that our love was strong enough to cope with whatever life threw at us—for better or for worse?' His blue eyes shimmered damply. 'I felt as if my life had ended the day you walked out.'

Then he turned and kept going, striding away.

It was the worst possible moment for Carrie to run slap-bang into the truth—that she couldn't bear to face the future without him.

But it was too late. Max was so angry he wouldn't listen to her. And even if she did try to explain he wouldn't believe her.

'Can you at least tell me where you're going?' she called, running after him.

'I don't know,' he snapped. 'I guess I'll find another hotel.'

'You don't need to, Max. Mum's given me her key. I'll go to her place.'

He stopped, apparently caught out by this sudden intrusion of practicality.

'OK. I don't care,' he said with an angry shrug. 'Whatever suits.'

# CHAPTER THIRTEEN

THE MUSTER AT Riverslea Downs, with long days in the saddle and nights sleeping rough, was over. The cattle had been rounded up, yarded and sorted, and now the huge road trains that would take the stock to the sale yards were ready to leave.

A loud wheezy hiss broke the morning stillness as the compression brakes were released. Then came the roaring rev of the motors, and slowly the massive vehicles rolled forward, each pulling three trailers loaded with Riverslea Downs cattle.

Max stood with Barney, watching as the trains slowly disappeared down the track, sending clouds of red dust in their wake.

'That's over for another year,' Barney said, shoving his Akubra hat back from his forehead with a weary hand. 'I can tell you, I'm bushed.'

'You've worked hard, old fellow,' Max told him. 'You need to take it easy for a few days.'

'Won't argue with that.'

The men enjoyed a cuppa together on the homestead veranda, yarning as cattlemen did about the muster, about the weather, the condition of the cattle and of the country they'd travelled over and the prospect of a decent price at the markets.

They didn't talk about Carrie. She'd become a taboo subject since Max had returned from Sydney.

Barney had learned the hard way, having tried twice to ask Max where she was and whether she was coming home, but he'd nearly had his head bitten off both times and hadn't asked again. For which Max was grateful. Not that Max didn't think about Carrie every minute of every day and night.

Her absence was a huge gaping hole inside him. The busy days in the saddle and the nights spent swapping yarns with the stockmen around the camp fire had served as a partial distraction, but Carrie had always been there—a permanent ache in his heart.

Max knew he had to shoulder the blame for their separation. It was hard to believe he'd actually been so angry he'd walked out on Carrie after she'd finally told him the real reason for her bewildering behaviour. He should have rejoiced that her motives had not been driven by a lack of interest or love but by the very opposite.

He'd been so blindsided by the raw fact that she'd kept her condition a secret. He'd been hurt that she hadn't wanted to share such a deeply important problem. Surely couples survived such tragedies by pulling together? But instead of turning to him for support Carrie had chosen to isolate herself in her own private world of misery.

The discovery of this in Sydney had hurt him so deeply that he hadn't bothered to offer her sympathy or comfort. He hadn't even given her a chance to explain her reasoning properly. He'd marched off in a cloud of self-righteous anger. And now he'd virtually been out of contact with her for nearly a month.

Of course over the weeks since then he'd nursed his share of regrets. At the time he'd been shocked. Shocked by her sad news, shocked for Carrie, for himself and for his own dreams of a family.

But the one factor that lingered and saddened Max beyond bearing was that Carrie had convinced herself she must leave him simply because she couldn't bear his child.

It hadn't made sense then and it still didn't make sense. But at least he now understood the pain that had led to his wife's irrational thinking. It was the same deep pain that had sent him storming off, abandoning the woman he loved with every fibre of his being. The woman he'd vowed to love and protect.

If the plans for the muster hadn't been so firmly in place he would have tried to delay it while he paid attention to his marriage. But all the stockmen, including a camp cook, had already been hired, the supplies and the freight had been ordered, and Max had promised to help Doug with the Whitehorse Creek muster as well.

He would have let too many people down if he'd shifted the dates. His personal disaster had been put on hold.

But the whole time he'd been away he'd been foolishly hoping against hope for a miracle—that Carrie might have tried to contact him. Last night, when he'd finally arrived back at the homestead, he'd driven straight down to the mailbox. Standing at the edge of the track, checking the envelopes by the light of a torch, he'd found plenty of bills but no letter from Carrie.

Clover hadn't even been there to greet him, as he'd

taken her to Whitehorse Creek to be minded by Meredith for the duration of the muster. Inside the house, he'd headed to the phone to check for messages. There had been nothing from his wife. In the office, he'd booted up his computer, but Carrie hadn't sent him an email either. In almost a month there'd been no contact at all, and Max felt like a dead man walking.

But now, at last, all his business commitments were behind him, and in the clear light of day Max knew that if he wanted any chance of winning Carrie back there was only one thing to do.

The waiting room at the fertility clinic held its usual contingent of pregnant women. Carrie kept her gaze averted from their rounded tummies. After the nightmares that had haunted her over the past few months she tried not to think about her last visit here, or the tests in the hospital that had preceded it.

She sat in a corner, paying assiduous attention to a fashion magazine. The clothes were beautiful. Carrie had mostly lived in jeans for the past three years and she'd lost touch with the latest trends, so there was a great deal to catch up on.

She wished she felt more interested in hemlines and fabrics. Wished her mind wouldn't keep wandering, thinking about all the action she'd been missing at the Riverslea Downs muster.

The big muster was always so exciting—the highlight of the year. She'd been thrilled the first time she'd joined in, riding off over the vast plains, helping to coax straying cattle out of gullies or scrub, then steering the thundering herd towards the stockyards. Best of all, at the end of a long hard day there'd been crisp, clear Outback nights beneath a canopy of dazzling stars…and Max…

'Mrs Kincaid?'

Carrie started when her name was called. She was instantly angry with herself for letting her mind drift to Riverslea Downs. She should have been collecting her thoughts and composing her response for when the counsellor asked her why she'd come. Now it was too late.

She was flustered and nervous as she was shown into the counsellor's office. But she soon realised it was less like an office than a comfortable living room, with brightly coloured sofas and prints on the walls. Instead of a desk, a medical examination table and filing cabinets there was a coffee table and a tall pottery urn filled with autumn leaves.

Rising from one of the sofas, a woman aged around fifty, with short dark hair and warm dark eyes, smiled at Carrie. She was wearing a green turtleneck sweater and white jeans. Gold hoops in her ears matched the bangles at her wrists, and as she walked towards Carrie there was a kindly light in her eyes, a friendly warmth to her smile.

'Hi, Carrie,' she said, deepening her smile. Her bangles made a pleasant tinkling sound as she held out her hand. 'I'm Margaret.'

Carrie returned her smile. 'Hello, Margaret. Pleased to meet you.'

She sensed immediately that this was someone she could talk to, and she felt the tension roll from her shoulders.

It was a chilly, windy day when Max arrived in Sydney. The late autumn skies were bleak and grey, and leaves blew along footpaths and piled in gutters. Dressed in a charcoal knitted sweater and jeans, Max was feeling almost as grim as the weather when he knocked on his mother-in-law's front door.

The panelled door was painted in full-gloss black, with a copper-gold doorknob, and two perfectly trimmed topiary trees in grey stone pots were positioned on either side of the formal entrance. It was a stark contrast to the straggling purple bougainvillea that climbed over the timber trellis and railing on his homestead's front veranda.

The doorbell, when Max pressed it, sent a musical cascade rippling into the depths of the apartment. He braced himself when he heard footsteps, wondering if it would be Carrie or Sylvia who opened the door.

'Max!' His mother-in-law looked startled. 'Good heavens.' She touched a perfectly manicured hand to her perfectly groomed silver hair. 'What are you doing down here? Are you looking for Carrie?'

*A brilliant deduction*, he thought, unable to throw off the cynicism that always coloured the way he viewed Carrie's mother. But he spoke as pleasantly as he could. 'That's right, Sylvia. How are you?'

'Oh…' Nervously, she pulled the two sides of her navy blue cardigan into line. 'I'm well, thank you. Recovered, but still on medication.'

'You're looking well.'

'Thank you,' she said faintly. 'But I'm afraid I can't help you if you're looking for Carrie.'

Max frowned. 'What do you mean? Isn't she here? Staying with you?'

'She *was* here. She was here for several weeks, actually, looking after me when I came home from hospital. But I'm quite well now, and Carrie decided to move out and get a place of her own. A nice little flat like she had—before—'

'Before we were married,' Max finished for her, forcing the words past the rock of pain in his throat.

'Yes.' Sylvia had the grace to look uncomfortable.

Dismay poured through Max, as chilling as icy rain. This news was worse than he'd feared. 'So Carrie must be staying somewhere new,' he said. 'I assume she's been in touch?'

'Not for several days.' Sylvia stood for a moment with her hand on the doorknob, regarding Max with a worried frown. 'I must admit I'm concerned about her,' she said. 'I knew she was upset about the marriage break-up, but I thought she would start to pick up after a week or two. Instead, she seemed to get worse.'

Twin reactions of alarm and hope held Max on a knife-edge. 'Sylvia, may I come in? I think we need to talk.'

With an unhappy nod she stepped back to let him through the doorway. He followed her down the carpeted hallway to her lounge room—a rather charming but decidedly feminine room, with delicate antique furniture upholstered in brocade and vases of flowers and china ornaments on every available surface.

Max had only ever been in here a couple of times, and he remembered how uneasy he'd always felt—as if he was too big and boisterous and might break something.

'Take a seat,' Sylvia said, offering him an armchair which at least looked sturdy enough to hold him.

Max sat with his back straight and his legs carefully crossed.

'Would you like tea?' Sylvia asked.

'No, thanks.' He was too anxious to hear about Carrie. 'Sylvia, I have to apologise,' he said next, preferring to be clear about his position from the outset. 'I made a hash of things when I was down here in Sydney. Carrie probably told you about our argument. I'm afraid I was angry and I overreacted. I went back to Riverslea without saying goodbye.'

His mother-in-law's jaw dropped and she looked completely puzzled, as if she hadn't a clue what he was talking about. 'I'm sorry,' she said. 'When *were* you down here in Sydney?'

'I brought Carrie straight down here as soon as we heard about your heart attack,' he said.

Sylvia continued to look puzzled. 'You came, too? How strange... She never mentioned that.'

This was *not* a good sign. Max supposed he couldn't blame Carrie. Why should she admit that he'd turned around and abandoned her within hours of arriving here?

'Carrie was leaving you, wasn't she?' Sylvia asked next, with her typical bluntness.

Max nodded grimly. 'That was certainly her plan before she fell off that horse and forgot that she'd ever met me.'

His mother-in-law's mouth tightened. 'Yes, that's when everything went wrong.'

*On the contrary*, thought Max, remembering how those few days of Carrie's amnesia had delivered him back his loving wife. He'd come within a hair's breadth of restoring his happy marriage before he'd stupidly let it slip away again.

He swallowed nervously, tapped his fingers on the gold and cream brocade arm of his chair. 'Sylvia, I'm assuming Carrie's told you that she can't have children?'

The woman looked so suddenly stupefied Max was worried she'd have another heart attack.

'I didn't mean to shock you,' he said.

'I'm all right.' But Sylvia had lost her usual poise and confidence. She seemed to shrink before his very eyes. 'Can she really not have children?' she asked, in a small frightened voice.

'No, I'm afraid she can't.' Max spoke gently now. It was bad enough that Carrie had never talked to him about this, but he was stunned that she hadn't confided in her mother. 'There's a problem with her uterus. A malformation.'

'Oh, my poor baby.' For the first time since Max had known Sylvia Barnes she looked shrunken and old.

'I'm sorry,' he said. 'I was sure Carrie would have talked to you about it.'

'You would think so, wouldn't you?' She pressed three fingers to her quivering lips and drew a sharp breath, as if she was struggling not to cry. Then she shook her head sadly. 'I'm beginning to think there must be a great deal that I don't know.'

Max had *not* expected to feel sorry for his mother-in-law, but he understood the shock and pain she was fielding. At this moment he almost felt as if he and The Dragon were on the same side. They both loved Carrie deeply, and they were both desperately hurt that she'd rejected them when she'd needed them most.

With admirable dignity, Sylvia rose from her chair. 'Why don't you come into the kitchen, Max? I'm afraid I need that cup of tea, after all. And while I'm making it you can talk to me about my daughter.'

So Max gave her his version of events over recent months at Riverslea. To his surprise, he wasn't interrupted. Sylvia looked chastened as she listened. The news of Carrie's infertility and the fact that it was a condition her daughter had been born with seemed to have shaken her certainty, her belief that *her* way was the highway.

'I must admit,' she said as she poured him a second cup of tea, 'I just assumed Carrie was following in my footsteps when she began to fall out of love with Riverslea Downs. She had been so stubborn about wanting to marry you and wanting to live in the Outback. I suppose I'd been expecting her to come to her senses and realise her mistake. When it happened I felt as if my misgivings were totally justified.'

'Carrie was very convincing,' Max agreed.

'She had me as a role model,' Sylvia admitted, somewhat guiltily. 'But I can't believe she decided that she had to leave you because she couldn't give you a child—' Fresh tears shone in her eyes and she gave a sad shake of her head. 'The poor girl can't have been thinking straight.'

'No,' Max agreed. 'I don't think she was. She was trying to carry the whole burden on her own, when it should have been a problem we shared.'

'Yes…I suspect Carrie would benefit from some kind of counselling. You probably both would.'

Max knew she was right. He wasn't keen on the idea of counselling—for him, seeking that kind of outside help went against the grain…he liked to think he was quite capable of sorting out his own affairs. But he would do anything to help Carrie, to salvage their marriage.

'I came to Sydney to find Carrie, to do whatever's necessary,' he said.

'Ah, yes.' Sylvia looked thoughtful. She drew a long breath and let it out slowly. 'I must confess I did lie to you before. I *do* know where Carrie's staying.'

'That's fan—'

She cut off his relieved response with a sharply raised hand. 'But I'm sorry, Max,' she said quickly. 'At the moment I don't know whether Carrie wants to see you, so I can't just hand over her address.'

Fortunately Max cut off the swear word that had sprung to his lips. 'For heaven's sake,' he said instead. 'Carrie's my *wife*. I *love* her.'

He and his mother-in-law had come a long way today. By a minor miracle they'd reached a kind of understanding bordering on respect—something Max had never thought possible. But right now he felt a surge of the old frustration. Would Sylvia *never* be able to trust him?

'It's not the end of the world,' she said now, and her smile was not unsympathetic. 'You have Carrie's phone number.'

'Yes. Not that she's answering.'

'Well, I'll let her know that you're here in Sydney and that you'd like to see her. If she wants to speak to you she'll get in touch. That's reasonable, isn't it?'

'Of course it is.' He suppressed a sigh.

Two days later, however—the longest days of Max's life—Max still hadn't heard from Carrie. He was at his wits' end. Short of hiring a private detective, there was little he could do but wait. But common sense told him that if his wife was going to get in touch she would have done so by now.

After another night of dining alone, and probably drinking too many single malts, he flew back north. Alone. He'd thought he already knew what it was to feel desolate, but any previous sadness he'd experienced had been a mere drop in the ocean compared with the sea of misery and despair that swamped him now, as he faced life without Carrie.

The drive from Townsville to Riverslea Downs had never seemed so long, and it was dusk by the time he arrived.

Max had always loved taking the last bend on the winding bush track and coming into the open country that offered the first sight of the homestead. His home.

He especially loved this time of day, when a golden glow shimmered above the western hills and long shadows spooled over the paddocks. But today the scene looked gloomy and unbearably lonely.

Until this moment, the isolation of his Outback home had never bothered him, but now he could only think how solitary the house looked, and he pictured the long empty months and years ahead, stretching endlessly into a lonesome future. There wasn't even a dog to greet him. Clover was still being cared for at Whitehorse Creek.

He parked near the front steps, grabbed his overnight bag from the back seat and went into the house. He hadn't bothered to lock it, and he shoved the door open, dumped his gear and went quickly from room to room—not taking in details, merely flipping on lights in an effort to cheer himself up.

When he reached the back door he stood looking out at the orchard trees that screened the vegetable garden, and at Barney's cottage, where a light was glowing in the purpling twilight.

He saw Barney standing near his front steps, sending him a straight-armed, cheerful wave. At least *someone* was pleased to see that he was home.

Max waved back. 'It's just you and me now, old fellow,' he muttered.

He was turning to go back inside when he caught a flicker of movement out of the corner of his eye. Near the orchard.

A kangaroo, perhaps?

Max looked harder. Surely it had been a human figure?

A slender shape emerged from the shadows and his heart leapt like a kite in high wind. A woman in jeans and a blue checked shirt with brown shoulder-length hair was coming towards him.

Then his vision grew blurry and he had to swipe at his eyes with the back of his hand. But he knew.

Carrie was hurrying across the grass, dragging off her gardening gloves and shoving them into the back pocket of her jeans.

# CHAPTER FOURTEEN

CARRIE WANTED TO run to Max, to leap into his arms, but he hadn't moved from the bottom step and her courage failed her.

He looked so stern, possibly upset, as if he might not be pleased to see her—which was more than possible. He was frowning.

'How long have you been here?' he asked as she reached him.

'I arrived yesterday. I caught a bus from Townsville to Julia Creek, and then managed to get a lift out on the mail truck.'

'I've been in Sydney, looking for you.'

'I know. Barney told me. I'm sorry, Max. It all felt too messy to try and sort it on the phone. I needed to see you face to face.'

But now that she was here, face to face with Max, she didn't feel quite so brave. Max wasn't frowning any more, but he wasn't smiling either.

A pool of yellow light spilled from the kitchen, splashing over him, outlining his dark hair and his big shoulders as he stood on the bottom step, blocking her access to the house.

'I thought you were living in a flat in Sydney,' he said.

'Did my mother tell you that?'

'She did, yes.' He folded his arms over his considerable chest.

'I let her think that. If I'd told her I was coming back here we would have had a fight.'

'I see. So why *have* you come back, Carrie?'

He looked as formidable now as he had the last time she'd seen him in Sydney, when she'd made him so angry.

Was he still angry? Carrie knew she couldn't blame him.

'Max, are we still fighting?'

'I don't think so,' he said. 'But I want to know why you're here.'

'I came to apologise.'

He gave a sad shake of his head. 'Because you can't have a baby? Carrie, you don't have to apologise for that.'

Just hearing him say the word *baby* caused a painful wrench deep inside her. But she was stronger now, armed with the counsellor's good advice. She knew that her pain was perfectly normal. *Legitimate* was the word Margaret had used.

'I'm sorry for the way I handled that bad news,' she said.

Max shook his head. 'I wasn't much better. I overreacted as well. That's why I went back to Sydney. To find you.'

'So I guess we're not fighting, then?'

Now, at last, he smiled. 'I guess not.'

Carrie released her breath in a sigh of sweet relief, knowing that she could now tell him the real reason she'd come home. She could cut to the heart of the matter.

'I'm here because I love you, Max. I love you so much. More than ever. And I'm hoping that we—'

'Shh.' In one stride he was beside her, pressing a finger to her lips. 'It's OK, sweetheart.'

Before she quite knew what was happening he had slipped an arm around her shoulders, another under her knees, scooped her into his arms and started carrying her up the stairs and into the house. As soon as they were inside he closed the back door, shoving it with his boot and shutting out the night.

Leaning back against the door, he drew her to him, wrapping his arms around her and holding her close so she could feel the entire, wonderful length of his body.

'Welcome home, Carrie.'

'It's so good to be here.'

When their lips met they kissed gently, in a shy hello, but it flowed as easily as the blood in their veins into a deeper kiss—a kiss with heart and soul. A kiss to banish despair.

A kiss to build hope.

'I love you,' Carrie told him again. 'You know that, don't you?'

'Of course I do, my darling girl.'

'I've been to see a counsellor, Max.'

He tucked a strand of hair behind her ear. 'That was a clever move.'

'She had lots of helpful things to say that I'll tell you about eventually. She made me feel heaps better.'

'That's the best news yet, Carrie.'

Now that she'd started, she needed to tell him more. 'Being told I was infertile came as a terrible shock. I should have got help.'

'Darling, you should have shared it with *me*.'

'Yes—instead of damming it up and blaming myself.'

'You were too stressed to think straight.'

'I guess… Now my decision to leave you, to set you free, sounds crazy, but at the time it felt like my only option.'

'It's OK,' Max said, and gently kissed her forehead, her cheek, the curve of her neck. 'Just so long as you're here now, and here to stay.'

He let his broad hands slide possessively down her back to her waist, and then traced the curves of her hips. The movement bumped the gardening gloves she'd shoved in her back pocket and they tumbled to the floor.

He chuckled. 'You've already started gardening?'

'I couldn't help myself. I bought a host of seeds in Sydney and I wanted to get the soil prepared. But I should have been inside, showered and shampooed and waiting for my husband, with something smelling wonderful in the oven.'

'I hope the counsellor didn't tell you that?'

'No, of course she didn't. Although she *did* warn me that the future will have its bad moments. She said that infertility is like grief. The sadness comes in waves. There'll still be sad days. For both of us. I think a part of me will always grieve for the babies we can't have.'

'Yes,' he said gently. 'Me, too.'

He drew her to him again, cradling her head close to his chest so she could hear the comforting rhythm of his heart.

'But I'll never be as sad as I was when I thought I'd lost *you,* Carrie.'

'Oh, Max.' Despite the warmth of his arms around her, Carrie shuddered. 'I can't believe I ever thought that was a good idea.' Now she laid her head against his shoulder, touched her fingers to his jaw in a loving caress. 'I guess it was lucky I lost my memory.'

Max held her closer. 'I'll be giving thanks for that for the rest of my days.'

a good one. Max rose and leaned against the settee, too tired for breath to be anything other than a light touch of a sleepy creature.

Max stood alone, filled with the thought that she might only days . . .

# EPILOGUE

*Two years later...*

ANOTHER MUSTER AT Riverslea Downs had come and gone. Carrie had been the camp cook, and she was really pleased with the meals she'd prepared on the camp fire. She'd produced stews and curries and golden syrup puddings, as well as the usual corned beef and damper. And there'd been plenty of praise from the visiting stockmen.

It was good to be home again, though. So good to throw their stiff and dirty clothes into the laundry, and complete luxury to indulge in a long, hot and soapy bath and to cover herself in creamy moisturiser.

Carrie emerged from the steamy bathroom feeling like a new woman, to find Max hovering in the hallway, excitement burning in his bright blue eyes.

'I found a message from Sally on the phone,' he said. 'She's still pregnant! She's passed the three-month mark!'

'Oh, my God!'

Carrie stared at him in amazed disbelief. She'd thought of little else during the weeks they were away. It had been The Most Amazing Moment *Ever* when Max's sister had visited them on her return from the UK and sat at their kitchen table, looking all serious and concerned, as she offered to be a surrogate mother for their baby.

They'd been stunned at first, and then scared of the possible heartbreak, but finally so deeply grateful and elated.

During the muster Carrie had been hoping like crazy that all would be well with Sally in Sydney—that their little frozen embryo had survived the all-important weeks after the transfer to Sally's womb. But Carrie had also been terrified, and braced for disappointment.

'Sally said to check my emails,' Max said. 'There's an ultrasound picture, but I wanted to wait so we could see it together.'

'Oh, Max!' Carrie squealed, and hugged him—but she hugged him quickly, because they were both so eager to get to the computer.

Together, they hurried to the office. Max had already downloaded his emails, and now he clicked on the attachment in the message from his sister.

And there it was—a black and white image showing a tiny, perfect baby. *Their* tiny perfect baby. Curled up like a bean.

Carrie had to dash the tears from her eyes. 'Isn't it beautiful?' Her voice was all high-pitched and squeaky with emotion.

Max was grinning. 'It looks a bit like an alien.'

She gave him a playful slap. 'They all look like that.'

'Yeah, I know.'

'I wonder if it's a boy or a girl,' she whispered.

'It doesn't matter, does it?'

'No, of course it doesn't matter. And I don't think I want to know until it's born. It will add to the suspense and the excitement.'

'Can we *bear* any more suspense and excitement?'

Carrie turned quickly to see if Max looked worried, but he was grinning hard enough to make his face split. She threw her arms around him again, hugging him hard.

'Can you believe it? Our own little baby by Christmas?'

'I think it's starting to sink in.'

'Isn't Sally the most wonderful sister ever? I hope her morning sickness isn't too bad…'

'Sal wouldn't complain,' Max said, with a hint of brotherly pride. 'She's a good sport.'

'She's amazing,' Carrie agreed. 'We should phone her and thank her again.'

'We should,' Max said. 'Just as soon as I've kissed the most ravishing mother-to-be since the dawn of time.'

Carrie widened her eyes in amused disbelief. 'Since the dawn of time?'

'In the southern hemisphere, then.'

Carrie had experienced many happy moments in her husband's arms, but she'd never been more elated than she was now as he drew her close and kissed her.

When he released her, she sent him a cheeky smile. 'Perhaps I'm the most ravishing mother-to-be on Riverslea Downs?'

'No doubt about that,' he said, and kissed her again.

\* \* \* \* \*

# MILLS & BOON®

## *Cherish*™

**EXPERIENCE THE ULTIMATE RUSH OF FALLING IN LOVE**

0116/23

*'The perfect Christmas read!'* - Julia Williams

Jewellery designer Skylar loves living London, but when a surprise proposal goes wrong, she finds herself fleeing home to remote Puffin Island.

Burned by a terrible divorce, TV historian Alec is dazzled by Sky's beauty and so cynical that he assumes that's a bad thing! Luckily she's on the verge of getting engaged to someone else, so she won't be a constant source of temptation... but this Christmas, can Alec and Sky realise that they are what each other was looking for all along?

Order yours today at
**www.millsandboon.co.uk**

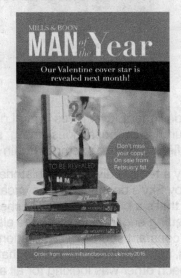

# MILLS & BOON®

## Want to get more from Mills & Boon?

Here's what's available to you if you join the exclusive **Mills & Boon eBook Club** today:

✦ *Convenience – choose your books each month*
✦ *Exclusive – receive your books a month before anywhere else*
✦ *Flexibility – change your subscription at any time*
✦ *Variety – gain access to eBook-only series*
✦ *Value – subscriptions from just £3.99 a month*

So visit **www.millsandboon.co.uk/esubs** today to be a part of this exclusive eBook Club!